MW00748479

Pr

"Fast-paced exci
from beginning

"Threads of several plotlines and deep underlying
sensuality are skillfully woven into the fabric of a
carefully crafted story whose complexities add to the
drama. This is a one-night read."
—*RT Book Reviews* on *Lord of Sin*

"Haunting, chilling, sensual and magical, this tale
of forbidden desire is as old as time, yet modern,
accessible and spellbinding."
—*RT Book Reviews* on *Lord of Legends*

"With heroines as powerful as her heroes, stories that
combine adventure, mystery and passion and a unique
understanding of the community of the wolf, Krinard
taps into reader fantasies perfectly."
—*RT Book Reviews* on *Luck of the Wolf*

"The author intertwines…deception, betrayal, and
suspense to form an incredible overall story."
—*Harlequin Junkie* on *Shadowmaster*

Praise for Debbie Herbert

"Highly recommended for fans of both romance and
paranormal genres."
—*Goodreads* review on *Siren's Treasure*

"The clever blending of mermaid myths and Native
American legends sets the Dark Seas miniseries apart
from other stories dealing with the supernatural. With
fascinating characters and wondrous details, every
scene in *Siren's Call* is compellingly riveting."
—*Goodreads* review

Praise for Susan Krinard

Susan Krinard has been writing paranormal romance, science fiction and fantasy for nearly twenty years. With *Daysider* she began a series of vampire paranormal romances, Nightsiders, for Harlequin Nocturne. This *New York Times* bestselling author lives in Albuquerque, New Mexico, with her husband, Serge, her dogs, Freya, Nahla and Cagney, and her cats, Agatha and Rocky. She loves her garden, nature, painting and chocolate…not necessarily in that order. Visit her website at susankrinard.com.

Books by Susan Krinard

Harlequin Nocturne

Nightsiders Series

Holiday with a Vampire 4
"Halfway to Dawn"
Daysider
Nightmaster
Shadowmaster
Night Quest

Harlequin HQN

Come the Night
Dark of the Moon
Chasing Midnight
Lord of the Beasts
To Tame a Wolf

Visit the Author Profile page
at Harlequin.com for more titles.

SUSAN KRINARD

AND

DEBBIE HERBERT

Night Quest

and

Bayou Shadow Hunter

HARLEQUIN® NOCTURNE™

If you purchased this book without a cover you should be aware that this book is stolen property. It was reported as "unsold and destroyed" to the publisher, and neither the author nor the publisher has received any payment for this "stripped book."

Recycling programs
for this product may
not exist in your area.

ISBN-13: 978-0-373-60229-2

Night Quest & Bayou Shadow Hunter

Copyright © 2016 by Harlequin Books S.A.

The publisher acknowledges the copyright holders
of the individual works as follows:

Night Quest
Copyright © 2016 by Susan Krinard

Bayou Shadow Hunter
Copyright © 2016 by Debbie Herbert

All rights reserved. Except for use in any review, the reproduction or utilization of this work in whole or in part in any form by any electronic, mechanical or other means, now known or hereinafter invented, including xerography, photocopying and recording, or in any information storage or retrieval system, is forbidden without the written permission of the publisher, Harlequin Enterprises Limited, 225 Duncan Mill Road, Don Mills, Ontario, Canada, M3B 3K9.

This is a work of fiction. Names, characters, places and incidents are either the product of the author's imagination or are used fictitiously, and any resemblance to actual persons, living or dead, business establishments, events or locales is entirely coincidental.

This edition published by arrangement with Harlequin Books S.A.

For questions and comments about the quality of this book, please contact us at CustomerService@Harlequin.com.

® and TM are trademarks of the publisher. Trademarks indicated with ® are registered in the United States Patent and Trademark Office, the Canadian Intellectual Property Office and in other countries.

Printed in U.S.A.

www.Harlequin.com

CONTENTS

NIGHT QUEST

Susan Krinard

With special thanks to my editor, Leslie Wainger,
for her patience and editorial expertise;
and to Serge, who will never give up on me.

Prologue

Some thirty years after the signing of the Treaty between human and Nightsider, or Opiri, forces, human Enclaves and Nightsider Citadels maintained a sometimes uneasy peace. Territories were well established, and the neutral Zones between were regularly patrolled by Citadel and Enclave agents.

The agents were of two specific genetic types. The half-breed Daysiders, or Darketans, day-walking Opiri, were born of human fathers and Nightsider mothers. Previously considered mutants, they had human coloring and extra-human speed and strength, but possessed the standard need for blood.

The half-blood dhampires, offspring of human mothers and Opir fathers, were of a different genetic type, with "cat-like" eyes and the ability to walk in daylight, while also possessing full Opiri speed, strength and acute senses. A percentage were dependent on blood, while some were able to digest human food.

Though both Daysider and dhampir agents were charged to prevent potential enemies from entering their respective territories, they could not prevent the establishment of illicit colonies.

In California, humans and progressive Opiri founded mixed settlements in which humans and Nightsiders could live in peace and cooperation. These new colonies were for the most part left alone by both Citadels and Enclaves. Farther north, in the former states of Oregon and Washington, humans established heavily guarded compounds inhabited by militias more devoted to killing stray Opiri than maintaining the peace.

Their victims were primarily exiled Opiri known as Freebloods. Most Freebloods were humans who had been bitten and turned into Opiri by powerful Bloodlords and Bloodmasters after the beginning of the ten-year War, first serving as vassals to their sires and then, after being replaced by other vassals, released from the bond created by the process of conversion.

Freebloods within the Citadels were forced to compete for human serfs in order to establish a Household and gain rank. But though, by treaty, the Citadels were compelled to send convicts to their former enemies, the supply of such convicts began to dwindle, and competition for the serfs became a significant problem.

As a result, hundreds of Freebloods were exiled from the Citadels to survive in any way they could. These Freebloods, running in packs, became a significant threat to human and mixed colonies, often stealing humans or killing Opiri colonists.

At the same time, certain Citadels began to see the necessity of changing the Opir way of life in order to deal with the ever-shrinking supply of accessible human blood. Some Opiri spoke of the need to abandon the taking of human blood in favor of animal blood, while others favored a new war. Meanwhile, the mixed colonies continued to grow and spread, offering a new alternative of peaceful coexistence based on the voluntary sharing of blood.

It was, of course, inevitable that these competing philosophies would come into conflict.

—from the Introduction to *The Armistice Years:*
Conflict and Convergence

Chapter 1

Timon.

Garret Fox knelt beside the footprints scattered in the dirt, tracing the smallest with his fingertip. They had paused here, the kidnappers, and the little person to whom the footprint belonged had briefly touched ground before being swept up again.

Still alive, Garret thought. He dragged his hand across his face, scraping against the four-day beard he hadn't had time to shave off, and got to his feet. Fear for his son made him ignore the deep ache in his muscles, the rawness of blistered feet, the heavy autumn rains that penetrated his coat and pried icy fingers under his collar. He hardly noticed the sting of the scratches across his face and hands where branches from trees and bushes had scraped his skin.

Speed had been far more important to him than caution. He wasn't interested in concealing his trail. Neither were the rogues ahead of him. They felt safe now, nearly two hundred miles away from the colony they had raided. Safe because they had left complete chaos in their wake, and every adult human or Nightsider had been needed to clean up the mess and protect the other children.

The rogues believed they had nothing to fear from a single human.

Garret adjusted his pack, reassured by the weight of the VS-134 rifle—the highly effective and notorious weapon known as the "Vampire Slayer," whose use was strictly forbidden except in cases of extreme emergency.

And that was why this had happened, Garret thought bitterly. Timon had paid for the colony's philosophy of nonviolence and indiscriminate acceptance of every potential settler. Garret had no compunction about using deadly force to save him.

If Roxana had been alive, she would have done the same. Timon was all he had left, the only thing in the world that gave meaning and purpose to what remained of his life.

I will get him back, Roxana, he promised.

He set out again, though dawn was still hours away. Rain turned to sleet with the unseasonable cold. The moon was bright enough for him to see by, but he didn't need to rely on it completely. He'd spent years not only honing his body and skills to fight enemy Nightsiders, but also in developing his senses of hearing and touch to help him move in darkness. The night would never be his element, but he had long ago reached a truce with it.

As darkness gave way to sunlight, he moved more quickly. As each day passed, the trail had led him deeper into wild country that seemed to grow colder with every mile, far from any human Enclave, Nightsider Citadel or free colony.

Time and again, he lost the trail and then picked it up, losing ground by night and gaining by day. Along the way he found the bodies of solitary humans drained of blood, their hollow shells cast aside, and each time he spoke a few brief words over the dead before he forced himself onward. His supply of dried foods shrank steadily, but he didn't dare search for some isolated homestead or settlement to replenish his stores. He sought clean streams to fill his canteen, gathered edible greens and caught whatever game he could find.

At the end of the second week, his stomach hollow and his gait uneven with exhaustion, he knew he had fallen far behind. Still he drove himself on. He began to see more human settlements—not mixed colonies, like Avalon, but high-walled, paramilitary compounds with heavily armed militias whose sole purpose seemed to be hunting down and killing rogue Freebloods. Garret avoided them, as he had avoided the less warlike settlements he passed.

Fifteen minutes before dawn on the first morning of the third week, near what used to be the city of Eugene, he heard the distant sound of a woman's scream.

He didn't pause to think. Dropping to his knees, he shrugged out of his pack and removed the components of the VS. With shaking hands he assembled the rifle and looped its strap over his shoulder. If the woman was being harassed by Nightsiders, the Vampire Slayer might be all that stood between her and an ugly death.

The sound of a twig snapping brought Artemis to attention. She grabbed her bow, her hunt unfinished, and ran toward the denser forest and one of the many refuges she had built for herself in the area she had chosen as her territory.

If it hadn't been for her hunger, she might have been clearheaded enough to notice the humans before she ran into them. If there had been one less human, she might have taken them down before they trapped her.

But there were five, all armed with automatic rifles, and they had thrown the wire netting over her before she could do more than raise her hands. Each segment of the weighted net was razor sharp, and though a thousand small cuts couldn't kill an Opir, the damage would prevent her escape.

"You were right, Coleman," one of the men said. "Never would have believed we'd find a female bloodsucker living alone out here." He looked at the sky. "Just about sunrise. We might still get her back—"

"Why?" a younger man asked, holding his section of the net with thickly gloved hands. "She ain't no spy."

"Dean's right," a third human said. "She wouldn't be out here alone near sunrise if she was. She won't have no useful intel. Might as well take care of her here."

Artemis barely heard their voices. The wire burned wherever it touched her skin and sliced through her clothing, but she tried to focus on calculating her best means of escape. One of these humans would surely be careless enough to loosen his grip on the net, giving her a few seconds to fight her way out. Blood loss might be great, but if she could grab even one of these monsters…

"Watch out!" the first male said as she lunged toward the loosest part of the net.

"Burn her!"

Something jabbed against Artemis's neck, and a paralyzing shock jolted her nerves and froze her muscles. She felt her useless body being dragged across the ground and through the mud, the wires cutting deeper as the humans found a patch of dry earth far from any hint of shade.

The sky had grown pale in the east. The sun was minutes away from rising, and her body ignored every command her brain tried to send it. She was aware of increasing pain as the humans jostled the net and anchored it to the ground, driving stakes into the earth to pin its edges so tight and close that she wouldn't find even the smallest opening.

Still, she tried. The paralysis broke, and she flung herself up and against the stinging web, cutting what remained of her clothes to ribbons and shredding the skin of her hands while the guttural laughter of the humans echoed inside her skull.

Then they stepped back, denying her what little shelter their shadows might provide, and watched the first rays of the sun strike her bleeding fingers.

She didn't intend to scream. She fought it with all the discipline and self-control she had learned both in the Citadel and as an exile in the wilderness.

But her own cry deafened even the laughter of the humans, and the last thing she saw was the bright hair of a man with green eyes blazing like emeralds in the rising sun.

For a few fleeting seconds Garret considered the possibility of leaving the Opir woman to her fate. There were five men, all carrying modified assault rifles, and numerous knives and bladed weapons. It would be impossible to approach them without being seen.

He'd faced similar odds before and met them head-on. But he had expected a human woman, not a Freeblood. For all he knew, the female might be among the most vicious rogues in this patch of wilderness, as bad as those who had taken his son.

And if anything were to happen to him now, there would be no one to look for Timon. No one to save him from whatever fate the rogues intended for him.

But the militiamen were torturing the woman, and that was far beyond the pale of what Garret could accept. He had no doubt of what Roxana would have done if she were here.

Kneeling behind a screen of shrubs, Garret separated

the VS into its component parts and returned them to his pack. Raising his hands above his head, he walked out into the clearing. Almost as one, the militiamen lifted their rifles and pointed them at his chest.

"Human," Garret said in his mildest voice, trying to ignore the muffled moans of the Opir woman in the net. "Peace."

Two of the men lowered their rifles. The others held steady. The eldest of the bunch, grizzled and scarred, stepped forward.

"Who are you?" he demanded, his hand on the butt of his hunting knife.

"My name is Garret Fox," Garret said. "I'm looking for my son, who was taken by rogue bloodsuckers." He glanced at the Freeblood in the net. "Have you seen any children in the area?"

The leader looked at his comrades. They shook their heads.

"We ain't seen no kids outside our compound," he said, his eyes narrow with suspicion. "Or any bloodsuckers except this one." He kicked at the body curled up on the ground, and Garret fought the instinct to stop him. "Your son, you said? Where you from?"

Garret estimated that he had no more than a few minutes before the sun was high enough to kill the Nightsider woman. He didn't have time for conversation.

"South," he said. "I've traveled a long way."

"Looks like it," one of the younger men said. His eyes were small and cruel. "If bloodsuckers took your kid, he's probably dead."

"Shut up, Dean," the grizzled man said. "How'd it happen?"

"We were out hunting," Garret said, staying as vague as possible. "Maybe this female knows something. Will you let me question her before you kill her?"

There were murmurs of protest, but the leader silenced them with a wave of his hand.

"Get her out of the sun," he ordered his men. He met Garret's eyes. "You got five minutes. Here." He tossed a shock stick to Garret, who snatched it out of the air. "Use this if she don't cooperate."

Garret edged closer to the leader as the other men dragged the net into the scant shade of a nearly leafless bush. "She probably won't respond to more pain," he said. "Let me tell her that you'll give her a quick death if she cooperates."

"Why should she believe you?"

"I was the interrogator in my compound," Garret said. "Even with *them*, persuasion can be effective."

"Why should I give her a quick death?"

"I didn't say you had to keep my promise."

The grizzled man bared his teeth in a grin. "Five minutes, like I said."

"Thanks." Garret turned toward the net, but the leader grabbed his arm with a callous hand.

"You got guts to travel out here by yourself," he said, "and you look like a good fighter. You married?"

The grief was almost as fresh now as it had been four years ago. "No," he said.

"Then you might be welcome to join us if you decide not to go back south again."

"After I find my son, I may take you up on your offer."

"My name's Claude Delacroix. Find the old town of Melford and wait by the bridge over the creek. Someone'll find you and bring you to the compound."

"I'll keep that in mind." Garret pulled free, firmly but politely. "If you can keep your men away, I'd appreciate it."

"Will do." Delacroix gestured to his crew, cast Garret another assessing look and followed them.

Well aware that the militiamen were watching every

move he made, Garret crouched by the net. The Opir woman's pale skin was striped everywhere with narrow lacerations, her jacket and pants were little more than scraps of fabric held together by a few threads, and the hand tucked half under her chest was blistered and red. Her hair, a rich shade of ivory, was just long enough to cover her face.

No matter what she was or what she might have done, Garret thought, she didn't deserve *this*.

"Listen to me," he said, leaning as close to the net as he dared. "I can help you get out of here, but you'll have to do exactly as I say."

Slowly she lifted her head. Her eyes were dark amethyst, unexpectedly and extraordinarily beautiful. Her body was slender, her face delicate and fine-boned, but there was nothing weak in either. The defiance in her eyes told him that anyone who made the mistake of thinking her fragile would quickly regret their assumption.

"I heard what was said," she said. "You are lying."

The misery in her voice cut straight through Garret like the razor wires that cut her body. "Where I come from," he said, "we don't leave people to be tortured to death."

"People?" she said with a brief, hoarse laugh. "Is that what you think I am, human? A *person*?"

"*They* obviously don't think so," he said, tilting his head toward the militiamen.

"You wish to interrogate me, but I have nothing to tell you."

"Do you live in this area?"

Her full lips remained stubbornly closed.

"You don't know anything about a pack of rogues with a human child?" Garret asked.

"No."

"I know his kidnappers came this way, but I lost their trail. You must have sensed them."

"I did not."

"Where is the rest of your pack?"

"I have no pack." She coughed, turning her face away. "If you have any of your supposed human mercy in you, let me have the quick death the other humans will never give me."

"Is that what you want?" he asked. "To die?"

"I cannot help you. Why would you offer me any other alternative?"

He glanced over the top of the net. The militiamen were muttering among themselves. Garret's five minutes were almost up.

"You have two choices," he said. "Trust me, or force me to hand you over to them. And I don't want your death on my conscience."

She tried to brush her hair out of her face, but the movement cracked the burned skin of her hand, and her expressive eyes blurred with pain. "What do you want me to do?"

"What's your name?"

"If it matters… Artemis."

He showed her the shock stick. "Artemis, you'll have to pretend I'm using this on you. Be convincing. I'll flip the net back. You come out, grab me and drag me into the woods."

"You believe I will not kill you?" she asked with obvious astonishment.

"Will you?"

"They will shoot both of us."

"It's possible. But I think I've persuaded them to believe that I'm one of them."

"Yes. You are *human*."

Garret held her gaze. "I hope you'll choose to live."

With another quick glance at the militiamen, Garret raised his voice in a harsh question and pretended to jab the stick into the net. The Opir woman began to convulse very convincingly, and as she did Garret grabbed two of the weights with his gloved hands and flung the net back over itself, leaving a narrow gap at the bottom.

Artemis was injured and in great discomfort, but she moved very fast, scrambling out from under the net, grabbing him by the shoulders and half dragging him toward the woods. He dropped the shock stick. Sunlight struck her, and she swallowed a cry. The weakness of her grip told Garret that she wouldn't be able to keep up the pretense for long, so he made a show of helplessness, struggling as if she had complete control of him.

A bullet whizzed past his ear when they were still a few yards from the woods' edge. Garret shouted and raised one hand in a plea as the woman continued to tug at him, her fingers beginning to slip from his coat.

"A little farther," Garret said. "Once we're inside the woods, run."

Artemis stumbled, and Garret twisted to push her toward the trees. The militiamen were jogging after them now, deadly silent and ready to shoot. Garret and the Freeblood reached the shade, and she staggered, her breath sawing in her throat.

"Go!" Garret said.

"They'll kill you," she said hoarsely, refusing to move.

"For being an idiot and allowing you to escape? I don't think so."

She didn't have time to answer, because the men were almost on top of them. Artemis grabbed him around the neck and dragged him deeper into the shadows. He could have escaped easily, but he played along, gasping for air and digging his heels into the dirt.

"Come no closer!" she shouted. "I will kill him!"

Chapter 2

The militiamen slowed to a walk. Delacroix signaled a halt. He met Garret's gaze.

"I'm sorry," he said, "but I can't let her escape." He lifted his rifle and aimed at the center of the woman's forehead.

"She knows where my son is!" Garret rasped. "Let her go, please!"

Delacroix hesitated. "Your son is no more important than the people this bloodsucker will kill."

"I will release him if you give me five more minutes before you follow me," Artemis said.

Bending his head toward the man next to him, Delacroix spoke in a low voice, listened to his comrades and nodded.

"Five minutes," he said, checking his watch.

Without warning, Artemis released Garret, pushing him toward the men, and sprang into a run. Almost immediately the militiamen started after her.

"Wait," Garret said. "I thought you said—"

Delacroix signaled a halt. "You think we'd keep a promise to one of *them*?" he asked. "Don't you want the info you say she has?"

"Yes, of course," Garret said, rubbing his throat as he got to his feet. "But if you go into those woods after her, she'll have the advantage."

Two of the men aimed their rifles at him. "Who *are* you?" Delacroix asked again.

"A former serf from the Citadel of Erebus," Garret said. "Do you know what that's like? Any of you?"

The men exchanged glances. One lowered his gaze. Another spat.

"This is my fault," Garret said. "Give me one of your weapons and I'll get her myself."

"She'll have even more of an advantage over one hunter," Delacroix said. "Why aren't *you* carrying a gun?"

The VS seemed to burn a hole through Garret's pack and into his coat. "I had one," he began, "but—"

"Take off your pack," Delacroix said.

"Why?"

"You're hiding something, and I want to know what it is."

Garret lunged at Delacroix, grabbed the man's rifle in both hands, yanked it away and slammed the butt into the leader's face. Without slowing, he struck the next man in the neck and then reversed the rifle.

Two of the others began to shoot, but Garret had already moved out of their path. He shot one of the men in the hand, forcing him to drop his rifle. The youngest one yelled and charged at Garret wildly. His heedless rage gave Garret the chance to kick the weapon out of the boy's grip before he could pull the trigger.

But another rifleman and the one he'd struck in the neck were almost on top of him. Someone flashed by him, a small figure who took the two men down so quickly that Garret couldn't see how she'd done it. He didn't take time to think it over. Shrugging out of his pack, he uncoiled the rope hanging from the metal frame and cut it into five lengths. By the time he turned back, all the militiamen were on the ground—alive, but weaponless and either unconscious or disabled.

He met Artemis's gaze briefly and knelt beside Delacroix, who was moaning as he began to wake up. Garret rolled him over and tied his hands securely. The Opir woman helped him with the other men, her face and body shielded by an oversize hooded daycoat that was thick enough to protect her from the worst of the sun. She wore equally heavy gloves. Garret could only assume that she had kept the day clothes close by in case she was caught out of the woods after dawn.

He checked on each of the men when he was finished. Two of them were already struggling and cursing, while Delacroix and his second-in-command were bleary-eyed and disoriented. The youngest glared at Garret with undisguised hatred.

"Listen to me," Garret said, crouching in front of him. "I'm going to set you free. You go back to your colony and tell them to come fetch their people."

The boy pulled hard against the ropes around his wrists. "You gonna leave them out here for the rogues to eat?" he demanded.

Garret glanced at Artemis. "Are there any other Opiri in the area?" he asked.

"No."

"You *believe* her?" the boy said, his face twisted in amazement.

"No Opiri are going to attack you in sunlight. Your people should be able to return with plenty of time to spare before dark."

"Traitor!" the boy spat, tears running down his cheeks. "We'll hunt you down."

Garret moved behind the boy and cut through the ropes. "Take your pack," he said, "and go."

For a moment he thought the boy would stay and try to fight, but even *he* had enough sense to realize he didn't have a chance. He grabbed the pack and ran off, his pace much too fast to maintain for more than a few minutes.

"You will pay for this," Delacroix said, his words a little slurred. "We kill sucker-lovers around here."

Garret ignored him. He gathered up the weapons and backed away until he was in the woods again. Artemis went with him. He noticed that she was carrying a bow in one hand and a quiver full of arrows in the other.

"Thank you," Garret said roughly, trying to adjust the rifles' straps so that he could carry them all at once to a place where the militiamen wouldn't find them. "You can go."

"You saved my life at the risk of your own," Artemis said, her eyes reflecting crimson under the hood of her coat.

"I told you—"

"That you would not leave someone to be tortured," she said. "But I still do not understand why you would turn against your own kind to help one of mine."

Anger and grief clogged Garret's throat and tore at his heart. "I knew an Opir who did the same for us."

Her brows drew down and her lips parted as if she were about to ask how such a thing could be possible.

And then she collapsed.

Artemis woke to pain. Tiny filaments of agony circled her limbs and waist, her chest and neck. And her hands...

"Easy," the human said as she tried to sit up. He eased

her back down to the bed of fallen leaves on which she'd been lying.

Instinctively she resisted, irrational panic flooding her body. But he refused to let her up, and she realized that he was strong enough to impose his will.

Human or not, he was dangerous. She had seen him fight. He moved almost as fast as an Opir.

"You're already healing," he said, his brows knitting in a frown, "but if you push yourself, you'll slow it down. We don't want to stay here any longer than we have to."

She disregarded the "we" and compelled herself to relax. "Where are the men?" she asked, casting about for their rank scents.

"It's only been a few hours." He glanced over his shoulder, and for the first time Artemis saw that they were far into the forest under a thick canopy of cottonwoods, protected on two sides by boulders that stood beside a small creek. She realized that she was wearing unfamiliar clothes that were much too large for her, carrying the oddly pleasant smell of the human who had saved her. Her daycoat and gloves lay neatly folded within reach; her knives, bow and quiver were farther away. It would take some effort to get them.

She might have just enough strength to surprise the human, grab her things and run.

"You don't have to be afraid of me," the man said, his eyes tracking her gaze.

"I am not afraid of you...*human*."

"My name is Garret Fox," he said, seemingly indifferent to her mockery.

"There is no need for you to stay," she said. "It would be best if you did not."

"Why? Are you planning on attacking me when my back is turned?"

The question seemed hostile, but his face was impassive. Too impassive to be credible. "If you believed that," she said, "you would never have brought me here."

"That's right," he said, dropping back into a crouch. "Saving my life just to kill me wouldn't make much sense."

She began to formulate an answer, but all at once she found herself lost in the extraordinary green of his eyes, like the moss clinging to the sides of the boulders. His dark red hair brushed the back of his collar, as if he hadn't cut it in some time, and there was a shadow of darker hair on his jaw and upper lip. His features were strong but not coarse, his mouth mobile but decisive.

By human standards he was very attractive. And Opiri appreciated human beauty well enough to seek out serfs that bore the same qualities this man exemplified, such as his lean, fit body, broad shoulders and easy grace.

Artemis had never owned such a serf. She had never owned a serf at all, though she had been strong enough to stake out her own Household in Oceanus, if that had been her intent.

Now, in a haze of pain and caught in the snare of this human's gaze, she wondered what it would have been like to own a man like this. What it might have been like if he were her Favorite, and they—

The man jerked away, and she realized that she had been touching his hand with her raw fingertips. His reaction had been so violent that she expected to see distaste on his face, but there was only confusion, as if he had been taken unaware by more than just the touch itself.

Artemis, too, was bewildered. Her fingertips tingled, and a series of small shocks ran through her arms and deep into the core of her body. Physical sensations she hadn't experienced in many, many years.

And through that touch she felt something else. Something that she thought she'd been rid of for a very long time. An emotional aura flared briefly around Garret Fox, as red as his hair, fed by all the anger and passion his expression concealed.

The aura vanished quickly, but her shock lingered. The ability she had worked so hard to erase—the ability to sense and feel the emotions of others—had returned with a vengeance, and a human had reawakened it.

But how could that be possible, when her brief dealings with her own kind since her exile had had no effect at all?

Fight it, she told herself. *If it takes hold again...*

"Lie still," Garret said, as if nothing had happened. "And keep that hand covered."

She lifted her chin, hoping that he hadn't noticed her bewilderment. "I am not accustomed to taking orders from your kind."

"Call it a suggestion, then." He cocked his head. "Why *did* you come back for me?"

"Do I not owe you my life?"

"Most of your kind wouldn't feel bound by a debt to a human."

"You said another Opir had helped you."

Artemis could hear the steady rhythm of his heartbeat break and then resume at a slightly faster pace. "She was a remarkable person," he said.

She. "What was her name?" Artemis said, trying and failing to control her curiosity.

"Roxana." He shifted his weight and looked away. "Which Citadel did you come from?"

"Why does it matter?" she asked. "Do you plan to interrogate me now, where you will not be interrupted by my untimely death?"

"You *are* an exile, aren't you?"

She wondered why he had chosen that word when he might as easily have called her a "rogue bloodsucker." It was how he had spoken of her to the other humans.

And how most humans thought of Freebloods, or Opiri in general.

Opiri. Nightsiders. *Vampires.*

"What else would I be?" she asked.

Her supposedly rhetorical question provoked a raised eyebrow and a keen look. She knew what was going through his mind: the same thing that was going through hers, but in reverse.

Both sides in the ongoing conflict between humans and Opiri had scouts and spies in the vast, supposedly uninhabited areas between human and Opir settlements, usually known as "Zones." Most of the human colonies' scouts and agents were mixed-breed Opiri, called dhampires. But a few pure-blood humans were skilled enough to survive in the Zones, even against Nightsider opponents.

Garret could easily be one such human. But he was too far from the nearest human Enclave to be one of their scouts, and she would bet her life—again—that he didn't work for any of the militias.

"I am not an operative for any Citadel," she said, answering his unfinished question.

"I believe you," he said. "You were alone when those men found you?"

"I told you I was."

"You also said you knew nothing about a human boy in this area."

"I do not." She hesitated. "This boy is your son?"

"Timon," he said.

"I am sorry," she said, realizing that she truly meant it. "I would help you if I could."

He met her gaze. "You can."

Alarmed by thoughts of what he might ask of her, she forgot her pain. "I am leaving," she said, propping herself up on her elbows. "Do not try to stop me."

"You aren't going anywhere," he said, getting to his feet.

"I may be injured," she said, "but you appear to be unarmed except for a hunting knife, and even now I am stronger than any human."

"I wouldn't bet on it. Sit down, before you—"

Artemis climbed to her knees. Agony like a spear of sunlight drilled into her skull. Her mouth was dry, though she suspected that Garret must have given her water. She swayed, and all at once he was beside her, supporting her, holding her. He was warm and solid, and she could hear the steady beat of his pulse, the throbbing of his blood in his veins. The shock she had experienced earlier returned with his touch, a raw electric current that attacked her mind and body as if she had literally been struck by lightning.

"I said you weren't going anywhere," he said, gripping her more tightly when she tried to jerk away. He eased her down to the ground. "You'll need blood or you won't fully recover."

His matter-of-fact statement gave her a very different kind of shock. Humans didn't despise Opiri only because of their attempt to conquer the world but also because the very idea of feeding on blood was an abomination to their kind.

He did not offer you his *blood*, she thought wryly. But where else did he think she would get it, in her condition?

"Wherever you lived," she said, "it must be very unlike the human compounds in this area."

He pulled his pack close so that he could reach inside, and she caught a glimpse of a rifle stock, a kind she didn't recognize. It wasn't one of the weapons he'd gathered from the militiamen, then hidden. Apparently he wasn't unarmed, after all.

"I assume the local militias kill every Nightsider they find," he said.

"Yes," she said. "They consider it their divine purpose

to hunt down as many Opiri as possible. Do you find that strange?"

"The militia compounds see packs of vicious predators, and the rogues only a source of food. An eye for an eye."

Now she heard in his voice what she'd sensed in his mind and seen in his aura: simmering anger fed by a deep fear that was not for himself.

Don't think about his feelings, she reminded herself. *Don't let them get inside you again.*

But she knew it wasn't that simple. Her shields had fallen, and she had to build them back up again. As quickly as possible.

"What was it that your famous peacemaker once said?" she asked, forcing herself to remain calm. "'An eye for an eye makes the whole world blind.'"

His laugh reflected his obvious surprise at her knowledge of human philosophers. "Very clever," he said. "Most Opiri don't have much interest in human wisdom. Are you one of those rare Nightsiders who see humans as more than barbarians, killers like the militiamen or potential serfs?"

"How else should I regard them?"

"Forgive me for my foolish question. Tell me—why don't you live with other exiles?"

"It is not in the nature of Freebloods to live in packs," she said.

He searched through his pack, and the scent of his skin—his blood—drifted toward her. "Not in the Citadels," he said.

"And how do you know so much about our lives inside the Citadels?"

"Inside the Citadels or out," he said, "Freebloods spend most of their time struggling constantly for dominance, so they can build Households of their own. That's the entire basis for their existence."

"It is not the basis for *my* existence," she said.

"Because you don't want to fight?" He withdrew a wrapped object from his pack. "Somehow, I don't think you live apart because you're afraid of being killed by your own kind."

"I am not."

"Then there's something else about your fellow Freebloods that you don't like. Do you hunt humans?"

The direct question startled her. "No," she said, without thinking.

"That would explain it, then." He opened the package to reveal several strips of dried meat, and Artemis's stomach clenched with hunger. "I knew you were different when I first met you."

"How would you know that?"

"Instinct."

The same kind of instinct, she wondered, that had made *her* trust *him* so quickly? "And if you had determined that I was like every other Freeblood," she asked, "would you have let me die?"

His very green eyes met hers. "But you aren't," he said. "I've met Opiri who didn't believe in living on human blood on principle, and others who just didn't believe in taking it by force. Which type are you?"

He spoke, Artemis thought, as if he had engaged in long, philosophical discussions with other Opiri, and that idea was flatly ridiculous. Wasn't it?

"Many Freeblood exiles do not know how to live without human blood," she said. "But most do not kill."

Garret offered her a piece of jerky. "Too bad the ones who don't kill can't—or won't—stop the ones who do."

She pushed the offered food away. "Are you so certain they have not tried?"

"Have *you*?" he said, searching her eyes.

"I want what is best for my—" She broke off and took a deep breath. She had no reason to tell him what she had attempted and failed to achieve in Oceanus. He would never believe it was possible.

"You hate us, just like the militiamen do," she said, covering her confusion with anger.

"*Us* is a very big word," he said. "I don't hate *you*."

He was right, she realized. She couldn't sense any personal hostility from him. To the contrary, he was intrigued by her, genuinely interested in knowing more about her life. She was afraid to look any further.

"I am still a Freeblood," she said.

"But you're no rogue," he said, setting the knife down on a flat rock beside him.

She was almost tempted to let him go on thinking that she was superior to her own people. *Different*, as he claimed. She found that she wanted his good opinion.

But if she let herself believe that she was better than the rest, she would betray her own principles. Freebloods only needed to be shown, guided, by one who had seen a little way beyond the bars of the prison they so blindly accepted as the limit of their lives.

Guided not by emotion, but by rationality. She didn't need her unwanted empathic ability to tell her that Garret was controlling feelings that might have paralyzed him if he set them free. In that, they were frighteningly alike.

"Where do you come from?" she asked. "From all you have said, it cannot be anything like the local compounds."

"I live alone."

"Without the protection of your own kind?" she asked. "Is that how you lost your son?"

Her cruel question had been meant to provoke an unguarded response—any response that would help her understand him—but all it did was open her mind to the ache of his sadness.

"It is my fault," Garret said quietly.

The red aura flared around him again, and Artemis cov-

ered her face. It made no difference. She wasn't seeing it
with her eyes but with her heart. And now all she could
feel was his pain, his sorrow, his terrible sense of loss.

She had known loss, too. But nothing like this. Not
since she had been human herself.

"I am sorry," she said, dropping her hands from her
face. "Have I convinced you that I know nothing of this
abduction?"

Staring at the dried strip of meat he still held in one
hand, he gave a ragged sigh. "Yes," he said.

His simple answer almost made her doubt his honesty.
But the "talent" she'd tried to bury insisted otherwise.

If she was wrong...

A fresh stab of hunger caught her unaware, and she
sank back to the ground with a gasp. Garret set down his
scanty meal and leaned over her.

"You've spent too much time talking and not enough
resting," he said.

"And whose fault is that?" she whispered.

"I should have been more careful."

She did her best not to notice the concern in his voice,
his worried frown, the compassion he should not feel for
one like her. Whoever and whatever he was, son or no
son, she had to get away from him. The temptation to feed
was terrifyingly strong in the wake of her injuries. If she
should hurt him...

"You should continue your search," she said, turning
her face away, "and I must return to my shelter to collect
my things and move on before the other humans find me."

He ran his hand up and down his left sleeve. "Your
physical state is obviously deteriorating. How far do you
expect to get this time?"

"Far enough."

"And then?"

Shivering with animal desires she could barely contain, Artemis moved to gather her things. "I am going. Do not follow me."

"It won't work." His footsteps were almost silent as he moved behind her. "In a few minutes you're going to collapse."

"Then what do you suggest?" she asked, spinning to face him. "I see no other—"

"I obviously didn't make myself clear," he said. He pushed up his left sleeve. "I'm offering an alternative."

Chapter 3

His meaning was terrifyingly clear, and suddenly Artemis was furious—at her own helplessness; at his inexplicable generosity, in spite of his valid reasons for despising her kind; at a world that had created such a bizarre set of impossible circumstances. Her mind and emotions and physical senses reacted all at once, making her excruciatingly aware of the body she had so admired.

Even thinking of taking his blood aroused not just her hunger for nourishment but for other things, as well. Her imagination began to spin scenarios that could never be. Her empathic talent burned more brightly—extending fingers of amethyst light, *her* light, toward Garret—and he began to breathe more heavily.

Vivid images sprang into her mind: lying beside Garret, naked in his arms as she sank her teeth into his neck; moaning in pleasure as the blood flowed over her tongue and he guided her down on top of him; urgency building as her hunger exploded into an unbearable need to feel him inside her, giving as she took, taking as she gave...

She came back to herself, her body hot and throbbing, to find him looking at her with that steady gaze, his eyes so clear that she could see every shadow passing beneath the surface. No pain now, no anger, no sorrow. Only need. And desire.

Desire for a Freeblood. For *her*. She looked from Garret's hungry eyes down to his broad chest and lean waist, and then below, where the evidence of his response was so readily apparent.

And *she* was responsible. *She* had to put an end to it.

"How can you do this?" she asked. "How can you bear to let an Opir take your blood? Is it because of this Roxana?"

"I've done it before," he said, his hunger still burning in her mind. "I have no reason to fear it."

She wondered again where he'd come from. He hadn't always been alone, not with such a casual attitude about donation. But if he had ever lived among Opiri...

"If I take your blood," she said, "what do you expect in return?"

"Your help in finding my son."

His blunt response took her aback. She felt the completely unexpected and irrational disappointment of realizing that he was being generous only because he wanted something from her. Something he had probably wanted from the very beginning.

If she gave in now, she would be throwing away the very principles she had worked so hard to establish since her exile.

"I cannot accept," she said. "I must go."

Garret's expression changed again, as if he were waking from a deep sleep and had forgotten where he was. His aura folded in on itself and vanished. He rolled down his sleeve, returned to his pack and began to shift things inside it, clearly pretending to keep himself busy so that he wouldn't have to deal with her. She watched him, her muscles frozen, knowing she would never see him again.

"I will lay a false trail," she said, pulling on her daycoat with clumsy hands. "If the humans do find our tracks, they will follow mine. I'm sure they would far rather kill me than you, traitor though they may name you." She stumbled a little as she took up her bow. "As your own people say, good luck."

An instant later she was running…throwing all her energy into every step, hoping that the initial burst of speed would carry her beyond his reach before she lost her breath. She knew it was time to abandon the area completely, and not only because of Garret. She had to get away from the possibility of any human or Opir contact, and lose herself in a place so remote that not even the most desperate Freeblood exiles would claim it.

True to her word, she laid a false trail, though it took a good deal more of her energy than she could afford. When she reached her temporary shelter, a small cave in the side of a hill, she gathered up her few possessions and left as quickly as she could, dizzy but still able to maintain a regular pace.

Every step carried her farther and farther away from the human who had inexplicably saved her life, then turned it upside down. Her heart seemed to drag several feet behind her.

By the time she left the woods a few hours later and reached the narrow path that paralleled the old northbound Interstate 5, a cold, driving rain had begun to fall. Normally it would not have bothered her; Opiri had lower body temperatures than humans, but their efficient metabolisms and greater strength enabled them to bear adverse conditions for longer periods.

But her energy was draining away a little more with every hour that passed. Hunger gnawed at her constantly. The weather didn't make her attempt to find game any easier, and she soon discovered that something had frightened away most of the local wildlife…a situation that might suggest an Opir pack in the area. She needed to avoid such packs at all costs.

As sunset approached, she sat down on a boulder under a stand of pines at the edge of a wide meadow and simply waited. The light began to fade. Nocturnal creatures would soon be venturing from their dens and hiding places, giving her another chance. Whatever came, she would have no choice but to take it.

Something large moved through the undergrowth on the other side of the meadow, an animal powerful enough to disregard any need for stealth.

A bear and her half-grown cubs emerged from the trees. The sow rose up on her hind legs, nostrils flaring, while the cubs tumbled about and cuffed each other in play.

Artemis caught her breath. She had seen plenty of bears before, but something in the scene touched her in a way she hadn't expected.

She rose slowly, careful not to attract the bears' attention, and prepared to set off again, feeling as if she had become detached from her body. Pebbles rolled on the ground behind her. She spun around, lost her balance, and then righted herself as she belatedly grabbed at the waterproof case of her bow.

Garret was standing a few feet from the boulder. He had thrown back the hood of his coat, and his wet auburn hair had darkened to a deep brown. His strong face seemed sculpted out of the rain itself, but he seemed no more disturbed by the weather than the bears were.

What disturbed Artemis was that he had approached almost as silently as an Opir. Once again she was surprised at his skill. Surprised—and furious that she had been caught off guard.

The only thing she had to be grateful for was that she perceived him only through her physical senses, not her mental ones. There was no aura to distract her.

Is that truly all you have to be thankful for? an inner voice demanded.

"What are you doing here?" she asked aloud. "Were you following me?"

"Did you finish your hunt?" he asked.

"Leave," she said, taking an aggressive step toward him. "Leave this place, before I must force you to go."

He looked her up and down with those keen eyes. "Why are you so afraid?" he asked softly as the rain continued to pelt down on his head and shoulders. "Is the prospect of helping me find a lost child so repugnant to you?"

A human child, she wanted to cry out. *Why should I care?*

But how could she lie to him, and to herself?

"You would ask me to hunt my own people," she said.

"They're barely 'your people' at all."

"But they are. And I believe they have a chance at a better future than what they face in the Citadels or as exiles."

He arched a brow. "You didn't mention this before."

"Why should you listen?"

"What does this 'better future' involve, Artemis? Teaching the rogues to follow your example and refuse to take human blood? Convincing them that humans aren't animals, aren't just another form of prey? How would they consider that an improvement on their lives now?"

She shook her head sharply. "There is so much you cannot possibly understand."

"I understand that you follow an ethical code of conduct that stretches to include humans, and that you live alone because you won't share your life with barbaric killers."

"I will not debate this with you," she said, knowing that she'd made a mistake in bringing her philosophy into the argument. "If our positions were reversed," she said, "would you lead me to humans *I* might choose to kill?"

"When did I say that I planned to kill anyone?"

"You have made your feelings about Freebloods very clear," she said, "and you will not hesitate to use any means to save your son."

"You're right," he said, matching the challenge in her voice. "But I'm not seeking revenge. If I can get Timon safely back without resorting to violence—" He broke off and took a deep breath, his gaze shifting to a point somewhere behind her.

She glanced over her shoulder. The bear had obviously seen them and had reared up again. Her formidable teeth flashed in her brown muzzle.

"Is that what you were hunting?" Garret asked.

Artemis licked the moisture from her lips. "I had no plans to attack them," she said, grasping eagerly at the change of subject.

"But you haven't found anything else."

"That is not your concern."

Garret set his pack down against the boulder. "I think you need my help," he said.

Growing sick with hunger and the scent of the blood pumping beneath his skin, Artemis stopped herself from falling against the boulder by a sheer act of will. "You cannot help me," she said.

"Do you object to taking human blood, even if it's freely given?"

"Freely given—at a price," she whispered.

"You live in the wilds. I'm well trained, but you're faster and have keener senses than I do. Even if you won't come with me, you can point me in the right direction. That's all I ask."

His voice began to fade in and out, the sound replaced by a thrumming behind her ears. She tried to convince herself to hold to her convictions, her vow never to take human blood again.

But philosophy would always fail when survival was at stake.

"Come with me," he said, holding out his hand.

No longer able to resist, she stumbled toward him. He picked up his pack and kept just ahead of her, leading her under the shelter of a stand of close-growing alders. Without quite knowing how she got there, she found herself on the damp ground beside him.

Garret removed his coat and then his shirt, neatly folding both garments and laying them across his pack. Her head began to pound, and she found herself staring at the muscles of his shoulders, arms and chest—an ideal image of human masculinity. There was nothing vulgar in the way he displayed himself, but she felt need pulsing not only in her belly but also between her thighs.

As she struggled with growing delirium, he removed a rubber cord from his pack, tied it around his arm above his biceps and flexed his hand into a fist, raising the veins in his wrist. His forearm was corded with muscle, the kind achieved only through hard manual labor.

But then she looked up at his face and noticed the pulse beating in his neck. Her mouth watered. She knew that he was no serf to be taken by the throat, though the desire to bare her own body, press it against his and sink her teeth into his neck was nearly more than she could endure. She looked at his mouth, the lips slightly parted, and wondered what it would be like to kiss him.

She hadn't kissed anyone in over a century.

"Are you certain…this is what you wish?" she asked, her voice raw with thirst.

He didn't seem to hear her. He ran his finger along

the length of the most prominent vein in his arm and met her gaze.

"Are you ready?" he asked.

A thread of sickness coiled through her belly like a parasitic worm. "I should not—"

"Are you afraid you'll hurt me? I promise that won't happen."

She licked her lips. "I can't."

Garret held her gaze. "You're afraid of losing control, aren't you? Whatever you think you might do, I'm prepared for it."

"Perhaps... *I* am not."

"You've run out of options, Artemis. Take my blood— or die."

His words were more than merely a warning. They were certainty, and Artemis knew he was right. It was a kind of blackmail, but he must know that in her desperation she might still overpower him and take what she needed.

He *trusted* her.

One time, she told herself. Then she would be strong again, and she would have learned from her mistakes.

Unable to fight her instincts, she grabbed his arm just below the elbow and bit into his wrist, barely remembering to temper the force of the bite before her teeth pierced his skin. He didn't so much as flinch, nor did he look away.

As his blood flowed over her tongue, Artemis felt something quite extraordinary. It wasn't at all like taking blood from the Citadel's public serfs, provided to Freebloods solely for the purpose of keeping them alive...barely. Nor was it similar to the times she had been compelled to feed from humans before and during the War, before the establishment of the Citadels.

That had been necessity. *This* was a far more intimate act, not merely a bargaining chip.

Intimate. That was the word, the sensation, the emotion,

that overwhelmed her. Her body grew warm with the rush
of vital nourishment and the headiness of lust.

Only after she was sated did she dare to look up. Garret's aura was alive, a scarlet halo visible only to her mind.
His eyes were like faceted emeralds, cool and hot all at
once. His chest rose and fell quickly, and she could smell
a distinctive change in his earthy, masculine scent.

Lust. It was happening again…his emotions were invading *her* mind, feeding her desire as hers fed his in an
endless cycle.

Bending to his arm again, she sealed the wound. Her
tongue lingered on his skin, tracing a line down to his
palm. He made a sound deep in his throat, and she felt
herself being pulled toward him. Her heart seemed ready
to leap from her chest into his. She closed her eyes and
pressed herself against him, her breasts exquisitely tender. He adjusted her to straddle him, and she could feel
his hardness thrusting against her through his camouflage pants.

Then he turned his face aside, pushed her away and
jumped to his feet. She did the same, trembling when she
should have been at her strongest, and wiped her mouth
with the back of her hand.

Wrong, she thought, *all wrong*. Garret had knocked her
so far off balance that she wasn't sure she would ever find
her footing again.

"That should be enough to help you finish healing,"
he said, reaching for his shirt as if nothing had happened.
"But we'll need to move soon."

"We." For a moment, she had almost forgotten.

This was a bargain. Now she had to fulfill her part of it.

Chapter 4

Artemis's lovely face turned utterly cold.

Garret wasn't surprised. She justifiably believed that she'd been blackmailed into helping him. She'd taken his blood only because she knew she had no other choice, and he would have done nearly anything to get her help.

But he also knew that she had been struggling ever since he'd rescued her...struggling with the same impulses and emotions he'd been feeling almost from the moment of their first meeting. Emotions most Nightsiders denied, believing them to be the bane of inferior humanity.

Yet when she'd taken his blood, he had experienced the kind of intense physical attraction he hadn't felt since Roxana's death. He'd been painfully aware of Artemis's petite but generously curved body, the quickness of her breathing, the deep mystery of her dark eyes. He had held her against him, feeling the heat of her arousal matching his, imagining her soft moans as he stroked her naked skin...

He cut off the thoughts before they could carry him into dangerous waters. In the end, he'd rejected his own lust. As the leader of Erebus's human Underground, he had always striven to be disciplined, watchful and patient. Roxana had made it almost easy.

Artemis didn't. What was it about her that stirred his body and soul to such an inexplicable degree? Knowing that she was different from other Freeblood rogues couldn't account for this strong, almost uncontrollable reaction. What had started out as a compulsion to save an intelligent being from an act of barbarism had quickly evolved into something else, something he didn't want any more than she did.

If he were making the decision only for himself, he would go his own way and let her go hers. It would be far better for both of them.

But Timon came first. His well-being was a thousand times more important than the relief of any small discomfort his father might experience along the way. No price was too high.

He had to gain Artemis's trust and keep it. Until Timon was safe.

"I'm sorry," he said, grabbing his coat. "I should have remembered that we'll both need to recover before we move on." He pulled on the coat and zipped it up with slightly numb fingers, aware that he had begun to tremble from loss of blood. The ground seemed to tilt toward him. He'd forgotten what it was like to give so much blood at one time.

"Are you ill?" Artemis asked, a little of the coldness leaving her eyes.

"Nothing that an hour of rest won't cure," he said. "And if you move too fast after taking so much blood, you're likely to have problems yourself."

She studied him with a frown. "I am in no danger," she

said. "But I see that you are not steady enough to travel. You had better sit down."

With a brief nod of acknowledgment, Garret slid to the base of the tree and leaned his head back against the trunk, grateful that they'd independently made the decision not to mention what had happened during the blood-taking.

"I don't expect you to stand guard for both of us," he said. "Wake me if I start to drift off."

Artemis chose a tree a little distance away and sat beneath it, holding herself erect and alert. "You are a strange human," she said.

"I thought you'd reached that conclusion when we first met," he said, closing his eyes.

"I know why you saved my life and shared your blood, or at least why you claim you did. What I do not understand is why you are so willing to reveal weakness."

Garret wondered if she was trying to make him angry. She didn't know him well enough to realize that he'd been through far too much to let pride influence his actions.

"I've already put my life in your hands many times over," he said. "If I didn't trust you—"

"No," she interrupted. "I have always heard that free human males believe themselves to be stronger than females in every way, and will do anything to avoid revealing any physical or mental impairment before one of the opposite sex."

Garret opened one eye a crack. "How do you know?"

"It is common knowledge."

"The same way it's common knowledge among humans that all Nightsiders are vicious killers?" He laughed shortly. "Not all human males feel the need to prove that they're invulnerable."

Artemis reached for her own small pack and unhooked her canteen. "It would be foolish to attempt it with a female Opir."

"I'd like to think I'm not a fool," Garret said.

"Would you have begged for my help, if I had been unwilling to give it?"

"Would that have made you feel better?"

"It would only have proven how much you wish to find your son."

"Then you have no more interest in having power over me than I do in having it over you. Which makes you exactly what I judged you to be."

"I still do not accept your 'judgment.'"

Garret rolled his head to observe the bears, who had apparently determined that the human and Nightsider were no threat and resumed their search for food. "Why didn't you go after them when you needed blood?" he asked. "It wasn't fear that stopped you, was it?"

"I was not afraid," she said, indignation in her voice.

"But something about them made you hesitate." He straightened, wishing he could sleep but determined to keep Artemis engaged. "They are a family."

She shrugged, though he could see that he had struck true. "Many creatures belong to what you call 'families,'" she said. "I cannot spare all of them."

"Do you know how long the female black bear protects her cubs?"

"I am not ignorant about the behavior of the creatures that live in the wild."

"One and a half years," Garret said. "These cubs are less than a year old. They'll go into torpor with her pretty soon, and then they'll be with her through the spring. No one can fault a bear's skill at parenting." He met Artemis's gaze. "When were you converted?"

"What has that to do with—"

"Did you have children?"

Her body stiffened. "I don't remember."

"You don't remember, or have you chosen to forget?"

"Even humans leave the past behind," she said.

"We try," he said, thinking of Roxana. His throat felt thick and full. "Do you remember what love is?"

"I…"

Garret unfastened his coat's padded chest pocket, withdrawing the battered photograph in its transparent envelope.

"This is Timon," he said. He rose and reached out to hand her the picture, and she accepted it with obvious reluctance. It had been taken before Roxana's death; Timon was smiling, a ball in his hands, and his best friend and cousin, Alessa, at his side. With his red hair and violet-gray eyes, Timon looked human.

There was softness in Artemis's face as she gazed at the picture, a softness that Garret had glimpsed only once or twice when she was at her most unguarded. Now she touched the picture with the tip of her finger, her lips curving in something like a smile.

"This picture was taken in a time of peace," she said. "Who is the other child?"

"Her name is Alessa. She's the daughter of my sister Alexia and her husband, Damon." He tucked the photo back into his pocket. "Alexia is half Opir. A dhampir."

Artemis stared at him. "Your father was a—"

"We had different fathers. I assure you, I'm fully human."

"But your sister—"

"Was born in the Enclave of San Francisco, after our mother found refuge there. She married a human in the Enclave, and I was the result."

Wrapping her arms around her chest, Artemis looked away. "I know…" she began. "I know it is an ugly thing, what our males did to your females during the War."

"It wasn't my intention to bring up the time before the Armistice," Garret said, regretting his slip.

"But surely Alexia was an agent for the Enclave, like all those of mixed blood."

"She left that life long ago. All I want for Timon is the freedom to live as he chooses, when he's old enough to make that decision. I'd hoped this would help you to understand."

"I always understood," she said in a near whisper.

"Then help me track the rogues who stole my son, and then return to your life. I won't trouble you again."

Her mouth tightened. "You will not expect me to fight for him?"

"I won't ask what you can't give."

They both fell into an uncomfortable silence, and Garret knew that it didn't matter whether or not they talked about what had happened between them. It was there, hanging in the air, haunting them, mocking them. An odd sensation seemed to tickle the surface of his brain, and all at once he was reliving the endless moments of lust and desire, hopelessly entangled with Artemis's need for blood and the memories of saving each other's lives.

"Artemis," he said, desperately resisting the urge to touch her, "I swear on Timon's life that what happened today won't be repeated."

It was clear that she understood him. She felt for the tree trunk at her back, fingers digging into the rough bark. Her breath came in short, sharp bursts.

"No," she said. "It will not."

They both looked away at the same time, and Garret released his breath. She said that now, and she must truly believe it.

But the connection between them couldn't simply be explained by the sharing of blood. He had wanted her in a way he hadn't wanted any woman since Roxana, and she'd wanted *him*. The blood was only the catalyst.

His mind refused to speculate further.

"I think we should go," he said, pushing himself to his feet. "If we walk slowly for a while, I'll be back to normal in a few hours."

"Surely you are not ready," she said. "It is nearly dark."

"As long as I stay close enough behind you, we can travel at night. It'll be harder for you by day, and we need to keep moving as long as we can." He hesitated, choosing his words carefully. "You can hunt along the way, and I'll do whatever I can to make things easier for you by keeping my distance."

Easier for both of us, he thought. But Artemis had already turned her back on him and was self-consciously examining her arrows, leaving him to wonder if they could both hold to their promises.

They started north in silence, setting out along a woodland trail commonly used by both men and Opiri passing through the region once known as the Willamette Valley. Artemis took the lead, casting her senses wide for any trace of Freebloods. The rain had obliterated most animal tracks in the area, and she knew it would perform the same service for any two-legged creatures.

However, she didn't have to rely only on sight. The scents of the wet forest were almost overwhelming, and she could track the movements of every animal—reptile, bird and mammal—that passed anywhere near them. Ironically, now that she no longer needed to hunt, she could hear tiny feet pattering over the pungent earth, and through the weeds and fallen pine needles, the rustle of wings in the undergrowth and deep among the branches.

But no Freebloods, and no humans.

As good as his word, Garret remained some distance behind. Yet he might as well have been clinging to her back; she could hear his rough breathing, the muffled tread of his boots, even the beat of his heart. And she could smell him, a pleasant scent that seemed to complement the aroma of freshly washed vegetation.

She could also smell his blood. As full darkness fell and he moved closer to take advantage of her night vision, she realized that the situation would not become any easier. One taste of his blood had been enough to make her crave it again. If she didn't find a way to ignore him, the journey would soon become intolerable.

As intolerable as the memory of other cravings…and the way he had turned her own unwanted emotions against her by asking her about her former life. About children, and loss, and forgetting.

And love.

As she walked, she concentrated on rebuilding the crumbling barriers inside her mind. By dividing her consciousness between observing their surroundings and reconstructing her mental shields bit by bit, she could almost forget Garret for minutes at a time.

After several hours of unceasing rain, stillness fell over the woods. Artemis slowed her pace. She knew this area well; after her expulsion from Oceanus she had lingered here, well outside the borders of the Citadel's territory, hoping that she might locate other exiled Freebloods and persuade them to accept her philosophy. She'd soon discovered that the outcasts had no interest in anything beyond survival.

She looked over her shoulder as she and Garret passed through a clearing where a cluster of ruined buildings stood, relics dating to sometime before the War. Garret was moving unsteadily, though his pace had never flagged. She came to a halt and waited for him to catch up.

"It's after midnight," she said as he drew level with her. "We should stop so that you can rest and eat."

He met her gaze from underneath his hood. "I'm not tired," he said.

"Nevertheless, you must have food. Wait here. I will hunt."

Before he could protest, she slipped away into the darkness where he couldn't follow. She brought down two rabbits in rapid succession and carried them back to the abandoned buildings.

Garret looked up, his eyes shadowed with exhaustion. "The goddess of the hunt returns," he said.

There was a complex note to his statement, not mockery but something more lighthearted. Belatedly, she remembered what it was. Teasing. And there was real admiration behind his words.

Admiration that deeply unsettled her.

She laid the rabbits down on a broken chunk of concrete and crouched beside it. "If I were a goddess," she said, "I could guarantee that a fire would be safe. As it is, I can only suggest that maintaining your strength is probably worth the risk."

"My future strength is worth nothing if we attract a pack of Freebloods or militiamen," he said. "Did you see or hear anything?"

"Freebloods *have* passed this way, but not in many nights."

"Then I'll risk the fire."

He removed a lighter from his pack and began to gather kindling. She went to look for fallen branches, and by the time she returned he had a small fire going. With quick, efficient movements, he skinned and cleaned the rabbits and suspended them from a long sharpened branch over the fire.

"You're welcome to share this with me, if you have an appetite for meat," he said, the firelight dancing in his eyes and carving his face out of the shadows.

"There is little enough for you, and I am not hungry," she said. "Eat, and I will patrol the area."

"Thank you, Artemis."

She ducked her head and pretended to examine her bow.
While he finished cooking his meal, she paced out several
wide circles around the ruins, listening as much as watching. By the time she returned, the fire was out, the remains
of the rabbits had been buried and Garret was fast asleep.

He trusts me, she reminded herself with more than a
little wonder. It was likely that he hadn't intended to sleep,
but his body had insisted, and his instincts…

His instincts told him that she would be there to wake
him if any danger threatened them.

Squatting beside him, she studied his face. Now that he
was asleep, she was even more aware that his usually calm
demeanor was only a kind of mask. He mumbled something that sounded like a name. She couldn't quite make
it out, but his muscles were tense, and she could feel distress radiating from him along with his body heat. Grief
beat against her new and fragile mental barriers.

"Garret," she whispered. "It is only a dream."

His eyelids fluttered. He expelled a short, harsh breath
and then relaxed into normal sleep. The pressure inside her
head disappeared, and she realized that learning to block
him was no longer a matter of mitigating the uncomfortable turmoil his emotions created in her thoughts. It had
become a necessity.

Still, a part of her longed to stroke the damp hair from
his forehead, to tell him that all would be well and there
was no need for bad dreams.

If she surrendered to such impulses, anything that happened afterward would be entirely her own fault.

An owl hooted somewhere above her and glided out of
the trees. It dived into the tall brown grass, and something
squealed. The strong taking the weak. The world fell into a
deep hush, as if in mourning for the fallen. Another sound
came faintly to Artemis's ears. No animal had made it.

She entered the woods on the other side of the ruins and listened for a repeat of the cry. It came again, softer than before, a moan of someone in pain.

Unbearable pain, forcing its way into Artemis's mind. She paused to brace herself and searched for the source.

She found the Freeblood lying half tangled in a mass of blackberry bushes, one arm caught in the brambles and his body twisted awkwardly. There was a gaping wound in his neck, too severe to heal on its own. The bite of another Opir.

Dark eyes rolled toward Artemis as she approached cautiously. He made a sound in his ruined throat. Most Opiri maintained the appearance of the age they'd been when they were converted, and this one appeared to have been turned in his late teens. Perhaps, she thought, after the end of the War.

"I will not hurt you," she said, though she knew such an assurance would probably mean nothing to an exile. He jerked as she drew nearer, his hands clenching and unclenching.

She didn't try to ask him what had happened. She could guess well enough. He might have been dying for hours, and his body's attempts to heal would have driven him to starvation.

"Brother," she said, dropping to her knees beside him. "Can you hear me?"

If he did, she thought, she had a feeling that things were going to get a lot more complicated.

Chapter 5

The boy's mouth opened, but all that emerged was another groan.

"I know you suffer," she said. "But I can ease your discomfort." She laid her hand on his cool forehead and bent over him. She placed her mouth on his neck, releasing a little of the healing chemicals she had used on Garret. He tried to resist her, but he didn't have the strength to fight for long. After a few moments he relaxed and closed his eyes.

Artemis withdrew and sliced her wrist with her smaller knife. While the blood of a pure Opir could not nourish another full Opir, it would temporarily ease his raging hunger. She offered her wrist and let him take what he could.

When he was finished, she pressed her palm to her wound until it began to close, and then touched his forehead again. It was slightly warmer, but she knew he had little time left.

"Listen," she said, stroking the boy's pale hair out of

his face. "I am seeking a pack of Freebloods who might be carrying a human child with them. Have you seen such a pack?"

Confusion crossed the young Freeblood's face. "Human?" he mumbled.

"A child, who never did any Opir harm."

"Why...you care?" he whispered.

"Because I believe that it is not our true nature to kill each other over humans, or take life, even human life, simply because we can."

With unexpected strength, the Freeblood grasped her wrist. "I...saw...the child," he said. "I was...with..."

She covered his hand with hers. "Where?"

Both she and the Freeblood heard the approaching footsteps before he could answer. The young Opir flinched. His fear nearly paralyzed Artemis, and only her rational assessment of Garret's essential character permitted her to keep her objectivity.

"Stay back," she called to Garret without looking away from the Freeblood's panic-stricken eyes. "He won't hurt you," she said to the boy.

Disregarding her warning, Garret circled around the bushes to stand just on the other side. "He was with *them*?" he asked. There was no pity in his voice.

The young Opir pushed against her, the urge to flee warring with his body's need for blood. Artemis held him down.

"What is your name?" she asked him.

"P-Pericles," he croaked.

"Pericles," she said, "this human is called Garret Fox. He saved my life from other humans who would have killed me."

"Where is my son?" Garret demanded.

"Garret," Artemis said sharply. She cupped the dying

Freeblood's head in her hands. "Pericles, where did you see the child?"

Pericles closed his eyes again. "Make the human go."

Ruthless in his suspicion, Garret moved to stand behind her and gazed down at the boy with his hand on his knife. "Where is he?" he repeated.

Shifting her body, Artemis placed herself between human and Opir. Garret felt like a looming thundercloud at her back.

"Don't come any closer," she warned.

"Answer me," Garret said, stepping around her.

Artemis stood and turned, her face only inches from his. "It would be very foolish if you and I were to fight now, when we may learn something of use to us," she said.

They stared at each other until the Freeblood gurgled in a way that sounded very much like death. Darkness swirled up in Artemis's mind.

The boy's time had run out.

Pushing all thoughts of dying aside, Artemis knelt beside him again. "It's all right," she said gently, cradling his head in her arms. "Garret, if you provide him with a little blood, he may be able to speak."

She expected refusal. Instead, he crouched beside her and gazed at the boy, his jaw working. He began to draw his knife from its sheath. Artemis caught his arm.

Garret jerked away and cut his wrist. "Tell me where I can find my son," he said to Pericles.

"Take it," Artemis urged. "His blood cannot cure you, but if you help us, at least one of your people will remember you with honor."

Licking his dry lips, the boy stared at the dripping blood in fascination. "North," he said. "Beyond… Oceanus's territory, across the… Columbia River." He choked. "Wa-Washington."

"Why?" Garret asked. "Why are they taking my son so far away?"

"I…" Pericles closed his eyes, beginning to lose consciousness. With a quick glance at Artemis, Garret offered his wrist to Pericles. The young Freeblood's mouth clamped on his flesh. Garret winced but held steady, and Artemis found herself battling both her own unexpected hunger and Garret's heightened emotions.

After a minute the boy's head fell back onto Artemis's arms, and he went still. The echo of his pain faded from Artemis's mind. Then there was only an emptiness where he had been for such a short while.

Somewhere in the darkness, an owl hooted. Perhaps, Artemis thought, the same owl as before. She laid the boy's head on the ground and closed his eyes with a sweep of her palm.

"Thank you," she said to Garret. She took his arm and sealed the wound. Garret hardly seemed to notice.

"He was with the ones who took my son," he said, his voice hoarse with anger.

"And they left him here to die," she said.

"They are rogues, and so was he."

"Yet you showed him mercy."

"To find out what we needed to know. It's unlikely he'd have done the same for me."

Garret had not felt the boy's very real fear of him, Artemis thought. She wished *she* had not. She lifted the boy in her arms and carried him to a place under the trees. She laid him out there, his hands folded across his chest, and stood over him for a few moments. Garret waited silently behind her.

"I know you don't believe it," she said, "but this boy was also a victim. I do not think he has been Opir for more than a few years."

"That makes it worse," Garret said. "He doesn't have

the excuse of having had decades or even centuries to forget what it was like to be human. He chose to join a pack of rogues and kidnap a human child."

"Did it occur to you that he might have needed to join a pack in order to survive?"

"Like *you* did?"

His sarcasm bit hard. "It is because I am older that I could do what he could not," she said.

"You can't make excuses for every rogue who commits crimes against humanity."

"Many of your kind would say that I have committed such crimes merely by existing."

Garret gripped her arm and turned her to face him. "Those humans would be wrong," he said.

"How many would have saved *my* life?" she asked, trembling at his touch.

"I would not be the only one."

"And I believe that only the worst of my kind would harm a human child." She pulled her arm from his light hold and strode back to the ruins.

"Artemis," he called after her.

She stopped without turning. "I do not wish to quarrel," she said.

"Neither do I," he said. His moon-cast shadow fell over her, and she felt his breath stir her hair. "We obviously don't understand each other very well yet."

"Perhaps it would be better if we did not."

"Our survival might depend on it."

She swung around to face him. "What is it that you do not understand?"

"I heard you tell Pericles that you believe it isn't in your people's true nature to kill each other over humans, or take human lives just because you can."

"Why is that a surprise to you?" she asked.

"Are you really concerned about saving humans, or only about Freebloods killing each other?"

Without answering, she broke into a fast walk back to camp, where she began to gather up her things. Garret did the same, though he moved more slowly. Artemis thought she sensed regret in his mind. He checked again to make certain the fire was out, and that the rabbit carcasses and entrails were well buried, not that an Opir hunter couldn't have smelled them if he'd been searching.

But there was still no sign of intruders, so Garret withdrew a folded sheet of paper from his pack, and carefully smoothed it across the cracked and overgrown floor of the building, right where a shaft of moonlight illuminated the ground. Artemis recognized a precise drawing of the western half of the former state of Oregon.

"If I judge correctly," he said, pressing his fingertip to a spot on old Highway 99E, "we're right about here, roughly twenty miles south of Albany." He glanced up at her for confirmation.

"Yes," she said, grateful for the need to focus on practicalities. "That is also my estimate."

"And ten miles north of Albany is the southern border of Oceanus," he said, indicating a large black square on the eastern slope of the Coast Range. "We have only limited information about this area. Do you know how far inland their territory reaches?"

"Why do you think *I* can tell you?" she asked.

"You were exiled from Oceanus, weren't you?"

"How do you know?"

"Because we've learned that most exiles stick pretty close to their home territory. There are only a few small Opiri outposts between Oceanus and the northern California Citadel, Erebus. And I know you didn't come from Erebus."

"What of the rogues who stole your son? Were they not from Erebus, nearer to your colony?"

"As near as I can tell, they were from a Citadel some distance away. They were acting out of character. It's all a mystery." He withdrew his hand and clenched his fist on his thigh. "From what the Freeblood—Pericles—told us, the rogues are taking Timon across the river into old Washington. God knows why. But if he was right, they'll probably have to cross the Columbia River near Portland, where one bridge is still supposed to be intact. They'll follow the path of least resistance, the I-5 corridor."

"But that will also be a more exposed route," Artemis said. "Oceanus itself may be situated in the foothills of the Coast Range, but its territory reaches across the valley to the western slope of the Cascades. The rogues will be summarily executed if they are caught." She tapped the map with her fingertip. "They might have gone farther into the Cascade foothills to avoid any chance of meeting a patrol."

"And that's much rougher terrain," Garret said. "If we can find a more direct route across the territory, we may catch up with them, or even get to the Columbia before them."

"Or we may be captured," she said. "I am of no use to them, so they will kill me quickly. But they will either take you as a serf or, if they think you are dangerous enough, execute you as an example to other humans."

"No surprises there," Garret said, carefully folding the map. "But I don't expect you to take unnecessary risks on my behalf."

"You always knew I would be taking such risks."

"Yes," he said, meeting her gaze. "But I'm prepared to release you from our pact."

"Because we quarreled?"

"I was wrong to interfere between you and the Freeblood. And I have no excuse for saying what I did about your motives for helping your fellow Freebloods. But my son must come first."

"Then nothing has changed," Artemis said, feeling another jolt of his worry and pain. "The most logical route to Portland is also the shortest, but there is still no guarantee that the rogues have not chosen the same route."

"Agreed."

"So we continue to parallel Interstate 5 for the time being."

She shrugged into her pack and returned to the path, leaving the young Freeblood to the elements and the scavengers that would return him to the earth.

Three days' cautious travel brought them to Oceanus's southern boundary. They crossed the Willamette River at Albany and continued north, roughly paralleling Interstate 5, to the rural city of Salem—which, like most other pre-War human cities, was a mishmash of half-fallen buildings and bare foundations, overgrown parking lots, cracked streets and patches of woodland that filled every available space in between. The river and a long line of hills stood between them and the western half of the valley and the Coast Range.

Patrols of Opiri and Daysiders from Oceanus would have to cross those hills to find them, Garret thought, and the presence of such a patrol on their side of the Willamette would be a matter of very bad luck.

At the moment, he and Artemis were observing from the edge of what had been a wide street bordered by parking lots and the remains of large, warehouse-style buildings. The woods ended here, replaced by scattered, smaller trees and shrubs, and resumed a thousand feet to the northeast.

Artemis rose from a crouch, shaking her head. "Nothing new," she said.

Garret concealed his frustration. Artemis had been vigilant; as they'd traveled, varying the hours between night and day, she had found numerous indications that Free-blood packs had passed this way. The "when" was more difficult to pin down, and there had been no clear signs of the presence of a human child.

He's still alive, Garret told himself. *He's a fighter. And they must have a reason for taking him so far.*

"Garret." Artemis laid a gloved hand on his shoulder, her dark eyes catching reflected light under the shelter of her hood. It was the first time they'd had any physical contact since they'd left Pericles, and suddenly he was immersed in the warmth of her body and the indescribable scent of her skin drifting out from beneath her heavy cloak. His heart began to race as it had when she had taken his blood, triggering the same startling current of desire and longing he had felt before and had struggled to ignore ever since.

Her fingers began to shake, and she withdrew her hand. "It's still early," she said. "We can be halfway across the territory before night falls."

"How long since you've taken blood?" he asked, breathing deeply to slow his heartbeat and suppress his arousal before it became too obvious. "You haven't hunted for yourself since you took mine, have you?"

She shook her head in a distracted way that worried him. He'd expected her to hunt at least once during the times they'd stopped to rest, but he'd begun to suspect that she'd neglected herself because of his eagerness to keep moving.

"Go now," he said, "I can wait as long as it takes."

"Later," Artemis said. With an abrupt, almost clumsy motion, she hitched up her pack and headed north toward the next patch of forest. Garret jogged to catch up, and then strode ahead of her. He could see far better in daylight than she could, and though the chances of ambush seemed small, he wasn't prepared to risk her walking into one. The Vampire Slayer, though still hidden in his pack, was close enough at hand that he could pull the segments out, assemble them and fire in less than a minute.

Sooner or later Artemis would find out about the weapon. He just hoped it wasn't because he had to kill a Nightsider right in front of her eyes.

They cleared the ruins of Salem by midday and began to travel in a more northeasterly direction, moving well away from the river and mountains to the west. Garret kept a constant eye on Artemis, watching for any sign of weakness that would indicate an urgent need for blood. But she continued to behave as if everything were normal, and he knew that forcing the issue wouldn't do anything to gain her cooperation.

At last they crossed the old six-lane freeway, passing through former pastures, farmland and orchards that had given way to mixed conifer and deciduous forest. Several times Artemis detected the scent or tracks of Opiri moving in groups, but again there was no indication that they carried a human prisoner. They met no patrols from Oceanus. It seemed to be going almost too smoothly until, soon after sunset, Artemis began to weave and stumble again.

Garret was looking for shelter where she could safely rest when she jumped the thicket of wild roses that stood between them and barreled into him, dragging him to the ground. Her hood barely stayed over her head.

"Opiri!" She flung her body across his as if to prevent him from rising.

His pack—and the VS—were trapped beneath him. He lay still as her breath puffed against his cheek, the gentle curves of her body seeming to fit against his like a missing piece of a puzzle falling into place.

"How close?" he asked.

Artemis turned her head, her lips inches from his. "Close," she said. "It is fortunate that the wind is with us."

"Patrol? Or rogues?" he asked.

"I believe they are Freebloods. I think there is a human with them, but—"

"Timon!" Garret began to rise, but she held him back with all her obviously waning strength.

"Don't be a fool!" she said. "If they have him, it won't do us any good to rush right up to them and try to take him."

Closing his eyes, Garret worked to regain his composure. Artemis was right. God knew what the Freebloods might do with Timon if they felt threatened. If it even *was* Timon.

"Yes," he said. "I'm all right."

She stared into his eyes for a long moment and then rolled off. Keeping low, he got to his knees and looked over the top of the thicket.

"You won't see them," Artemis said, kneeling beside him. "They are some distance ahead." She slid him a glance out of the corner of her eye. "You know I have a far better chance of getting near them without alerting them."

"Not when you haven't fed," he said.

"I am well," she said.

"You'll have to take my blood again."

"No."

"You're being irrational, Artemis."

"I will not do it."

"Then you'll have to stay here while I scout, or you could get both of us killed."

"I tell you I am well!" she said, her voice nearly rising from a whisper.

He took her face between his hands, though he knew what it might do to both of them. "Are you so disgusted by what happened between us that you'd ignore your own health and risk your life?"

The moment he finished speaking, he realized how desperately he wanted her to say no.

Chapter 6

Her breath caught, and so did Garret's. Fear and desire surged through his body, and it almost seemed as though they were her feelings as well as his. She was afraid of him, and of herself. Afraid she would take, and give, too much. She sensed that he was desperately afraid for her. Not because she could help him find Timon, but—

Artemis pulled away, her face paler than it had been a moment before. "When we know whether or not your son is with these Opiri," she said, "I will do whatever is necessary. For the moment, you must let me go ahead."

"No," he said. "We go together."

"So that you can protect me?"

He knew how she would react if he admitted the truth. Yes, he wanted to protect her, as much as he'd ever wanted to protect Roxana. And he'd been in a far less advantageous position to help Roxana in the Citadel where he'd been a serf and she his mistress.

"If you're not in your right mind, you'll need my protection," he said. He glanced up at the sky. "It's nearly sunset. In a few minutes you won't need your heavier clothes, and you'll be able to move faster. But don't make a move without me, Artemis. I mean it."

She gave him a scathing glance. "And to think I had thought you a human male without undue pride in his own abilities."

"It's *your* pride I'm worried about. Let's go."

Bent nearly double, they ran northeast, Artemis pausing twice to get her bearings. A quarter mile on, she stopped again and threw back her hood. Only a trace of pink light lingered over the hills to the west.

"The Opiri are somewhere beyond those trees," she said, pointing at a wide stretch of mixed woodland. As she began to move forward, Garret knelt to check the VS parts in his pack.

He rose again and trotted after Artemis as she slipped from tree to tree as lightly as a leopardess. She was nearly crawling when they reached the border of the woods. He dropped to his belly behind her. An area of nearly unbroken grassland stretched ahead as far as he could see.

"Do you see the rogues?" he said, squinting into the darkness.

"No, but I know where they are." Her voice held a new note, and the hair prickled at the back of Garret's neck. "They are camped less than two hundred yards from here. There are seven, perhaps eight, of them, and—"

"Timon?"

"I…sense that there is more than one human in the area."

He tensed to move again. "We have to get closer."

"Wait." Her nose wrinkled. "These Opiri are ready to fight. They are expecting to attack or be attacked."

"Attacked by whom?"

"The humans, perhaps," she murmured. "Whoever they

may be, they are remarkably foolish to venture within the Citadel's borders."

"And my son could be caught in the middle of whatever's about to happen."

She turned to meet his gaze. "If the Freebloods have protected him so far, they will not let him be hurt. And if the humans should win…"

"We can't stand by and let this—"

"We must. If we die, who can save Timon?"

Clenching his teeth, Garret tried to weigh the options objectively. Artemis was right. Whoever the humans were, they would want to help a human child, and in a fight, the rogues would keep Timon out of the way. He and Artemis would probably have a better chance of grabbing Timon when the battle was decided one way or the other.

"I know this is against your every instinct," Artemis said. "I am sorry. I will go ahead, and see if—"

"No," he said, pulling her down when she attempted to move. "Can we get any closer without the Nightsiders sensing us?"

"No. In fact we have to go back to be safe," she said.

She retreated. Garret lingered a moment, listening, but his human senses were not acute enough to gather any additional information. Reluctantly, he followed Artemis to a point well within the shelter of the woods but close enough to the grassland that she could monitor what was happening there.

They waited as the long minutes went by, sitting a long arm's reach apart from each other. Garret was constantly, painfully aware that Artemis was very near but not quite close enough to touch, and that he badly wanted to touch her. Even in the midst of so much uncertainty, those feelings refused to go away.

An hour passed in silence, and then another. Artemis's head began to droop, and her breathing grew shallow. Garret moved closer to her. He noted a new transparency to her pale skin, a dullness in her hair and a deepening of the shadows under her cheekbones and closed eyes.

"Artemis," he said, carefully touching her shoulder.

She jerked awake, her body snapping into a defensive posture far more slowly than it should have. She blinked, recognized him and clambered to her feet.

"What has happened?" she demanded.

"Nothing, as far as I can tell," he said. "But you were falling asleep."

"I wasn't—" She broke off and strode away through the trees. Garret waited ten minutes and then got up to follow her.

He found her at the edge of the woods. "Nothing has changed," she said as he crouched beside her.

"That's right," he said. "You still need what you need. We have to be ready to move quickly."

"You will become weak if I take too much."

"I trust you to take only as much as is safe for both of us."

They stared at each other, and Garret could see her struggling with arguments he knew she didn't want to make. Arguments that had nothing to do with her fear of his becoming weak. But she knew he was right, and she was the first to look away.

"Very well," she said. "But we should use the other wrist."

Garret hesitated, reexamining the decision he'd made. He couldn't pretend that there wasn't a risk in giving her much more intimate access to his blood.

But she would derive nourishment from his throat more efficiently than she would by taking blood from his wrist. And if he couldn't trust her now, he might as well let those Opiri in the field kill him themselves.

He led her back to their camp, removed the blanket from

his pack and laid it down at the foot of a tall pine. Then he removed his coat and unbuttoned his shirt. Her gaze flew to his hands, watching his progress with apparent fascination, and he found himself suddenly self-conscious. He could sense her need as if it were his own.

"What are you doing?" she asked in a slightly strained voice.

"Just what we agreed," he said.

Removing his shirt, he folded it and laid it on the ground behind him. He rested his palms on his thighs and settled into the calm, detached state that had always served him well when he had worked with the human Underground in Erebus. He would need all that detachment to treat this feeding like any other.

He tilted his head back, took a deep breath. "I'm ready," he said.

"You are…" Artemis stammered. "You expect me to…"

"It's fast, and it's practical," he said, staring up into the green boughs overhead. "The sooner we're finished, the sooner we'll both be ready to take whatever action is necessary."

"How many times have you done this?" she asked.

"Often enough to know what I'm doing."

He waited, holding himself ready, until he felt the heat of her body close to his, her breath sighing over his skin, her lips brushing his throat.

"Are you certain?" she asked softly.

"Look at me, Artemis."

Whatever she saw in his eyes apparently frightened her, and she almost bolted. But he grabbed her hand, and she settled down again, panting and trembling. Her teeth penetrated his flesh. She moaned as his blood began to flow, and he felt desire take hold exactly as he had prayed it wouldn't. He reached out to clasp his hands around her waist. He found the hem of her tunic and slipped his fingers beneath, sliding his palms over the skin below her ribs.

Then he paused, because she hadn't asked for his touch, because he knew that she was not Roxana. But Artemis gripped his wrist and held his hand where it was.

She was too far gone to stop. And so was he.

The moment Artemis tasted his blood, she knew it was too late.

She felt his warm breath stirring her hair, heard the rapid drumming of his heart, smelled the surge of his lust and only drank the more deeply, caught up in an ecstasy more overwhelming than any she had known before.

Even the last time he had given his blood, it hadn't been like this. She'd underestimated the impact of taking it directly from his throat. An intimate act, she'd thought when she'd first met him, one he surely wouldn't share with her.

And yet here she was, and her body and mind were opening to Garret, abandoning all caution, renewing the intense emotional connection she had wanted so badly to extinguish. She had forgotten what it could be like, how quickly one could lose control with the right partner. And she had never taken blood during what humans called "making love."

But now, when Garret touched her bare skin, she felt his excitement as well as her own. She was being carried away by a current she couldn't stop, delirious with feelings and sensations that superseded mere arousal or the sensual stimulation that so often accompanied feeding.

She wanted him. She wanted to possess him, to be possessed by him, to join in complete physical union. What happened afterward…

No. The unraveling thread of her sanity begged her to remember what she could lose, what she could do to Garret. Once she stepped onto this path, she might never find her way back again. A single reckless act might finally shatter any hope she had of closing the gate against Garret Fox.

But sanity had no hope when Garret's fingertips discovered her nipples and teased them into firm, sensitive peaks. His blood soothed her tongue. Erotic images shaped in Garret's mind slipped into hers as his fingers slid down her belly and to the waistband of her pants. He unfastened the fly and dipped inside. Callous skin touched tender flesh. She shifted her body, urging him to explore as she continued to drink.

Garret stroked her with one hand while his other worked at the buttons of her shirt. Cool air washed over her breasts, and she straightened as his emotions told her what he wanted to do. Acting entirely on instinct, she sealed the bite and leaned back, giving him complete access to her breasts.

When he took her nipple into his mouth, she moaned at the incredible sensation of his reaction as well as her own, desire doubled and redoubled as he suckled her hungrily. His other hand found its way between her thighs and grazed the tight little bud where pleasure was almost like pain. She gasped, and he gasped with her.

Somehow her pants came off and she was straddling his thighs, rubbing against the taut bulge of his erection. She felt herself floating, guided to the ground by strong arms, lying on her back with her thighs parted.

The touch of his lips and tongue in her most sensitive place drew a muffled cry from her throat, quieted only by some distant sense of self-preservation. She seemed to recall something like this happening long ago, but the past was as unreal as the future. Garret knew exactly where and how to use his tongue to tickle and tease, drawing out each caress with rapid flicks and long strokes.

She arched her back, begging him with her entire body.

He turned his attention to her breasts and continued his ministrations while she felt for the waistband of his pants.

"Garret," she whispered, filling her mind with the emotional images of taking and being taken. His aura erupted around him, emitting tongues of flame that strained toward her. Her own aura flared for the first time, a blue-tinged amethyst radiance that opened to accept the thrust of his fire as her body was ready to accept his.

Garret was more than ready. Her hand found him, large and very hard. The intensity of his need—hers—multiplied a thousandfold.

For a moment there was nothing between them. Nothing at all—no boundaries, no barriers, no walls. He eased himself over her, gazing down at her with his weight braced on his hands and his hips between her thighs.

Again she saw herself through his eyes, less a distinctive shape than an aura enclosing the interwoven strands of her emotions. But the image began to take form, and she glimpsed her face: eyes closed, lips parted, hair wild and tangled about her shoulders.

And beautiful. Beautiful in a way she could never have imagined. It was the face she'd seen in mirrors before her exile and sometimes in the imperfect reflection of water, but bathed in a gentle light that softened the blue of her aura to a silky violet. Violet water, smooth and untroubled.

Garret caught her lips with his, exploring the terrain of her mouth, coaxing her to open for him. With a low moan of surrender, she parted her lips, and his tongue found its way inside. He curled it around hers, sucked, kissed her more deeply than she would have believed possible.

Violet transformed to deep, hot purple. She pushed her fingers into his hair and bit lightly into his lower lip, drawing blood. He adjusted his position so that a single thrust would make them one at last.

Something remarkable happened then. Feelings she

barely recognized bloomed in her mind, so astonishing that, at first, she didn't know how to name them.

But not all the memories were dead. There were no times, no places…only the joy and happiness and exhilaration of the single thing she had sought and found and lost before the change. The thing she wanted again, here within her grasp.

Everything else vanished. There was no more need to struggle, to aspire to anything greater than this. Her emotions swelled to obliterate all other desires. She would float in this perfect world forever, in endless bliss and exultation.

She had found what the humans called heaven.

But there was a bubble of disturbance in the flawless pool of eternal rapture, a devil in this paradise. It picked and prodded at her, mocking her with warnings she could not quite shut out.

There is no heaven for Opiri.

"Artemis," Garret said. His voice was hoarse and urgent, his mind spinning on the edge of euphoria. She knew that all she had to do was speak a single word, and every other voice would be silenced.

So would her dreams and hopes for her people. She would no longer care about them, because she had what she wanted, all she would ever want.

Forget them, she thought. *You owe them nothing.*

But her past would not be silent. *They are your people*, it said. *How can you abandon them for a human?*

"No," she whispered.

All we fought for destroyed, because of you. Because of him.

Garret's face came into sharp focus, blazing with elation. *He* could destroy nothing, but he could give her—

"Roxana?" he murmured.

She saw her own face again…saw it change, felt Garret's bewilderment and her own turmoil as that other face slipped over hers like a mask. Eyes too dark, hair too long, features too...

"No," Garret said hoarsely. The stranger vanished, but the sheer weight of his emotions—regret, grief, confusion—bore down on her with such force that she thought they would crush her. Illusion shattered. Shock worked as no careful discipline could have done.

She pushed him out—out of her heart, her mind, her very being—and slammed the wall down between them, severing all emotional ties, all the feelings that had tempted her into relinquishing the new way she had sought to win for her own kind.

The feelings that had nearly made her surrender to a human who saw another face even as he prepared to possess her.

Chapter 7

Artemis scrambled to her feet, snatching up her pants as she bolted away from him. Garret's face was drained of color, and though she could no longer sense his emotions, she saw the stark pain in his eyes.

For her, or for himself?

Roxana.

Somehow Artemis dressed, gathered her weapons and fled without looking at him again. She ran recklessly toward the border of the woods, as if by simply putting physical distance between herself and Garret she might undo the past hour and forget.

But she knew it was not possible to regain that safe sense of living in a fortress that could never be breached. There was no undoing *this*. The gate had closed, but she knew that she could never take Garret's blood again. It wasn't simply a matter of becoming dependent. Death would be preferable to losing herself, losing all she believed had made her what she was.

Garret had asked her if she remembered what love was. She hadn't been honest then. She remembered the physical and emotional closeness that accompanied complete faith in another: a lover, life partner, the one she could not live without. Garret had made her experience some of those feelings again. His blood, his touch, had engulfed her in passions she had left behind for a greater, nobler purpose.

But there was no reality behind those passions, no foundation. Garret's invocation of that other name was proof enough of that.

Had that other woman been so different from her, though? Ivory hair, eyes the color of rich, purple wine—the distinctive traits of any Opir save for the newest converts.

Artemis filled her lungs with pine-scented air, and then expelled her agitation along with her breath. The only purpose in analyzing her emotions was to rid herself of them. If she could not be an impartial, dispassionate teacher, she could not help her own people break the chains of savagery that bound them to lives of degradation and self-destruction.

She slowed as she approached the field, focusing her attention on her surroundings. There was no sound, no movement in the sea of grass, but she knew the Freebloods and humans were still there.

Stretching out on her belly, Artemis rested her cheek against the cool earth. This was a test. If she truly considered the fate of her kind more important than anything else, she could leave this place and let Garret find his own way to his son, facing the dangers of capture and death alone.

But she could no more leave him than she could erase her empathic "gift." The test did not ask her to choose which commitment was more important. It asked for proof that she could remain by Garret's side and not lose herself again. If she succeeded, then she might be capable and worthy of carrying out her mentor Kronos's great dream. The one he had died for.

She was preparing to return to Garret when a flock of birds exploded from the tall grass, followed by the report of many guns firing in unison. She froze as cries of pain and terror and rage rent the night, and the thump of flesh meeting flesh accompanied the rising scent of blood.

"Timon!"

Garret staggered up behind her, his pack dangling from his shoulder by one strap. His face was pale, his breathing shallow. Artemis trapped her concern in a cage of logic, grateful that she could not feel what he felt, trying not to imagine what he had thought when she left him without explanation.

"I am certain that Timon is well," she said calmly. "You have lost a great deal of blood, and you have been running. You must rest."

He looked at her as if she had lost her sanity, let the pack drop to the ground and knelt beside it. He fumbled inside with shaking hands, withdrawing a handgun.

"You cannot go out there," Artemis said. "Certainly not with that."

There was another scream, but Garret never so much as glanced up. He set the gun aside and withdrew several components of a weapon Artemis didn't remember ever having seen before. He pushed the pieces together, pausing several times when his clumsy fingers lost their grip. When he was finished and raised the weapon to check his work, she knew what it was: the only projectile weapon the humans had produced that could kill an Opir with a single shot to almost any spot on the body.

"No," she said. "You will be killed before you can ever use that thing."

"There's no other choice." He met her gaze as he got to his feet. "Don't try to stop me."

"I said the same thing to *you* once," she reminded him. "I believe I managed to make it ten feet before I collapsed."

Jaw set, Garret stepped out into the darkness. He had gone perhaps three yards when one of his legs gave out from under him and he fell to his knee. Another spatter of gunshots blotted out whatever sound he might have made, and then a deep hush fell, even more absolute than the silence that had come before.

Garret clambered to his feet, swinging the rifle back into position. Artemis joined him. She sniffed the air, and it was as if she could *see* what had happened as surely as if she had been in the middle of it.

"Let me go ahead," she said. "If there are any survivors, I can move more quickly to do whatever must be done."

"Together," he said grimly.

Artemis knew that trying to stop him would be pointless. He was already moving again, ready to shoot at anything with pale skin and sharp incisors. All she could do was hope that she was right about his son.

Before them lay a scene of utter carnage. Bodies were scattered across the field, mostly Opiri, seven or eight of them lying in pools of dark red. There were several humans, dressed in the mottled clothing of militiamen. Their annihilation had left abstract, scarlet patterns on the grass and shrubs around them, attesting to the violence of their deaths.

Timon was not with them.

He squeezed his eyes shut, waiting for his heart to resume its normal speed. After a few moments he opened his eyes again and examined the battlefield. He'd seen such violence before, but somehow this seemed worse, as if he might have prevented the killing with a few well-chosen words in the same way he'd once rallied and encouraged members of the human Underground in Erebus.

He glanced at Artemis. Her face was expressionless. She, too, must regret the killings, but he had no way of knowing what else she thought.

And she wasn't going to tell him. Now he knew that she had been correct to hesitate before taking his blood again. If it had only been a matter of physical attraction, he might have been able to hold himself aloof. He had deceived himself into thinking he could donate without being affected by her the way he'd been the first time— wanting her, wanting to be inside her, to claim her for his own in a way he had no right to do.

But it wasn't just her beauty and his desire for her that had created the danger. It wasn't even a matter of his admiration for her courage and determination, and for the compassion he had once believed no Freeblood was capable of feeling.

There was more to it, much more. It had been as if they'd joined in some profound meeting of minds and hearts, a union of a kind he'd never imagined was possible, a bond stronger than any he could remember experiencing in his life.

Except with Roxana.

He had seen Roxana's face, serene and untroubled, at the very moment when his inexplicable joy was at its highest. There had been no recriminations in that face, no censure of his need for Artemis, but the grief had come anyway.

And he'd spoken his wife's name.

The strange connection between him and Artemis had shattered, and she'd run as if the mere sight of him disgusted her.

He'd wondered then if she'd abandoned him. He wouldn't have been shocked if she had. He'd betrayed her. They had both wanted comfort in the midst of fear and savagery, and he had denied her even that small relief.

But she was still the same Artemis. Apparently they would go on as if nothing had happened. Go back to where they had begun.

"Something is moving," she said, cutting across his thoughts. She pointed west. "Over there, away from the others."

Lifting the rifle, Garret started forward, placing his feet carefully so that he wouldn't stumble again. A dozen yards on, he saw the grass quiver and heard the faint rustle of something still hidden from his view.

"Come out," he said, raising his voice.

The grass stilled.

Artemis glanced at him. "There are two," she said. "One is human."

"Get up—slowly," Garret said, breathing fast. "We won't hurt you."

A pair of hands rose above the grass, showing themselves empty of weapons, and then a head appeared—white hair, pale skin, dark eyes. A young face, little more than a blur in the darkness.

Garret aimed at the Freeblood's head, vaguely aware of Artemis's muffled protest.

"There is a human with you," he said. "Let me see him."

Another figure rose beside the Freeblood, much shorter and smaller, the head barely reaching the rogue's rib cage.

A child.

"Move away," Garret said to the Freeblood, gesturing with the barrel of the VS.

The rogue hesitated, biting his lip, and then edged sideways. The child made a low sound Garret couldn't quite make out.

"She is calling for him," Artemis said. "She's not afraid."

She. Tremors seized the muscles of Garret's arms, making the rifle shake. Not Timon, but given what had happened here…

Artemis walked ahead of him. "It's all right," she said in a voice perfectly pitched to soothe and reassure. "You can come out. No one will hurt you or Pericles."

Pericles. Garret stifled his surprise. "Send the girl ahead," he said.

"Her name is Beth," Pericles said, his hands still high above his head.

"Beth," Artemis repeated. Garret caught up with her and lowered the rifle. Slowly the girl emerged from the grass, her steps uncertain as she glanced back at the Freeblood.

But not in fear, Garret thought. He shifted the strap of the VS, pushing it behind him. "It's okay," he said to the girl, beckoning cautiously. Once she was within reach, he swept her up and retreated several yards. Artemis went with him.

"Pericles," the girl protested in a thready voice. She felt as light as an infant in Garret's arms, ragged and filthy, and with a face so dirty that he never would have known her gender if Artemis hadn't told him. Aside from her apparent concern for the Freeblood, she hardly seemed aware of her surroundings. He pressed her head gently against his shoulder.

"Artemis," Garret said, "you take Beth back to camp. I'll watch the rogue until we can figure out what to do about him."

"'Do about him'?" she echoed, meeting his gaze. "Apparently we saved his life. He has shown no hostility, then or now."

"Or maybe he let us think he was dying. And now he has a human child with him. How do you think that happened?" Garret heard the anger in his own voice and made an effort to moderate his tone. "I won't kill him," he said. "Not until we know what he has to do with this massacre."

"The child," Artemis said sharply. "She can hear you."

"I doubt she understands," Garret said, stroking the little girl's hair. "Beth, will you go with this lady?"

Beth blinked and met his gaze with bewildered brown eyes. "I'm lost," she said.

"We'll take care of you now. I promise."

The girl's unfocused stare shifted to Artemis's face. "Okay," she said, holding out her arms.

With uncharacteristic awkwardness, Artemis took the child and cradled her against her chest. Beth sighed and snuggled closer, tucking her head under Artemis's chin.

Garret turned to look for Pericles, but the Freeblood had already slipped away. Garret cursed under his breath.

"Go back to camp," he said to Artemis. "I'll be right behind you."

Moving as carefully as if she were holding a delicate porcelain doll, Artemis made her way back into the woods. Garret held the VS ready until they had reached the camp. Artemis set Beth down on the blanket and arranged it around her, using one of Garret's spare shirts as a pillow. She turned on his small lantern, poured a little water out of his canteen, wet a scrap of cloth and began to bathe the girl's face.

Memory cut through Garret's mind like a blade through a barely healed wound. Roxana, leaning over Timon, smiling and whispering in his ear. Roxana, doting so tenderly on the child that had come of a forbidden yet enduring love.

Garret saw that same tenderness in Artemis's face.

He cleared his throat and tried to focus on the child. In the light, he could see that Beth appeared to be about five years old, small for her age, and far too thin.

"How is she?" he asked, propping the VS within easy reach against a nearby tree trunk.

"She does not seem to be injured," Artemis said without looking up. "Perhaps we can get her to drink a little water."

Garret knelt on the other side of the blanket. Beth opened her eyes and blinked several times.

"How are you feeling, Beth?" Garret asked, smoothing matted hair away from the girl's face. "Does anything hurt?"

"Pericles?" she said.

"He's…away," Garret said. He rummaged through his pack, pulled out the first aid kit and gave Beth a brief but thorough examination. Except for a few shallow scratches and a bruise or two, she seemed unharmed.

When he was finished, Artemis propped Beth's head up and coaxed her into drinking a little water. Garret removed his coat and laid it over the blanket for extra warmth. Within minutes, the girl was deeply asleep.

"She's exhausted," he said, gesturing for Artemis to join him a little distance away. "She's probably in a state of shock."

"What else can we do for her?"

"Until we know what the rogues did to her…"

"We do not know that they did anything."

"She's in very poor condition."

"She cannot have been hurt if she has so little fear of Opiri."

Artemis was right, Garret thought. Beth was dirty and underfed, but the rogues hadn't harmed her. That was important.

That gave him hope for Timon.

"Garret?" Artemis reached out as if to touch him, dropping her arm only at the last minute. "They will both be all right. We will make sure of it."

We. He looked into her eyes, but all he could see was her usual honesty.

"You were very good with Beth," he said. "Thank you."

"You entrusted her to me, and yet you are surprised?"

Her voice was pinched, and he realized he'd hurt her again, even though she would never admit it.

"No," he said. "I'm not surprised. You've done this before, haven't you?"

"You must rest," she said, turning away. "I will look for Pericles. Try not to shoot me when I return."

If there had been any humor in her voice, Garret might have laughed.

Two hours later, Artemis found Garret sitting beside the girl, watching her quietly. He glanced up as she approached, shooting to his feet when he saw Pericles walking freely behind her. His gaze swept from her bow in its case to the rifle propped against the tree.

"It is all right," Artemis said quickly. "He means no harm."

"I want to help," Pericles said, moving to her side. "Is Beth all—"

"Stay back," Garret snapped as the young Freeblood took a hesitant step toward the little girl. He looked Pericles up and down. "How did you survive when we left you in the south?"

"I don't know." Pericles wet his lips. "You must have saved me with your blood."

"Where is my son?"

Artemis couldn't *feel* Garret's anger, but she knew him too well to mistake his mood. "There was a misunderstanding," she said calmly. "When we questioned Pericles before, he thought you were asking about Beth."

"So *she* was the one he stole," Garret said. "That makes it so much better." He took a step toward Pericles.

"What was he doing with her out there after the battle? How did he survive *that*?"

Pericles edged behind Artemis. "The Freebloods who died are the same ones who left me for dead. After you saved me, I tracked them here to make sure that Beth was all right."

"Then you saw the battle," Garret said. "Who were the humans?"

"Militiamen. They found the pack south of here and followed them until the Opiri turned to fight."

"But you weren't part of the fighting?"

"I was only in the area because of Beth."

"Pericles had the task of caring for Beth, until the pack leader turned on him," Artemis said.

"It's true," Pericles said meekly. "I tried to keep her clean, get her enough to eat. But when I tried to get her away they—"

"You were with a pack of rogue kidnappers, and you tried to help her escape?" Garret asked, disbelief in his voice.

"Is that so astonishing to you," Artemis asked, "when *I* was willing to help you find your son? Is it so impossible to believe that there might be more than one Opir capable of such concern?"

Garret looked at her as if her words genuinely surprised him. "What makes you believe him?" he asked.

"What made you believe *me* when I promised to go with you?" Artemis said.

"I'm sorry about your son," Pericles said, shuffling from foot to foot like a hare torn between lying still and leaping away from the fox lurking nearby.

"Sorry?" Garret said, clenching his fists. "It was a pack just like yours who took him." His eyes widened. "My God." He sank into a crouch beside Beth. "My son *and* Beth."

"Yes," Artemis said, her heart aching for him in spite of all her efforts to remain detached. "Pericles told me they are taking children, Garret. Not only Beth and Timon, but many others."

Garret dragged his hand across his face, and then fixed his stare on Pericles. "Why?" he asked. "Where are they taking them?"

"To the north, as he said before," Artemis said. "He knows nothing else."

"Pericles?" Beth whispered, beginning to sit up.

"I am here," he said, venturing out from behind Artemis.

Garret didn't move.

"At least let me give her something to eat," Pericles said. He reached inside his torn shirt, and Garret tensed.

Artemis held out her hand. Pericles gave her a packet of waxed paper and a small pouch. "It isn't much," he said, "but it's all I could find."

"Nutrition bars," Artemis said, looking inside the packet. She opened the pouch. "Seeds, nuts and dried fruits."

"Can I see her now?" Pericles asked.

After a long hesitation, Garret stepped out of his way, and Pericles crouched beside the girl. She reached for his hand and clung to it tightly.

"I am sorry I wasn't here to help you earlier, Beth," Pericles said, squeezing her fingers very gently.

Freeblood and human child began to speak in low voices, though Beth's words were brief and strained. Garret stared at them, one contradictory emotion after another sliding across his face in rapid succession.

"She obviously trusts him," Artemis said, when she and Garret stepped aside to talk. "Are you prepared to trust me again?"

He looked from her to Pericles. "When we helped him,

you called him 'brother.' I know you believe in a new future for your kind. How can *you* be objective?"

"Is it so difficult for you to imagine that what you see here is no more or less than the truth?" she asked. "Or will you deny that such relationships are possible?"

Chapter 8

Artemis had intended simply to make him see reason, but her question had the unexpected effect of forcing her to relive that moment when she had believed there *could* be more between an Opir and a human than blood and sexual desire.

Joy. Happiness.

And then she remembered that other face…

"Are you basing that question on *our* relationship?" Garret asked softly.

She couldn't bring herself to speak of what she suspected of Garret and Roxana. "Pericles believes as I do, Garret," she said. "He shares my hope for a better future."

Garret sighed. "I trust you," he said. "Where did the rogues find Beth?"

"A human colony on the coast. A place called Coos Bay."

Unsealing the outer pocket of his pack, Garret removed

the map and spread it across his thigh. "That's over two hundred miles southwest of here," he said.

Artemis knew what he was thinking—how far a southward journey would put him behind in his search for Timon—but he didn't say it aloud. He folded the map and returned it carefully to the pack.

"Did you look at the bodies?" he asked, getting to his feet.

"I found Pericles before I had the opportunity," she said.

"I want to get a better idea of what happened," he said. "I'm going out there."

"You are nearly night-blind," she protested.

"There's still a little moonlight," he said, "and I've done well enough so far. While I'm gone, try to find out everything Pericles knows about these children."

"I believe he has told me—"

"Artemis," he said, meeting her gaze, "if he knows anything he *hasn't* told you, we have to get it out of him—everything he's seen and heard regarding these abductions."

Neither of them moved. They stood half in, half out of the small circle of lantern light as if nothing else existed beyond them.

"There was still no sign of Citadel patrols when I found Pericles," Artemis said when the silence had stretched too long. "Nevertheless, this battle may have attracted attention. Please, be careful."

"I will be." He smiled, and she was glad that he couldn't feel her fear for him. As long as he didn't try to touch her...

He didn't, though his hand rose to the level of his waist before he dropped it again. He stepped outside the light and grabbed his rifle. Pericles's head snapped up in alarm. Garret ignored him and strode into the woods.

Pericles scrambled to his feet. "Where is he going?" he asked.

"To examine the battle site," Artemis said. "Beth is well?"

"Sleeping." He hunched his shoulders. "The human hates me."

"He's afraid for his son," she said. "But the better I know you, the easier it will be for him to understand."

"Understand what?" Pericles asked, a little shaky as he sat down again. "That I wasn't lying when I said I cared about Beth?"

"And that Freebloods are not all barbarians. You are proof that my mentor's goals are possible."

"No one in my pack cared about what happened to the others, or to the humans they met."

"Perhaps they were not as strong as you are, Pericles." He laughed. "Strong?"

"There are different kinds of strength." She sat down beside him. "You have only been Opir for a few years. It is easier for the youngest, who still remember their old lives, to accept a new way."

Pericles brought his legs to his chest and draped his narrow wrists over his knees. "I'm still not used to this. Maybe I'll never be."

"You are not alone," she said. "Not as long as you are with me."

"I know." He gnawed on his lower lip. "What about Garret? Does he know about what you did in Oceanus?"

"He does not," she said. "I wish to explain it myself, when the time is right."

"I won't say anything," Pericles said quickly, eager to please. "If you trust the human, so do I."

And so, Artemis thought, two who might be enemies were relying entirely on her to keep the peace. It seemed ironic after what had happened in Oceanus, where she had failed so miserably. She got up to pace, listening intently for Garret's return.

"You're really afraid for him, aren't you?" Pericles asked.

"Garret can take care of himself."

"Even that weapon wouldn't be enough if he came up against a patrol."

She rounded on him. "Did you see one and neglect to tell me?"

"No!" he said hastily. "I haven't seen any patrols." His gaze tracked her as she strode back and forth. "Have you… taken his blood?"

"Yes," she said curtly. "But only out of necessity."

"You didn't…force him?"

"Does it seem to you that such a thing would have been necessary?"

Pericles shook his head. "Why did you decide to help him find his son?"

"Garret saved my life from humans in the south. I owe him a debt."

"Oh." Pericles hugged his knees. "What are we going to do now? I want to make sure Beth is okay."

"As do we," Artemis said. "But you have not explained the circumstances of her abduction, or how you know that other children are being taken to the north." She sat beside him again. "Why is this being done?"

"I don't know." He clasped his hands together. "I only heard—"

He broke off as the sound of Garret's quiet footsteps announced his return. Still gripping the rifle, he dropped into a crouch beside Pericles and Artemis. His face was calm, his expression flat.

He must have seen ugly things out in the field, Artemis thought, but he had left emotion behind and become all unwavering purpose again. He barely seemed to notice her.

But he was safe.

"Heard what?" he asked, staring at Pericles.

The young Freeblood leaned away from Garret. "Our leader—Chares—wanted to find more children to deliver, to prove that our pack was better than the others who were doing the same thing."

"Other packs," Garret said in a monotone. "To whom were you supposed to deliver the children?"

"To a Bloodlord. Maybe a Bloodmaster. But someone very powerful. I heard that he might be in Canada, in the mountains. British Columbia, I think."

"And you didn't think to mention this until now?" Garret said, his fingers tightening around the barrel of the rifle.

"I'm sorry," Pericles whispered, his gaze darting between Garret and Artemis. "I was afraid."

"What were *you* getting out of this, you and the other child-stealers?"

"Chares never said," Pericles said meekly. "He didn't know what this Bloodlord wanted with the children. But we were supposed to keep Beth well and untouched until we reached this place in the north. There must have been some kind of reward."

"What else?"

Pericles looked at Artemis as if for reassurance. "There's a reason why the pack took Beth, and didn't want any of the other children from that particular colony."

"What do you mean?"

"Your son…he isn't a full human, is he?"

Artemis cast Garret a startled glance. He swung the rifle around, butting the muzzle up against Pericles's chest. The young Freeblood stopped breathing.

"How did you know?" Garret asked in a soft and very dangerous voice.

"Because the pack wouldn't have taken him otherwise. The Bloodlord in the north doesn't seem to…want normal human children."

The scent of Garret's hostility grew stronger, laced with a tinge of fear. Artemis curled her fingers around the rifle's barrel and pulled it away from Pericles's chest.

"If they do not want human children," she said to the young exile, "what *do* they want?"

"Mixed-bloods, like Darketans."

"Daysiders?" Garret said, using the human word.

"But Darketans aren't of mixed blood," Artemis protested. "They're mutations of normal Opiri, which is why they can walk in daylight."

Garret cast her an indecipherable look. "Beth is Darketan?" he asked Pericles, lowering his rifle.

"That's what the colonists told Chares."

"But you said she came from a human colony!" Artemis said. "What would an Opir mutation be doing there? Was she a prisoner?"

"Not a prisoner," Pericles said, breathing steadily again. "She looks human, and Darketans don't require blood until they're older, but…" His voice dropped very low. "The pack didn't have to raid the colony to get her. Some humans there sold her to us."

Garret's face went pale. "My God," he said. "Humans selling children."

"Opir children," Artemis said, thinking aloud. "I do not understand. It is true that Darketans do not have all the privileges of full Opiri in the Citadels. But Beth is far too young to have escaped a Citadel and found her way to this colony by herself."

"There's a far more likely explanation," Garret said, "but it may not be easy for you to accept."

"What is that?" Artemis asked with a twinge of alarm.

"What you said about Darketans being mutations…it isn't true. They're as much mixed-blood as the dhampires who work for the human Enclaves."

"You are wrong," Artemis said, shocked by his suggestion.

"The rulers of the Citadels have led you to believe a lie. We in the colonies only recently learned the truth when a high-ranked Bloodlord from Erebus chose to join us. He told us that Darketans are taken early from their mothers, trained as soldiers and forced to serve as daytime spies for the Citadels. It's possible that Beth was sent out of the Citadel to avoid that fate. But it's far more likely that her mother and father escaped, and sought refuge in the colony."

"Opiri...seeking refuge in a human colony?"

"Only the mother would have been Opir. The father was human. It's the opposite with dhampires—their fathers are Opiri and their mothers are human."

"But this is impossible," Artemis whispered. "All humans in the Citadels are serfs. No female Opir would permit... Any such child would be destroyed by command of the High Council!"

"They aren't," Garret said. "The Citadels don't dare admit it, even to their own citizens."

Artemis jumped to her feet. "I do not concede that what you say is true. We would know. Humans would sow dissension in the Citadels by spreading such rumors."

"What bothers you most, Artemis?" Garret asked, his expression grim and sad. "That this might be a lie created to undermine Opir society, or that female Opiri might allow themselves to be impregnated by male humans?"

Unable to answer, Artemis leaned heavily against the nearest tree. Garret had no reason to lie to her. He must know that she would find this information—

Timon, she thought. She remembered when she had first seen the boy's photograph. She had never doubted that he was human.

But if the rogues only wanted half-blood children...

"Why would the rogues think that Timon is a half-blood?" she asked.

"Artemis," Garret said with a low sigh, "you know the answer."

She slid down the trunk and sat with her back to the tree. "You mated with an Opir female," she said.

Garret pressed his hand over the pocket where he carried Timon's picture, as if someone might snatch it away from him. "Yes," he said.

"Roxana," she said, remembering her earlier guess.

"She was my wife," Garret said.

An Opir who had turned against her own kind to help one of his people.

Irrational anger overwhelmed Artemis's shock. "You said you lived alone," she said. "But I knew that could not have been true. You were too easy with me." Her eyes felt hot and dry. "Why did you lie?"

"I'm sorry, Artemis," he said. "It wasn't the right time to tell you the truth."

"You mean that you feared I might not help you if you admitted your former relationship with a female Opir?"

"I never intended to hide it from you."

"But you did. What else have you not told me? Where did you come from?"

Garret looked at her, and she saw the pain in his eyes.

"In old California," he said, "there are colonies where humans and Nightsiders live together in peace. I came from one of those colonies. We named it Avalon."

"I have heard of such places," she said, finding her composure again. "I thought they were forbidden."

"And I'm sure the Citadels in the north plan to keep it that way," Garret said. "Erebus has only accepted them because their Council realized that the colonies were no threat to them."

"But humans are free in these colonies, are they not?"

"Opiri and humans live as equals."

"How do the Opiri get their blood?"

"Through cooperation."

"And that is why you found it so easy to give yours to me?"

"No one is compelled to donate, but everyone—humans *and* Nightsiders—contributes to the general welfare of the colony." His lips thinned. "Unless the Nightsiders happen to forget where they are."

The bitterness had returned to his voice, and Artemis sensed that he spoke from very personal experience. She tried to imagine what life would be like for Opiri in such a settlement. They would have to change their habits and customs completely, and the motivation for such a change could only be a philosophical commitment to equality.

She knew that Opiri with egalitarian beliefs did exist, even in the Citadels. They generally kept their opinions to themselves, but if they left their Citadels or were exiled, they might seek places where they could live their ideals.

But could they maintain those lofty ideals in the face of constant temptation?

Isn't that what you would demand of your fellow Freebloods? she asked herself. *To discard what they have known and begin afresh?*

But she had never asked her people to live among humans. It was a recipe for disaster. As it had been when she and Garret had become too intimate. When he had called his wife's name.

A wife he had spoken of in the past tense.

She didn't ask him for more details. She couldn't bear to feel his sorrow, and the longer she remained with him, the more she had to struggle to keep her empathic barriers in place.

"The only human settlements in the north are the militia compounds," she said, trying to focus on more practical matters. She turned to Pericles. "They would never have permitted an Opir female among them."

"It wasn't like that," Pericles said with a quick, uneasy glance at Garret. "They didn't try to shoot us when we approached the gate. Their defenses weren't very strong. The men who sold Beth to us did it to keep us from attacking, but they didn't want anyone else in their compound to know what they were doing."

"And what of her parents?"

"They were never mentioned."

"But they could have been there," Garret said. "Maybe someone decided to start a mixed Nightsider-human colony in Oregon, in spite of the danger."

"That would be madness," Artemis protested.

"It takes a kind of madness to attempt something that's never been done before," Garret said. He gazed at Beth thoughtfully. "We have to decide what to do with her. We can't bring her with us to find Timon, but if her parents and the rest of the colonists didn't know that she was being sold to Freebloods, they'll take her back."

"Two hundred miles in the wrong direction," Artemis said.

Cradling the rifle in his arms, Garret seemed to lock himself away, torn between two equally terrible choices. Return the child to her home and hope for the best, or carry her on a dangerous journey to the north, possibly right into the arms of those who wanted her so badly.

"I'll take her back," Pericles said in a small voice. "She knows me. I've cared for her this long, and if it's just the two of us…"

"You can't defend *yourself*, let alone Beth," Garret said harshly. He began to pace. "Covering two hundred miles each way will take at least three weeks, probably more, even if we push ourselves."

Three weeks, Artemis thought. Three weeks' lost time

in Garret's search for his son, and an exhausting pace that would leave them all drained and weary by the time they returned to the borderlands of Oceanus.

"Let *me* go," Artemis said. "You know where to look for Timon. If you head toward British Columbia, you are certain to find—"

"Leave you alone?" Garret interrupted. "No. We still don't know anything about these colonists."

"It is my risk to take."

"No." Garret met her gaze, and her barriers slipped just enough to let her feel his agony. "There seem to be many Freebloods involved in this child-stealing, and whoever takes Beth to her home has to be ready to fight off several at once and protect her at the same time." He closed his eyes, and Artemis began to reach for him, no longer caring what effect the contact might have on her.

Her fingertips brushed his arm. He flinched and opened his eyes.

"We will take Beth back to her people," he said.

Chapter 9

Closing her hand around his, Artemis willed him to feel her sympathy. She had known that Garret couldn't sacrifice one child for another, even if one of them was his own son.

"He'll be all right," Garret said in a voice that suggested he was trying to convince himself. He squeezed her hand. "He'll be all right."

A long silence fell. Reluctantly, Artemis released Garret's hand. When Pericles finally spoke, his voice was little more than a whisper.

"Will you let me come?" he asked "We can take turns carrying Beth."

"Aren't you afraid of humans?" Garret asked coldly.

The young Freeblood lifted his chin. "I promised to protect Beth and failed. Now I have another chance."

Garret visibly weighed the boy's statement. "How long since you've fed?"

"I... I hunted before I found Beth."

"Humans?"

"No! I'm… I believe the same things Artemis does."

"That's good, because you won't be getting any more blood from me."

"I never expected—"

"We will hunt game along the way," Artemis interrupted. "You and Beth will require food, as well. The rations Pericles carried will not last long, and I doubt your dried meats will be proper nourishment for a child."

Garret nodded his thanks. "As Pericles suggested," he said, "we'll take turns carrying Beth and move as fast as we can without exhausting ourselves, or her. And when it comes to dealing with any humans we meet, you both keep out of sight unless I say otherwise."

"Understood. As long as *you* stay out of sight if we meet Opiri."

"We'd better hope we can avoid them completely," Garret said.

They packed up quickly. Garret broke his rifle apart and tucked it in his pack. He looked in on Beth, stroking her hair and checking her pulse and breathing. The little girl barely did more than murmur drowsily when Pericles lifted her from her blankets and neatly devised a sling to hold her on his back.

It almost hurt to watch them, though Artemis was very careful not to let a hint of emotion show in her face or voice. Neither Pericles nor Garret—especially Garret— would ever know what she had felt when she'd held a child in her arms again.

South, Artemis thought. *Think only of the goal, a promise kept and freedom afterward.*

The three of them crept out of the woods, on the alert for Opir patrols. Garret agreed that Artemis should take the lead, while he fell to the rear and Pericles trotted be-

tween them, Beth securely cradled on his back. Garret
tried to focus his attention on their surroundings, but he
couldn't get his mind off what Pericles had told him of the
kidnapped children and the unknown Bloodlord's mysterious purpose for them.

Timon was strong and brave. But he was still a child.
The thought of his fear and bewilderment tore at Garret,
constantly threatening to gut his hard-won dispassion.

But he knew he couldn't indulge in worry that would
slow him or make him careless. He had to be ready to turn
back north as soon as Beth was safe.

In the meantime, he and Artemis would remain close
to each other, at least physically, for an extra few weeks.
He'd told her only a part of his past with Roxana and the
mixed colonies, and he knew he couldn't keep her in the
dark forever.

But to reveal everything would open a Pandora's box of
emotion he wasn't prepared to deal with so soon after the
last fiasco. He knew he'd hurt Artemis when he'd called
Roxana's name. She had tried to keep her distance ever
since, but at times, as on many previous occasions, she had
seemed strangely attuned to his emotions. When they'd
discussed Beth's fate, Artemis had touched him in an act
of comfort, though it must have taken real courage to make
herself so vulnerable with him.

That they had come to care for each other was not an
issue. But he couldn't read her mind. He wondered if she
could understand that he had once lived with an intimacy
built not only on sharing blood, desire and mutual respect,
but also on love. The love of a man for a woman, regardless of race or kind.

Love he never expected to feel again. But as they traveled, he was constantly aware of Artemis moving quietly ahead of him, her body swaying with natural grace,
as lithe and strong and beautiful as a white tigress. Like

a lioness, she would fight to defend those she considered her family. And, like a lioness, she was untouchable, forever beyond his reach.

He was grateful when necessity forced him to push Artemis out of his thoughts and concentrate on keeping his footing in the dark.

They traveled by night and by day, Pericles swathed in heavy clothes and a cloak foraged from Beth's fallen captors. Though they switched off carrying Beth, the young Freeblood insisted on taking her two-thirds of the time. No one spoke of weariness or rest until it was clear they could go no farther, and often it was more for Beth's sake than for their own.

They cut south for a day, and then traveled west along Highway 20 toward the ocean. That road wound through forested hills, and the trek took longer than Garret had hoped.

But their strength held. They met neither humans nor Opiri, and Artemis took Pericles hunting at regular intervals, returning with meat for Beth and Garret, while they apparently subsisted on animal blood.

When they reached the ocean, they made camp just off the beach in the fallen town of Newport. The sun was setting over the sea, a touch of nature's glory that not even the War and its aftermath could destroy.

"It is beautiful," Artemis said, as Garret readied the fire and Pericles rested a little distance away. "Though I lived in Oceanus, I never saw the sea."

"Our colony was—is—near the ocean," Garret said, "but you never get tired of something like this."

She smiled at him, and his heart turned over. In the peace of the moment he felt the absurd desire to take her hand and hold it in his. She must have guessed what he was thinking, because she clasped her hands in her lap and stared out across the beach.

"How are you feeling?" she asked abruptly. "Have you had enough rest?"

Garret fed more twigs to the tiny flame. "You don't have to worry about me," he said with a wry twist of his lips. "I know my limitations, *and* when I come too close to exceeding them."

"I did not mean to imply…" She cleared her throat. "Your endurance has never ceased to surprise me."

"I guess I should take that as a compliment."

Beth, lying on a pile of blankets a few feet away, began to whimper in her sleep. Without thinking, Garret gathered the girl into his arms and held her against his chest, humming under his breath.

"That is a pretty song," Artemis said, her voice wistful. "I used to—"

She broke off and looked away quickly. *Used to what?* Garret thought. Used to sing? It wasn't a common activity in the Citadels, though some took up music when they came to the colony.

Could she be speaking of her former human life?

"It's a lullaby Ro— I used to sing to Timon," Garret said. "Beth's asleep. Do you want to hold her while I finish with the fire?"

Hesitantly, Artemis reached for the little girl. She held Beth gently, her lips curving up in a tentative smile.

"She's so fragile," Artemis said. "Sometimes it amazes me that humans can survive in this world at all."

"Homo sapiens have gotten along well enough for over 150,000 years."

"Yet some adapted better than others. You were a leader in your colony, were you not?"

Maybe, Garret thought, it was time to tell Artemis the truth. Now, when they were at ease with each other.

Suddenly Artemis jerked up her head. "Someone is approaching," she said.

A moment later Pericles was sitting up on his bedroll, his nostrils flaring. "What is it?" he asked.

"Humans," Artemis said. She held Beth out to Garret. "I should go see."

"How many?" Garret asked.

"More than two, but less than ten," she said. "If they are militia…"

"I'll talk to them," Garret said. "The last thing we need is a firefight, and you know I can communicate with these people on their terms."

"Yes," Artemis said, "I know. But—"

"But you and Pericles stay here and look after Beth until I give the okay."

Artemis opened her mouth to protest, shook her head and subsided. She wouldn't look at him as he rose from the small fire, and her jaw was set.

Knowing that there was nothing he could do to satisfy her except return in one piece, Garret tucked his handgun under his coat and headed out in the direction she had indicated.

She'd been right in her estimate. Nine humans, ranging in age from early teens to late middle age, were huddled together under a stand of wind-beaten spruce a few hundred yards north of the camp. They were underdressed for the weather and the stiff ocean breezes, their clothing primarily made up of loose pants, long tunics and the occasional cloak. They had no weapons except for a couple of knives.

Serfs, Garret thought. Runaways, almost certainly from Oceanus.

The fact that they had escaped at all was a miracle. But that they'd come so far with so few resources was a testament to their fortitude and conviction.

Garret was doubly glad that he hadn't brought Artemis and Pericles.

"Hello," he called out, stepping into clear view and holding his arms out at his sides.

Immediately two men and a woman in their twenties or early thirties jumped up and confronted him, their faces creased in alarm. Garret walked toward them, his arms still well away from his weapon.

"Peace," he said. "My name is Garret Fox. I used to be a serf, just like you."

"They're heading to Coos Bay," Garret said.

Artemis stared at him. "Serfs?" she said. "Serfs who escaped from Oceanus?"

With a sigh, Garret sat down and poked at the embers that were all that remained of the fire. "They had a little help," he said.

"I do not understand," she said.

"From inside the Citadel," he said. "Is it so difficult for you to believe that there are humans willing to risk their lives for freedom, or Opiri who might help them?"

Artemis shook her head slowly. "I never heard of such a thing in Oceanus, though I—" She pushed her hair away from her face. "Are you suggesting that these are not the first?"

"They didn't discuss it in any detail, but there have probably been others."

"And surely the Council must know that there have been escapes." She met Garret's eyes. "They would kill any Opir who dared to break the Citadel's laws."

"If I was a serf, would you help *me*?"

She clenched her slender hands in her lap. "I would do everything in my power to see that you were not harmed."

"As a Freeblood, you'd have no control over my condition. And you were taught to believe that the keeping of serfs is part of the natural order of the world."

"What I was taught ceased to matter long ago," Artemis said.

"And you don't want to take human blood. You've never told me why."

Abruptly she looked up at him. "You asked me if I was more concerned about saving human lives or only about Freebloods killing each other," she said. "I do not believe that Opiri should be dependent upon human blood. It is a weakness in us, a source of corruption and violence that harms both my people and yours."

Garret sank down beside her. "Then you're opposed to the practice of serfdom primarily for the benefit of your own people."

She flinched as if she sensed his disappointment. But he knew he had no right to feel that way; the very fact that she was against human slavery for any reason put her far ahead of most Opiri. Even Roxana, in the beginning…

"I understand now," he said. "I'm a corrupting influence."

"No!" She shot to her feet. "You… You and I…it is different."

"Because I'm not actually a serf?"

Artemis began to tremble, and Garret cursed himself for his clumsiness. "I'm sorry," he said. "I've asked a lot of you. But I'm going to have to ask a little more."

Almost before he'd finished speaking, Pericles called from the beach. "They're coming," he said.

"We'll be traveling with the refugees," Garret said. "They're headed to the same colony, and it'll be easier for us to take Beth in with a group of serfs seeking a safe place away from the Citadels." He laid his hand on Artemis's shoulder. "Can you deal with that?"

"Will they not be frightened of me and Pericles?" she asked in a very soft voice.

"They've heard that Coos Bay might be a mixed col-

ony," he said. "They're prepared to deal with peaceful
Nightsiders. But I've given them certain assurances that
you can be trusted."

"What assurances?"

Garret hesitated. "I didn't have time to consult with
you," he said, "so you'll have to act a part until we've returned Beth to her caretakers."

Her shoulder tensed under his hand. "What have you
done, Garret?"

"I've told them that you're my wife."

Artemis took the offered hand, careful not to grip the
serf's fingers too firmly. The woman smiled with obvious
unease and quickly dropped her hand, but not before she
had unwittingly triggered Artemis's empathy.

After the long days of attempting to suppress her emotional connection to Garret, Artemis was surprised that
merely touching another human could have such an effect.
But the emotions of the former serfs were strong and unguarded, in spite of their reticence around her. They were
afraid and uncertain, and yet brave and resolute...willing,
as Garret had said, to risk everything for the mere possibility of freedom.

Artemis smiled at one of the male serfs and edged away
as Garret began to speak with the group. Her anger with
him had gradually subsided, but she was left to play a
role she was ill prepared for—pretending to be his mate.
In spite of his efforts to shield her from any real intimacy
with the serfs, she still had little idea of how to behave as
the Opir "wife" of a human.

The fact that the humans accepted her, she thought, was
due more to Garret's efforts than her own playacting...ef-
forts that included frequent brief touches, many smiles,
and words of affection meant to prove his devotion to her.

He was so good at it that, for moments at a time, she believed he really meant it.

"How are you doing?" he asked, drawing her aside. His hand on her arm made her breath catch, and something of his feelings transferred into her mind: relief, determination and pride—in *her*.

"You should tell *me*," she said, managing what she hoped was a persuasive smile. "Have I convinced them that I am your devoted mate?"

"You've even convinced *me*," he said lightly, though his gaze was anything but casual. "They've fully accepted our background story, and they're sure you've always believed that serfs should be free."

Artemis ducked her head. "Will we wait for daylight to travel again?"

"They're prepared to leave now, and if we stick to the highway we shouldn't have any difficulty. Pericles will carry Beth until he becomes tired."

"And what am I to do?"

"I hope you'll stay at my side," he said. His green eyes were like the sea itself, calm one moment, stormy the next. Now they were dark and mysterious, holding a world she imagined lay deep beneath the surface of the ocean.

And she could feel everything she had tried to shut out, a maelstrom of emotion that left her gasping and desperate to get away—or to fall into Garret's arms as if she truly were wife and lover and the chosen companion of his heart.

A *human* heart.

She broke free. "I will travel beside you," she said formally. "I will play my part for as long as it is necessary."

His eyes clouded. "I know you will," he said.

He walked away, and Artemis stared after him, wondering what she had done…and what she was becoming. As often as she resisted it, the empathy fought to return.

But that "gift" wasn't the source of her feelings now.

She put the thought out of her mind and retrieved her pack as Pericles secured Beth to his back with the sling and Garret finished speaking to the serfs. The group formed a loose column, and Garret nodded to Artemis, indicating that she should join him.

After a time, she took drag to watch for pursuit. A few of the serfs cast uneasy glances over their shoulders, but none of them faltered, and by dawn they had traveled over fifteen miles south on Highway 101, hugging the coastline.

Four days and nights later, they approached Coos Bay. Remarkably, the tall bridge crossing the eastern portion of the bay was still intact, and, except for its lack of inhabitants, the city beyond it seemed to have missed most of the War entirely.

Pericles, who knew the location of the colony, led them south and west across deserted suburbs and through a forest to a cluster of buildings that had obviously once been a public facility. An old, almost illegible sign identified it as a community college. The forest growing alongside the buildings provided the compound with a natural defense.

Closer to the buildings, the colonists had built a flimsy stockade around a section of the college, though not one that could hold off a concerted attack by Nightsiders who wanted to get in. Only a few humans were patrolling the stockade, and their weapons seemed to be in poor condition.

"They've been lucky," Garret said, stretched out beside Artemis in the small clearing among the trees and underbrush. "No one's been interested in going so far out of their way to bother them."

"Except for the rogue kidnappers."

"Yes," he said. "Artemis, I want you and Pericles to stay outside while I go in with the others. We still don't know the exact circumstances of how Beth came to be with the rogues. We need to find her parents first. If only a few of the colonists were involved in selling her, we'll be exposing them when we return Beth, and that could get tricky. I want you to be safe."

"Surely these people can be no threat to me."

"Believe me, Artemis," he said, "you don't have the experience to judge. Will you stay here?"

Reluctantly, she agreed. But as Garret went to join the other serfs, she couldn't shake the feeling that matters were not going to turn out quite as they hoped.

Chapter 10

"**B**eth's mother isn't here."

Garret crouched beside Artemis, gazing at the humans with whom he'd been speaking moments before. They stared in his direction, heads together in conversation, and then returned to the compound through the door in the stockade. It closed with a finality that made her very glad that Garret was with her again.

"What happened to her?" Pericles asked, quietly coming to join them.

"The colony is not what we hoped," Garret said. He turned back to Artemis. "We expected a mixed colony of humans and Opiri. Until fairly recently, it was."

The heaviness in his voice put Artemis on the alert. "Where are Beth's parents?" she asked.

"Her mother was a Freeblood from Oceanus," he said, "and the father was a serf she helped to escape. They came to this colony in search of a sanctuary where she could give birth." Garret grabbed a twig and snapped it in half.

"Beth was born here, and soon afterward her mother died of an infection, one of those few that are fatal to Opiri."

"A sad fate for the child," Artemis said.

"And for her husband. He raised Beth with the help of his sister, who had come to the colony before him. There were six or seven other Opiri in the colony at the time."

"But they are not here now," Artemis said.

"Four years after the death of Beth's mother, her father left on a hunting trip. He never returned. Not long after that, the colony…" He sighed. "They didn't tell me this, not officially, but I was able to figure out the truth. I don't know why, but the human colonists gradually made the Nightsiders aware that they weren't welcome, and one by one the Opiri left the colony. In the end, Beth was the only colonist who had Nightsider blood."

Feeling a little ill, Artemis closed her eyes. "Who cared for her?" she asked.

"Her aunt. She has Beth now."

"She'll keep the child?" Pericles asked.

"She didn't know that certain members of the colony wanted Beth gone, as well, or that they intended to trade Beth to the rogues," Garret said, his lips thinning in disgust. "But she seems to have her suspicions."

"I don't know what they said to Chares," Pericles said, "but he decided not to risk attacking the colony once we had Beth."

"And the men who sold her are still in the colony?" Artemis asked, baring her teeth.

"If they are, they're keeping a very low profile. The leaders here didn't know what had happened to Beth, but they did know that the rogues who had approached the colony suddenly decided to leave and that was when her absence was noted. They sent out search parties, but gave up after two days."

"We should not leave her here, among such people," Artemis said. "How does her aunt expect to protect her?"

"She believes she has allies in the colony."

"But are they enough? The fact that the humans virtually drove the Opiri away suggests otherwise. You spoke of peace between Opiri and humans in colonies such as this, and yet here is proof that such a thing cannot last."

"It's only proof that these people couldn't handle living at close quarters with Nightsiders," Garret said. "Every one of the colonists here is a former serf, and none of them have forgotten their lives in the Citadels."

"And you find this easy to understand?" she demanded.

Garret gazed at her in silence, and a little of his emotion leaked through to her. She tried to shut off the connection, but not before she realized that he was considering whether or not to trust her.

After all the time they had spent together, she found it remarkably painful to sense his doubts. She was angry, yes, but it was more than that. Her chest ached, and her ribs seemed to contract into a tight, hard coil. She had agreed to all his plans, even playing the part of his—

"I was a serf in Erebus," he said, interrupting her thoughts. "So I do understand their resentment. Even their hate."

Astonished by his confession, Artemis scrambled to her feet. "*You* were a serf?" she asked.

"For many years. I saw how most humans were treated in the Citadel." He pushed his hair away from his face. "I was lucky. I was chosen by a Bloodmistress who treated her serfs well. But most serfs in Erebus were regarded as cattle, as they are by most of your people."

The ache in Artemis's chest spread throughout her body, twisting her stomach into knots and making her head throb. Garret seemed so superior to the serfs she had seen in Oceanus, or the men and women they had found in the town on the beach. He had courage and will equal to that of any Opir.

But she knew he could not be the only human like this.

"I'm not very different from those people in there," he said, as if he'd read her thoughts. "I was sent as tribute from the San Francisco Enclave because I'd committed the crime of trying to help other convicts. I was just like the other serfs, except that I learned to love my mistress. And she learned to love me."

Suddenly Artemis knew what he was about to say. "Roxana was your mistress," she said.

"Yes." He took a long, slow breath. "Roxana and I cared deeply for each other almost from the beginning. She treated me as an equal in private. In public, we had to play a game. But when she became pregnant…"

"You had to hide her condition," Artemis said, forgetting her own anguish.

"They would have forced her to give up the child and raised it as Darketan. Roxana would have been punished, and of course I would have been executed as an example to the other serfs."

"So you escaped."

His gaze grew unfocused, looking into a past Artemis could scarcely imagine. "Yes. Because serfs and Opiri were prepared to risk their lives to help make it happen. We had an Underground in Erebus, humans and Nightsiders trying to make serfs' lives easier and sometimes help them escape brutal masters. I joined it before Roxana and I… Before we became lovers. When she found out, she became part of it and met with other Opiri who were willing to help. Eventually they were able to get us out of Erebus, along with dozens of other serfs." His voice thickened. "Timon was born in freedom."

"And then Freebloods stole him from you." Artemis sank back into a crouch. "If you had told me this earlier…"

"Would it have made a difference? I'm the same man either way."

"Yet you hesitated to reveal your past," she said. "Did you think I would refuse to help you if I knew?"

The slight rustle of undergrowth marked Pericles's sudden disappearance, and Artemis realized that the young Freeblood had felt like an intruder in a very intimate world. She wished she could run after him.

Coward, she thought. She was ashamed of having felt a twinge of disgust at the idea of a Bloodmistress bearing a human's child; she couldn't bear to acknowledge the possibility that she might have treated Garret far worse than he deserved if she had realized he was an escaped serf.

"You gave your blood to me, even though you knew so little of me," she said softly. "How is it that you could trust me at all?"

"If it hadn't been for Roxana and the other Nightsiders I knew in Erebus, I might not have," he said. "But as I said, I was fortunate. Many serfs have nothing to help them survive but hate, even after they escape."

"Then how could these serfs bear to come near me?"

"It wasn't easy for some of them, but they knew I would never have married a Freeblood if I didn't believe she could be trusted."

"And the colonists?"

"I don't know what they might have experienced that turned them against the Nightsiders here, but—"

"It makes them no better than Opiri in their prejudice. More evidence that expecting humans and Opiri to live together in harmony is a foolish dream."

"I've seen it work," he said. "I've learned that civilized, rational Nightsiders and humans are far more alike than they want to acknowledge." He looked into her eyes. "You and I, Artemis, are not so different."

His words filled her with a kind of nonsensical joy, as if

they had somehow relieved her of the burden of this new and unexpected guilt. It wasn't quite so simple, of course, but she was grateful. Grateful and warmed by the acceptance in his eyes.

She had learned to value the judgment of a human. *This* human.

For a moment she dared to open her mind, to let the empathy awaken again. Garret's aura flared around his head, radiating heat like a fire. The heat was not merely sexual but inextricably intermingled with emotions that frightened her with their potency.

But she remembered how it had ended the last time, when Garret had spoken another name. She hesitated, torn between giving way and holding back. At last she leaned forward and kissed him. Then his arms were around her, and he was returning the kiss with a passion that filled her mind and redoubled her own need for him.

"Artemis," he murmured into her neck, tracing her ear with his lips and tongue. She could so easily have cast aside all her fears, stripped off her clothes and relieved him of his. But there was another need even more pressing. She felt him recognize and accept that need gladly, suppressing his own.

She had fought so rigorously to keep this from happening again, but now all her former worries seemed unimportant, of no greater interest than the way she cut her hair. Her defenses crumbled. She kissed his face from forehead to jaw, sucked on his neck without breaking the skin. She licked his shoulder and then grazed the base of his neck with her teeth. When she bit, he exhaled as if he had been holding his breath and whispered words she couldn't quite understand.

She drank lightly, because she didn't want to make him weak for the return journey to the north. But something happened she hadn't expected. She felt not only the vibrant blaze of his emotion—a pleasure as sensual as any joining of bodies—but also a slight but noticeable change in the taste of his blood, a change that made the sharing almost painful in its intensity. It was far more than mere nourishment; it rolled over her tongue like the sweetest ambrosia, unlike anything she had ever tasted before.

When Artemis realized what seemed to be happening, her heart stuttered to a stop. Surely it couldn't have occurred so quickly. Surely it was all in her mind. Blood-bonds didn't occur until an Opir had taken a human's blood for some time, and then only under extraordinary circumstances.

Even if it was only beginning to happen, she had to stop it.

She sealed Garret's wound, her hands trembling on his shoulders. He opened his eyes, and she thought they had never been so bright, so vibrant with life.

Did hers look the same? Could she ever expect to feel this euphoria again, this magical strength that came from something sweeter than any blood?

Not with Garret. Never again with him. She must hold true this time. She must not permit—

Someone loudly cleared his throat. Artemis and Garret broke apart, and Pericles crept into the tiny clearing, looking everywhere but at them.

"What is it?" Garret said, his voice gruff with frustration.

His face still averted, Pericles crouched at the edge of the clearing. "Beth's aunt is outside the stockade," he said. "She wants to speak to you."

Garret's expression turned grim. "Wait for me here," he said to Artemis.

"Something is wrong, isn't it?" she said, pushing aside her fear. "What haven't you told me?"

Hiding his gun under his coat, Garret met her gaze. "I

don't know. But it's strange that Beth's aunt would want to speak to me now."

"I am coming," Artemis said. "Beth is as much my concern as yours, and now that it is dark you have no advantage over me."

"All right. But please, Artemis…trust my judgment. Stay behind me."

With a powerful sense of foreboding, Artemis followed Garret and Pericles toward the colony walls. A small human woman was standing just outside the gate, her arm around a little girl.

Beth.

The woman looked past Garret into the darkness, as if she could see Artemis in the shadows. "I am sorry," she said, tears in her voice. "I thought the colony would accept her back. But there has been something wrong here since Beth disappeared. Certain men of this colony…" She bit her lip and hugged Beth more tightly. "I can't trust them. I don't think Beth will be safe here."

As if she only half understood her aunt's words, Beth smiled at Garret and yawned. Garret looked back at Artemis. His anger was palpable.

"Please," the woman said, "take Beth away with you. You can find a better place for her, a place where she won't be the only one of her kind." Tears rolled down her cheeks. "I want her to be happy. Please help us."

"Why would she come with us?" Garret asked. "She'll want to stay with you."

"But I can't protect her," the woman said. She pulled a small packet out of her pants pocket. "I have something to…quiet her down. I've already given a little to her, and if you give her the rest, she'll be calm until you've taken her far from here."

"We're going on a dangerous journey," Garret said. "Do you understand what you're asking?"

"You took good care of her. You know how to deal with people who aren't... Who don't fit in. I would not entrust her with anyone else but the ones who saved her life."

Artemis stepped forward. "We will take her," she said, glancing up at Garret. "We will keep her safe."

Garret met her gaze and took her hand in his. "My wife is right," he said. "We'll do all we can to help her."

"Thank God," the woman said, clearly struggling to hold back her sobs. "Please, take her before I—"

Artemis stepped forward and held out her hand. Beth took it, innocent trust on her face. Pericles joined them, draping a cloak over the little girl's jacket.

"Is anyone apt to follow us?" Garret asked.

"They only want the problem gone," the woman said bitterly.

"Then we'll leave within the hour," Garret said. "We have a few preparations to make."

"Thank you," the woman said. She pushed a sack into his hands. "These are some of Beth's things." Abruptly she rushed to Beth and planted a kiss on the girl's forehead. "Be good, Bethy."

She rushed back inside the wall and closed the gate behind her. Beth stared after her in bewilderment, and Garret looked down at the small packet in his hand.

"I hope we won't have to use this," he said.

Artemis lifted the girl into her arms. "Let us make sure we do not," she said. She carried Beth back to the clearing. Beth stirred restlessly and called her aunt's name once, then dropped into a light sleep.

Laying the girl down on a blanket, Artemis waited for Pericles and Garret to join her. Garret's expression was dark, as if he had a bad taste in his mouth. Pericles was very quiet.

"They would harm a child?" Artemis demanded. "Even though she is half human?"

"They wouldn't harm her," Garret said, "but her life wouldn't be a happy one."

"In other words, this is another case in which humans and Opiri cannot live together in harmony."

He sidestepped her statement. "The important thing is that we must find a safe place to take her."

"Your own colony," Pericles said hesitantly.

Garret closed his eyes. "Another two hundred miles to the south," he said. "Timon—"

He didn't finish, but his despair was a living thing in the air between them.

"There must be a place to the north," she said. "What of the human Enclave of SeaTac? I have never been so far north, but perhaps they would take her in."

"A long and difficult journey," Garret said. "And there's no guarantee that they would accept her."

"There's another place," Pericles said. "It's still in the north. But it's on your way to the river crossing into Canada."

"What is this place?" Garret asked.

"A compound on the Willamette River in the old city of Portland."

"Portland?" Artemis said. "I heard that the last human settlement there was destroyed ten years ago."

"They built a new one. Chares talked about it. It's guarded by strong walls, nothing like this place. The people there are very well armed."

"A militia compound?" Garret asked. "But Beth is half Opir."

"Chares said the Portland compound uses mixed Opiri and human patrols. They coexist peacefully." Pericles hesitated. "There's only one problem. They hate Freebloods. Chares said they've been under siege by rogues working for the Bloodlord in the north, so *he* wouldn't go anywhere near them."

"Beth is not a Freeblood," Artemis said.

Garret's expression softened as he looked down at Beth. "I don't want to leave her in a place where such prejudice exists," he said, "but you may be wrong, and I can't put off finding Timon any longer." He met Artemis's gaze. "I won't let either one of you fall into their hands. If you're still willing to come with me."

"How do we get to this place, Pericles?" Artemis asked.

"I don't know exactly where it is," Pericles said, "but I know it's on the river in the old city, close to a bridge they can guard easily."

A little of the tension went out of Garret's body. He pulled the map from his pack. "So we return to our previous route and continue past Salem along the Willamette until we reach Portland. Once we've seen to Beth, we'll continue northeast to the bridge over the Columbia at Government Island." He folded the map. "We'll still have to pass Oceanus, but our luck held the last time. It's our only option."

Pericles nodded. Artemis stared at the map. It would be a long walk to this other colony, but at least they would be going in the right direction. Garret needed that goal now, the belief that he would finally find his son.

But she would have to fight doubly hard against feeding from Garret now that she understood the consequences of what had happened between them at the last blood-taking. It would be painful and unpleasant, but there was still a chance to break the cord before it became too strong to sever.

"If we're ready...?" Garret said.

Lifting Beth into the sling on his back, Pericles nodded. Artemis donned her own pack.

None of them looked back when they left the walls of the colony behind.

Chapter 11

Garret's hopes were fulfilled, and twelve days later, foot-sore and weary, they reached Oceanus's northern border without incident. Their road had taken them back to the winding Willamette, and they had agreed to keep to the east side of the river as they approached Portland.

For most of the journey Beth had been quiet and co-operative, seemingly content to be with her rescuers and only occasionally calling out for her aunt. Between them, Garret, Artemis and Pericles kept her clean, comfortable and well fed with meat and any edible plants they could find. Pericles remembered several games from his human life, and Garret told her stories he'd once told Timon. Artemis made it her business to hold Beth as often as possible, as committed to Beth's welfare as any mother would be.

As Roxana would have been.

But it was not Beth who Garret was worried about. As each day passed, he had noticed changes in Artemis's appearance and energy. After a few days' travel, her face began to look drawn. Halfway to Salem, she began to stumble occasionally, and by the time they reached their camp south of Portland, her eyes were clouded and her lips pinched with discomfort.

Garret knew the signs. She obviously wasn't getting enough blood from animal sources, but she refused to ask him for what she needed. He'd thought she was over that particular inhibition after Coos Bay. Instead, it seemed to have gotten worse.

Still, he kept his thoughts to himself as they forded the Clackamas River and found a sheltered area where the remains of a bridge disappeared into the forest on its way to the ruins of a string of towns, suburbs and small cities stretching in an almost continuous line toward the Columbia River. Pericles set Beth down under a tree, and Garret removed the girl's food from his pack.

"We have somewhere between ten and twelve miles to go," he said, giving Beth a carefully harvested handful of late blackberries.

"We should hunt," Artemis said. She gathered her bow and checked her arrows.

"Let Pericles go ahead," Garret said. "I'd like to speak to you."

Her face took on the stubborn look he knew all too well. "It is better if we hunt while it is still dark."

"I'll scout for game," Pericles said, slipping into the trees.

Garret held Artemis's gaze. "I know what's wrong with you," he said bluntly. "You're starving yourself again. Why?"

"I don't know what you—" She broke off and jumped to her feet. A second later Garret's more limited human senses alerted him to movement in the trees. He dropped his pack and scrambled for the pieces of the partially assembled VS.

The muzzle of an automatic rifle pressed into his skull from behind.

"Stand down," a soft, cultured voice said.

Garret released the VS. He knew the rifle's wielder was Opir and that his chances of bringing the Nightsider down were slim. He looked for Artemis. Even as he watched, a woman—clearly dhampir, dark-haired and stocky, with the typical "cat eyes"—and a male Nightsider of indeterminate rank dragged Artemis out of the woods. All three of them bore the marks of a vicious scuffle.

And they were not alone. Garret's Opir guard grabbed the sections of the VS and tossed them to someone out of the range of Garret's sight.

"There's a kid here," another voice, rough and human, said from Beth's direction. Garret pulled his hunting knife from its sheath and twisted to sink it into the Nightsiders leg. The Opir kicked the knife away, grabbed Garret by the throat and slammed him against the tree.

"Back off, Varus," the human said. "Don't hurt him."

Without argument, Varus let Garret go. A whip-thin human with a short wiry beard and several scars appeared in front of Garret, and others closed in around him: a mix of humans, Opiri and dhampires, all armed and clearly working together. Garret managed to catch a glimpse of Beth, who was sitting up and staring at the human woman kneeling close to her.

"Leave her alone," Garret said, calculating the best angle of attack. "Who are you?" he asked the thin man. "What do you want?"

"My name's Cody," the man said.

"Why did you attack us?" Artemis asked, the dhampir's pistol poking into her ribs.

"We don't plan to hurt you," Cody said, meeting his stare. "But if you try to attack one of us again, we might have to."

Unwilling to risk Beth's or Artemis's safety, Garret raised his hands above his head. The human woman bent to pick Beth up, but the little girl jerked away and ran toward Artemis.

"Where's Pericles?" she cried, grabbing Artemis around the legs.

"Are there other people with you?" the leader demanded.

Thank God, Garret thought, that Pericles had taken his small pack with him. "Pericles's her stuffed toy," he said, cautiously meeting Artemis's gaze. "She lost it."

Artemis stroked Beth's hair. "If you touch her—" she began.

"Let the girl go to Rachel," the thin human said, indicating the woman who had been talking to Beth earlier.

"What do you want with her?"

"The question is what *you're* doing with her."

Garret forced himself to relax. "My name is Garret Fox. We're trying to take this child to safety. If you're what I think you are, you'll either let us go or help me."

"Take her to safety?" the dhampir asked. "From what?"

"We found her amid the bodies of Freebloods and humans who'd slaughtered each other. She was the only survivor. We were looking for a settlement willing to take her in and care for her."

"And where would that be?" the thin human said.

"We heard that there was one in old Portland, on the Willamette River," Artemis said.

"Where did *you* come from?"

"Far south of here, from a colony where humans and Opiri live together in peace," Garret said.

"Why didn't you take the girl back to your own colony?" the dhampir asked Garret.

"We were much closer to Portland," Garret said. "And we're looking for another child, taken from our colony by rogue Freebloods." He glanced at the dhampir. "I have no reason to lie."

"You would if you're one of the humans selling children to the packs," Cody said.

Given what had happened to Beth, Garret was far less shocked than he might have been. Still, he felt bile rise in his throat at the idea that other humans might do the same thing…and that he was being accused of it.

"He hasn't sold any children," Artemis said with a scornful laugh.

"You're a Freeblood, are you not?" Varus asked.

"Aresia is a Bloodlady from Oceanus who has found a new life in our colony," Garret said, giving Artemis a quick and meaningful glance urging her to play along. He didn't want anyone recognizing her as a Freeblood now. "She has nothing to do with those rogues."

Hard, unblinking eyes examined him as if he were one of the ubiquitous and immense yellow slugs that lived beneath the leaf mold. Garret looked from one suspicious face to another. There was no chance that he and Artemis could fight their way out of this one.

But if these people were concerned about kidnapped children, they wouldn't hurt Beth, whatever they might think of him and Artemis.

"If you are who I think you are," he said, "you're what we've been looking for. Will you help Beth?"

"He asks if we'll *help* her," the dhampir woman said with a twist of her mouth.

"Can it, Sonja," Cody said. "You," he said to Artemis, "let the girl go, or we'll have to hurt your friend."

"I have good things to eat," Rachel said, holding out a crisp, firm apple to Beth. "I'll bet you're hungry."

Artemis knelt and held Beth gently by the shoulders. "These people are going to help us," she said. "You go on to that lady there. She'll take care of you for a while."

She looked up and fixed Varus with a severe gaze. "Don't be afraid of these Nightsiders. They aren't like the ones who took you."

"I'm not afraid." Beth thrust out her lower lip. "Where's Pericles?"

"I'll find him for you. I promise." She released Beth to Rachel, who gave Beth the apple.

"Both of you," Cody said to Garret and Artemis, "turn toward me."

With a quick shared glance, Garret and Artemis did as they were told. Rough hands wrenched Garret's arms behind his back. Artemis's body was coiled and ready to spring, but she knew as well as he did that they had to go along until fighting, however doomed, became their only option.

"Good," Cody said. "Keep cooperating and we won't have any problems."

"The child we're looking for is still out there," Garret said. "The longer you hold us, the longer he'll be alone with those monsters."

"You'll get to speak your piece when we get to the compound."

"How far?"

"You should be able to figure it out, if you really were looking for our colony." Cody turned away, and the muzzle of a gun prodded Garret in the back. Sonja gathered up Garret's supplies and stuffed them into his pack, while Artemis's Nightsider guard threw her hooded daycoat over her. The other full-blooded Opiri put on their own. Keeping Garret and Artemis apart, the patrol spaced themselves out to cover all possible angles of attack and keep an eye on their prisoners at the same time.

As they moved northeast through the overgrown suburbs and low, forested hills, the Willamette River always to the west, Garret watched and listened for Pericles. He would find out soon enough what had happened, if he didn't already know.

Garret hoped for the boy's sake that he would stay well away from them and their captors. He managed to catch Artemis's eye from time to time when their guards moved slightly out of formation. He knew that she was looking for Beth. He was, too, occasionally catching glimpses of the girl's dark hair.

Cody called for frequent stops to allow Beth to rest, so the going was slow. But Artemis still looked wan and pale, and Garret knew that if she got much worse he would have to beg these people to give her blood. She would certainly never ask for herself.

The group crossed the Willamette over a barely intact bridge at a place called Ross Island, and then continued west to the hills framing the southern portion of old Portland before continuing north again.

By the time the sun was at its apex, they had paused on a ridge overlooking the river, which glittered like a silver ribbon in the sun. Cody consulted with Sonja and several of his other compatriots, pointing toward the sprawling ruins in the valley below. Varus, Beth, Rachel and two others split off and descended at a fast pace. Artemis moved to follow, but her guard had already anticipated the attempt and jammed the muzzle of his gun into her neck. Garret's guard did the same to him.

"Don't worry about her," Cody said, addressing both of them. "If you pass muster, you'll see her again soon."

Garret followed Cody's gaze, squinting against the glare of sunlight on water. The four men and women with Beth were only specks against the slope of asphalt, concrete and faded autumn grass.

Cody held a pair of binoculars up to Garret's eyes, giving him his first glimpse of their destination: the high walls of a fortress on the river shore, built almost on top of a bridge that connected the western half of the fallen city with the east.

"Delos," Cody said, a note of pride in his voice. He glanced at the others. "Let's go."

Like almost every settlement, mixed colony or militia compound Garret had ever seen, Delos was a garrison designed to hold off an army of enemies if the need arose. But it seemed even more martial than most: the battlements were bristling with weapons, including what looked like a cannon and an array of machine guns. The eastern wall of the fortress literally butted up against the riverbank, with the bridge accessed by heavily guarded rear gates.

If Avalon had been protected this well, he thought, he might never have lost Roxana or Timon. But once the front gates swung open, he could see that the interior was not so different from Avalon's, with rows of barracks, a wide central commons for colony meetings, social gatherings and entertainment, an extensive garden, storage units, and a handful of smaller buildings that served as administrative offices.

"Is this what we were looking for?" Artemis asked Garret, twisting to see around the guards.

"I hope so," he said. "Are you—"

She held up her hand and looked across the commons, her eyes narrowed under her hood. Garret followed her gaze. Halfway across the central plaza, Rachel held Beth in her arms as she consulted with a tall woman in a much-mended lab coat.

"The doctor," Cody said, coming to join Garret. "She'll put Beth to rights."

"One of us should go with her," Garret said. "She'll be frightened without us."

"No can do. We'll have to confine you until the boss can

talk to you." He narrowed his eyes. "You sure you don't have anything to tell me? Something you might have forgotten before we left your camp?"

"Let us speak to your leader," Artemis said.

"In time," Cody said, his attention already focused on something else.

"I think we have the same enemies," Garret said. "The child I'm looking for is—"

Cody turned and walked away before Garret could finish. Sonja took his place and grabbed Garret's elbow.

"Do yourself a favor," she said, "and don't try lying to the boss."

"Garret!" Artemis called as her guards escorted her across the commons.

"Where are you taking her?" Garret demanded.

Sonja didn't answer. She and Garret's other guards waited until Artemis was out of sight, and then dragged him in the same general direction. People at work—humans, dhampires and presumably Daysiders, who could tolerate the sun—paused in their building, repairing, harvesting and sweeping to watch Garret and his escort pass, but he was clearly not much of a novelty. If Delos was anything like Avalon, they would have seen many people come to them in hopes of finding refuge.

Or maybe, Garret thought grimly, *arriving as prisoners*.

"Where have you taken Aresia?" he asked again, deliberately slowing his pace.

"You don't need to know that right now, though I'm sure she appreciates your concern," Sonja said. "Just remember that her treatment depends on your good behavior. And vice versa."

Muscles knotted with the compulsion to search for Artemis, Garret barely maintained his composure. The guards half dragged him past the rows of barracks to a windowless building near the eastern wall of the fortress.

An armed sentinel unlocked the door and stepped aside as Garret was pushed into one of several small, dark rooms with a tiny barred aperture set in the door. He stumbled into a cot set against the wall, and the cell door slammed shut before he could straighten and turn back.

"Wait!" he called, pressing his face against the bars. "If you're worried about the children, I can tell you where they're taking them!"

No one answered. The outer door closed. Garret knew perfectly well that it would be futile to bang on the cell door, so he walked the perimeter of the tiny room, looking for a means of escape. He wasn't surprised to find that there wasn't one. This place had obviously been built to hold Opiri, who were stronger than any human.

Garret sat on the cot and assessed his situation. Unless his captors were as bad as the militias and intended to try to sweat the "truth" out of him by confining him in a cold room without food or water for a few days, he doubted that he would be left alone too long.

But if Artemis was left without blood...

Garret lay back, closed his eyes and quieted his mind. He woke to the sound of metal scraping metal as someone unlocked the outer door. He rolled off the cot and jumped to his feet.

The cell door swung open. Cody and Varus stood just outside, rifles aimed at his chest.

"The boss will see you now," Cody said, jerking his gun toward the door.

Garret moved past them out of the jail. The sun was on the decline, and he realized that he'd slept far longer than he'd planned. His mouth was dry and his head ached, but he was already planning what to say to the "boss." He knew how to be very diplomatic when he had to be.

And if diplomacy didn't work, he would find something that did.

His guards' destination was another of the freestanding smaller buildings near the front of the colony, but Cody stopped midway to stare at a commotion near the colony's front gate. Garret swore under his breath as several Opiri dragged a cloaked and hooded Nightsider inside the stockade. Pericles hung limp between the arms of his guards, but he seemed unharmed and in one piece.

Garret knew better than to acknowledge him now. First, he had to find out what the hell was going on. He ignored the activity near the gate and didn't stop until they reached the building. Cody held the door open and pushed Garret in front of a plain pine desk, a battered chair and a wall covered with detailed maps of the area, each one marked with notations and pins.

While they waited Garret listened to the raised voices outside and clenched his teeth against his anger and worry. "Keep me informed," a masculine voice said somewhere behind the door at the back of the room. Then the door opened, and a man walked in to stand behind the desk. He looked at Cody expectantly, barely sparing a glance for Garret.

"We have something of a crisis, Cody," he said. "You'll have to—"

"Daniel?" Garret said.

Chapter 12

The man stared at Garret, clearly as startled as *he* was. Daniel moved around the desk to clasp Garret's shoulders. "What in hell are you doing here?" he asked.

"I could ask you the same question," Garret said, relief replacing his astonishment.

"Sir, you know this man?" Cody asked.

Daniel shot him a weary, impatient look. "You're usually a keen observer, Cody. Perhaps you need more time to rest between patrols."

"No, sir," Cody said, flinching at Daniel's sarcasm.

"*This* is the man you reported as being a potential child-stealer?"

"There seems to have been a misunderstanding," Garret said.

"Apparently," Daniel said. "Uncuff him, Cody."

Clumsy in his haste, Cody released Garret's hands. Garret rubbed his wrists, thinking about Artemis and Beth.

Hold on, he urged Artemis in his mind. *This won't take much longer.*

"You're far from your home ground," Daniel said, stepping back.

"So are you," Garret said. "It's been a long time."

"A strange time," Daniel said. He gestured toward a chair behind Garret. "Tell me what happened."

Garret perched on the edge of the chair and studied Daniel's face. It was clear that the past few years hadn't been easy on the man who had been a fellow serf in Erebus. Born into slavery, Daniel had been treated brutally for much of his early life in the Citadel and had learned to behave like any good human: quiet, obedient and controlled. He had only revealed the extent of his rebellious side when he had learned that his master, the Bloodmaster Ares, was actually his father, and that in spite of his appearance, he wasn't human. He'd risked his life to save Ares from his enemies, and had helped Roxana and Garret get dozens of captive humans out of the Citadel.

He had escaped with them, only to be overwhelmed at first by the vast world outside the Citadel's high walls. He'd adapted quickly, but the man who stood before Garret now had clearly done far more than merely adjust to a strange and hostile environment. He'd become like the soldiers who followed him: battle-tested, wary and tempered by hard experience.

Garret knew he was fortunate that Daniel wasn't his enemy. "I assume Cody told you most of it already," he said. "Your people found us traveling with a little girl about twelve miles southeast of here and apparently assumed we'd kidnapped her."

"My soldiers have reason to be suspicious," Daniel said, taking his own seat behind the desk. "Other humans in the area have been seen working with the rogues."

"Working as in side by side? You can't believe that they'd be traveling together."

"But you were with an Opir," Daniel said. "If I had been there, I never would have suspected you, of course." He steepled his fingers on the desk. "You were trying to get the child to safety?"

"We heard there was a mixed settlement somewhere near the river in Portland. If I'd known you were here—"

"Fortunately," Daniel said, "I was elected commander three years ago." He glanced at a paper on his desk. "I assure you that Beth will be well looked after. Who is the woman?"

Garret took a long, careful breath. "Aresia is a fellow colonist from Avalon, a former Bloodlady from Oceanus. She's no threat to anyone."

"Cody tells me that you are searching for another child."

"My son, Timon. He was taken from Avalon by rogue Freebloods nine weeks ago."

"I'm sorry. Aresia volunteered to help you find him?"

"She did."

"Then she is welcome here." Daniel tapped his fingers on the desk. "We knew the rogues have been stealing children wherever they can find them, but they must be ranging far if they've reached Avalon."

"Yes," Garret said tightly. "Have they stolen any of yours?"

"No, but only because we've taken steps to make sure they don't get the chance. We send out regular patrols to look for packs that might have children with them."

"And the humans who are helping them."

Daniel's eyes turned cold. "I was told that you know where the rogues are taking the children."

"North, over the border to Canada. Some kind of stronghold in the mountains."

"Yes. There are rumors that this stronghold is a Freeblood encampment, but we don't have any details." Daniel's fists clenched. "Even if we can't provide you with much additional information, we may be able to spare a few fighters to help you after we've dealt with the current problem."

"The Nightsider you just brought in?"

"You saw him?"

And I told Pericles that I wouldn't let him fall into their hands, Garret thought. "Not clearly," he said. "What has he done?"

"There's a good chance that he's one of the rogue scouts who look for vulnerable settlements to raid."

"We didn't encounter any rogues on the way here."

"They come in waves, and we're in a lull at the moment." Daniel frowned. "We have reason to believe that the prisoner has been a spotter for the child-stealers. He locates settlements and colonies where the others can break in."

It seemed, Garret thought, that this was a day for nasty surprises. "You've seen him before?"

"He's been described to us in considerable detail."

Garret almost spoke up then, but something in Daniel's manner convinced him to wait. "What do you do with prisoners?" he asked.

"Question them about our enemy's intentions. I don't expect them to tell the truth."

"And then?"

"We can't afford to keep them here for long."

A chill settled at the base of Garret's spine. This was definitely not the old Daniel. "It seems almost personal with you," he said.

"Opiri like my father and our people here can be trusted. Most Freebloods can't." Daniel cocked his head. "You don't hate them for what they did to your son?"

"Yes," Garret said, "and for what they did to Roxana. Raiders killed her four years ago."

"I'm sorry. I don't have to tell you how highly I thought of her. Does Ares know?"

Garret tried to remember the last time he'd seen Daniel's father and Ares's mate, Trinity, who like Garret had come from the Enclave of San Francisco. "Ares left Avalon not long after you did," he said. "I don't know where he is now."

"I understand." Daniel rose abruptly. "For the time being, you'll be assigned quarters and everything you'll need until our patrols report that it's safe for you to leave."

"And Aresia?"

"We'll release her on your recognizance." Daniel ran his hand over his face. "But this isn't like Avalon. We have strict rules here and tend to be suspicious of strangers. I'll make sure everyone knows you're guests, so feel free to talk to anyone in the colony if you have questions." He cocked his head. "Do you prefer shared accommodations with your companion or a separate room?"

"Shared will be fine," Daniel said. "I…should have told you that she is my wife."

"I see," Daniel said in a neutral voice. "I'll arrange it."

Garret nodded his thanks. "After you've released Aresia," he said, "I'd like to speak to the prisoner. He may know something about Timon."

"We know how to get that kind of information very quickly," Daniel said. "There's no need to dirty your hands."

"We're talking about my *son*."

With an unreadable glance at Cody, Daniel nodded. "Find me or Cody when you're ready."

"Thank you." Garret offered his hand.

Daniel took it, gripping hard. "Good luck," he said. Concealing his deep disquiet, Garret followed Cody back outside. Daniel might be a little too eager to find guilt in Pericles, but it wasn't as if Garret or Artemis had known the boy for more than a few weeks. If he was what Daniel had claimed…

"I'll take you on a short tour of the camp, and then to the Bloodlady's holding cell," Cody said, interrupting Garret's thoughts. "Your quarters should be ready within the hour."

"You seem to trust Daniel's judgment without question," Garret said.

"He's kept us alive," Cody said. "That's good enough for me."

Artemis knew that Garret was coming before he set foot in the prison. She breathed in his scent and closed her eyes. Though she hadn't been mistreated in any way and didn't expect that the soldiers would seriously harm Garret, she'd had grave doubts about the nature of this colony. Though it did appear to be one of those in which Opiri and humans lived and worked together, the soldiers' behavior suggested that it was little better than a typical militia compound—run with military precision, bound by almost rigid order and tainted by overt hostility toward outsiders.

"Where is she?" Garret's voice demanded from outside the building.

She inhaled sharply. Garret wasn't alone, but his words were clear and strong.

Perhaps there wouldn't need to be any violence, after all.

The key turned in the lock, and the door to her cell swung open. Garret stood framed in the light seeping in from the outer door, straight and still. Footsteps receded, and in an instant Garret's arms were around her, and he was pressing his lips to her neck as if he were the Opir and she the human donor. He released her quickly and closed the cell door behind him.

"They set you free," she breathed, pulling him down on the cot beside her.

"They've set us both free," Garret said. "We have the run of the colony."

She took his hand. "How did you manage that?"

"I know the man who runs this place."

"You *know* him?"

"I knew Daniel in the south. And I know why we were brought here as prisoners. Apparently there are humans helping to steal children for the rogues."

"Humans?" she asked. "Like the ones in the other colony who sold Beth?"

"I don't know if they're connected in any way," he said, "but the soldiers who found us thought I might be one of them. They've seen more than one kidnapped child pass through this area, and have been intervening whenever they can."

"And they thought a human would work so closely with a Freeblood?" she asked.

"You're not a Freeblood, remember?" he said, touching her face with his fingertips. "You're the Bloodlady Aresia. And I'd like to keep pretending that you're my wife."

Her heart thumped heavily in her chest, but not with fear. "You think I would be in danger if they knew who I really was?" she asked.

"They've been under nearly constant attack by Freebloods," he said. "They've seen citizens killed by rogues who have no regard for human life." His hand slipped down to her wrist, and he lifted her hand as if to expose the cuff marks that had already disappeared. "If they'd hurt you—"

He broke off, but he didn't need to finish. Artemis knew

what he'd wanted to do, because she would have done the same thing herself.

Too many feelings, she thought. His very nearness made her entire body vibrate with desire—and hunger. The barriers in her mind were holding, but barely. In such a crisis, it would be all too easy to let go.

Stop, she told herself. *Think*.

"Was your colony like this?" she asked.

"No. Avalon's leaders didn't take the necessary steps to protect its citizens, including my son. Daniel has corrected that problem here."

"By assuming guilt in any Freeblood they bring in?"

"I told you that Delos has been continuously attacked. Their suspicions are not unjustified." He hesitated. "There are no Freeblood colonists here."

"Your friend's decision?"

"The colonists'."

"Human colonists?"

"Opiri as well." He cleared his throat. "I'm sorry, Artemis. There's one more thing. They've taken Pericles."

"He must have been following us," she said. "You told your friend that he was with us?"

"No. Daniel seems to think Pericles is a spy for the child-stealers. They say he's a scout who looks for vulnerable settlements with half-blood children."

"Surely you do not believe this?" she asked.

"We've taken Pericles's word about everything that happened to him and Beth. The part about her colony was true, but we've only assumed that the rest of what he told us is also the truth."

Artemis lowered her voice with an effort. "Before we came here, you believed that Pericles was like me. Yet now you would accept the judgment of those who assumed *you* to be a criminal?"

Garret got to his feet and paced across the cell. "You're convinced Pericles has been telling the truth."

She gripped the edge of the cot until her fingers ached. "Did you wonder if *I* might also have been lying to you?" she asked. "If perhaps I knew about Pericles's true purpose and was protecting him from you?"

"No. Never." He returned to the cot and looked down at her, deep creases between his brows. "I *do* think even you might have been deceived."

Could he be right? Artemis thought. If Pericles had fooled her, how could she ever be certain that any of her fellow Freebloods could learn a new way of life, completely separate from the influence of the Citadels and the old customs?

"Will you tell them how he helped Beth?" she asked. "Or will you stand by and let them punish him for crimes he may not have committed?"

"I'll do what I can for Pericles," Garret said. "But if we can't get him released, we still have to go on with our search."

"And what if I should choose to admit that I am a Freeblood like him?"

"To punish me?" He took her by the shoulders, squeezing just enough so that she knew how serious he was. "If you do, I won't be able to leave you. And I can't stay here, Artemis. I've delayed far too long already, and Timon…"

He had pushed his worry for his son so far back in his mind that Artemis had been mercifully spared from sharing his fear. Now it flooded over her again, freezing her blood and filling her mind with the terror of unbearable loss.

Close your mind, she told herself. But even when she tried to block him out, the echo of his emotion was still within her. The effort left her breathless and dizzy.

I won't be able to leave you, he'd said. And he'd meant it.

Her knees gave way.

"Artemis!" Garret said, easing her back down on the cot.

"I'm fine," she said, scraping her hair away from her face. "Garret, promise me one thing. Ask the commander to let Pericles and me speak to him with Beth present. Let him *see* Pericles's compassion for her, and her feelings for him."

The expression in Garret's eyes shifted from worry to one of deep consideration. "That's a reasonable request," he said. "I'll tell Daniel everything we know about Pericles, and ask him to give Pericles a chance to speak for himself. That's all I can promise."

"That is all I ask."

For a time, neither of them spoke.

"You know I didn't intend to cause you pain," Garret said at last.

"I know."

He expelled his breath. "It's time to get you out of this cell. You and I have been given our own quarters, if you have no objection to staying with me."

"You know I have not."

"Good. I think you need rest." He pulled her up. "You need blood, too."

She tried to pull away from him, but he put his arm around her shoulders and didn't let go. "Come," he said gently.

The compound looked very different by night. Torches and lanterns atop high poles had been lit to accommodate the few humans moving about, and Artemis could identify far more Opiri, as well as a few dhampires. Some of the colonists glanced her way, but none showed any overt signs of suspicion or hostility.

It was almost as if the entire tenor of the place had changed now that the humans had retreated into their barracks. To an Opir, Artemis thought, darkness smoothed away the rough edges and lent an air of civilization absent in the presence of daylight.

But she knew that was her own prejudice speaking. The Opiri who had taken her and Garret had been no more sympathetic than the human patrollers. As far as she was concerned, that was only more proof that mixed colonies created a poisonous atmosphere for both humans and Opiri alike, a place where ordinary suspicions only festered and increased with proximity.

Garret seemed blind to such possibilities. He took her elbow and led her to a cluster of small, cabin-like buildings branching off from a path near a sandy area that Artemis assumed to be some kind of training ground. He stopped before the smallest cabin, opened the unlocked door and stood aside to let her precede him.

The single room was furnished with a cot, a desk and a chair. The wall behind the desk was covered with pinned maps, a few handwritten lists and what looked like a child's drawings, scribbled in charcoal. Artemis's pack lay on the cot, along with her knife and bow.

She stopped just inside the door and leaned against the wall, trying not to stare at the bed. She hadn't slept in one for many years.

But she wasn't thinking of sleep just now.

The room suddenly seemed very small. Too small to contain her and Garret at the same time. She tried not to look at him again, though she would have felt his presence even if he had been halfway across the settlement.

"I asked if you could bathe," he said. "I can escort you to the women's bathhouse. And Daniel has arranged for us to have clean clothes while ours are washed."

"Very hospitable of him," she said. "But then I am a Bloodlady, not a monstrous Freeblood."

"Artemis—" Garret began.

Someone rapped on the door. "Fox?" a man's voice called.

"Daniel must be ready to see us earlier than I expected," Garret said. "Are we all right, Aresia?"

He was asking again if she agreed to his deception, Artemis thought. But what choice did she have, if she wanted her words to be acknowledged and accepted by Delos's tyrannical human commander?

She followed Garret outside, where Cody was waiting for them. He turned away without comment and set out along the torch-lit path toward the commons.

Their destination was one of the separate buildings near the barracks. Inside it stood a large table and a dozen chairs—a conference room, Artemis guessed, currently unoccupied except for a single light-haired human.

The colony's leader rose from his chair, looked Artemis over with a frank, assessing stare, and gestured for her and Garret to be seated.

"Lady Aresia," he said tersely. "I won't waste your time with trivialities. I assume Garret informed you of the situation here. I apologize for our error."

"I understand the reason for it," she said, drawing upon the gracious manners of a Bloodlady. "But we have certain concerns about your other prisoner."

"The Freeblood, Pericles," Garret said. "I should have told you before that we've been traveling with him, and have every reason to believe that he has severed any ties with the rogues who are taking the children."

"In fact," Artemis said, "he had been caring for the little girl, Beth, even before we met him. He is no criminal."

Daniel tilted his head in acknowledgment. "I am sorry to disappoint you," he said. "We interviewed him in depth and called witnesses who had seen him with other children, delivering them to packs headed north. This testimony upheld our original assessment of his guilt."

Chapter 13

"You mean that you have already tried and sentenced him," Artemis said.

"I intended to ask you to let him talk to Beth in your presence," Garret said. "You'd see that he never harmed her. He protected her from other Freebloods and saved her life."

"Even if he was sincere in his feelings for the girl," Daniel said, "his behavior with her does not mitigate his previous bad acts." He met Artemis's gaze with a probing stare. "I admit to wondering why a Bloodlady is so intent on defending a mere Freeblood rogue. The elite of the Citadels regard them as hardly better than animals."

"You're speaking to my wife, Daniel," Garret said, half rising.

Artemis held up her hand. "I am no longer of the Citadel," she said, "and I clearly have greater hope for *all* my people than you do."

"Pericles could have betrayed us at any time on our way here," Garret said, "but he didn't."

"He ran from our patrol," Daniel said.

"Given the circumstances here, he would have had reason regardless of his guilt or innocence."

Daniel's face was grave, but there was no regret in his light blue eyes. "We have too many enemies outside our gates, and no margin for error. I'm sorry, but we cannot set him free."

Artemis began to rise, but Garret stopped her with a firm hand on her arm. "What do you plan to do with him?" he asked.

"Keep him confined, for the time being. When I return, we will make the final decision."

"Return?" Garret asked, speaking again before Artemis could protest.

"I'll be going with you to find Timon."

Some wordless, very private communication passed between the two men, a reflection of a shared past that Artemis knew she could never fully understand. She felt strangely bereft.

At that moment, she hated Daniel for more than his ruthlessness.

"With so many enemies at the gates, as you said, won't you be needed here?" Garret asked.

"There are many competent men and women who can take my place," he said. "As a dhampir, I can be of use to both of you."

"A dhampir?" Artemis said, startled out of her anger. "But your eyes…your teeth…"

"There are a few dhampires who don't have the usual features, and Daniel's father wasn't the usual kind of Opir," Garret said, sliding his hand down her arm to clasp her hand. "His father was a Bloodmaster in Erebus."

"Erebus?" Artemis echoed. "How is that possible?"

"We were serfs together," Garret said. "But Daniel was born in the Citadel."

"And you were permitted to live?" Artemis asked Daniel.

"My father, Lord Ares, didn't know who I was until shortly before Garret and I escaped from Erebus. Only his greatest rival knew of my true parentage, and he kept me alive to spite Ares."

"Then you have good reason to despise my people."

"I don't, Lady Aresia. My father and his Opir allies helped save my life, and the lives of many other serfs." He glanced at Garret with a slight frown. "You didn't tell her everything."

"Evidently he did not," Artemis said, freeing her hand from Garret's. "But I wonder, Daniel, if your experiences have not made it easier for you to pass overhasty judgment on the least-powerful Opiri who fall into your hands."

"Aresia," Garret said, "you have no idea what he suffered in Erebus, and what it took for him to get to where he is now."

"Garret overstates his case," Daniel said to Artemis. "I am sorry that your traveling companion is not who you believed him to be."

Garret stared at the tabletop, his fist clenching and unclenching on the chair. "Daniel, what if Pericles could help us track down some of these other packs? Would you reconsider?"

"He would require constant watching," Daniel said. "We can't do that and concentrate on finding your son."

"Let me speak to him," Artemis said, beginning to rise. "There must be a way for him to prove that he has changed."

"That will not be possible," Daniel said.

"What do you think she'll do?" Garret asked, leaning over the table. "Help him escape?"

"Would you?" Daniel asked her.

"Either you trust my judgment or you don't," Garret said to Daniel.

"Stop," Artemis said. "I am not a child to be argued over." She pushed away from the table, nearly upsetting her chair, and strode out of the room.

Walking blindly, she started across the commons. She avoided contact with the colonists she passed, including the Opiri. Pericles was being held in some detention facility, and she knew she could find it easily enough by scent, if not by simply looking for it.

But it would surely be guarded, and she wasn't prepared for another confrontation. She walked once around the camp, observing silently, and then returned to the cabin. She threw open the door and walked inside.

Garret was already there, one of the child's drawings in his hands. He didn't seem to hear her come in. She knew he was thinking of Timon, and her anger drained away.

"I did not intend for the conversation with your friend to end as it did," she said.

He looked up slowly. "I should not have spoken to you as I did, especially in front of Daniel." His gaze focused on her face. "You look even worse than before," he said, setting the drawing on the desk.

"What is it you humans say?" she asked. "You are like a hen with one chick."

"I would never mistake you for a chick, Artemis," he said with a wry smile. "Not even an eaglet. I'd say you're fully grown."

She felt her tension give way to the soothing warmth of his voice. She sat on the cot. "I know you did what you could for Pericles," she said. "I thank you for that."

He knelt beside the cot. "I'm sorry I couldn't do more." He took her hand, turned it over and kissed her palm. The brush of his lips startled her as much as if he had never

touched her with his mouth, though she remembered every
caress with excruciating clarity.

Apparently his memory was equally keen, for he
quickly let her go, rose and stepped back. "I know how
you feel about Delos, and Daniel's judgment," he said.
"You have doubts about humans and Opiri living together.
There are times I've had the same doubts. I told you that
Avalon made mistakes. So did Beth's colony. Daniel has
managed to avoid those mistakes." He moved to the door.
"There's something I'd like you to see."

Reluctantly, she went with him. They followed one of
the paths between the individual cabins back to the commons, passing a dozen dhampires and Opiri engaged in
hand-to-hand fighting. Lights flickered behind the small
windows of the barracks, suggesting that their human oc-
cupants were engaged in their own evening activities.

"This is the mess hall," Garret said, indicating a building about half the size of the smallest barracks. "Many of
the human citizens are eating their evening meal."

Artemis balked. "If it is a human place…"

"Everyone is welcome." Tugging gently on her hand, he
led her to the mess hall and opened the door. Immediately
Artemis was struck by a blast of scent and sound—humans
of every age gathered around long tables, eating with obvious pleasure, engaged in dozens of conversations, laughing and clearly enjoying themselves. In addition to the
tables, there were clusters of mismatched, much-mended
chairs scattered around an open area at the far side of the
single room, also occupied with people lost in discussion
or playing unfamiliar games on smaller tables.

The contrast to what Artemis had seen outside was
great, but most surprising was the presence of children.
Children with adult kin, or playing with balls, cloth dolls
and wooden horses.

And not all of the children were human. Artemis saw

that several had the distinctive eyes of dhampires, and once she had noticed them, she also realized that there were a number of full-blooded Opiri among the humans. One male Opir was at the table opposite a human female, gazing at her with rapt attention, while a dhampir child sat beside him, scribbling on rough paper with a piece of charcoal and kicking his legs vigorously under the bench. In the open area, a female Opir was holding an infant on her knee while a male human looked on with obvious pride, as if the child were his own.

Garret followed her gaze. "That's what Daniel is trying to save," he said. "He's doing what my former colony failed to accomplish—protecting children like these, providing the only kind of settlement where civilized Opir and humans can live in peace without the constant fear of attack."

He took her hand again and led her to the couple with the infant. The female Opir glanced up with a smile of such open welcome that Artemis was astonished all over again.

"You must be Garret," she said, "and Aresia."

"Welcome," the human father said, standing to greet them. "I'm Johan, and this is my wife, Deineira."

"And this," Deineira said, lifting her squirming baby, "is Sophia Johanna."

"Quite a mouthful," Johan said with a grin. He offered his hand to Artemis. She took it gingerly. A flush of heat raced up her arm, carrying the human's emotions into her mind: pride, contentment…and love, powerful enough to breach her empathic barriers.

While she was recovering from the intensity of Johan's feelings, Deineira abruptly pushed Sophia Johanna into Artemis's arms. Artemis had no choice but to hold the squirming, blanket-wrapped bundle, cradling the round head and swaddled bottom against her chest.

She looked down into the chubby, wide-eyed face, and the memories she had fought so hard to contain came rushing back. Holding her own infant in her arms, only days before the first Opir she had ever met had nearly killed her. The infant she had lost because Kronos had saved her life by converting her, forcing her to leave her human life behind. Her life, and everything she had loved.

With the greatest of care, Artemis bent to return Sophia Johanna to Deineira's arms. "Your daughter is beautiful," she murmured.

The Bloodlady beamed, no trace of Opir reserve in her eyes. "She is, isn't she? She will grow up to walk in daylight, like her father."

Artemis's vision blurred, though there was no physical reason for it. She looked for Garret, who was eating what humans called a "sandwich" and talking to Johan between ravenous bites. Artemis realized, with a twinge of guilt, that she hadn't given enough thought to Garret's physical needs. Now, at least, he had decent food and a real chance to rest.

He couldn't have known what seeing Deineira's family and holding the infant would do to her. He'd asked her about children once, and she'd evaded his question, as she'd evaded so many others.

Garret had wanted to make a point, and he had succeeded.

"Lady Aresia," Johan said, briefly touching her arm. "You are ill."

"No," she said, overwhelmed by his genuine concern for her. "I'm only a little—"

"Hungry," Johan said. "I know the signs. You have not been feeding."

Artemis knew that she couldn't lie to Johan. There was a quiet wisdom in him that defied any attempt to deceive him.

"You need not tell me why you have not taken your husband's blood," he said. "It is none of my business. But let me help you. I have not made a donation in three days and will not suffer for it."

Startled, she stared into Johan's eyes. "You would give me your blood?"

He lifted a brow. "It cannot be so different in the colony you came from, surely?"

"No," she said quickly. "No, not at all."

"Then, please." He gestured to three doors in the back of the hall.

"But your wife..."

"She suggested it."

Artemis felt faint. There was clearly nothing sexual in the invitation, and it was possible that taking blood from another human would solve the problem she had been facing since Coos Bay. If it did, she could honestly tell Garret that she was well and did not need *his* blood. There would be no need for dodging his questions again and again.

She looked around for Garret. He was nowhere to be seen. What would he think if he knew what she had done? Would he consider it a betrayal?

"Come, now," Johan said. He nodded to Deineira, who smiled at Artemis, and started toward the back of the hall. Half in a daze, Artemis followed him into one of the small rooms, comfortably furnished with a couch and a pair of chairs.

The entire procedure was almost clinical, and she felt not the slightest arousal or any sense of real intimacy, in body or mind. Johan's mind seemed focused on pleasant thoughts that matched his mellow personality, and all Artemis felt was profound relief.

When it was over and Johan was rolling down his sleeve, she thanked him and hesitated at the door.

"I envy you and Deineira," she said softly.

"Our Sophia?" he asked. "I have no doubt that you will have a child of your own when the time is right for you."

Unable to bear his sympathy, Artemis fled the room. She still saw no sign of Garret. She returned to the cabin and lay on the cot with her arm over her eyes. The door opened, and Garret's boots crossed the floor. Wood scraped on wood as he drew the desk chair close to the bed and sat down.

"What is it, Artemis?" he asked. "If I'd known seeing the children would upset you so much…"

"I'm not upset," she said.

"Sometimes you're very good at hiding your feelings," he said, "but this isn't one of those times."

"I know why you took me to see them," she said. "You wanted me to understand what it was like with you and Roxana. And Timon."

She felt the movement of air as he reached toward her and then dropped his hand before he made contact. A profound ache filled her body.

"It was like that, for a while," he said. "But not at the beginning. It wasn't until we escaped Erebus that we could live as equals and try to give Timon a good life."

Artemis swallowed. "What happened to Roxana, Garret?" she asked.

"She died fighting rogue Freebloods, defending our colony. Timon never got a chance to know his mother."

Remembering how she had berated Garret for not telling her about Roxana in the beginning, Artemis felt a terrible remorse. She swung her legs over the side of the cot and brushed his hand with her fingertips. Emotion overwhelmed her, and sensory images flooded her mind: two kindred spirits bound together, bright lights in a great darkness, gathering other lights to themselves, projecting warmth and hope and joy.

And then the sundering, the unbearable loss, one of the bright lights extinguished in pain and fear. And the other soul…crippling bereavement that altered everything—

more devastating than slavery or any other ordeal, save one: the disappearance of the child he and his mate had created.

Shuddering violently, Artemis fell back on the cot. "I see why you would despise us, those of my rank. I, too, would hate."

Garret knelt beside the cot. "I blame myself for what happened to Roxana and Timon," he said. "When we founded Avalon, we were too idealistic, too invested in the philosophy of peace to take the necessary precautions. We accepted nearly everyone who came to us from the Citadel and Enclave, human or Nightsider. That was a mistake." He laced his hands together, gripping with such force that his fingers turned red and his knuckles white. "Some of the bad ones, the humans, were only trouble-makers, antisocial. But others, especially the Freebloods, assumed that they could simply take what they wanted without giving what was required of them in return. Still, we believed they could be taught to discard their old ways. Roxana was the biggest idealist of all of us, and she had the courage to stand by her convictions. She had faith. But she was wrong."

Barely able to endure the bitterness of his grief, Artemis covered his rigid hands with hers. "The Freebloods betrayed you," she said.

"They betrayed all of us. They opened the gates to rogues. We killed nearly all of them. But even afterward, the council didn't do enough to make certain it never happened again. When the raiders broke through to steal Timon, they got away with it because too many of the colonists wouldn't compromise their *principles*." He laughed hoarsely. "I should have taken Timon away from that place long ago, before…"

"But you still want what *they* did," she said, "or you

would not have protected me from the militia in the south, or taken me to see Deineira and Johan tonight."

"I believe in a philosophy that doesn't destroy itself," he said, his jaw so tight that the words seemed barely able to escape.

Daniel's philosophy, she thought. No wonder Garret admired this colony for protecting its citizens as his old one had not.

How could she blame Garret for doubting Pericles… or for expecting her to abandon him after he'd saved her from the militiamen?

Slowly and carefully, she withdrew her hands. "Perhaps you would like to be by yourself now," she said. "I can—"

"No," he said. "I wanted to tell you all this because there's no more need for secrets between us. It's all in the past."

But it is not, she thought. The distress was still there, raw and throbbing. She could give him comfort with words, but beyond that…

She was afraid of where such comforting might lead. Afraid to let down her guard, lower the gate, cross the moat she had dug around herself. Now that there was so much more between them than the empathy and their mutual desire…

But she was well fed now. There was no danger that she would slip. If she didn't reinforce the bond again, surely it would continue to fade.

Stripping her mind of all thought beyond the moment, she put her arms around his shoulders. He stiffened, sighed and buried his face against the curve of her neck. His anguish flowed into her like blood, and her body seemed to absorb it, striving to heal the wound that refused to close. Garret held her as if he believed she was the key to his mortal salvation, and she pulled him down onto the cot, the wish to heal and the need to feel flesh against flesh blending to become one overwhelming compulsion.

"Are you sure, Artemis?" he murmured. "You don't have to do this, just because I—"

In answer, she kissed him. After a moment he yielded, slipping his tongue inside her mouth. She took it gladly, hungrily. He eased himself over her, resting his weight on his hands, grazing her breast with his chest. Even that slight contact brought her nipples to aching peaks. Everything they had done in the woods returned to her in a burst of light and lust.

His lips left hers, brushing her cheeks and teasing the lobe of her ear. He suckled ever so gently, tugging, awakening a sympathetic response in her nipples.

"Garret," she whispered.

He withdrew. His face was flushed, his eyes unfocused.

"Touch me," she said. "*Touch* me."

He rolled onto his side, watching her face as he rested his palm just above her breasts. Her heart felt as if it would leap right into his hand. He teased loose the uppermost button of her sturdy, shapeless shirt and parted the plackets. His fingers slid into the gap and traced tiny circles, sending wild shivers along the length of her spine. Garret was not so hesitant after that. He undid one button and then another, discovering that she wore no bra. He grazed one nipple with his fingertip. She arched and gasped. He lifted her and slipped the shirt back over her shoulders. Then he eased her back down and began to stroke her breasts, the calluses on his fingertips only heightening the erotic sensation. She bit her lip and closed her eyes.

"Am I too rough?" he asked.

She took his wrist and pressed his palm over her right breast. He bent over her and flicked his tongue over the peak of her nipple. Pleasure radiated outward to every point of her body, and a rush of heat blossomed between

her thighs. She tilted her head back, breathing deeply as
he drew her nipple into his mouth and suckled more vigorously, moving from one breast to the other until both were
thoroughly tender and the smallest touch set her gasping.
She was so lost in sensation that she moved more by instinct than thought when he reached down and unzipped
her pants. He slipped them down over her hips, leaving
her underpants the only physical barrier between him and
her naked flesh.

Her emotional barriers, too, were giving way. His sorrow was beginning to ease. Giving herself, letting him
give, was a balm to his grief. And to her own.

Thought gave way to pure sensation as his fingers
slipped inside her underpants and found the slick wetness beneath. She moaned, and he stroked the swollen
lips at her entrance, running his fingers up and down the
cleft without probing deeper. It was the sweetest torment,
unbearable excitement.

Her pleasure heightened his and echoed back to her.
She whimpered as his thumb slid over the nub that could
bring so much ecstasy. He pinched and released, stroked
and withdrew. Artemis began to shudder.

It was coming too soon. She didn't want it, not this
way, not with him still outside her. Even when he found
her entrance and slid his finger into it, she kept enough
of her sense to remember how much she needed to know
that he had become a part of her.

"You're tight," he said. "So tight."

"Garret, I… I want…"

He kissed her lips and forehead, and began the caresses
all over again. Then he was removing the last of her clothing, and his warm breath was where his fingers had been.
His mouth pressed against her, and then his tongue glided
over the same moist, plump flesh his fingers had explored.
She couldn't stop the cries of pleasure as he flicked his

tongue up and down, licking up the wetness with relish, thrusting his tongue inside until she could think only of feeling his hardness filling her to the brim.

She didn't have to find the words. His desire and tenderness filled her mind. When he paused, it was only to remove his clothing and lie naked beside her.

Almost shyly, she reached down to touch him. He inhaled sharply, raised himself onto his arms and crouched over her, his hips above the cradle of her spread thighs.

Let go.

She let him feel everything she had withheld from him since their last sexual encounter. His eyes widened, a look of wonder crossing his face. His aura awakened, shimmering over his head and shoulders. With infinite care he eased down, the head of his cock, hot and full, just grazing her. When he entered, it was like a homecoming, a fulfillment of dreams she had never held long enough to discard.

The rhythm was gentle at first, testing her readiness. He leaned down to kiss the corner of her mouth. "Artemis…"

Then he said no more. He tilted back his head and moved more quickly, gliding in and out more forcefully but never so strongly as to cause her anything but the utmost pleasure. She found herself moving with him, arching into his thrusts, joining a dance whose steps she had almost forgotten. Their emotions intertwined, strengthened each other, built toward a pinnacle of joy just as before. The ecstatic tension expanded as Garret's motions grew more urgent.

Artemis knew it was nearly over, and she didn't want it to be. She tried to hold him inside. He paused, breathing fast, and then thrust again, shuddering as he reached his completion. She experienced it as if it were her own. Her hips lifted, and she cried out, waves of indescribable sensation pulsing outward from her core.

Garret withdrew and rolled onto his side, one arm draped possessively over her waist.

"My God," he breathed. "What's happening to us?"

Chapter 14

It wouldn't be so difficult to tell him now, Artemis thought, gradually settling back into her own body. She ached, inside and out, but the joy was there, pushing the pain and sorrow out of her mind—and his.

But she couldn't spoil this moment with explanations that might make him consider the implications of what she—they—had done. If she told him of her empathic abilities and the new bond between them, this peace would come to an end. Even if he accepted, there would be questions. Too many questions.

So she remained silent. His arm lay heavy on her ribs, and his breathing slowed into the cadence of sleep. She turned her head to look at his face. So peaceful now, the harsh lines of experience and adversity softened with contentment. He didn't hear her as she collected her clothes, put them on and left the cabin.

She was fortunate. There were still Opiri and a few humans about, but they only glanced at her and went about their business.

After a brief search, she found Pericles in a small building similar to the one in which she had been imprisoned. If there had been a guard, he had abandoned his post. No one saw her break the lock and enter.

"Artemis?" Pericles said from behind the cell door.

"Yes," she said. "Are you well?"

"They haven't hurt me." The door creaked as he leaned against it. "They questioned me. They believe I've been involved in stealing other children."

"Have you?"

"No! They have me confused with someone else."

She laid her palms flat on the wood as if she could draw his innermost thoughts through the door and feel the truth of his words.

"We tried to make the commander understand how you saved Beth and helped us take care of her," she said.

"It didn't do any good, did it?"

He sounded so small and sad that Artemis was racked by a fresh pang of guilt. "Many of the colonists have spoken against you," she said.

"I'm not who they think I am," he said, his voice rising. "Why would I have come anywhere near this place if I thought they would accuse me?" He gulped in a breath. "Artemis, tell them that if they let me go, I can help them. I can make myself useful to some other pack and try to learn more about why they want the children. If I can get to this place in the north, maybe I can report back to you before you arrive."

Artemis closed her eyes. "Pericles—"

"They'll have to kill me, Artemis," he said. "They won't let me go, and they can't keep me in this cell forever."

Daniel had said that Pericles's fate wouldn't be determined until he returned from helping Garret find Timon, but Artemis had never doubted what he meant. Pericles would die.

Unless she set him free.

She backed away from the door and leaned against the opposite wall. A mistake now would not only betray Garret but possibly put other half-blood children in danger.

Even if she tried to use her empathy now, it had never worked as a simple lie detector. She had to rely on her own judgment. If she surrendered all belief in that judgment and assumed that Pericles was the villain Daniel believed him to be, she would lose the dream she had refused to abandon for so long.

"There's something else," Pericles said, his voice dropping to a whisper. "Did you know that they've got other Freeblood prisoners here, in another building?"

Artemis started. "What?"

"I think it's a secret from everyone but a few of their leaders. There are five of them, and I was in a cell next to them for a little while, before the humans took me out to question me."

"They must have been captured during one of the rogues' attacks on Delos."

"The prisoners say they weren't part of any attack and were taken because they were mistaken for the ones who are trying to break in. They say that the rogues outside want to kill them, because they're opposed to what the child-stealers are doing."

The story sounded utterly implausible to Artemis. "Opposed? In what way?"

"The same way we are. Why should we be the only ones?" He took a breath. "Listen to me, Artemis. They're like these colonists, working against the thieves, but from a different direction. Isn't that important?"

A bud of hope formed somewhere beneath Artemis's

ribs. "Have you ever met these Freebloods before?" she asked.

"I didn't see their faces," Pericles said. "Their voices weren't familiar."

"Then why did they confide in you?"

"I don't know," Pericles admitted.

"What did you tell them about yourself?"

"Just that I was being held for things I didn't do."

"Did they know how you came to be here and think that you could help them?"

"I don't know!" Pericles said, frustration rising in his voice. "They said that when they tried to explain why they were in the area, the leaders here didn't believe them, just like they don't believe me. Or you."

"Garret's wife, a Bloodlady, was killed by Freeblood raiders."

There was a thump from behind the door as Pericles sat heavily on his cot. "He had an Opir mate?" he asked. "I didn't know."

"I did not know, either, until a very short time ago," she said. "You can see that he has reasons for mistrusting Freebloods."

"But he still helped us," Pericles said. The cot creaked as he got up again. "Why are the leaders here keeping these prisoners a secret? What if they *know* these Opiri really are working against the rogues but can't admit that there are Freebloods who aren't their enemies?"

"You are suggesting some kind of conspiracy," Artemis said. "Daniel, the leader of the colony, has no love for Freebloods, either, but I see no reason to believe that he would deliberately hide evidence that some might be allies."

"Then why did you tell him that you're a Bloodlady? You must not have believed he'd treat you fairly if you told him the truth."

She wondered how Pericles had learned what Garret

had done. "It was Garret's decision," she said. "He did not consult me in advance."

"But you aren't a prisoner, are you?" Pericles asked with uncharacteristic bitterness.

"You assume too much," she said. "You still know only what other Freebloods have told you, without objective evidence of any kind."

"You want to believe that we can live differently than we always have," Pericles said. "You're looking for Freebloods who can see something beyond their own ability to obtain serfs and rise to become Bloodlords. Maybe these prisoners are what you've been looking for.

"Talk to them," Pericles urged. "Just listen to what they have to say."

"I doubt I would be permitted to see them if they are being held in secret," Artemis said. "But I will do what I can."

"Thank you," he said.

His relief was so obvious that Artemis was glad that she could give him some measure of peace at such a terrible time. But now she had to determine how to gain access to the other prisoners.

Asking Daniel directly was out of the question, and she wouldn't expect Garret to intercede for her, which would undoubtedly arouse suspicion.

Keeping low, she peered out the jail door. The guard, if there had been one, hadn't returned, but there was a change in the air, an electric tension that didn't make sense to her until she saw a woman running from one of the barracks, a rifle clutched in her hands.

Alarm. Fear. The rise of adrenaline in bloodstreams, the instincts of fight or flight.

She shrank back inside the door until the woman was out of sight and then slipped out. As she worked to hide the damage to the lock, raised voices echoed across the compound, and other figures—male and female, human and Opir—began to spill out into the commons from the surrounding buildings.

Something was wrong, and Artemis suspected she knew what it was. She was just turning back toward the cabin when Garret walked into view, obviously looking for her. As she raised her hand to catch his attention, a bell began to ring from somewhere along the walls. Colonists armed with rifles and compound bows dashed toward the front gate and ramparts.

Garret saw Artemis and jogged toward her. "Where have you been?" he asked, gripping her arms. His concern swept over her, possessive and a little afraid. "When I woke up, and you weren't there…"

"I wanted to walk a little," she said, her body responding almost instantly to his touch and his scent and the vivid memory of their lovemaking. "I didn't mean to worry you."

"I know you can take care of yourself," he said. "But I don't like to think I did something to scare you away."

"What you did," she said, "was anything but frightening. But I…" She hesitated, faced by an unpalatable decision. "I was too inclined to continue, and I knew you needed your rest."

"You thought I wasn't up to it?" he asked, drawing his fingers over her cheeks and lips. "You look much better. I hope I had something to do with that."

A part of her reveled in the desire in his voice and mind, the slightly rough texture of his fingertips, the way his body so clearly reacted to her presence. She wanted to run back to the cabin and begin all over again.

But the bell was still ringing, and neither one of them could ignore what it must portend. She covered his hand with hers and clasped his fingers.

"What has happened?" she asked.

A little of the brightness left Garret's eyes, and his

emotions darkened. "A Freeblood attack," he said. "Daniel knew another one would be coming soon. There's not much chance that the rogues can break in, but everyone who can fight is taking up defensive positions."

"Does Daniel know why these rogues continue to attack when they have so little chance of succeeding?" she asked, thinking of what Pericles had told her.

"We didn't discuss it," Garret said with a frown. "But whatever they want, they have to be reminded that they're the ones who suffer most in these attacks. If enough of them die, they may give up."

Artemis looked away. "I'm sorry," Garret said, clearly meaning it, "But they're as much a threat to you as to anyone else here." He cupped her chin. "You're not expected to fight, but I have to help the colonists. If you want to do something, you can stay with the children and the noncombatants who are looking after them. I'll be on the stockade."

He kissed her, hard and fast, and then was gone. Artemis felt cold inside, as if his kiss had pulled all the warmth out of her body. Letting him fight alone felt utterly wrong to her, and she knew it wasn't impossible that he could be hurt.

But the odds were small, and the colony didn't appear to be in any serious danger.

There was still another way she might make a difference.

Coming to a decision, she began to search. Pericles had said that the prisoners were hidden, so it didn't seem likely that they would be in the obvious place.

In the chaos of the colonists' response to the rogues' attack, no one seemed to notice that she was heading away from the battle. Nevertheless, she walked briskly and with a show of purpose until she was among the storage buildings and more extensive gardens close to the northern wall, where the compound abutted the river and the fortified bridge. A handful of soldiers were patrolling the parapet there, but their attention was focused outward.

Artemis moved among the buildings, listening and scenting the air. If Daniel meant to hide the prisoners from the Opiri colonists, he would have needed to muffle smell as well as sound.

In the end, she found that only one of the buildings was guarded. A single apparently human soldier paced back and forth in front of the door, his attention clearly focused on the sounds of the battle he hadn't been permitted to join.

Unless the structure contained some treasure of greater worth than the children of Delos, Artemis thought, it must hold the secret prisoners.

Now she had another choice to make, and a dangerous one. Under the circumstances, she couldn't imagine that the guard would simply let a stranger in to see captives she should not even know existed. But if she forced her way in...

Artemis almost turned back. But a powerful feeling of something very like compulsion sent her running between the doused torches, creeping in the shadows and using all her survival skills to reach the side of the building, just out of the guard's sight. She waited until her breathing was steady again and then inched forward until she was only a few feet away from the soldier.

She struck the human with carefully measured strength, caught him as he began to fall and laid him out on the ground. A set of keys hung on his belt. She found the right one, opened the lock and carried the guard inside the building, laying him down gently.

She knew at once that Pericles had been correct: there were five Opiri here, each one in a separate cell.

"Who are you?" a male voice asked. The others shifted and murmured.

Of course they would know by her scent that she was not their usual guard, Artemis thought. She hesitated again, wondering how to begin.

"You are one of us," the voice said. It held a vibrant, commanding note that suggested an Opir of age and experience, reminiscent of a Bloodlord or Bloodmaster rather than a typical Freeblood.

It was also eerily familiar.

"I spoke to Pericles," she said, bypassing unnecessary explanations. "He conveyed to me what you had claimed about your opposition to the rogues who are stealing half-blood children."

There was a measure of silence as the speaker absorbed her words. "What Pericles told you is correct," he said. "But who are *you*?"

"Someone who also opposes the rogues," she said.

"But you are not human."

"I am Opir," she said.

"Not from this colony."

Artemis approached the speaker's cell. "How do you know?" she asked.

"You are the Opir who arrived with the human, are you not?"

Realizing she had already revealed too much, Artemis saw no reason to lie. "Yes," she said.

"And you trust Pericles?"

"I did not know that he was an accused child-stealer."

"So the humans claim," the speaker said. "What is your relationship to the human who came with you?"

Naturally the Freeblood would detect Garret's scent on her body. "We are searching for a child taken by the rogues," she said, dodging his question.

"Then that is why the half-blood commander came to question us."

"Did you tell him what you told Pericles?" she asked.

"We told him and were not believed." Artemis heard fabric rustle as he moved behind the door. "They will not believe we could be working for a common cause."

"And how are you doing this?" she asked. "Are you fighting those who steal innocents? Are you freeing children?"

"We are still gathering others who share our beliefs," he said, "convincing them that this wholesale abduction will only lead to another war that may destroy us all."

"And that is your sole purpose? To prevent another war?"

"No. That is, not all of it. We believe that Freebloods need not be rogues, killing each other over humans and accepting either a short, brutish life or a constant struggle to maintain status in the stagnant world of the Citadels. We believe there is another—"

"Another way," Artemis interrupted. "You sound very much like someone I used to know."

"I *do* know you," he said. "I know why you were exiled from Oceanus."

"Then everything you say is merely tailored to win my sympathy," she said. "I cannot help you." She spun on her heel and headed for the door.

"Wait!" he called after her. Fingers scraped at the hatch over the aperture cut into his door. "I know you have a gift. Touch my hand."

She froze, her heartbeat slamming to a halt. Almost as if drawn by some ancient sorcery, she drifted back to the cell door and opened the hatch.

The face she saw through the opening was not one she recognized. But when he pushed long, slender fingers through the gap and she touched them, she knew.

"Kron—" she began.

"My real name is not known here," he said. "I go by the name Nomos. The world believes that Kronos is dead,

and now I am known as a Freeblood. But if you still believe as I do, you realize that the words I speak are true."

Artemis didn't bother saying it wasn't possible. It
clearly was. Kronos had not died in challenge. He had
left Oceanus alive. He had changed his face—with genetic manipulation, or with surgery—and his name. He
was in hiding.

And he was…he *must* be doing the work he claimed,
the same work she had tried to take up in his absence.

*What if they know these Opiri really are working
against the rogues but can't admit that there are Freebloods who aren't their enemies?* Pericles had asked. She'd
scoffed at the idea of such a conspiracy. But now?

"Can you get us out, Artemis?" Kronos asked. "I fear
that if you do not, our fate will be the same as that of every
other Freeblood prisoner Daniel and his soldiers have ever
taken alive."

She closed her eyes. The question was no surprise to
her. What came as a shock was the depth of feeling she
still had for her former master, the sense of obligation and
loyalty even his supposed death had not erased. Kronos
had been family to her when all her old human connections had vanished along with her humanity.

"I know you must feel I abandoned you," he said. "I
escaped, leaving you to do the work in Oceanus. I only
learned much later that you had been exiled. I spoke to
many Freebloods, and heard that you were in the south. I
was hoping to find you, Artemis. To have you at my side
again."

"You were looking for me when you were captured?"
she whispered.

"It was one of my goals," he said. "As the humans say,
'in the wrong place at the wrong time.' But now we can
work together to end this madness and lead the most op-

pressed Opiri from the path of ruination." He pressed his face close to the aperture. "You are our only hope."

Backing away from the door, she wrapped her arms around her chest. Old loyalties and new. They were in direct conflict, and she knew she had no hope of convincing Daniel that these Opiri were speaking the truth. Though she might make Garret believe her, she would only force him to turn against his friend.

"It is the human, isn't it?" Kronos asked, sympathy in his voice. "You have some affection for him. Pericles said that he saved your life."

"He did."

"And yet it is more than that. You were never like my other vassals, Artemis. In so many ways."

She banged her fist against the wall. "Rogues are attacking the colony as we speak," she said. "There is no time—"

"No time," he repeated softly. "Help me, Artemis."

"And if I do? What will *you* do?"

"Go north. Try to discover a way to organize a resistance to this Bloodlord who takes children. I have developed contacts over a wide region, and you know that I can make other Opiri listen to me. That is why they tried to kill me in Oceanus. Let me try, Artemis."

He was right, she thought. If anyone could persuade other exiles to turn against the child-stealers, it would be Kronos. He could be instrumental in saving Timon and every other child who had been taken. He could unite Freebloods as she never could, even with her abilities. And in any case, her empathy had proven to be far more a burden than a gift.

"I will," she said. She glanced at the guard who, to her great relief, was beginning to move slightly. "This may be your only chance to escape. But you must swear to me,

Kronos, that you will not harm any of the people in this colony as you leave it."

"If we must fight," he said, "we will take great care not to do lasting harm to anyone here."

Artemis knew she couldn't ask for more. And since she would be with him and his disciples, she would do everything within her power to make sure that such fighting wouldn't be necessary.

Stepping carefully over the guard, she looked out the door. The battle outside clearly hadn't ended, and there was still no sign of colonists in this part of the compound. Backed by the river as it was, the eastern wall had been left untouched by the attacking Freebloods. But the sky had taken on the faintest tint of light, and soon the rogues outside would be compelled to retreat.

She unlocked the door to Kronos's cell. She didn't waste any time dwelling on his changed appearance or their strange reunion, but quickly released the other four Freebloods. The two females and two males were clearly ready to move as soon as Kronos gave the command.

"There will be no room for mistakes," she said to them, hoping that Kronos had chosen his allies well. "We must get to the woods before daylight. We will go straight over the wall and into the water."

"We?" Kronos asked.

"I am coming with you."

Chapter 15

"You will abandon your human friend?" Kronos asked.

"The guard didn't see me," she said, "but Daniel will certainly realize that I am the one who released you. If I allow Garret to defend me, I will put him in an untenable position."

Kronos nodded gravely. "And Pericles?"

"We have no time to save him," she said, fighting desperately against paralyzing grief, anger and guilt.

"It is unfortunate," Kronos said, "but I believe that he will gladly make the sacrifice."

Artemis grabbed one of the daycoats hung outside the cell and tossed it to Kronos, while his disciples claimed the others. There wasn't one left for her, but she trusted in her well-honed ability to get to cover before the sun rose.

"I will go first," she said, "and try to distract the guards on the wall. Stay behind me until I give the signal."

She left the building as she had approached it, crouching low as she ran, and made straight for the eastern wall.

"You!" she called, waving at the nearest of the four guards. Once she'd caught his attention, she said, "I was sent to tell you that rogues have gotten into the compound, and that all soldiers must report immediately to the front gate!"

The dhampir hesitated, eyes narrowed as he studied her face. "Lady Aresia?" he asked. "Why did they send you with this message?"

"No one else could be spared. Daniel says that you must come!"

Someone behind Artemis darted forward, passed her in a blur and launched himself up the stairway close to where the dhampir stood. The guard never saw him coming. The dhampir fell onto the parapet walk, and the Freeblood crouched beside the still body, his expression tense with excitement and fear.

Furious that the exile had acted without her signal, Artemis started forward. But the other three guards were charging the Freeblood, and Kronos's disciples leaped up the steps to confront them. Artemis joined them in time to watch the brief struggle, prepared to interfere the instant one of the exiles acted too forcefully.

But they were skilled, and kept Kronos's promise. They took the soldiers down with carefully calibrated blows that rendered them temporarily unconscious, as she'd done with the guard at the storage building. She quickly checked the dhampir's pulse, and found it strong and even. He would wake within minutes.

"We must jump," she said as Kronos came to stand beside her. He nodded and signaled to the others. Together, the six of them leaped over the wall. Shouts of anger rang from the stockade.

Artemis rolled as she struck the ground and plunged over the riverbank into the water. The bridge loomed over her to the right. Kronos splashed down beside her, and she heard the others nearby. They turned left, wading parallel to the bank as bullets cut the surface of the river directly behind them.

Then, suddenly, the barrage stopped. Artemis could no longer hear raised voices or the chatter of weapons. The sky was growing lighter. Trees bunched thickly along the riverside beyond the area the colonists had cleared around the walls, the only real shelter in sight.

She and Kronos clambered onto the bank and ran toward the hills to the west, his followers on their heels. She began to feel ill halfway across the clearing, and by the time they made it to the trees she knew that her body was rejecting the blood she had taken from Johan.

It isn't the blood, she thought. It simply wasn't the *right* blood.

She kept running alongside the others as they weaved their way through the remains of a once-thriving city. Dawn brightened the sky behind them. At last they found an old warehouse with three walls, a back door and part of its roof intact, and settled deep in the shadows. Artemis found herself panting and sweating, her stomach struggling to empty its contents.

"Have you not fed?" Kronos asked, crouching beside her.

"How did they feed *you*?"

"Animals," Kronos said. "But of course that is how we have been getting our nourishment for some time now."

Artemis knew him too well to miss the slight curl of his lip when he spoke the words, but she was deeply relieved. Of course they had agreed on the need to end Opir dependence on human blood, but that had been a matter of philosophy rather than practice within the Citadel, where there were no other sources available. She could not have accepted his hunting humans outside it.

"I am well," she insisted. "But you must keep moving. It

would be best for you to continue into the hills and wait for nightfall to cross the Willamette. The colonists will soon be after you, and they have the advantage of daylight."

He frowned. "Why do you say 'you'?" he asked.

Artemis realized that she didn't know exactly when she'd changed her mind. It wasn't the sudden illness, but she was just as certain now that she had to go back as, less than an hour ago, she had been about leaving.

"I can't go," she said. "I should have stayed and tried to explain."

"They will never believe you." Kronos cupped her cheek as Garret had done, but his touch seemed icy on her flushed skin. "You say this only because you believe you will slow us down, but I will not lose you again."

"I'm sorry." She got up, swayed and straightened with a hand braced against the crumbling wall. "I must go back."

"No." He rose and stood in her way as she moved toward the remains of the fallen wall. "Whatever you feel for this human is not worth your life."

"There is shade enough in the forest," she said, "at least for a time. If I cannot stand by my convictions—"

Kronos jerked up his head, silencing her with a raised hand. The sharp rustling of leaves outside the warehouse walls brought the other Freebloods to their feet.

"Human," Kronos said. "He is not making much effort to conceal his approach."

He. She took a breath and shivered. "Go," she said. "I will meet him."

"Artemis—"

"Go!"

With a slow shake of his head, Kronos gestured for the others, who still wore their daycoats, to follow him out the back doorway. Artemis emptied her stomach, cleaned her face and waited tensely.

Garret stepped across the rubble of the fourth wall,

his silhouette framed against sunlit trees. He wore heavy clothing, his pack, and her bow and quiver. The VS was slung over his shoulder.

She caught a flash of relief on his face, and then his expression hardened. He looked toward the rear door. "Where are the others?" he asked.

"Gone." She shivered again. "I take full responsibility for their escape."

"Why did they leave you behind?"

"I stayed of my own accord. I had hoped—"

"Don't hope," he said. "And don't try to explain. The attack on the colony is over, and there are already two patrols out searching for you and the prisoners. Since they believe you're my wife, I said I'd look for you."

"How did you explain...?"

"I didn't."

"I will not resist," she said, starting toward him.

"I'm not taking you back."

"If we return, I can try to explain, and you will not become a traitor to your friend and his people."

"I won't let them treat you like a criminal."

"Did I not betray *you*?" she asked.

"You must have had a reason for what you did."

"And if you cannot accept my reason?"

"I've made my choice."

He held her gaze for an uncomfortable length of time. She stared down at her feet, utterly vulnerable to the emotions he unconsciously projected so powerfully.

He knew what he was doing, and what it meant for his own future.

And still he chose *her*.

"We're getting away from here as fast as we can," he said into her silence. "We can't cross the Willamette at Delos, and if we go west to one of the closer bridges we could run right into the patrols. We'll have to try the northwest St. John's Bridge." He unslung the rifle, removed the pack and her weapons, and then pulled off the heavy, hooded coat and tossed it to her, revealing his usual heavy jacket. "We have about six miles to go. Don't let that slip." He nodded at her bow and quiver. "Get your weapons."

Breaking into a jog, he headed northwest parallel to the river. Artemis pulled on the coat, retrieved her weapons and fell in behind him.

"I cannot let you do this," she said.

"You can't stop me," he said, "unless you plan to leave me here half-conscious, like those guards."

"Are they all right?"

"Yes. I'm guessing you did your best to make sure of that."

She felt light-headed. "I am glad," she said.

He stared straight ahead. "I think we'd better pick up the pace. Can you keep up?"

"I was not injured."

Garret began to run, choosing the clearest path between the trees and dodging the thick patches of undergrowth. Artemis listened for pursuit and heard movement some distance behind. She had no idea if the followers were rogue Freebloods or colony soldiers, and she didn't want to find out.

What had become of Kronos?

"We're coming to the end of the woods," Garret said, slowing down as he spoke. "Put your hood up."

She did as he asked. The woods ended abruptly at the edge of a vast expanse of fallen buildings, disintegrated asphalt and cracked concrete, through which smaller trees had forced their way. Sunlight beat down on the broken surface like a hammer.

Garret grabbed her arm and roughly pulled a pair of oversize gloves over her hands. "With luck," he said, "the rogues will stay well away from here, and Daniel's patrols won't expect us to cross open ground. We may get a little farther ahead of them."

"Garret—" she began.

"Let's go." He took her hand, and then they were flying across the urban plain, Garret pulling her along as if he were some unstoppable machine. She nearly fell several times, and only his desperate strength kept her on her feet. They paused once or twice in the shade of structures that hadn't completely crumbled, but he kept them moving with relentless determination.

When they reached the wooded area on the other side of the tract, Artemis was only slightly burned where the coat and hood had slipped once or twice, but she was weak from her reaction to the blood, and the world rushing by began to tilt and spin. Garret slowed, swept her up in his arms and continued to run until it was obvious that he had exhausted his own strength.

They collapsed near a thicket of densely interwoven brambles. She could smell the river nearby, but the scent only made her empty stomach heave again. Garret drew his hunting knife and hacked at the branches, making a shallow hollow into which he could push her. She resisted, realized it was futile and let him tuck her into the cramped space. Breathing hard, he laid the rifle on the ground beside him and pulled off his pack.

"Drink," he said, pushing a canteen into her hands.

She held the canteen and stared at it blankly. "You should go back," she said. "Daniel said he would help you find Timon."

He turned his head just enough so that she could see his strong profile against the dim light filtering through the trees. "We can't stay here long," he said. "It would be better if you rest."

"Did he blame you for my escape?" she asked.

"It doesn't matter."

"But I want you to understand. One of the prisoners was the Bloodlord who saved my life over two centuries ago, when I was human, after the Opir who nearly drained my blood left me for dead."

"It sounds like a long story," he said. His voice was heavy, and she realized how fantastic the explanation must sound.

"I know it seems to be an amazing coincidence," she said earnestly. "But I had thought him dead for years. I was not only his vassal for decades…he gave me reason to live when I had lost everything." She leaned toward Garret. "You have always wondered why I maintained such faith in my fellow Freebloods. Kro—" She paused, remembering that Kronos was using an alias. She felt she had to respect his wishes, even with Garret. "Nomos wanted to alter the inequitable structure of Opir society. The work he and I carried out together was based upon the idea that Freebloods might be taught a better way than they know in the Citadels, and that such a way might lead to peace with humanity and true freedom for all."

"A way that didn't involve dependence on human blood."

"Yes."

Garret ran a hand through his stiff hair. "I knew he couldn't have been a Freeblood himself."

"He had his own Household in Oceanus, but he was compelled to leave the Citadel because of his teachings. He has been posing as a Freeblood to evade his enemies. Believe me, Garret, he was the last Opir I ever expected to meet."

The emotions she sensed from Garret were so contradictory that she couldn't begin to untangle them. Fresh queasiness settled in the pit of her stomach.

"Did he tell you that I questioned him?" he asked.

"Yes. He said he tried to convince you and Daniel that he was opposed to the stealing of half-blood children."

"We had no reason to accept his story."

Her throat felt as if invisible hands had slipped a rope around it and were tightening it bit by bit. "Nomos is a good Opir, Garret."

"He wants to prevent another war...or so he said."

"That has always been his goal," Artemis said. "And mine."

For the first time since they had made love again, Garret's aura flickered to life, dancing wildly around his body. "I was sure you felt you had a good reason for helping them escape." He looked up through the tattered leaves at a patch of bright morning sky. "Do you know where Nomos has gone?"

Just for a moment, she doubted him. She considered the possibility that he wanted her to tell him so that he and Daniel could track Kronos down, recapture him...

Garret's aura contracted like a wounded animal seeking shelter. He looked at her, a peculiar expression on his face.

Then his emotions hit her all at once, and she knew how badly she had wounded him with her unfounded, unforgivable doubts. Doubts *he* had felt as clearly as she felt his pain. The queasy sensation in her belly turned to full-blown nausea.

He had not only sensed her feelings the way he sometimes seemed to do when they were closest, she had *projected*, pushing her emotions outward without conscious effort. He could not have defended himself from them without learning to build mental barriers of his own.

The emotional bond made it so simple to forget that she could do such things as easily as she might brush his skin with her fingertips. Their link was by no means growing weaker, in spite of her efforts.

And now she knew that accepting other human blood

was not the solution. The blood-bond had already taken hold, in spite of her best efforts. The empathy had made it all the more powerful.

But she didn't dare tell Garret. Not yet. It would be possible to subsist on animal blood for the time being, though it would not be pleasant.

She crawled out of her shelter, determined to face her fears, and projected her regret, hoping that he would absorb and accept it as easily as he had her ugly distrust. "I only know that he also intends to travel to the north," she said.

The tension eased from Garret's face, but his aura remained flat and inert. "If you trust this man so much," he said, "then maybe you'd be better off rejoining him. I don't hold you to your agreement to help me find Timon."

The words seemed angry, but she sensed no blame. He was not trying to punish her. Still, she nearly doubled over with sickness.

"You *want* me to leave you?" she asked.

Denial sent Garret's aura into another turbulent dance. "I want you to understand that I know I've been hard on you," he said. "I had no right to expect you to be other than what you are."

"I *did* fail you," she whispered, "but not because you expected too much."

"I put you in an impossible position," he said. "I won't do it again."

Artemis turned her head aside and retched again. At once Garret was with her, his arm around her, supporting her head with a gentle hand.

"What's wrong?" he asked, nearly smothering her with his self-recrimination.

Weak and shaking, she tried to push him away. "The sun," she said.

"No." He stroked her hair away from her face. "Artemis, I know you took blood in Delos, but clearly something went wrong. You're not keeping it down."

She wondered how he had learned about Johan's donation. She sensed no anger or jealousy from him, only deep concern.

"There was no need to go elsewhere for blood," he said. "You could have come to me anytime."

"I…didn't want to impair you before we left Delos," she said, scrambling for an explanation. She met his gaze. "Garret, no matter what I have done up to this moment, my loyalty has not altered since the day I promised to come with you. As long as you want me by your side, I will never leave you again."

She felt something inside him let go. His aura flowed over and around her, soft and fierce at the same time. He wiped her mouth with a cloth and cradled her head in the curve of his shoulder.

Against all reason, Garret had believed her. *Did* believe her. And he still wanted her.

"There is something more I must tell you," she said, burrowing more deeply into the protective curve of his body. "Pericles was the one who urged me to speak to the prisoners. He was persuaded by my mentor's story before I knew who Nomos was. Or who he pretended to be. I am no longer certain of Pericles's motives."

"It's a little late to worry about that now. I let him go."

She wriggled out of his arms. "What?"

"I think it was all a setup," he said, his humor evaporating. "I think Daniel still believed you were an enemy, and that you'd tricked me into trusting you. He left Pericles unguarded and only one soldier to watch the other prisoners, expecting you to try to communicate with them. He just didn't anticipate that the rogues outside would cause so much of a distraction, and that you'd be so efficient in helping the other Freebloods." He cleared his throat.

"I don't know if he actually believed that Pericles was a child-stealer, but I can't accept anything he told me without wondering how much of it was true."

Real anguish radiated from his mind. If his speculation about Daniel was correct, then his friend had never trusted *him*.

"Perhaps he meant only to protect you," she said.

"Or you were right when you said his experiences made it easier for him to pass judgment on Opiri enemies who fall into his hands."

"Will Beth be safe there?"

"Daniel will protect her with his life. I'm sure someone in the colony will adopt her."

Artemis closed her eyes. "Where is Pericles now?" she asked.

"I told him to run. I don't know where he went." He glanced up at the sky again. "We should move. Do you need blood?"

The idea of telling Garret the truth about the blood-bond still terrified her. *Soon*, she told herself. *Soon*.

"No. I…only had a slight reaction to the other… To Johan's blood. I took enough nourishment."

To her vast relief, he didn't pursue the matter. They gathered their things, and continued west and north through tracts of woodland, decaying city blocks and open areas where buildings had collapsed like fatally wounded soldiers. The shattered road they followed passed through an increasingly narrow neck between the hills and the river. Artemis warned Garret when she heard sounds of pursuit, but those who followed them never seemed to gain much ground. Artemis began to wonder if Daniel was letting them escape.

The thought did not comfort her.

The sun was beginning its westward arc when they reached the bridge Garret had identified as the St. John's.

Except there was no bridge at all—nothing but a few pylons still standing on either side of the river.

"We're out of luck," Garret said. "There aren't any other bridges farther west than this one."

She looked up at him. "Can you swim?"

"It must be a good eight hundred feet across here, and I don't know how strong the current is."

"Yes, but can you swim?"

He met her gaze. "In the Enclave, we used to go to Ocean Beach. It was cold, and the currents were dangerous, but we used to dare each other to swim as far out as we could. I usually won."

"I happen to be a very good swimmer. I believe I can beat you," she said, pretending her body hadn't just decided to declare war against her.

Chapter 16

Garret's approval rode on waves of warmth and admiration. Artemis basked in it the way a human might bask in the sun, forgetting the hollow feeling in her body and the hunger that had returned with such a vengeance.

"We'll need to wait until nightfall," he said, "or you'll be too exposed. But I accept that challenge."

She smiled. Moving as quickly as an Opir, he grabbed her and captured her mouth with his. Her knees nearly buckled with the force of her desire and relief and happiness. And *his*, pouring into her through their kiss. Hard muscle—and more—pressed against her, raising an exquisite ache in her nipples and between her thighs.

When they separated at last, she could still feel him all through her body. And it wasn't enough. She wanted to find the nearest shelter, fall with him to the ground—soft or hard, wet or dry—and join with him, with no thought to the consequences.

But Garret had more sense than she did. He led her

away from the river in search of a safe place to wait out the rest of the day. The hours passed with no sign of their pursuers, and at sunset they returned to the riverbank.

It was a hard swim. Artemis was most concerned about Garret's exposure to the frigid waters of the river, but he swam strongly and reached the other side without faltering, beating her by two yards. She insisted that they build a small, sheltered fire while their clothing dried. He slept the sleep of exhaustion while she watched, and by dawn they were ready to move again.

Before the detour to Delos, they had originally planned to cross the Columbia River at Government Island. But they agreed to take a chance on the shorter route to the bridge at Hayden Island, some five miles to the northeast. They cut across a neighborhood that had been old and worn even before the War, then waded through a slough and a soggy wetland onto the abandoned marina beside the Columbia River.

The bridge itself was impassable. A large portion of the first span had tumbled into the river, leaving half a mile of unbroken water from the buckled road on which they stood to the bank of Hayden Island.

"The damage seems recent," Artemis said. "Could the colonists have destroyed it in order to prevent the child-stealers from traveling north by this route?"

"It's possible," Garret said, a grim set to his mouth. "We have to assume that the bridge is down on the other side, as well. It'll be much too wide to swim across there, even if the currents aren't too powerful and we make it to the island. We'll have to head for the bridge at Government Island and hope it's still standing."

"If the colonists know of this," Artemis said, "they may be waiting there."

"It's a chance we'll have to take." He squinted at the sun. "It's only about ten miles to the southeast as the crow flies, but we don't want to push too hard, or we'll be use-less if it comes to another fight." He eyed her critically. "Artemis…"

"I am well," she said. *But not for much longer.* "Let us continue as long as we can."

He nodded, accepting her word, and gestured for her to precede him.

The Glenn L. Jackson Memorial Bridge was empty.

Not, Garret suspected, that it had been that way for long. Though portions of the span had fallen away and the rest was badly rusted, the buckled road rising onto it was guarded by a small, fortified brick building, barely large enough to house a dozen people but strategically placed so that no one could pass without coming under fire.

"Do you sense anything?" he asked Artemis, who crouched beside him in the thick brush encroaching on the old freeway.

"No," she said. She wrinkled her nose. "There were humans here not long ago. Opiri and half-bloods, as well. But they have been gone for some time, perhaps as much as half a day."

"If Daniel got word to them to stop us," he said, "they wouldn't have deserted their post."

She gazed at him, a trace of anxiety lingering in her eyes. He guessed what she was thinking. Sometimes it felt as if he knew every single thing she was feeling.

Including what she felt for *him.* He wasn't sure when it had happened, just as he wasn't sure when he'd realized how much he cared for her. The way she'd looked after Beth and Pericles, her courage, her capacity for compassion, the way it felt when he and Artemis made love—with all the closeness and joy that came so easily to them when they touched—had convinced him that his ability to care for another woman hadn't died with Roxana.

Still, though he couldn't conceive of feeling this way about any other living woman, there was a hole in his heart that had scarred over, impenetrable and hard as stone. Inside that hole were words he couldn't speak, that he never expected to speak again.

But that didn't change his need for Artemis, even though he feared that this ugly conflict might finally come between them.

Not if she keeps her word never to leave me, he thought. If they survived all this, if he got Timon back and found some way to make Artemis happy…

"I do not smell blood," she said, relieving him of thoughts he didn't want to examine too closely. "At least not…" She hesitated, biting her lip. "At least not in quantities that would suggest death."

"No bodies, and no killing," Garret said. It should have been good news, but he knew—as Artemis clearly did—that something was very wrong.

"Did Nomos pass this way?" he asked.

"I think—" Artemis released her breath in a sharp puff. "There *are* Opiri nearby," she said.

"Where?" he asked, scanning the area intently.

"Behind us."

They rose and turned as one, facing south toward the labyrinth of intersecting freeways and ramps that ended at the riverbank.

"We can try to cross before they get to us," Garret said.

"There are several of them," she said. "If they are hunting us, they will not stop."

"And if they catch us on the bridge or the island, we'll be at a disadvantage."

Artemis picked up her bow and nocked an arrow. Garret checked over the VS and held it muzzle down, but he could see Artemis stiffen.

"I won't use it unless I have to," he said. "If they're rogues, I may not have a choice."

"And if they are from the colony?"

"I won't let them take you."

"Garret—" she began. She broke off, lifting her head. "They are not enemies."

He knew what she was about to say. "Nomos," he said.

"Yes." She lowered the bow. "They are no danger to either one of us."

But how the hell did they get here after us? Garret thought.

Releasing his grip on the rifle, he tried to relax. He'd chosen to suppress his doubts and accept Artemis's faith in this Opir. Now he had to put his commitment to the test.

"I will meet him," she said, starting forward.

He put out his arm to stop her. "Wait."

The Opiri emerged from the woods rising around the freeway—nine, not the five who had been imprisoned in the colony. There wasn't enough light left for Garret to make out faces, but he didn't doubt that the one in the lead was Nomos.

"It is all right," Artemis said. Her voice was breathy with excitement. Before Garret could stop her again, she began to run toward the Opiri. They stopped when Artemis reached them, and she gestured toward Garret with an expressive wave of her arm.

The leader inclined his head, and the Opiri continued toward Garret, Artemis speaking to her former sire with great animation as she walked beside him. It was obvious to Garret that the two Nightsiders had been very close. He could see the rapport between them even though he couldn't hear their conversation.

No wonder she had set him free.

His body chose that moment to ignore the advice of his mind and he tensed up again, instinctively preparing for a fight. Or a challenge to a rival. A challenge any Night-sider would sense within a dozen yards of him.

He let the rifle swing back on its strap and held himself still as Artemis and Nomos approached. Now that he was no longer in a cell, the Opir—with his handsome, ageless face and long white hair drawn back in a queue—seemed more like the elite Bloodmasters Garret had known in Erebus. He exuded authority and the natural arrogance of his kind.

And when he looked at Garret, there was no particular friendliness in his eyes, even when he smiled with his teeth carefully hidden.

"Garret Fox," he said, extending his hand in the human way. "Artemis has spoken of you in the most glowing terms. It's fortunate that we have been given the opportunity to meet again under more favorable circumstances."

"I assume you weren't lying about stealing children."

"Garret," Artemis said, casting him a reproachful glance.

Nomos laughed. "You have courage, even when you aren't on the other side of a cell door," he said. He nodded at the VS. "Or is it the weapon that gives you such confidence?"

Artemis stepped between them and glared at Nomos. "If it is your intention to bait Garret…"

"I apologize," Nomos said, brushing his fingers across Artemis's cheek. "My experiences in Delos have somewhat soured my mood." He nodded regally to Garret. "You saved her life. That alone earns my gratitude."

Shove your gratitude, Garret thought. But he knew he was being irrational. The sight of Nomos touching Artemis fed his visceral dislike, but he couldn't trust his emotions where she was concerned.

Belatedly Garret remembered the outpost and looked over his shoulder. No sound, no movement. If there had been a single living soul left in the place, they would have reacted by now. And Nomos would know that, just as Artemis had.

"You needn't be concerned with those who kept watch here," Nomos said, following his gaze. "We convinced them that retreat was the better part of valor."

"You were here before?" Artemis asked, taking a step away from Nomos. "You attacked them?"

Garret touched the barrel of the VS, and Nomos's eyes snapped down to Garret's hand.

"There is no need to be alarmed," the Nightsider said. "I believe they meant to prevent you from crossing. We told them to abandon their station and they would not be harmed." He met Garret's stare. "We even escorted them part of the way back to Delos, so that there would be less chance of their being attacked by rogues fleeing the failed attack on the colony."

"You went back," Artemis said, "even though you said those same rogues wanted to kill you for opposing them?"

"Now that we are free, we are capable of protecting ourselves," Nomos said. "And as we wish to stop our fellow Opiri from provoking another war, it would hardly do to drive the sentinels from shelter and leave them vulnerable." His gaze returned to Artemis. "Have you forgotten the rest of what I said? You can still help me end this threat and save the misguided, desperate Freebloods who have fallen under the power of this madman in the north."

Garret stiffened. "Artemis is with *me*," he said.

"Garret," Artemis said, turning to face him, "Nomos has offered to help us find Timon."

"Has he?" Garret asked, making no attempt to hide his suspicion.

"Of course I would not attempt to interfere with your plans in any way," Nomos said with another smile. "I merely thought that I could be of assistance, and you have proven yourself unlike those humans who, like the leader of Delos, hate all Opiri because of the actions of the worst of us."

"Daniel isn't human," Garret said. "And he doesn't hate all Opiri, but he's had plenty of experience with 'the worst of you.'"

"Garret," Artemis said. She laid her hand on his arm and looked at her mentor. "Nomos, you do not know—"

"It's no matter," Nomos said, speaking to Garret over her head. "I am aware that you and Daniel were serfs, and that you have reasons for your opinions."

"You must have had a longer conversation with him than I realized," Garret said to Artemis.

"I said nothing of that," Artemis protested.

"Do not blame her," Nomos said. "I had already heard of Daniel and determined his motives."

"And what have you determined about *me*?" Garret asked him. "That I don't have a chance of getting my son back without your help?"

Nomos shook his head. "I am not here to bicker with you. I have offered my assistance, and you may accept or not as you choose. But I would suggest that you cross the river quickly, in case Delos sends a larger party to deal with us."

"He's right, Garret," Artemis said. "We should cross while we can."

"And we must hunt," Nomos said. "It would be better if we did so on the other side, if you can tolerate our company for a brief while."

Artemis looked at Garret steadily, watching to see if he would accept her reassurances. He knew he couldn't disappoint her.

"I have no objection," he said. "Artemis said you saved her life when she became an Opir. I'll be very interested to hear the rest of that story, if she's willing to tell it."

"Then let us be on our way," Nomos said. "Oh, and I should correct a misapprehension. My name is Kronos. Nomos was a name I used to conceal my identity from those who wished to kill me. But I am out of their reach—for the present."

He walked past Garret and Artemis, his men and women behind him, and continued onto the bridge until he and the others were lost in darkness.

"I am sorry," Artemis said, reaching for Garret's hand. "I should have told you more about him on our way here. You were not prepared, and neither was he."

"You didn't know we'd meet him again. I didn't exactly make things easier for you."

"And he..." She hesitated, and then rushed on. "He knows of my connection to you, and he does not completely approve."

"I gathered as much. The feeling is mutual."

She released his hand. "Garret, I will not be fought over as if I were a—"

"Serf?" he said, injecting a little humor into his voice for her sake. "Does he think I'll hurt you, or just that I'm not good enough for you?"

"I do not know what experiences he has had since he escaped Oceanus. He never mistreated humans there, but now he knows what it is like to be hunted by them."

"Why didn't he try to contact you once he escaped?"

"He did not exactly escape. They believed that he had been killed, as I did. I was exiled only after he was declared dead, because of my attempts to carry on our work."

"I'd like to hear about your work," he said, "when we have time for a longer conversation."

Her lips curved in a smile, and he knew he'd said the right thing. "I am glad," she said. "I can tell you that I believe without doubt that Kronos means to resist the Bloodlord in the north and help us find your son, if you permit it."

"And you think he was telling the truth about the people at this post?" he asked.

"Kronos is not a killer." She took his hand again. "But if you choose to go on alone, just the two of us, I will support your decision."

Garret cursed silently. Of course she would. But he would be crazy to reject any advantage that could help him get to Timon, first impressions be damned.

"No," he said. "As long as you think it's safe, we'll take him up on his offer to travel together."

He bent quickly to kiss her, irrationally driven to remind her—and himself—that they had an alliance Kronos could try to break only at his own peril.

They stepped onto the bridge, passing by the post and continuing over the water. It was black as oil to Garret's eyes, and he could just make out the bulk of the island ahead. They walked through the dense woods and reached the other side of the island without meeting Kronos and his followers.

The second span had been repaired many times, and one fallen section had been rebuilt with wood that had begun to rot. Garret wondered if the Bloodmaster in the north would see to its continued repair to ensure that the flow of children wasn't cut off.

The thought made his stomach churn with rage. As always, Artemis caught his mood. She took his arm.

"We're almost to the other side," she said. "They're waiting for us."

"They must have decided that you'd persuade me to take Kronos up on his offer," Garret said drily.

"He said they had to hunt. Perhaps their need is urgent."

"I suspect that your needs are getting urgent, too," he said as they stepped off the road. "I don't care where you get the blood, as long as it does the job. Why don't you join them?"

"I can't leave you alone."

"If I set up camp close to the bridge, I can watch for anyone coming from the south."

"You will need to sleep."

"I can do that when you get back."

"I will bring you food. I'll speak to Kronos and let him know what we have decided."

They kept going, Garret behind Artemis as they followed the road. As she had predicted, Kronos and his band had stopped not far ahead.

Kronos didn't comment on Garret and Artemis's arrival except to smile at his former vassal and favor Garret with a brief but amiable nod. Artemis spoke to Kronos briefly and returned to Garret.

"He was about to go after the Freebloods he sent to scout for game," she said. "I am welcome to join them."

"Good," Garret said. "Tell him that I'm heading back to the bridge to keep watch."

"He will probably wish to send one of his Opiri to watch with you."

"Tell him that this human can take care of himself. And that it would be better if none of his people suddenly show up when I'm not expecting them."

Her gaze fell to the VS. "I will."

With obvious reluctance, she returned to Kronos. The Bloodlord looked at Garret, gave a very human shrug and beckoned her to accompany him.

The sight of them together triggered irrational jealousy in Garret, and he quickly walked away. Once he'd chosen a place from which to watch the bridge, he made himself as comfortable as possible with his blanket over his shoulders and his back against a tree trunk.

Tired as he was, he didn't intend to be taken by surprise the next time someone approached, friend or enemy. Without the constant distraction of immediate danger—

or of Artemis's engaging, alluring and often frustrating company—he had plenty of time to think of what had happened, and what was yet to come.

There had been too many delays in his search for Timon, and he blamed himself for that. If he'd been more alert, he and Artemis would never have been taken by Delos's patrol. There would have been no questions from Daniel and no trap set for Artemis.

But she also wouldn't have seen, with her own eyes, what it could mean when Nightsiders and humans lived in harmony and produced children together...wanted children, raised with love.

He rose abruptly, peering into the darkness toward the bridge, and swung the VS into firing position. Two figures came into view—a male and a female—their eyes catching the moon's faint light like those of night-prowling cats.

Freebloods, Garret thought, but coming from the north. Kronos's followers. They continued to approach until they were a dozen yards away.

"You watch well, human," the male said. "Better than most of your breed."

"What do you want?" Garret asked, holding the rifle steady.

"Why, only to more closely observe the human with whom Artemis seems so enamored," the female said. "Kronos has many questions."

"You weren't with him in Delos," Garret said.

The Nightsiders exchanged glances. "We were not taken prisoner with the others," the male said.

"Well, you'll have plenty of time to satisfy your curiosity," Garret said. "Artemis and I will be traveling with you." He smiled. "Assuming you have no objections."

"Why should we?" The male's gaze fell to the vicinity of Garret's throat. "Are you not from one of the colonies where humans willingly donate their blood to their Opir allies?"

Garret knew that look, and the intent behind the words. "Originally," he said, "but we had a slight difference of opinion."

"Perhaps you would feel safer with company," the female said, flashing her teeth. "The night holds many dangers for your breed."

"I'm fine. And I'm sure Kronos will appreciate your help in the hunt."

Nodding curtly, the male Freeblood made to pass by Garret. Garret turned to keep him in sight, but all at once the female came at him, attacking with superhuman strength and speed.

Chapter 17

Acting even before he could think, Garret reversed the rifle and swung at her. The butt struck her a glancing blow across the forehead, and she staggered. But the male was almost on him, and he had just enough time to turn the VS and jam the rifle's muzzle into the Nightsider's stomach.

The male snarled at him, and the female bared her fangs as she recovered and lunged toward him again. All he had to do was pull the trigger.

Kronos walked up behind the female and casually struck her across the neck. She gagged and fell, alive but disabled.

"You disappoint me, Flavia," Kronos said. He cast the male an icy glare. "Are you all right, Garret?"

"In perfect health," Garret said. "I assume you don't want me to shoot this one?"

"Xenophon has broken my law," Kronos said. "It is your right to kill him, if you wish."

"Step back," Garret said, pushing Xenophon with the

rifle. The Nightsider backed away, glanced at Kronos and then ran.

Garret let him go.

"Your mercy does you credit," Kronos said. He glanced down at the female. "I doubt that Flavia will give us any further trouble now that her companion is gone."

Garret lowered the rifle. "They meant to take my blood," he said.

"Yes. As I said, in attacking you they disregarded the rules I have laid down for my followers." He nudged Flavia with the toe of his boot. "Get up," he told her, "and join the others."

She scrambled to her feet and sprinted away.

"Where's Artemis?" Garret asked.

"I had hoped that you and I might speak in private."

"About her?" Garret asked, tensing up again.

Kronos strolled away, his hands clasped behind his back. "About what she and I have worked for and still hope to achieve." He stopped to gaze at the bridge. "She told you of our relationship and my feigned death in Oceanus?"

"She thought you were dead, but instead you abandoned her."

"Yes," Kronos said, regret in his voice. "I did not learn she had been exiled for some time, and I was unable to search for her until recently."

"Recently? As in before you were captured by the colony patrol?"

"Yes." Kronos faced him again. "She had been a close companion for two centuries, devoted to our cause. She spoke of that, as well?"

"She mentioned it."

"Ah." Kronos's eyes crinkled. "I confess that I do not fully understand the nature of your relationship with her. It does surprise me, however."

"That she could think well of a human?" Garret rested the VS against the tree and squatted beside it. "I picked up on your skepticism."

"She can be very loyal to those to whom she feels she owes a debt."

"Like the debt she owed you?"

Kronos brushed a fallen leaf from his shoulder. "I like your directness, Mr. Fox," he said, the formal address a kind of mockery. "I confess that I didn't learn to view humans as much more than chattel until I left Oceanus and experienced more of the world as it is now."

"You were involved in the War, weren't you?"

"On the sidelines, like most of my rank."

"Was Artemis forced to fight?"

"She didn't tell you?"

"I never asked."

"You *do* surprise me." Kronos ran a long-fingered, almost delicate hand over his loose hair. "We were fighting for what we perceived as our very survival, but all we desire now is peace." He nodded toward the rifle. "*You* do not seem so committed to peace, Mr. Fox. Neither did your fellow humans in Delos."

"You had something to say about Artemis?"

Smiling ruefully, Kronos bent to pick up a branch fallen from a nearby tree. "She told you that I saved her life. The Bloodlord who attacked her in the early nineteenth century had no interest in converting her."

"Neither one of you went into hibernation in ancient times with the rest of the Opiri?"

"No. And for most of the centuries until the Awakening of our kind, those of us who had remained active during the Long Sleep kept few servants and moved frequently. The Bloodlord had nearly drained her dry when I found her, healed her and converted her."

"Did she have children?"

Kronos's gaze was far away. "I believe she had a single child, and that it was given to a relative to raise."

"And you gave no more thought to it, or how she felt about it."

"As an Opiri, she could not have kept the child with her, nor remain with it." He focused on Garret. "Why? Has she spoken of it?"

"No," Garret said, concealing both his anger and his pity.

"Her old life came to an end, and I took her with me on my travels," Kronos said. "I came to see how remarkable and intelligent she was. She was my constant, loyal companion."

"But you didn't free her from vassalage."

"She would have been at far greater risk as a Freeblood. So many vassals and Freebloods died during the beginning of the War that Bloodlords and Bloodmasters began converting large numbers of humans to replenish our ranks of fighters. After the Citadels were founded, it was soon apparent that there were insufficient resources to accommodate all the Freebloods who *did* survive."

"Not enough serfs, you mean," Garret said.

"Even when the Armistice called for the human Enclaves to send their lawbreakers to serve in the Citadels, the majority was claimed by the elite. The number of public serfs available to provide blood to the lower-ranked diminished, as well. I saw that the life awaiting Artemis—a life of constant conflict, fighting her way to the position of a Bloodlady of property or dying in battle—was not worthy of her."

"And why would you, one of the elite yourself, feel concern for Opiri your kind consider little better than serfs?"

"I came to realize that our treatment of Freebloods

was a rot within the Citadels, a barbarity that had to be changed if we were to survive as a race. That was when I freed Artemis and we began to work together to encourage those changes."

"It obviously didn't work out quite as you expected."

The stick in Kronos's hands snapped with a loud crack. "Change requires sacrifice, Mr. Fox, and can only be accomplished in small steps if it is to last. I spoke out on behalf of the Freebloods. I suggested that it would soon become necessary to redistribute our resources more equitably. I was blamed for fomenting rebellion among them."

"So the leaders of Oceanus arranged your death?"

"I was challenged again and again in rapid succession, as my enemies attempted to wear me down and eventually kill me. Fortunately, I had allies who were able to help me feign my death and get me out of Oceanus. I had hoped that Artemis, with her bravery and skill, could carry on with my work."

"Even though you must have known her life would be in constant danger."

"You underestimate her strength."

"That's the last thing I would do."

"Has she taken your blood?"

The question was both unexpected and intrusive, as if Kronos were asking for the intimate details of his and Artemis's lovemaking. "How is that any of your business?"

"Because she was fully committed to ending the traditional consumption of human blood."

"She never expected that to work in the Citadels," Garret said.

"We had been discussing that very problem when I was challenged," Kronos said. "I know that she wished to set an example for her people. Now that she is outside the Citadel, any violation of her principles would arouse great conflict within her."

That, Garret knew all too well. "She's not taking my blood now," he said shortly.

"I am glad to hear it. We would not want further misunderstandings between you, Artemis and my disciples if we are to travel together. They are forbidden from taking human blood as long as they follow me, but Flavia and Xenophon were provoked by the belief that Artemis had sole access to you."

"You can tell them they're wrong."

"Yet my followers will continue to see you and Artemis in close contact."

"They'll have to get used to it."

"You seem to be losing your temper, Mr. Fox. Is it possible that you have something to prove, not only to Artemis or to me, but to yourself? Do you wish to possess her, perhaps to display your ability to control one of my kind? Or can it be possible that you actually believe you love her?"

"I'm damned sure that *you* don't feel anything like that for her."

"You are dodging the question. Of course you must realize that Artemis cannot return your feelings, but she is committed to standing by you for the time being, and she will constantly feel obligated to protect you from any of our people who express the slightest hostility toward you." Kronos plucked a dangling yellow leaf from a branch overhead. "You will be prepared to do the same for her, but though you have an abundance of courage, you lack our strength and speed."

"She'll let me know if it becomes a problem. I trust her judgment, or we wouldn't be here now."

"Perhaps that is true, Mr. Fox. You are not totally lacking in experience with Opiri females."

Garret felt for the rifle and stopped, clenching his fist. "What are you talking about?"

"Believe me when I tell you that I do regret the loss of your wife."

"Artemis told you?"

"There are other ways of learning such things, especially when you have my connections."

Making certain that the VS remained within easy reach, Garret got to his feet. "Do you know who killed my wife?"

"Not at all. But her work to aid human serfs was known even outside Erebus, and with so many rogues running wild, rumors spread. It is no small matter to take the life of a Bloodlady of her status."

Garret began to shake. "If I ever find out that you know anything about this…"

"Your threats do not impress me, Mr. Fox. But I assure you that I will inform you if I hear anything at all." Kronos looked to the north. "I only ask you to remember that such relationships between Opiri and humans are by nature both complex and dangerous. And where Artemis is concerned, you have not faced the final test. Her true devotion is to her people. Will you stand in her way when she does what she must?"

Before Garret could answer, Artemis arrived, a brace of rabbits slung over her shoulder. She looked from Garret to the Bloodlord with an arch of her brow that conveyed worry more eloquently than any direct inquiry.

"I have brought you dinner, Garret," she said. "I hope I am not interrupting."

"We have had a most illuminating discussion," Kronos said. "But now I will leave you to your meal."

He strode away.

Artemis studied Garret's face. "You quarreled," she said.

"I'm sure that doesn't surprise you," he said, well aware that he wasn't able to hide his anger.

"Will you tell me why?" she asked.

Garret couldn't trust himself to speak. He slung the VS over his arm and took the rabbits from her. "Thanks for these. Did you get enough for yourself?"

"Did Kronos threaten you?" she demanded.

"He's very protective of you."

"You are not telling me everything."

"If I'm going to cook those rabbits," he said, "we'd better return to the others."

They fell into step and headed back to the place where Kronos had set up his temporary camp. Garret told her briefly about the Freeblood attack and what Kronos had told him about the reason behind it.

She stopped. "I am sorry, Garret," she said, her lip twitching above her upper teeth. "It will not happen again."

He took her arm and led her forward. "I don't want you fighting them, Artemis. It won't advance your cause. Kronos explained more about what you and he were hoping to accomplish in Oceanus."

She stopped again and wrapped her arms around him, pressing her cheek to his chest. Holding the rabbits awkwardly in one hand, he returned the embrace and closed his eyes.

"Garret," Artemis said, her voice muffled against his shirt. "I don't want you to hate Kronos."

He dropped the rabbits on the ground and put both arms around her. "I don't hate him," he said.

Her lips brushed the base of his neck, sending almost violent tremors through his body. "Whatever I am as an Opir," she said, "he is responsible for it."

"No one is responsible for what you are but you." He set

her back so that he could see her face. "And that's something pretty damned remarkable."

She gazed at him, her eyes bright and expressive. Her feelings seemed as real and solid as her lithe body and the tender lips so eager for his touch.

"Garret," she murmured, "have I told you that I—"

"Garret? Artemis?"

Garret started at the sound of the familiar voice and let her go. Pericles stood behind her, grinning, and as flush with health and happiness as any Nightsider could be.

"Pericles!" Artemis said. "How did you find us?"

"I'm sorry I didn't come earlier," Pericles said, looking from her to Garret, "but I was scouting for Kronos." He beamed at Garret. "After you set me free, I searched for him." His gaze darted back to Artemis. "He's amazing. He welcomed me, and I've been—" He broke off, like a child unable to keep his mind on one subject at a time. "You saved my life, Garret. I know you had to leave Delos because of that." He sobered. "I'm sorry."

"I knew what I was doing," Garret said, hoping he was right. "Did you see Daniel or any of the patrols who were hunting us?"

"I managed to evade them," Pericles said. "But as far as I know, no one else has seen them since we got close to the river."

"I am glad you are safe," Artemis said.

"Now nothing can stop us from finding Timon," Garret said.

And nothing, Garret thought—not paranoid humans, hungry Freebloods, or even his own doubt—was going to slow him down again.

But it wasn't quite that simple.

Garret had taken precautions to prevent another incident like the one with Flavia and Xenophon. He and Artemis had agreed that they should travel a little apart from Kronos's band and maintain some physical distance from one another, but it was obvious from the second night how much of a challenge it would be to stay apart. Garret was hyperaware of Artemis's presence as they crossed the border into old Washington State, and made their way through fallen cities, dense forest, and over hill and mountain. His body seemed attuned to hers to a degree he hadn't experienced with anyone else, including Roxana, and he always knew where she was relative to his own position at any given moment.

She seemed equally aware of him, and they would find themselves staring at each other across the small fires he made to cook game or to warm himself as the nights grew increasingly cold. He was haunted by vivid images of her supple figure, arms and legs wrapped around him, nipples peaked and tight against his chest as she took him inside her. There were times when he knew she was seeing the same images; her lips would part and her eyes become dazed with memory and hunger.

By unspoken agreement, they never discussed her taking his blood again. Even if she hadn't already inexplicably chosen to avoid it since Coos Bay, she had excellent reason to reject it now.

Sometimes, when she returned from a hunt with the other Opiri, Garret would see her locked deep in conversation with Kronos. Each time he swallowed his envy, and each time she returned to him, even if all they did together was sit quietly and companionably while the Nightsiders rested after their feeding.

Pericles spent nearly all his time trailing in Kronos's wake like an eager acolyte, accepting any attention with the kind of gratitude he'd once bestowed on Artemis. He seemed so focused on his new hero that he seldom spoke to her or Garret.

By night and by day they traveled, careful to stay hidden, always alert for other groups of Opiri. Their scouts observed more and more such packs the farther north they went.

And there were children. Stolen half-bloods, sometimes several with the larger packs. The first few times Garret and Artemis had argued in favor of saving the children, but Kronos had refused to help. There was nowhere to keep them safe, and there were far too many rogues to fight on equal terms.

But other Freebloods joined Kronos along the journey, most of them obviously acquainted with him and willing to follow his lead. They provided more information about the mysterious Bloodlord known as "the Master," and confirmed that he had gathered large numbers of Freebloods near a fortress, or possibly a castle, in the Canadian mountains, promising them some unknown reward for delivering the half-bloods.

Everything had been going smoothly—almost too smoothly, Garret thought—when several of Kronos's Freebloods returned with the human captives.

Garret was the first to see them and their captors hiding in the woods just outside the small clearing where the Opiri had made their temporary night camp. The three humans were dressed in camouflage uniforms, clearly soldiers or scouts of some kind. The Freebloods—Flavia among them—were arguing among themselves, and Garret listened from cover as they discussed taking blood from the humans right under Kronos's nose.

Knowing better than to confront them directly, Garret went looking for Kronos. He was speaking sternly to Artemis, whose face was unusually pale.

Garret interrupted the conversation. "You have Free-bloods flouting your laws," he said with a quick, probing glance at Artemis. "They've captured three humans, and plan to take their blood. I won't let that happen."

"Nor will I," Kronos said, getting to his feet. He and Artemis followed Garret to the hiding place, Garret automatically reaching out to steady Artemis when she stumbled several times along the way.

But he didn't get a chance to ask her what was wrong. The Freebloods had sensed their coming and were already arrayed in a defiant line, with the bound humans behind them.

"What is this?" Kronos demanded.

"We found these humans sniffing around the camp," Flavia said.

"And so you took them, against my express orders?" Kronos asked.

"They're spies, fair game," Flavia said. She sneered at Garret and Artemis. "We'll find out who sent them soon enough."

Garret positioned himself between Artemis and the Freebloods, cursing himself for having left the VS behind at his campsite. "I thought Kronos taught you a lesson," he said.

"He said that you were not to be touched," Flavia said. "But we know that *she* takes your blood even now."

"Why do you believe this?" Kronos asked.

"It is obvious," one of the male Freebloods said. "She barely touches the game we hunt. It repulses her. There is only one reason why an Opir will refuse animal blood. She must have a blood-bond with the human."

A current of shock raced through Garret's body. A blood-bond. It happened between some Opiri and their serfs in the Citadels, and among free Opiri-human couples. It was not rare, but it wasn't common, either. When it occurred, the body chemistry of both partners was altered, and all other sources of blood became unpalatable to the Nightsider.

But he'd never suspected that the growing closeness between Artemis and himself might be part of such a physical bond. Now her ongoing fatigue, in spite of regular hunts, made perfect sense.

Was she starving herself to set an example for Kronos's other followers, or because she rejected the bond itself?

Chapter 18

Artemis stared at Garret, her distress emanating from her body like a ragged halo. "It is not true," she said.

"Of course it is not," Kronos said. "Artemis abides by our compact."

The rustle of moving bodies followed his denial, and Garret became aware that they had attracted an audience. All but a few of Kronos's disciples were now listening intently, waiting to hear how the drama would play out.

If it went wrong, Garret thought, Artemis would face a crowd of angry Freebloods—and continue to starve until she died.

"Your feelings for the human are clear," Flavia said to Artemis, "as are his for you. How will you prove that you have no bond?"

"If it existed," Garret said, "I think I would know it."

"Your word isn't good enough, human," the male Freeblood said. He looked at Kronos. "If you cannot convince your chief disciple to follow your path, why should *we* obey you?"

Kronos stared at his challenger, and Garret could almost feel the power emanating from him. This was a Nightsider accustomed to being obeyed, exile or not.

But these were Freebloods, not his vassals, and they were far from the hierarchical structure of the Citadels.

"I will prove that you are wrong," Artemis said, stepping in front of Garret. He moved to pull her back and stopped, realizing that the wrong action on his part could provoke the Freebloods into hurting the human captives as well as attacking Artemis. His need to protect her might set off an explosion that none of them could contain.

"Yes," Flavia said, "prove it." She pointed behind her into the woods. "We have fresh game. If you take your full share of the blood and your body accepts it, we will know there is no bond between you and the human."

Artemis's heart felt slow and sluggish. She knew she was much weaker than she should be; Garret had noticed it days ago, but each time he had chosen to trust her rather than question her about her condition.

This was the price he paid for that trust, to learn from hostile Freebloods what she had known of and tried so hard to ignore since they had left Coos Bay: the blood-bond that had developed between them in spite of all her efforts to prevent it.

Now she was caught, and Garret was in terrible danger. He had denied that any such bond existed, but she knew that he had only meant to protect her, with no thought for himself. His mind was steady and unshaken, focused on saving her, even though he must know there was nothing he could do.

"Will you release the captives if I satisfy you?" she asked Flavia.

The Freeblood nodded. "If you prove you are still truly one of us."

Battling nausea, Artemis stepped forward. She felt Garret's silent protest and focused on projecting confidence back at him, hoping he would sense it as well as he did so many of her other emotions.

It will be all right.

Pushing all awareness of Garret out of her thoughts, she followed Flavia into the thicket of small trees and bushes. Her mind was assaulted with the emotions emanating from Flavia and her two cronies, their hostility, their envy, their contempt for Garret. Their hunger. And she felt the humans' emotions, as well: fear, anger, the drive to escape at any cost.

She was raw and open to all of them, her mental shields fallen to exhaustion and illness. She deliberately dropped the last of her defenses, the ones she had built against herself. The ones that controlled her ability to project her feelings. The ones that kept her from becoming something she despised.

It would be easy to make Flavia see what Artemis wanted her to see, believe what Artemis wanted her to believe. Extending the control to the others would be more difficult, but far from impossible.

But once she gave in to the temptation…

You have no choice, she thought.

"Do you intend to do this or not?" Flavia asked, baring her teeth.

Artemis moved forward slowly, the scent of blood strong in her nose. She followed Flavia deeper into the woods. The game was fresh, and Artemis did her best not to flinch at the knowledge that there had been no need to kill the creature.

She did what Flavia expected, though it sickened her. Through the sickness, she imagined herself passing Flavia's test without difficulty, projected that image to Flavia and the others just out of sight.

When she was finished, she still didn't know if she'd succeeded. She wiped her mouth and met Flavia's gaze, concealing her disgust at what she had done. What she'd *had* to do.

Her eyes unfocused, Flavia blinked several times and nodded with obvious reluctance. "You have passed the test," she said.

Artemis remembered to breathe. "Set the humans free," she said.

"Surely Kronos will wish to question them first."

"He did not ask," Artemis said, "and you gave your word."

With a sharp sigh and a nod to her followers, Flavia began to untie the first of the human prisoners. As soon as the others were free, the male with the uniform markings that designated the highest rank prodded them from their stupor, and the three of them bounded off into the forest. The leader looked back once, briefly meeting Artemis's gaze, and then vanished.

Artemis was left with the aftertaste of Flavia's angry disappointment in her mind as she walked back into the clearing. Garret was on his feet watching for her, while Kronos stood at his ease, his hands clasped lightly behind his back.

"The humans are gone," Artemis said, meeting Kronos's gaze. "There is no question of any blood-bond with Garret Fox. This does not mean that I will cease to regard him as an ally who saved my life and set me free when he could have delivered me to Delos."

The remaining Freebloods muttered among themselves, but none seemed inclined to question her further. The crowd broke up, the Freebloods drifting away until only Garret, Kronos and Artemis were left.

"What did you do?" Garret asked, moving closer to Artemis.

"She convinced Flavia and her lackeys that she does not share a blood-bond with you," Kronos said.

Garret pulled Artemis aside. "Is it true?" he asked. "Is there a bond between us?"

She knew that no matter what she told him, it wouldn't alter the truth. He only wanted confirmation of what he already knew.

And he feared for her...feared the hold Kronos might have over her, worried about how she would deal with the need for his blood when the risk of exposure was so great. Soon, even animal blood would be completely unpalatable to her.

"It does not matter if there is a bond or not," Kronos said before Artemis could speak. "Have you been breaking my laws?"

"No," Garret snapped.

"Then you must remain apart unless you are in full view of my followers."

"To hell with your noble philosophy," Garret said. "Do you think I'll let her starve?"

"There are ways of breaking such bonds," Kronos said. "It will not be easy or comfortable, but—"

"It's like breaking an addiction, but a hundred times worse," Garret said. "I've seen it. Artemis will be the one to suffer." He took her arm. "We'll go ahead on our own."

Artemis leaned against him, trying to clear her mind and get her ability under control again. She could influence the thoughts of others and cloud their minds, but she could not seem to think for herself.

"You do know what you have done to her, besides making her dependent upon your blood?" Kronos asked. "You have taken all choices from her."

"She has already made her choice," Garret said, his voice nearly a growl.

"Has she? Or have you made it for her?"

"I've never forced Artemis to do anything against her will," Garret said.

"Perhaps not deliberately," Kronos said. "But your emotions have constantly affected her. Your mere presence has influenced every move she has made."

"Even a blood-bond isn't that powerful."

"I am not speaking of something so simple." Kronos glanced at Artemis. "She is what you would call an empath. She can sense and even share the emotions of others. But surely you must know that by now, Garret Fox."

Garret stared into her eyes, and she felt him remembering times when he had almost believed he'd felt her emotions, even sensed her thoughts.

"Garret," she began, "whatever you may think—"

"I knew she possessed some degree of skill when I first saved her life by converting her," Kronos cut in as if she hadn't spoken, "but it was much enhanced by the change. In the years she was with me, she shared my emotions as well as my work, even when I believed I had lost all capacity to feel. She awakened a part of me that had long been dead."

Garret flinched, and Artemis caught a fleeting glimpse of Roxana. A part of *him* had been dead, too. He could feel the changes within himself—changes he had only begun to accept—because of her.

"Yes," Kronos said. "You and I have something in common, Mr. Fox."

"But it isn't just us, is it?" Garret asked Artemis, laying his hands gently on her shoulders. "Can you feel everyone? My God, how can you stay sane?"

"She can experience the feelings of anyone she comes into contact with," Kronos said. "She helped me understand the innermost needs and ambitions of the Freebloods we approached in the Citadels. When first I realized how much this made her suffer, I tried to shield her. As I should have shielded her from *you*."

"Shielded her?" Garret said. "My God. The War..."

"Indeed," Kronos said. "It is why I tried to keep her away from the battlefields. She was nearly driven mad by the savagery."

"I was not mad," Artemis protested, pulling away from Garret. "I am not as weak as he claims."

"True enough, my child," Kronos said, "it was your strength that enabled you to survive."

Garret's powerful desire to hold Artemis mingled with his fear of making things worse for her, but his pity was rapidly transforming into suspicion and anger—not at her, but at Kronos.

"So what happened in Oceanus, when you tried to spread your ideas?" Garret asked. "How was *that* protecting her from Opir savagery?"

"When Artemis and I were together, she was safe."

"Safe? You abandoned her."

"No!" Artemis said, moving to stand between them. "Kronos *did* help me."

"Help that obviously didn't last," Garret said.

Remembering how she had influenced Flavia's thoughts, Artemis tried to soothe Garret's anger. A dazed look came into his eyes, and Kronos cast her an inquiring glance. She realized what she was doing and stopped, horrified at how easy it was to reach for her forbidden talents just because it seemed the simplest course of action.

"I had to learn to manage my abilities," she said, trembling with self-disgust.

"Because anything less would eventually have destroyed her mind," Kronos said. "But you, Mr. Fox, must have fractured her armor and left her defenseless from you and everyone else."

"No, Kronos," Artemis said. "It would have happened sooner or later."

"Without the additional impetus of the blood-bond?" Kronos shook his head. "Mr. Fox knows I'm right."

Artemis recognized the precise moment when Garret began to accept everything that Kronos had told him. He tried desperately to mute his feelings—toward Kronos, toward the Freebloods who had attacked him, even toward her.

It only made things worse.

"How much do you care for Artemis, Mr. Fox?" Kronos asked. "Enough to leave her with me, so that I can teach her to master her abilities again?"

"P-please," Artemis stammered.

"Look at her!" Kronos said. "She is caught in your hatred of me, in the web of your irrational humanity."

"No!" Artemis said. "Garret, you must believe—"

"There is more," Kronos said, relentless in his honesty. "Artemis can also project her own emotions. She can share her feelings with others, cause them to experience her wishes and desires, even without conscious effort."

"And I refused to do it!" Artemis said. "Not in the Citadel, and not afterward."

"But you used that power on Flavia, did you not?" Kronos asked.

"Is this true, Artemis?" Garret asked, searching her eyes. "Can you manipulate what other people feel?"

His question felt like an assault, though he had every right to ask it. Could she have manipulated Garret in the past without realizing it, compelling him to save her from the militiamen and later "influencing" him into joining Kronos?

"I never did it when…when you and I were together," she stammered.

"Indeed," Kronos said, echoing her thoughts, "why should she try to influence your feelings, since, being such a very civilized human, you certainly needed no encouragement to save her life when you first met? And surely your devotion to her was reason enough for you to help her escape Delos and join forces with me and my disciples."

Artemis heard the stinging sarcasm in Kronos's words, the eagerness to sow doubt in Garret's mind. It hurt to know that he so badly wanted Garret gone that he would use any tactic to achieve that result. It hurt much worse to realize that Garret was now questioning everything he knew about her, weighing all their interactions, wondering if everything he'd done had been of his own free will.

"You're right," Garret said. "I didn't need any encouragement to get her away from the militiamen who wanted to kill her. I didn't need a blood-bond or any kind of push to help her escape from Delos, or trust her reasons for helping you get away."

Sucking in a sharp breath, Artemis went to Garret and leaned her head against his chest. He put his arms around her and held her lightly, his gaze never leaving Kronos.

Kronos smiled. The tips of his teeth were very white in the shadows. "I admire your loyalty, Mr. Fox," he said. "I'm quite certain that Artemis never abused her abilities. But she is still suffering because of them. And you."

Garret's face might have been carved from granite. "When we're alone," he said, "I'll ask her. And she'll tell me the truth."

"Unless she allows me to protect her as I did before, she will lose her sanity."

"You're wrong, Kronos," Artemis said, slipping free of Garret's arms. "I know you hate Garret. You would do anything to—"

"Your involvement with him has warped your senses," Kronos said. "I hold no hatred for him, or any human."

Perhaps, Artemis thought, her senses *were* warped, but Kronos was telling the truth. There was no hatred. Contempt, yes. Disgust that she had chosen the company of a human over that of her former lord and protector. And he emphatically wanted her by his side.

But there was something else. Something that floated just beyond her reach.

"Laying the blame upon Garret changes nothing," she said. She turned to Garret again. "I have no wish to separate unless it is your choice."

"It won't be that easy to get rid of me," Garret said, laying his palm against her cheek.

"Can you control your emotions, Mr. Fox?" Kronos asked, speaking over Artemis's head. "Can you change the very nature of your being?"

"It is not *his* responsibility to change," Artemis said, taking strength from Garret's trust. "I can learn to master my ability again."

"Do you still require further proof?" Kronos asked Garret. "Artemis, come to me."

"She isn't your vassal now, Kronos," Garret said.

Before Garret could react, Kronos bounded toward Artemis, swift as a timber wolf, and embraced her. She stiffened to fend him off, but almost at once the tumult in her mind subsided. Kronos's and Garret's emotions—and her own—dimmed to a manageable pitch.

"Look at her now, Mr. Fox," Kronos said.

Chapter 19

Though Artemis did nothing, it was clear that Garret saw what Kronos wanted him to see. His pain was a distant thing to her now, but she recognized it in his eyes, in the way a muscle jumped in his cheek.

Once, she had simply accepted that something about Kronos helped to shield her from the worst of the side effects of her abilities. Now it came to her that she had never understood how he did it, just as she now wondered how Kronos had so quickly convinced Garret.

"We can still help you find your son," Kronos said to Garret, "but you must stay away from Artemis. I will help her break the blood-bond, and—"

"Let me go, Kronos," Artemis said.

"You heard her," Garret said. "You can't hold her against her will. If you try, I *will* stop you."

"I will not let you die for his sake," Kronos said, stroking Artemis's hair.

Instinct claimed victory over discipline, and Artemis

acted almost without thinking. She turned her anger on Kronos, and he released her abruptly, his surprise almost comical.

Stunned by her own act, Artemis backed away. Garret was behind her, as solid as one of Delos's walls.

"We need to go," he said. "You have to take my blood, and we can't do it here."

"Think, Artemis," Kronos said, recovering from her emotional attack. "You and I understand each other as the human never will. Not because you are Opir and a Freeblood, but because you are beyond both."

His words made no sense to Artemis. But then again, right now nothing did. "If you think I will use this ability to win other Freebloods to our cause—" she began.

"I would never expect that of you," Kronos interrupted. "But I need—"

"Let's gather our things and get out of here," Garret said, grasping Artemis's arm. But when she looked at Kronos, she remembered the old days—his compassion for the Freebloods struggling to survive in Oceanus, his gentleness with her, his flawless logic.

What had changed him? Kronos had never been so possessive before, so determined to control her. How had she failed to see that Garret's concerns about her old master might have a basis in fact?

"Stay," Kronos said, extending his hand.

"Artemis," Garret said softly. "We'll find a solution."

She went with him. There had never been a question of that, though Kronos was clearly furious with her decision. Garret knew she was starving, and he would have physically attacked Kronos if the Opir had tried to hold her, with absolutely no regard for his own life.

But the intensity of his emotion was such that she couldn't separate it from her own. Once they had collected their things under the suspicious eyes of the other

Freebloods and left camp, her desire for blood had become indistinguishable from his feelings for her. They traveled for a full mile, Garret half supporting her, before they found a place for her to take his blood.

At first, it was like surrendering to her most primitive instincts: Garret baring his throat, her teeth piercing his skin, the blood flowing into her mouth. But then she felt the joy, the contentment, the feeling of utter completion enhanced by the blood-bond. She realized how much she had been missing Garret's arms around her. The idea of cutting herself off from his emotions suddenly seemed unbearable.

"Garret," she said when they were finished, "you have no reason to fear what I can do. I will never—"

"Don't worry about me," he said, shifting her into a more comfortable position in the crook of his arm. "Is it true that I broke down your mental shields and left you defenseless?"

"No," she said sharply. "Kronos exaggerated. I did begin to feel your emotions soon after we met. At times I was uncertain, but I was never helpless."

"But you *have* been affected by my emotions, my humanity."

"Do you think that is such a terrible thing?" She grabbed his hand, feeling hard muscle, calluses, the way his fingers closed around hers. "I realize now… Kronos thinks he knows me. But I am not the same as I was in the Citadel, when I worked with him."

"Kronos recognizes your courage and your skill," Garret said, "but he doesn't seem to realize that you have qualities he can't comprehend." He stroked his thumb over her lower lip. "Kronos won't succeed in teaching Freebloods to change their way of life, because he wants to dominate too much. He'll never set an example they can follow."

Artemis couldn't meet his gaze. She had come to the

same conclusion, and it hurt as much as Kronos's treating her like a vassal, bound to his will.

"Nothing he said could make me stop trusting you," Garret said, turning her face toward his. "The empathy wasn't only one way, Artemis. It also made me see you more clearly."

"Then you can forgive me for hiding this from you?"

"Humans and Opiri have another thing in common. They tend not to trust those who are different. You were protecting yourself by concealing what you could do, but you refused to rely on your other abilities to keep yourself safe." He looked at her very gravely. "I don't know if I can block my feelings from you, at least not quickly enough. You'll have to teach me to—"

"No." She smiled. "I don't want to be cut off from you ever again."

Garret took her in his arms and kissed her. His pride filled her to overflowing, and it was only their precarious circumstance that prevented them from following their most basic impulses.

"There is one thing I'd ask of you," he said when they had finally separated. "If your empathy will help us find Timon, will you use it?"

Jerked out of her drowsy contentment, Artemis played his question back in her mind. She had almost forgotten Timon in the drama of what had happened with Flavia and Kronos.

She felt a mingling of shame and anger, a part of her wondering why she hadn't thought of it herself, and another part—the old Artemis, who found it so difficult to trust—wondering if Garret found it so easy to accept her "talents" because he saw them as a means to get to his son.

Kronos had implied that Garret wanted to use her abilities, but Garret wasn't like Kronos. He wouldn't want her to use her mental powers to alter the thoughts and emotions of other beings.

Still, even after she had convinced herself of Garret's benign intent, she continued to feel uneasy. The first flakes of snow were falling as they broke camp and traveled side by side, moving quietly and without talking.

Near noon, when they paused to rest again, they had nearly reached the old Canadian border. The hilly landscape was only lightly dusted with snow, but the white-topped mountains of British Columbia—and the camp of the Master—still lay before them.

Artemis scouted ahead, heeding her sense that they were being watched. Their pursuer's emotions were so muted that she didn't recognize him until she was nearly on top of him.

Pericles froze in place when she found him, a little nervousness seeping through the strange but familiar barrier around his mind.

"Artemis," he said in a flat voice. "Are you all right?"

"What are you doing here, Pericles?" she asked. "Spying for Kronos?"

There was no reason to be so hard on him, and she regretted it immediately. But Pericles seemed not to notice her accusation; she almost felt as if he were looking right through her.

"Kronos is in trouble," he said slowly.

Immediately Artemis was on her guard. "What kind of trouble?" she asked.

"The other Freebloods turned against him," Pericles said. "Flavia said that he trusted you too much and broke his own laws by letting you consort with a human. They attacked him and left him in a bad way."

Artemis's alarm quickly gave way to confusion. Pericles's words were stilted, almost as if he were reciting by rote.

And that barrier…

"When did this happen?" she asked, setting aside her troubling thoughts.

"Soon after you left," Pericles said. "He's alone. I thought maybe you could help him."

Artemis glanced over her shoulder toward camp. The last thing she wanted was to leave Garret now, and this could all be a ploy by Kronos to get her back.

If it was a ploy, he might not be injured at all. But she couldn't bring herself to take that chance. Whatever he had said or done, she couldn't leave him to die if she could find any way of preventing it.

Briefly, she considered her situation. She had fed well not long ago. She carried the basic necessities in her pack, and she had her bow and quiver. She couldn't return to camp and try to explain to Garret why she was going back for Kronos, because he would surely try to stop her.

As long as she found him again in a few days, she wouldn't lose too much of her strength.

"Listen carefully, Pericles," she said. "I'll go back to find Kronos, but you must stay here and tell Garret why I've left. Tell him not to come after me. He needs to go on ahead. We have a good idea of where the Master's camp is located. Tell him I'll look for him there."

"I understand," Pericles said.

She gazed at him a moment longer, doubting both him and herself. But she had made her decision. Leaving Pericles to carry out her instructions, she set a fast pace southwest to Kronos's camp.

She found him alone and injured, just as Pericles had told her. Bleeding profusely, he had rolled under a clump of thick bushes, the dark red tatters of his clothes a testament to his injuries. But his wounds had closed, and he opened his eyes when Artemis knelt beside him.

"Pericles sent me," she said, gripping his hand. Pain

and anger and shame came from his mind to hers through their touch. "He said the others attacked you."

Kronos choked on a laugh. "Yes. I confess to being surprised that they left me alive." He squeezed her hand. "I knew you would find me again."

She wetted a piece of cloth with her canteen and wiped his face. "You will need blood quickly," she said. "It is fortunate that they also left you your daycoat. Rest here, and I will find game for you."

"Don't leave me alone," he said.

His vulnerability softened her toward him in a way she wouldn't have believed possible, but she knew she couldn't give in to pity. "You must have fresh blood to recover," she said, "and I will only be gone a very short time."

As she rose to leave, he touched her leg. "Garret?" he asked.

"I sent him on ahead."

With a long sigh, Kronos nodded and closed his eyes.

Artemis returned an hour later with a deer slung over her shoulder. She stood over Kronos and forced him to take nourishment, even when he turned away in disgust.

"A pity that Flavia's captive humans are no longer here," he said hoarsely.

"But you would never break your own laws by taking blood from them," Artemis said.

"No," he said. "I wonder if Flavia and the others caught them again."

"I hope that Flavia's stupidity in attacking you carried over to her hunting ability," she said. "No, don't try to explain. You asked for more than they could give, and they turned on you for it."

"What have I done wrong?" Kronos asked, lifting his head. "Artemis, you who know me better than anyone… how have I failed?"

"You haven't failed," she said, her body aching with his

regret and discouragement. "We knew this would never be easy."

He lay back again. "There is something you must know," he said, "in case I can go no farther."

"Of course you can," she said, alarmed by the thready sound of his voice.

"I know something of what this Master has planned," he said. "He is building an army."

"For what purpose?" Artemis asked.

"I do not know." Kronos coughed again. "But whatever that purpose may be, the Master will only bring harm to those you and I meant to save…the Opiri who know no other way but seeking rank through violence. And the end result will be terrible suffering for thousands of Opiri."

Artemis's breath grew short.

"What did you plan to do when you reached the Master's camp?" she asked.

"The Master has promised a reward to the Freebloods who bring the children and remain afterward. But, as we know, any leader can lose his followers, no matter how powerful he may seem." His laugh emerged as a bark. "I know that with so many Freebloods together in one place, some will have become disaffected and might listen to my words of peace. I had hoped to reach out to them in secret, with my own disciples to help me. But now…"

Artemis knew what he was going to ask, and she tried to harden her heart against him. But his despair and sorrow and hope had mingled so deeply with her own emotions that they overwhelmed the warmth and comfort she had felt with Garret.

"You want me to carry out your plan," she said.

"I cannot keep up with you now, and I know you will not abandon Garret Fox. But you can still be of great help to me. Once you arrive at the encampment, I would ask you to scout for any Freebloods who have come to oppose the Master and might be willing to listen to our philosophy. I would not expect you to act on what you learn, only to wait for me until I arrive."

"I will be helping Garret look for his son."

"You are resourceful enough to carry out two tasks at once. And it may be you can learn more about the children from Freebloods who are not completely loyal to the Master."

His words made sense, though Artemis wondered how he could draw so many conclusions based on relatively little information. All his assumptions might be wrong.

Still, she and Garret needed any information they could get.

"Can any Freeblood enter this encampment?" she asked.

"I heard that one must bring either a half-blood child or a human to add to their communal herd of blood-serfs," he said. "There may be other ways. You will have to determine what to do when you are there."

"Are you certain that you can travel on your own?" she asked him.

"I have recovered from much worse injuries."

"Then I'll do as you ask, if I can," she said. "I'll stay with you through the day and leave at sunset."

Kronos nodded and dropped off into the semiconscious state that served Opiri as sleep. Artemis went in search of game and water, and then returned to watch over her old mentor. By sunset, Pericles hadn't returned.

He's gone ahead with Garret, she thought. That was the only explanation that made sense. And yet she was left with that uneasy feeling she couldn't shake.

When she set out at last, all she could think of was being with Garret again. She only hoped that he understood why she'd gone back to Kronos, and that he would wait for her before he did anything rash in his eagerness to find Timon.

* * *

Garret looked down on the vast walled camp stretching across the river valley, turning to his field glasses again and again, wondering if Artemis had somehow managed to arrive ahead of him—as if he had any hope of finding her in the throng of Freebloods milling about like ants scouring the forest floor for their supper. A ridge of low hills formed a half circle around the camp, ending in the anthill—a cliff that towered over the sea of snow-dusted tents and awnings, surrounded by a royal guard of high mountains and topped with a structure out of some pre-War horror story.

A castle. That was what it appeared to be, anyway: all dark stone, massive gates and high turrets, a perfect home for a mythical vampire.

Or an egotistical, evil Nightsider who needed to make an impression on the thousands of Opiri who had been drawn here by the promise of reward for delivering the children. And maybe something worse yet to come.

These ants looked very much like an army. As a human, he would stick out like a sore thumb, even with the day-coat he had stolen from a small, untended campsite on the other side of the hill.

But he had to make his move soon, and he would much prefer to have Artemis with him when he did. He looked for her again. *She had to return to Kronos*, Pericles had told him. *She'll find you at the camp.*

Adjusting his pack, Garret began a careful descent down the hill. The moon was on the wane, but it was still close to full. Without it, he would have been nearly blind. His VS had disappeared from Kronos's camp before he and Artemis had left, and all he had now was a hunting knife, an ordinary handgun…and a well-trained but very human body.

When he was near the foot of the hill, he coated himself with a crust of snow and crawled low to the ground, pausing every minute to get his bearings. Now that he was close to the level of the valley, he could better see the scattered torches that indicated the presence of other night-blind humans. Here, they could only be serfs. Or prey, to be kept alive until they were used up.

Garret felt the burst of emotion before he could turn to face the Freeblood behind him.

"Garret," Artemis said. "I thought I'd never find you. I was afraid I—"

He grabbed her, pulled her down and kissed her hard. She melted against him, returning the kiss even though it was foolish and dangerous.

He didn't give a damn.

"Are you all right?" he asked, setting her back so he could see her shadowed face. "Pericles barely told me anything. I was afraid that Kronos—"

"Would convince me to stay with him?" She kissed him again. "He was injured, and I had to make sure he was all right. But that's all, Garret. I'll never leave you again."

He held her close for a moment, feeling the slow beat of her heart against his chest. She flinched, and at first he thought he was holding her too tightly.

But there was pain in her eyes, and it was not physical.

"What is it?" he asked.

"So many emotions," she said, clenching her teeth. "All these Freebloods together, and humans… I haven't felt this since I left the Citadel."

"How can I help?"

"I don't…" She hesitated. "Maybe there *is* a way. Let me focus on your emotions. Perhaps that will allow me to block out the others."

"What do you want me to feel, Artemis?"

She looked into his eyes, and he knew. He gave her all the devotion and affection he had reserved for only a few people in his life: Roxana, Timon…and Artemis. She gasped, and though—like all Opiri—she couldn't weep, he could feel the reflection of his emotions cast back at him, filling his eyes with the tears she was unable to shed.

For a few brief moments there was no barrier between them at all.

"By the blood of the Eldest," she whispered. "It is working." She began to laugh, and Garret laid his hand across her mouth.

"I'll give you all the strength I can," he said. "But we have to find out where the children have been taken."

Artemis signaled that she was in control again, and Garret removed his hand.

"Kronos told me more about the encampment," she said, her voice still a little breathless. "He thinks the Master is preparing an army, but we don't know where or when he plans to strike. Freebloods can get inside the walls if they bring a half-blood child or a human."

"There must be two thousand here already," Garret said. He paused to listen to the constant hum of voices from the camp. "We have to get inside the walls to find out if the children are there," he said. "Our only plan is obvious."

Chapter 20

Artemis had known that there was only one way to get inside the encampment, but still she shook her head.

"There must be something else we can try," she said.

"I assume they're holding captive humans to feed the Freebloods. They probably won't let you keep me, so the worst that can happen is that I get thrown into a pen with the other humans. At least we'll both be inside." He gripped her hand. "We'll figure something out once we're there."

But Artemis knew that there was one other possibility: convert Garret into an Opir. It still left them with the problem of the "entrance fee" to the camp, and in all the time he had been with Roxana, Garret had never chosen to become like her. There must have been a powerful reason for him to reject immortality with the woman he had once loved, so Artemis could think of no earthly reason why he would do it for *her*. It was far too much to ask. She couldn't even bring herself to suggest it…especially since a part of her badly wanted to make him just like her. Make sure he could never leave her, even when this quest was over.

I love him, she thought. It was no sudden revelation but a gentle movement of a puzzle piece into its proper place. The feelings had been there for a very long time. She was no longer afraid of the words.

But she could not force her love on him any more than she could make him love her. And though she knew he cared for her deeply and held her in great esteem, that wasn't the same.

If ever he came to love her, she would know it. And even if he did not, she would never regret these feelings. She would give Garret whatever he needed as long as both of them were alive.

"I must ask you to do one thing for me," she said. "Show me Timon."

His eyes caught the moonlight and glittered under his hood. "I've shown you what he looks like."

"Show me with your emotions. Perhaps, if we are anywhere near him…"

Without hesitation, Garret closed his eyes and let her *feel* Timon. His image was not a physical thing with clear features and solid shape but was built entirely of Garret's love for his son, an aura of tenderness and devotion and fierce vigilance. Guilt and fear were there, too, but she refused to let those darker feelings taint the rest.

"I see him," she said, her mind overflowing with memories as fragile as spring ice and as powerful as love itself.

Garret opened his eyes. "Did it help?" he asked.

"If we find out where the children are held," she said, "I think I will be able to find him." *If he is still alive*, she added silently, glad he couldn't hear her thoughts.

While she kept watch, Garret concealed his pack behind a jutting boulder, along with his knife and gun, covering each of them with handfuls of dirt and small stones. When he was done, he pulled Artemis into his arms again and kissed her, pushing his tongue between her lips, groaning deep in his chest. She opened her mouth and met him with equal passion.

"Artemis," he said, his lips trailing kisses over her jaw and neck, "take my blood."

She broke free. "Now? Are you mad?"

"We've been apart for nearly two days. You need it. If you don't feed, you'll become too weak to fight if we have to."

Weighing the risk of discovery against her hunger, Artemis nodded. "We must be quick," she said.

Euphoria flooded through her at the first taste of his blood. She felt her emotions pour into Garret, a sharing not of pain but of ecstasy, belonging and wholeness that needed only one simple act to complete. He tipped his head back and gasped as she drank, and his sudden arousal triggered her own. She shifted to lock her thighs around his waist. He arched up, his body hard and insistent.

This was how the world was meant to be, she thought. This was *life*, and she never wanted it to end.

But neither one of them was stupid enough to give in, no matter how urgent their desire. The path they needed to follow now lay through the encampment and hundreds of hostile Freebloods. To Timon.

Garret released her, though his hands lingered on her waist. "Are you ready?" he asked.

"I have no way to bind you," she said.

"I know how to behave like a human among undomesticated Nightsiders," Garret said, taking the sting out of his words by brushing a bothersome strand of her hair out of her eyes. "Don't give yourself away, whatever you do."

"Only if you promise to do the same."

Taking care to make certain that no one else was observing them, Artemis rose first. A group of Freebloods passed by, arguing hotly, completely unaware of her or the human at her feet. Once they had moved out of sight, Artemis motioned for Garret to rise and pushed him ahead of her. He glanced over his shoulder, and she saw his entire body change. His expression became worn and defeated, his body slumped. Only his mind told her that he was the Garret she knew.

The stockade was built of tree trunks stripped from the forest covering the surrounding hills. Perched on the barren cliff at the opposite end of the valley stood the mysterious castle, its silhouette marked with high, pointed turrets, crenellated walls and an imposing bulk that suggested unassailable strength. During the era when Artemis had been born, such monstrosities had been the creations of writers who told tales of haunted strongholds and mad villains.

This castle, like the ones in the novels, had been built to symbolize power…and evoke fear.

As she and Garret approached the wall of the camp, they found themselves among packs of Freebloods crowded outside, forced to intermingle as they jockeyed for position. Artemis noticed that some of the Opiri approaching the stockade were half-blood adults—not prisoners like the children, but walking freely among the full-blooded Opiri. She concentrated on blocking the seething clamor of the thousands of contradictory emotions that radiated from the vast encampment.

She took firm hold of Garret's collar and made straight for the gate, a crudely wrought, lopsided affair made of the same rough-hewn logs as the walls.

There were five Freebloods manning the gate, along with a single Darketan, who appeared human but smelled Opir. She didn't let the gatekeepers see so much as a flicker of doubt on her face.

"I have brought a human," she said. "Let me in."

The Freebloods glanced at each other with obvious

amusement. "Where is the rest of your pack?" the Darketan demanded.

"I need no pack to be of use to the Master," she said.

"Give the human to us," the Darketan said.

Artemis looked him up and down. "I take no orders from a Darketan."

"Give him up and we'll let you in," the tallest Freeblood said.

Garret stiffened, muscles tensing in preparation for a very one-sided fight.

"I will give him to the one in charge of the humans inside and to no one else," Artemis said quickly.

A low muttering started up behind her, restless Freebloods who doubtless hadn't drunk much human blood in recent days. "Silence!" the Darketan shouted.

Amazingly enough, the Freebloods quieted. The gate creaked open behind the sentries. They turned in angry surprise as a pair of female Opiri walked out, unaware that they had interrupted an increasingly hostile dispute.

Several things happened at once. Two of the sentinels tried to close the gate, one of the females shouted in protest, and Garret charged through the gap between the door and the wall.

Artemis sprinted after him, barreling past the gatekeepers before they could react. There was another crowd of Opiri just inside the gate, possibly drawn by the scent of human blood. Some of them were already running along a central lane between rows of tents and canopies, giving Artemis a good idea of which way Garret had gone.

While Artemis had never been as strong as some Opiri, she was very fast. She hurtled by the pursuers, lashing out at them with arms and feet as she passed. She opened her mind to Garret, willing him to let her know where he was.

She found him quickly enough, alerted only a few seconds before by his mental cry of warning. Three Opiri were dragging him into a tent halfway across the camp. He was resisting, buying time to urge her to stay away.

Artemis went directly to the tent and stepped inside. Seven Freebloods were crowded into the space, and she recognized them at once.

Most of Kronos's former followers seemed surprised to see her; Flavia and one other were openly hostile, while one looked shame-faced, as if he realized that she knew what he and the others had done to Kronos.

"Let him go," Artemis snapped, gesturing to Garret.

To her astonishment, the ones holding Garret released him. He straightened his daycoat with a sharp jerk and came to stand beside Artemis.

"It seems we've found old friends," he said with a curl of his lip.

"You betrayed Kronos," Artemis said to the Freebloods.

"It was Flavia's idea," one of the Freebloods—Mikohn—said to Artemis in a hurried burst of speech. "She thought Kronos was weak. She attacked him."

Flavia shot him a poisonous look. "We came here to look for the life Kronos couldn't give us," she said. "We knew his preaching would only get us killed if we came with him."

"And did you find what you were looking for?"

The Freebloods exchanged glances. "When we came here," Mikohn said, "we were told that we would become part of a new kind of life that the Master was making for all the Freebloods who agreed to follow him. We would share all the humans in common, no Opir getting more than another, and make raids on human colonies when we were strong enough. We would all be equals."

"As Kronos promised," Artemis said.

"You know what he made us give up," Flavia said. "He wouldn't have allowed any raids. We would have starved."

"And you were too afraid to leave Kronos without trying to kill him?"

Flavia opened her mouth but quickly closed it again. The rest were silent.

"How did you get into camp?" Garret asked.

"With your VS," Flavia said. "It seems that they can use weapons as well as half-bloods and humans."

"But we were wrong about this place," Mikohn said at last. "There aren't enough humans here to feed everyone. No one has seen the Master in many weeks, and some think he has abandoned the camp and his followers. A few Freebloods are trying to take over the camp as if they are Bloodlords." He glanced toward the tent flap. "There's talk of a war. We don't want any part of that."

Rebels, Artemis thought. Only she hadn't expected to find them so quickly, let alone run across Opiri she knew.

But if Kronos's former disciples were discontented after only a day or two of being in the camp, there were undoubtedly others. Freebloods still remembered how they had been used as cannon fodder in the War.

Artemis leaned against Garret, grateful for his solid presence at her back. "Where are they keeping the children?" she asked.

"If we tell you what we know," Flavia said, "what will you do for us in return?"

Artemis laughed. "What can I give *you*?"

"You can help us get out." Flavia shifted from one foot to the other and looked away. "I know how you fooled us into thinking you didn't take blood from the human."

Garret started. Artemis gripped his arm. "I do not know what you're talking about," she said.

"When we got here, I remembered what really happened, what you did to me," Flavia said hotly. "You made me believe something that wasn't true."

"You're mad," Artemis said, striving to breathe normally.

Flavia bared her teeth. "Kronos made us all mad to follow him. Is he like you?"

"What?"

"Can *he* make people do what he wants and believe what he wants them to believe?"

Startled, Artemis remembered how oddly Pericles had behaved when Kronos was injured. She had thought it strange at the time, but to suggest that his behavior had anything to do with an ability like hers...

"I have known him most of my life," Artemis said. "He has no such skill."

"But *you* do," Flavia said. "And now you will use it to make the guards let us out."

"You can't leave?" Garret asked.

"Once you come in, you are not permitted to go out again without a pass. Some of the guards at the front gate probably work for the rebels, and they want to keep us in as much as the Master's soldiers do. If the Master is truly gone, they need Opiri to rule over."

"Why don't the rebel Freebloods overpower the Master's guards?" Artemis asked.

"The guards have human VS weapons," Mikohn said.

"Do as we ask," Flavia told Artemis, "or we'll throw this human out into the camp."

"And I'll tell them that you plan to sneak out," Garret said.

"They won't listen to a human."

"They'll listen to another Freeblood," Artemis said.

"Do you want to know where the children are or not?"

The war within Artemis's mind echoed in Garret's, and she knew he understood. She despised and feared her power to control and deceive others. She would do nearly anything to avoid using it—anything but abandon Garret. Or the hope of rescuing Timon.

"Tell us where they are," she said, "and I give my word that I'll help you, as long as it does not involve harming others."

Mikohn and Flavia looked at each other. "Agreed," Flavia said. "The Master has been keeping the children in the castle. The rumors say that he is treating them well, but no one knows what he wants with them."

"The castle," Garret said, exhaling slowly. "From the look of it, it's virtually impossible to approach from any direction. How can we get inside?"

"That is not our concern," Flavia said. "We have told you what we know."

"There may be a way," Mikohn said. "The Freebloods who are trying to gain power while the Master is gone…it is rumored that they intend to go up to the castle in force and demand to know where he is. If they can show the camp that he has disappeared, and that only his personal guards remain to defend his position, then—"

"Where are these rebels?" Garret asked.

"They have established themselves in the rear of the camp," Mikohn said. "They have the largest tents. You'll find them easily."

"We have to join these rebels," Artemis said to Garret. "We have a better chance of getting into the castle as part of a group."

"You'll have to prove that you're strong enough to be an asset to them, but also that you're not a threat to their new power," Flavia said. "But again, that is not our concern. It is time for you to get us out."

Garret laid his hand on Artemis's shoulder. "Can you do this?" he asked in a low voice.

She covered his hand with hers. "I will," she said. She

addressed the other Freebloods. "We'll all go outside together."

After a brief hesitation, the Freebloods gathered behind her, Garret sandwiched between them to obscure his scent. The sun was rising, so Garret, Artemis and the Freebloods put up their hoods and made for the wall.

No one noticed them; there was some commotion at the gate that seemed to be occupying everyone's attention. As they drew nearer, Artemis heard Garret curse under his breath.

A dozen humans had apparently been captured, men and women in camouflage fatigues who stood with heads lifted and defiance in their eyes. They waited just inside the gate, surrounded by avaricious Freebloods who were obviously on the verge of grabbing any human within reach.

"These look like Enclave troops," Garret said.

"We cannot help them now," Artemis said. "We must—"

"Did you hear?" a young female Freeblood said, clutching at Artemis's arm. "A human army is coming, and the Master has deserted us!"

"Calm yourself," Artemis said, engulfed by the woman's very real terror.

"But now we will have to fight, and the Master is not here to lead us!"

"You should have considered that before you came here," Artemis said, fighting to separate the woman's feelings from her own.

The young female ducked her head and skittered away, hunched low and avoiding eye contact with any of the other Freebloods she passed.

"Stay close to me," Artemis murmured to Garret.

Garret did stay close, so close that he was nearly on top of her, ready to defend her from the slightest hostile gesture. His presence was a shield against the wildly fluctuating emotions of the Opiri around her, and she imagined herself in a position of authority, confident in her purpose. All she had to do was convince the distracted guards at the gate that she and those with her had to leave the camp on urgent business.

But as she felt for the minds of the guards among all the others, she felt sickness and revulsion surge up inside her, blurring her thoughts and making it impossible to focus. Garret caught her as she swayed, holding on to her under the cover of his daycoat. "You can't do this," he whispered. "When I yell, get the others out. Find Timon."

Before she could answer, he released her and stepped away from the group. "Human soldiers!" he shouted. "How many are coming? Hundreds? Thousands?"

As the human captives stared at Garret, other Freebloods turned toward him, their emotions swarming over Artemis—hunger, fear and alarm—as Garret's words penetrated the growing chaos. Flavia's group pressed in around her, on the verge of panic themselves.

Garret continued to mock the Freebloods at the gate, asking them how ready they were to stand against a human army carrying Opir-killing rifles like theirs. Artemis couldn't seem to move. In a moment, she thought, the guards would overpower and silence Garret, possibly kill him.

Closing her eyes, she focused her thoughts and projected the terror of death, of becoming trapped, of being pawns in a game the Freebloods didn't understand. There was no safety here.

The number of Freebloods moving in the direction of the gate began to increase, while the gatekeepers made a futile effort to stem the tide.

"Go!" Artemis said, shoving Flavia forward. "Run. Now!"

Kronos's former disciples broke away and sprinted for the gate. They lost themselves in the crowd. Voices rose in warning, and there were gunshots, followed by fighting that rapidly overwhelmed the guards.

Artemis grabbed a handful of Garret's daycoat and hung on. "We must go back into the camp," she said hoarsely.

"You're sick," he said. "You aren't ready to deal with the rebels when they storm the castle. I'll find somewhere for you to rest."

"No." She grabbed his hand and tried to draw him toward the rear wall. Her fingers trembled, and racking pain hammered inside her temples. "Someone will surely come after us if we do not move while the fighting distracts the guards."

With a terse nod, Garret half carried her back the way they had come. She couldn't feel his emotions through the clamor inside her skull, but his warmth and strength wrapped her in a cocoon that no outside force could penetrate.

As they ran deeper into the camp, dodging between tents to evade any pursuit, the noise of the battle at the gates began to fade. Artemis peered through the glare of daylight, looking for the large tents Flavia had mentioned.

They had nearly reached the rear of the camp when Garret came to a sudden stop. Clustered against the wall stood several tents that had been decorated to suggest that their owners were Opiri of rank and power. They were painted with symbols of dominance and arrayed with crudely carved standards atop staffs reminiscent of those carried by Bloodmasters in the Citadels.

As Artemis and Garret watched, two Freebloods in thickly embroidered daycoats approached the tents, arguing in low voices. Their emotions were hostile and angry, like those of Opiri on the verge of challenge.

The rebels, Artemis thought.

"Find the nearest empty tent," she whispered. "Hurry."

Garret went straight to the row of tents perpendicular to the rebels', paused outside of one, moved on to the next and gestured to Artemis. Keeping an eye on the arguing Freebloods, she followed him inside.

The interior was very similar to the one Flavia's group had occupied: a few pieces of camp furniture, a folding table and little else. Artemis crouched by the tent flap and listened intently.

"What are they saying?" Garret asked, crouching beside her.

"They are speaking of the challenge to the castle and how many Freebloods they have recruited to follow them."

"We'll have to quickly prove ourselves of use to them if we're going to join their group," Garret said.

"You know you cannot come with me," she said. "You will have to remain hidden while I am gone. I'll try to get you outside the camp, and—"

He met her gaze. "Did you think I came with you this far just to be left behind now?"

"Do you think they will allow a human to accompany them? They will simply seize you and keep you for themselves."

"They won't be able to," Garret said. "Because I won't be human."

Chapter 21

Artemis couldn't mistake his meaning. Her chest constricted, and she felt that, had she been human, she would have wept.

"It was inevitable," Garret said, holding her gaze. "We never discussed it, but you must have known all along. I can't go any farther as a human in this place. You have to convert me."

Struggling to quiet her own emotions, Artemis replayed that moment on the hill when she had considered and rejected this very option. "Do you know what you are saying?" she asked, spinning on her heel to stalk across the tent. "Do you understand that once this is done, it cannot be undone?"

"I understand," he said. "I've known it since long before I was sent to Erebus as a serf." He held out his hand to her. "I accepted all the ramifications long ago, when Roxana and I joined the colony and Timon was born."

She returned to him and knelt beside him. He stroked

her knuckles with his thumb, as if she were the one about to sacrifice everything she knew.

"I chose to remain human because I believed it was important to set an example for others, to show that we could live on equal terms with Opiri without giving up our humanity," he said.

"But now you wish to surrender that humanity? You can accept the complete transformation of your very nature, becoming dependent upon blood for the rest of your long life, never able to feel the sunlight on your skin?"

He brought her hand to his lips. "I endangered both of us, and Timon, by refusing to recognize the necessity of change." His fingers laced though hers, firm and unyielding. "I said we'd have to prove ourselves to these rebels. If it goes as far as a fight, the change will give me greater power and far better odds against any Opir."

"But do you know what else comes with the conversion?" she asked. "You will be my vassal, tied to me by a force even more powerful than the blood-bond."

"And once we find a way to join the rebels going up to the castle, you can claim the right to take your vassal with you."

"If these rebels had created vassals of their own, Flavia and Mikohn would have told us."

"They wouldn't have felt obliged to tell us everything. But once you've done it, Artemis, the rebels will have to accept it."

"If I can *make* them accept it."

"*We* will, and to hell with the rules of combat that forbid anyone from interfering in a challenge between Opiri. Getting into that castle is all that matters now."

So he thinks, Artemis thought. But would he feel the same when Timon was safe and he was faced with a world in which everything had changed? Would he come to re-sent her for holding power over him, even if she were to set him free the moment they had achieved their goal?

She saw that she had no choice but to play her final card. "I honor your courage," she said. "But courage will not save you if the conversion fails."

"I understand the risk."

"Do you? Are you aware that conversion by a Freeblood carries greater danger for the human than one carried out by an Opir of higher rank?"

"I know that some humans react adversely to conversion when it's done by a Freeblood," he said. "But it's not common for Freebloods to attempt it in the first place. I still believe it's a chance worth taking."

"You could die within minutes of my bite," she said, panic strangling her words. "You could become incapacitated, helpless."

"Nothing you've said changes my mind, Artemis." He cupped his hand around her chin. "Trust me."

She wanted to wail in protest. It shouldn't have been this way, done in haste and secrecy under conditions that would put him in far greater danger than almost anywhere else.

But he was strong. Strong and healthy and tenacious. His aura shimmered around him, red as flame, his determination feeding on his conviction and her faith in him.

"I will do it," she whispered.

"Thank you," he said. "Thank you for Timon's sake."

Surrendering to the inevitable seemed to take a weight off Artemis's shoulders. "The change is not immediate," she said briskly. "Your strength and speed will increase over time. You may even be able to tolerate sunlight for a few days, as your body adjusts. You should not require blood for at least twenty-four hours. But you must be very careful not to overtax yourself in the beginning, no matter how much you want to fight."

He nodded. "Do you need more blood before we begin?"

he asked. "I know mine won't be as nourishing for you after I'm changed."

"I will receive some blood during the process," she said.

"Enough to get you through the next few hours?"

"We'll worry about that later. For now..."

She met his gaze. "Prepare yourself as best you can, and I will do the same." She took several long, deep breaths and began to focus her thoughts on what she must do. Garret let his body relax.

They sat facing each other, looking into each other's eyes in a last, wordless communication. Artemis's heart was so full that she was afraid she would broadcast her emotions all over the camp, so she locked her feelings away completely.

"Are you ready?" she asked.

In answer, he bent his head back. Opiri had no real religion, but Artemis sent a plea to the universe and gently pressed her lips to his skin.

"Do it," he said hoarsely.

She bit down. His blood rolled over her tongue, and she completed the adjustments to the chemicals in her body that would provoke the conversion. Her vision hazed. Adrenaline raced through her veins, activating her instinct to create a new Opir, a vassal bound to her until she chose to set him free.

Garret's head began to jerk, and his eyes rolled back in their sockets. His teeth snapped together, and the tendons in his neck strained under his skin. Artemis realized that he was seizing, swallowed her panic and tried to stop.

But the process could not be halted. She tried to hold him steady, imagining that she was giving him more than the modifications that would alter his chemistry and his very nature. She gave *herself,* as well—all the vitality she had to spare, all the will and determination to survive.

Still it wasn't enough. She let all the barriers fall and

stepped *inside* him, carrying her love into the very center of his mind…the love that had become as real to her as the old dreams of Freeblood independence.

Gradually he began to respond. The tremors subsided, and the rigidity left his muscles. When she was certain she had finished her work, she closed off her emotions again and healed the wound, waiting for his body to accept what he had become.

Or for it to give up.

Sounds and smells passed in and out of her awareness. Lassitude crept over her, a weakness she had felt before and knew only too well.

Had the work of conversion, the first she had attempted in her two centuries as an Opir, been more than she could safely manage? Would she now require more blood before she could fight?

She snapped back to full consciousness when Garret made a sound deep in his throat and opened his eyes. He stared straight ahead.

"Artemis?" he murmured.

She shifted to sit in front of him, and he reached for her blindly.

"I can't see you," he said.

The small amount of blood she had taken from him seemed to curdle in her stomach. "It will pass," she said.

He felt for her face. "The light," he said. "It's too—"

The tent flap opened, and a tall Opiri walked in. He was bristling with rage; his eyes were black with it, and his large teeth were on prominent display.

There was no question in Artemis's mind that this Freeblood was one of the rebels who had asserted dominance in the camp. He reeked of the confidence that set the strongest Freebloods apart from others, and his emotions and his arrogant thoughts were all of power.

"Who are you?" he demanded. "What are you doing in my territory?"

Artemis rose to stand between him and Garret. "My name is Nemesis," she said, "and I have come to join the Opiri who are going up to the castle. You *are* one of them, are you not?"

"I've never seen you before," the Freeblood said, taking an aggressive step farther into the tent. "How do you know about us?"

"The whole camp knows," she said. "I have a need to see the Master, if he is here."

"Why?"

"I have reason to hate him, just as you do."

"We want only to find out what has become of him," the Freeblood said, suddenly cautious.

"That would also serve my purpose," she said. "What are you called?"

"I am Brutus," he said, "and we do not trust strangers." His nostrils flared. "Who else is with you?"

"Only my vassal," she said.

"Vassals are forbidden here!" Brutus snapped. "How did you get into the camp with one?"

"Perhaps I am clever enough to be of use to you."

"Where is your pack?"

"I have no need of other Opiri to protect me."

He laughed scornfully. "Why do you think we will permit you to join us?" he asked.

"I will fight for the privilege."

Brutus tried to step around her. "Let me see this vassal of yours."

Garret rose up behind her, though she knew he wasn't ready. His emotions were chaotic, and she felt without looking at him that he still couldn't see.

"A new convert!" Brutus said with a sneer. "Still mostly human. Did you make him in this camp?"

"It doesn't matter," she said. "I am prepared to defend him and earn a place in your ranks. Will challenging you be sufficient?"

"You would challenge *me*?"

"Do you lack the authority to give me a place in your delegation when I defeat you?"

"My reputation is well known. If you truly seek death, I will give it to you."

"Then I offer challenge, to take place within this tent. You and I, alone."

"Without witnesses? What game is this?"

"Would you risk a formal challenge in full view of the camp, when you do not yet have complete control of this place?" She arched a brow. "If you are afraid to fight without witnesses, you can always summon *your* vassals. Oh, but they are forbidden, are they not?"

"I have already proven myself," Brutus snarled. "I accept your challenge. And when you are dead, I will kill the vassal. Slowly."

Brutus attacked without warning, throwing himself at Artemis with his mouth stretched wide to clamp down on her throat. She was lighter and faster than he was; she slipped sideways, and he barely caught his balance before he crashed into the tent wall.

Still, he was fast enough, and his reach was far longer than hers. If it hadn't been for Garret, she might have failed before she began.

But she was all that stood between him and Brutus's frenzy. That fact alone seemed to replenish her energy, feeding her body and pumping new life into her muscles. She feinted, drawing Brutus away from Garret, and danced across the tent with a derisive laugh. Brutus swatted at her, fingers curled, but she evaded him again and darted under his guard to strike at his privates.

She had hoped to enrage him into clumsiness, but

she had miscalculated. She was too close to him, and he swooped down, seizing her neck between his long-fingered hands. She bit hard on his wrist, to no effect. His face descended toward her throat.

Garret slammed into him from behind, forcing him to release his hold. Artemis dropped to her knees and fell back, catching herself on her hands.

When she was on her feet again, Garret and Brutus were grappling like bears, the Opir snapping at Garret's neck. But Garret was holding his own, and it was clear that he was able to see well enough to focus on his opponent. His aura rose up in a halo around his head, scarlet tinged with purple, brighter than it had ever been.

Artemis didn't wait to find out how long his energy would last. She hurled herself on Brutus, grabbed a handful of his loose hair and bit his shoulder. With a howl more of outrage than pain, he reached back with one hand to dislodge her.

Moving with astonishing speed, Garret knocked Brutus's other arm aside and slammed his elbow into the Freeblood's gut. Artemis slid off Brutus's back, and Garret delivered a kick that caught the Opir in the middle of his chest and sent him flying across the tent. Brutus fell onto his back and lay there, stunned, like a turtle turned upside down.

Artemis and Garret reached the would-be Bloodlord at almost the same moment, Garret pinning him down with both hands while Artemis hovered over him, one efficient motion away from ripping into his throat.

"You're done," Garret said. His voice rasped and his arms trembled as he pushed down on Brutus's wrists, but Artemis knew he had passed the crisis.

In fact, he had done more than merely begin to change. His increase in speed and strength were only one sign, for when she met his gaze she saw that his green irises were ringed with vivid magenta, and his red hair was streaked with white. He smiled, and though there was no change in his teeth, she guessed it would not be long before they, too, revealed what he was becoming.

Brutus struggled to rise, heaving against Garret's weight. Garret hit him across the face with a clenched fist. Brutus subsided, blood trickling from his mouth.

"You…broke the laws of challenge," he croaked. "Your vassal…"

"Shall we tell the others that you were defeated by a small female Opir and a new-made vassal, or will you let us accompany you to the castle?" Artemis asked.

Such was Brutus's pride that the threat worked. He agreed to allow Artemis to accompany him to a meeting with the other "emissaries," which was to take place in one of the large tents in two hours.

Once he had left the tent, Artemis had to do something she very much wished she could avoid. "You'll have to stay in the tent until I return," she said to Garret.

He met her gaze, the magenta circles around his irises expanding and contracting erratically. "Is this your first order to your vassal?" he asked.

"Do you think I would ever use that against you?"

"No," he said, shaking his head. "Not you." He ran his hand through his hair, plucking a white strand and examining it with interest. His aura was quiet now, his emotions calm and dangerous. Artemis had no doubt that he would become such a formidable Opir that he could challenge any Bloodlord and win.

"Is your vassal permitted to touch you?" he asked with a wry smile. Without waiting for her answer, he pulled her close and kissed her. It lasted only a few seconds, but when it was over she felt stronger than at any time since she'd taken his blood on the hill just outside the camp.

The last time she would ever do so. Their relationship

would never be the same again. And she had no real idea what it would become.

The sound of a commotion outside shattered her reverie. Garret knelt by the tent flap and looked outside.

"Soldiers," he said. "Some are in daycoats, but there are half-bloods with them, all dressed in fatigues."

"The Master's loyal disciples?" Artemis asked, joining him.

"They're dragging the Opiri out of the big tents." His jaw set. "It looks as if the Master, wherever he may be at this moment, has learned about the little rebellion in his camp."

Artemis clenched her fists. "I do not think we can escape unnoticed."

"They may not check this tent at all," he said. "But there are too many to fight." Unexpectedly, he smiled, and Artemis didn't think it was her imagination that his incisors were just a little more pointed. "If they do take us, maybe we can convince them to escort us to where we want to go."

Artemis was considering the possibilities when she recognized one of the invaders: Pericles, dressed in a daycoat and standing apart from the soldiers. She gasped, and Garret gripped her arm to keep her from running outside.

"He's with the Master's forces," Garret said. "Why?"

Before she could answer, one of the soldiers dragged Brutus over to Pericles, who asked the rebel a brief question. Brutus pointed at the tent.

"Get ready," Garret said, pulling Artemis to her feet. "If Pericles is a traitor to Kronos, we may have no choice but to fight."

Chapter 22

The soldiers came right at the tent, weapons raised. Garret and Artemis stepped back to give themselves room. He clasped her hand briefly.

"Before you do anything rash," she said, "let me try to talk to Pericles."

Two soldiers lifted the tent flap but didn't attempt to enter. Pericles came in, and Artemis cautiously tried to read his emotions. They were as close to blank as she had ever found in any human or Opir.

"Artemis," he said, pulling back his hood. "I'm glad I found you."

"What are you doing here?" Garret asked, stepping in front of Artemis.

Pericles blinked. "I work for the Master," he said.

He didn't sound like himself, Artemis thought. "What of Kronos?" she asked. "How long have you been a traitor?"

As if he were wandering through a dream, Pericles

didn't seem to hear her. "The Master wishes to speak to you," he said.

"I thought he had disappeared."

"He has returned."

"You told him we were here?"

"Of course," Pericles said tonelessly. "He sent me to find you."

"But why would he want to see *me*?" she asked.

"He knows of your connection to Kronos and wishes to learn more of his philosophy. They want many of the same things."

"I never heard that Kronos wanted war," Garret said.

Pericles ignored him and continued to speak to Artemis. "The Master would prefer that you come willingly."

She glanced at Garret. He nodded slightly. This was their way into the castle, a more direct path than they could have taken with the rebels.

But if the Master knew about Kronos and had learned where to find his disciple, he might very well know *why* Artemis and Garret were here in his camp.

"We'll go with you," Artemis said.

"Good." Pericles ducked his head outside the tent and spoke to the soldiers. "We will leave right away."

The entire camp was nearly silent as the Master's soldiers escorted Artemis and Garret out through the gate. There were no more fleeing or fighting Opiri, though there were a few bodies scattered nearby, looking bleached in the morning sunlight. Other Opiri were dragging them out of the way as the soldiers strode past.

It was obvious that any open rebellion had been put down by the soldiers who now stood guard at the wall.

Once they had cleared the gate, the soldiers started up the narrow path that was the only direct approach to the castle on the cliff above, climbing a steep hill through the trees and then over bare scree where any attempt at attack could be easily prevented by a relative handful of defenders.

The path wound behind the castle and became a kind of narrow causeway, purposely designed so that only a few men or Opiri could approach at one time. The castle gate was high, wide and imposing, reinforced with massive sheets and hinges of steel that must have been salvaged from the remains of an old human town, dragged over some great distance along the river.

The castle itself was built, like the stockade far below, of heavy timber, but far more carefully worked and constructed. There were no windows except at the very tops of the four towers, and they were insignificant. But the painted wooden and metal embellishments and decorations above the gate and on the towers echoed designs from another time and place. A human time, long before the Awakening.

Unlike human-built fortresses, however, this structure was entirely protected from the open sky. The parapet walks were covered by heavy awnings, the rest by sloped roofs made to resist the snow.

As Artemis opened her mouth to speak to Garret, the gates swung open and a dozen of the Master's soldiers, dressed in fatigues and bearing rifles, walked onto the causeway, headed for the path below.

"More rebels to suppress?" Garret asked Pericles.

"There is much to be done," the young Freeblood answered cryptically.

Garret gripped Artemis's elbow, steadying her. The gates stood open, and their escort chivvied them into an empty, canopied bailey and forward toward the castle door.

The interior of the castle was as plain as the outside was imposing. The great "hall" of the keep was not the traditional large single room but a series of smaller interconnected chambers leading off into narrow corridors. Walls and doors lacked all decoration, and as Artemis and Garret moved deeper into the structure, it became more and more apparent that the castle had been built primarily to impress those outside it.

"Can you feel Timon?" Garret asked, his lips brushing her ear.

"No," she said. "And my sense of the others is dulled, as well. It almost seems as if something—or someone—is interfering with my ability."

Before they could discuss it further, they were ushered into one of the many small chambers, furnished with a recently upholstered couch and chair.

"You will wait here until the Master is ready to speak with you," Pericles said. "Do you require blood?"

Artemis met Garret's gaze. Considering the energy he had expended so soon after his conversion, he would need his first blood sooner than he might have otherwise.

But she was fairly certain their only option here would be to accept the blood of captive humans, and she knew that Garret would never consent.

"We need nothing," she said.

With a slight frown, Pericles studied her face a moment longer and then left the room.

"They didn't tie us up," Garret said, his gaze sweeping the room. "There's something strange going on here."

"Yes," she said. She reached for his hand, and he cradled it between his, his still-changing body almost feverish. "I wish I could see what it is. We may not have much time to find the children."

"What do you suggest?"

"I'm not sure. But perhaps…" She concentrated on Garret, and he started, his eyes widening.

"I heard that," he said. "I…*understood* you."

"Yes," she breathed. "We had a blood-bond before,

along with an empathic connection. Now the bond is based upon something even more powerful."

"And you want me to help you with your empathy? By focusing on my emotions again?"

"I used that technique to block out the feelings of the Freebloods and humans in the camp," she said. "This time I need to draw on your mind to enhance my own ability."

"I don't understand how *my* mind can help you."

"You have great inner strength," she said. "Like the... the roots of a very ancient tree, sheltering the weak and drawing life from the earth. I can anchor myself to those roots and reach out in a way I could not risk otherwise."

"If I have that kind of strength," he said, "I came by it the hard way." He hesitated. "What do you want me to do?"

"Artemis!"

She and Garret looked up as Kronos entered the room, his bearing and his mind filled with concern and relief. "I am very sorry to see you here," he said.

Artemis shot to her feet. "Kronos! What are you doing here?"

He took a seat on the chair and gazed at her as if he wanted to make sure that she was still in one piece. "I was taken when I approached the camp to learn more of the Master's plans," he said. "Apparently I was recognized by someone who remembered me as a leader of Freebloods and had heard of my philosophy."

"Pericles works for the Master," she said.

"So I have learned."

"You seem fully recovered from your injuries."

"I was fortunate—in that, at least," Kronos said. "But I did not have the resources to fight when the Master's soldiers came for me." He smiled crookedly. "I was given the opportunity to attend the Master here in his dwelling, or..."

"We were given the same choice," Garret said, rising

to stand beside Artemis. "The Master claims to want to speak to Artemis about your philosophy."

"There's been chaos in his camp," Artemis said. "Flavia and the others who abandoned you were trapped inside. We attempted to help them escape, but I do not know if we were successful."

"I saw Flavia fleeing the camp." Kronos lowered his voice. "It seems the Master is having trouble managing the Freebloods he lured here. But he is far from powerless." He glanced toward the door. "Under other circumstances I would be happy to speak to this Bloodlord and discover whether we share any common ground. Perhaps I might even have been able to persuade him to strike a more peaceful course."

"Not as long as the Master and his followers snatch innocent children from their homes," Garret said. "Do you know why he wants them?"

"Unfortunately, I doubt I know more than you. I assume it is still your desire to find them?"

"Yes," Garret said roughly. "If you have any ideas…"

"I do," Kronos said, addressing Artemis, "but first I have a confession to make."

"What confession?" she asked.

"About your gift of empathy."

She experienced a sense of foreboding so strong that Garret felt it and pulled her hard against him. "It has seldom been a gift," she said.

"It was what led me to you when you were dying two centuries ago."

"Because my mind called for help."

"Your emotions called me, yes. But why was *I* the one who came to save you?" He leaned forward, his hands clasped between his knees. "I, too, am an empath, Artemis. I learned early to control it, for such sensitivities can only hamper any Opir who wishes to rise to power.

But I sensed your dying, and I recognized in you one like myself."

For a moment Artemis was too stunned to speak. Kronos's emotions were pouring into her now—not because she welcomed them, but because he was *making* her feel them. Pride, triumph, confidence, ambition. For the first time she could see his aura, a deep purple halo hovering around his head and shoulders.

"You saved me because I am like you?" she said.

"Because I knew that one day we could work together for the betterment of our people."

Artemis's foreboding increased. "Does your empathy include the mental strength to affect others?" she asked.

"It does."

"Blood of the Eldest," she whispered, remembering what Flavia had asked her about Kronos's abilities.

"Pericles was under some kind of spell when you were injured and he came to find me. Was that you?"

Kronos relaxed, as if he had no concern at all about what she might discover. "Yes. I found that it was easier to make him understand what he had to do."

Garret's face was a grim mask. "Did you control Pericles when you two were in the same jail in Delos, so that he could convince Artemis to see you?"

"I only encouraged him," Kronos said.

"But now he works for the Master," Artemis said, "and he's behaving just as strangely."

"I have no explanation for that."

Unless the Master has the same powers Kronos does, she thought. But the idea that she, Kronos and the Master should possess identical abilities was sheer madness.

"What about Oceanus?" she asked. "You were always so skilled at persuading the Freebloods we attempted to recruit, but I assumed—" Her blood froze. "You asked me to help you understand the feelings of those who resisted our message."

"And so you did, unaware that you sometimes pushed beyond merely sensing into encouraging, as you did with Flavia when you convinced her that you took the animal blood."

"So all along I was pushing undecided Freebloods to obey you?"

"You and I wanted the same thing. We were attempting to save our race."

"But you never told me. You never explained. And after you died…"

"You shut out your talents, because you needed me to guide you."

"But *you* couldn't keep Flavia and the others with you!"

"Ah, Artemis. I lack the focused power of your gift. I can persuade, but not command. In this, I acknowledge you my superior."

"And now you want to use her again," Garret said, his voice a growl.

"What would you ask her to do in order to find your son?"

"I was going to ask him to help *me*," Artemis said.

"By employing your bond to enhance your empathy?" Kronos asked. He stared at Garret. "You are not far along, are you? Still not one of us. Your loyalty is entirely to the humans."

"He is my vassal," Artemis said, "but I do not control him. We work toward the same ends."

"Do you, Artemis?" Kronos held out his hands. "You wish to find his son. You wish to prevent a war, and lead Freebloods upon the right path, as we always did. If we can convince the Master—"

"By compelling him?" Artemis said. "Whatever you say, I have no such power."

"I can help you now, as I did in Oceanus." He smiled, and his aura lightened with something very much like joy. "Think of the good we can do here, my child. How many lives we might save."

"The children?"

"So much more than that, Artemis. Neither one of us can wield the power the two of us can when our minds and emotions join as one."

As she had proposed to do with Garret, Artemis thought, though on a much smaller scale. The idea of joining with Kronos disgusted her. He had already used her without her knowledge, deceived her for two centuries.

"I can see that the suggestion seems unpleasant to you," Kronos said. "But when we combine our abilities, we can change the world to match our vision."

Change the world. But she knew that he meant something more than improving the lives of beleaguered Free-bloods, saving the children, or even preventing another war. He had a grander vision.

Grand, and terrible. But she could only *feel* it, not see the specifics. She had no idea what he planned.

"How will you do this in the Master's house?" she asked. "For all we know his guards may have heard everything you just said."

"All the more reason to hurry," Kronos said. "We must act while we still—"

"Forget it," Garret said. He gently pushed Artemis behind him. "I never trusted you, and now you're talking crazy. Artemis's mind isn't a toy for you to play with."

"And what if I can save your son?"

"Not at that price," Garret said, though his voice nearly broke. "We don't need your help."

"Don't you?" Kronos said to Artemis. "Will you let the children remain captives of the Master, their fates unknown, because you are unwilling to try what I suggest?"

Fear washed through Artemis, quickly followed by anger. "I am prepared to try—but only for Timon's sake."

"No," Garret said. He turned her to face him. "I can't let you do it. I *won't*. We'll try it the way you suggested before. I'll be your tree, Artemis. Whatever you need to do, I'll give you everything I have."

"Artemis..." Kronos began.

She gazed into Garret's eyes. Their physical appearance was changing, but he was still Garret. Still strong-willed, courageous and resolutely set on protecting her.

"I must," she said softly. "I have to try, Garret, so that we can get the children out alive."

"And if Kronos is influencing you, even now?"

"Have I touched your mind in any way?" Kronos challenged. "Do you feel any compulsion?"

"No." Artemis laid her hands on Garret's arms. "Only for the children," she said.

Garret tried to dissuade her, not with words, but with the force of his emotions: his distrust, even hatred for Kronos; his driving concern for her; his certainty that Kronos's plan would end in disaster.

But through it all she could read his fear for his son and the other children, fear he couldn't conceal.

"Artemis," he said. "If you do this—"

The door opened, and Pericles entered with two of the guards.

"Kronos," he said, "the Master will see you now."

Kronos rose. "I am glad you are well," he said to Artemis. "I hope to see you again soon."

Shaking with anger, Garret turned to Artemis as the others left. "Kronos doesn't care about the children," he said. "He only wants a way into your mind, and then—"

"Garret," she whispered.

He turned toward the door. Pericles was still there,

though his face remained as blank as it had been ever since Artemis had met him again.

"The Master inquires again if there is anything you need."

"Pericles," Artemis said, approaching him cautiously, "how did you come to serve the Master? You were with Kronos before. What changed? Or did you always work for the Master, even when you saved Beth and we took her all the way to Delos?"

"I don't understand," Pericles said, stepping toward her.

"Were you spying on us? Is that how the Master knew about me and Kronos?"

Expressionless, Pericles turned to leave. Artemis saw Garret near the door, opening it a tiny crack to check the hall outside.

"I don't think you are a spy," Artemis said quickly, snatching at Pericles's arm. "Something's wrong. Let me help you."

Pericles flinched as if her hand had burned him, and she felt the first real stirrings of alarm.

"Look at me, Pericles," she said.

His clouded gaze met hers. Sharp pain sliced into her skull.

And she knew what she had to do.

Chapter 23

Artemis closed her eyes and, keeping a firm grip on Pericles, concentrated on all the things she had learned about him and admired when they had first met: his bravery, his willingness to change his way of life, his determination to defy his own people for the sake of a human child.

Then she looked for the invader in his mind. And found him, *part* of him, intertwined with the feelings that made Pericles what he was, corrupting them like spreading rot in a healthy grove.

Knowing that she had to work quickly, she tried to construct an image that would help her do what was necessary. She imagined the negative influence as a black thread entangled with a golden one, woven so tightly that only the greatest skill could pick the strands apart. She wove her own emotions into a third strand—crystalline blue—and searched for a weak place in the skein.

When she found it, she forced her thread between the other two, pouring her own emotions into it, all the compassion, trust—and love—that Garret had brought into her life.

Pericles moaned. His terror engulfed her. Her legs gave way, and she dragged him down with her. She lost all sense of herself as a separate being. Even breathing was agony. The black strand began to burn and shrivel.

She collapsed. When her vision cleared, Garret was crouched over her, and Pericles lay on the floor beside her. He opened his eyes. They were filled with bewilderment, but they were clear. He was himself again.

"Artemis," Garret said, supporting her head in his hands. "What in God's name did you do?"

"It's all right," she said, rubbing her temples.

Pericles sat up. "What hap—" he began. "Kronos." He covered his face with his hands. "He got inside my head."

"You freed him?" Garret asked Artemis.

"Yes," she said. *But if Pericles has been working for the Master...*

"Whose commands are you obeying now?" Garret asked Pericles, as if he'd heard her thoughts.

Pericles moved his head slowly from side to side, as if he wasn't sure that it belonged to him. "I don't know," he said. "But..." He looked toward the door.

"The guards aren't near the door," Garret said, suspicion rolling off him like waves of heat. "If they're listening, they're using a device, not their ears."

"What were you about to say, Pericles?" Artemis asked.

"I...think Kronos is working for the Master."

"Working for him?" Garret said. "How?"

"I don't know," Pericles moaned. "It's all mixed up inside my head."

"If Kronos is already involved with the Master," Garret said, "he's been deceiving us since you first met him at Delos." He looked at Artemis. "He wanted you here with him, and my search for Timon was only a convenient means of achieving his goal."

"But he can't support what the Master is planning," Artemis protested, nearly choking on the denial. "The idea of another war…"

"How can you know what's really in his mind?" Garret asked. "He can obviously hide his true feelings. He said he needs your help to influence the Master in some way. Is that really what he wants?" Garret forced her to look at him. "Why would he work for the Master in the first place, Artemis?"

"It's a trick," she said. "He heard of the Master's plans, offered his services to learn more…" She heard the pleading note in her own voice and tried to calm herself. "Even if he lied to us, he must have come to realize the Master was wrong. That's why he wants my help."

"He 'encouraged' Freebloods in the Citadel. He manipulated you. He made Pericles into a slave." Garret grimaced. "Do you remember what he said, Artemis? He said he learned to control his abilities because they would only hamper an Opir who wanted to rise to power. Isn't that what he's really wanted all along? Power? If he thinks he can get it through the Master…"

A grander vision, Artemis had thought when Kronos had spoken of changing the world.

Did he think he could destroy the Master, inherit his Freebloods and take command of a ready-made base of operations…all to establish the new way of life he had fought and nearly died for in Oceanus?

"Until I see proof," she said, "I cannot condemn him."

"Then be prepared to act quickly when you change your mind," Garret said.

They stared at each other, neither willing to look away first.

"Artemis?" Pericles said faintly. "Do you still want to save Timon?"

"Do you know where he is?" Garret asked, leaning over the young Freeblood.

"I…think…" With Artemis's help, Pericles got to his feet. "I think I remember seeing the place, but I'm not sure how to get there."

Garret sprang up and ran to the door. "The guards are still gone," he said. "It must be some kind of trap." He returned to Pericles. "If you're lying…"

"I don't sense the guards anywhere nearby," Artemis said.

"Are they so confident that we can't escape?" Garret asked. "I saw that kind of arrogance in Erebus, when I worked for the Underground. But we can't count on it."

"If the Master means to kill us, will it matter if we remain in this room or search for the children?" Artemis asked.

"Pericles, will you show me what you *do* remember?" Garret asked.

"I'll try," Pericles said, meeting Garret's gaze.

"I want you to stay here, Artemis," Garret said. "If you find a way to escape, I want you to—"

"This is becoming tedious," Artemis said with a weary smile. "I will not remain behind, and you cannot compel me to. In fact, *I* could compel *you*, if I wished." Her smile faded. "We will go together."

"I had to try," Garret conceded with a look that made her feel hot and cold at the same time.

"Where do we start?" she asked Pericles.

Pericles looked around the room. "There are dozens of small chambers all through the castle," he said, "and just as many halls and corridors. If I could just figure out where we are…"

Artemis opened her memory, seeking the emotional

imprint of Timon that Garret had left in her mind. The laughing, softly rounded face appeared to her inner vision, reverberating with all the love and devotion Garret felt for his son.

"I feel you," Garret whispered. He covered his eyes with his hand. "And I think I... I think I feel Timon."

She gripped his wrists. "Calm," she said.

"He's afraid," Garret said hoarsely. "My son. And all the others...so afraid."

Artemis closed her eyes. She caught the echo of what he was experiencing, the pain of feeling the suffering of the helpless and not being able to do anything about it. The sickness of losing himself in the emotions of others. Of his own son.

If she let herself, she would be caught in the same trap. One of them had to remain clearheaded for the sake of those same children.

"It's all right," she said, rubbing his arm. "I did not know this would happen when I converted you. Perhaps I should have guessed."

Garret uncovered his face. "What *has* happened to me?"

"When I passed on the substance that provokes the change, I think I...also gave you a little of my ability. I am sorry."

Garret pressed his palms to his temples and sank to his knees. "How do I stop it?"

"I can show you how to protect yourself," she said, kneeling beside him. "But if I do it now, you may lose all contact with Timon."

Gritting his teeth, Garret shook his head. "Then I... don't want it to stop." Tears glittered in his eyes. "God, Timon."

"Can you feel where he is?" she asked gently.

"No. There's too much—" He broke off, and she was engulfed by his grief.

Roxana was there, his wife, with her sparkling eyes and undeniable beauty. Loss. Rage and the desire for revenge against someone he had never found. Devastating loneliness.

"I am with you," she said. "You are not alone." She rested her forehead against his. "Try to focus. There is a point where the feelings are strongest. We must find that focal point, because the children will be there."

"I'll find it," he said, struggling to his feet. He offered Artemis his hand and pulled her up. She knew that his pain wasn't gone, but there was that familiar determination in his eyes that rejected all obstacles. His fingers traced her face, as if he were committing it to memory. "We'll do this, Artemis."

A kernel of absurd joy burst in her chest. They were in accord again, fully aware of each other and of themselves. Garret squeezed her hand, pressed his lips to her fingers and then just as quickly let her go, moving to the door at the opposite side of the room.

"Pericles," he said, his voice calm and level, "don't reveal that you're free of Kronos's influence. Allow whoever we meet to believe that you're our prisoner."

He looked at him mournfully but nodded. Garret tested the door. It was neither guarded nor locked. With Garret leading the way and Pericles between him and Artemis, they passed into a similar room and then entered a narrow corridor, dividing their attention between watching for guards and following their inner senses.

Remarkably, they met no one at all, not even the servants Artemis imagined a Bloodlord like the Master would require. There were many rooms and halls, some furnished, but none felt as if they had ever been occupied. The emotional core of the building still lay ahead of them.

So did the danger.

They had just entered what appeared to be a small meeting or dining area when Garret lifted his head. Artemis knew at the same instant what he was sensing.

"Timon," Garret said. He whirled around and ran for a door on the other side of the room. Artemis and Pericles hurried to catch up, and they plunged into another corridor that ended abruptly at a flight of steep, descending stairs. Garret bounded down the steps, only pausing at the bottom to make sure that the others had negotiated the stairs successfully.

But now they were faced with a new dilemma. Three more corridors—little more than tunnels—branched out from the small room at the foot of the stairs, each smelling of damp, cold earth and stone.

"Underground," Garret said. "They're keeping the children *under* the castle."

Artemis took a deep breath. "Join with me, Garret," she said. "We can find them."

He took her hand again. Emotions exploded like fireworks and then receded to a distant hum. Auras mingled without resistance or discomfort, her abilities and his— the power she had given him—blending as one in full awareness.

Then they were off again, Garret squeezing into a space barely large enough for an adult, human or Opir. It was only the entrance to a maze of bewildering turns and reverses, stairs and dead ends, clearly built to hinder attempts at rescue or escape.

But the builders had not anticipated an invasion of empaths. Garret found the correct path, and they finally emerged into a long, narrow room furnished with a single ornate chair near the center.

To Artemis, it felt as if the entire room had been emptied of air. She sensed the crushing weight of mountain and castle above as if it might collapse in on them at any moment.

Garret swore. "They're here," he said. "Timon—"

"Yes," Kronos said, coming around a corner with eight Free-and half-blood soldiers at his heels. "They are all here, and safe. The Master…" He glanced at Pericles, and a flicker of doubt crossed his face. "The Master is temporarily disabled."

"By you?" Garret demanded.

"With great difficulty, yes. I cannot say how long his condition will last."

"The Master wouldn't listen to your proposals?" Artemis asked.

"He would not hear me at all. He is too far lost in his dreams of power." He stared into Artemis's eyes. "I *must* have your help now. We can stop him before he goes any further."

Garret laughed. "Are you so certain you want to stop the Master, Kronos? Why didn't you kill him?"

"I am not a murderer."

"But if he's helpless, Artemis and I—"

Artemis silenced him with a gesture. An idea was developing in her mind, too terrible to acknowledge.

"Who are these soldiers?" she asked.

"I have brought them around to my way of thinking." Kronos looked at Pericles again. "Why is *he* with you?"

"He helped us find this place."

"Do not trust anything he says," Kronos said.

"Because he is no longer under your control?"

"His loyalties are suspect."

So are yours, Artemis thought.

Garret moved slightly so that Pericles was behind him. "Where are the Master's soldiers?" he asked.

"Most have left to deal with problems in the camp."

"What does the Master intend to do with the Free-bloods?" she asked.

"Invasion of the Citadels with a Freeblood army, to ensure that Freebloods are granted the rights of full Opiri."

"Then why have so many of them rebelled?" Garret asked.

"The Master was away too long. There are too many Freebloods in camp to dominate easily, and his personal charisma was holding them together. They began to doubt, to fear."

"Then he's not going to have much luck managing them now," Garret said.

"Do not underestimate him, vassal," Kronos said. "You do so at your peril."

"But you still won't kill him."

Artemis trembled with the effort to keep her feelings hidden. All she sensed from Kronos was perfect control and a distant feeling of triumph.

"I am not a barbarian," he snapped. "But we can stop any possibility of his succeeding in his plans. If we work togeth—"

"Release the children," Garret said, "and maybe we'll help you."

"I need none of *your* help," Kronos said, with a twitch of his upper lip.

"Bring them out," Artemis said, "so we'll know they're all right."

"They're far safer where they are."

"You're lying," Garret said, trying to get past Artemis. "They're terrified. You've done nothing to help them."

Artemis touched his arm, projecting sympathy and patience. "What do you intend to do when the Master is no longer a threat?" she asked Kronos.

"Help the remaining Freebloods, of course. Organize them properly, and teach them as we always planned."

Artemis ached with wanting to believe him. But he

could not easily have overcome a Bloodlord who had gathered so many Freebloods in a single camp.

"Garret has come all this way to save his son," she said.

"The children will only get in the way," Kronos said, his voice soothing and persuasive. "When the Master recovers, he could use them against us."

"I'll help you," Artemis said. "Show me what you want me to do."

"Artemis!" Garret said, reaching out to hold her back.

Without words, she tried to make him see what she planned to attempt. She had to make Kronos believe she trusted him, get him to let down his emotional guard.

Because if Kronos wanted so badly to join minds with her, there must be a way to use her empathy to stop him.

"Stay here, Garret," she said, avoiding his eyes. "Pericles, remain with Garret."

"Like hell I will," Garret said.

"Do not make me command you."

"No," Pericles said, pushing his way past Garret. "Don't believe anything Kronos says, Artemis. He'll do to you what he did to me."

"What *I* did to you?" Kronos said with a convincing display of surprise. "I no longer guide you. You serve the Master."

"Artemis freed him from *your* empathic influence," Garret said, taking a step toward Kronos.

"He didn't always try to control me that way," Pericles said. "I knew him long before he and I met in Delos." He looked from Artemis to Garret. "I lied when I said I lived in Oceanus."

"Be silent," Kronos growled.

"I was in the south of old California, near the Citadel of Angelus, when he came to the Freeblood exiles there with stories of a new life for us."

"When?" Artemis asked, unthinkingly reaching for the support of Garret's mind.

"About six and a half years ago," Pericles said.

Not long after Kronos's supposed "death" in Oceanus, Artemis thought, and around the same time as her exile. She felt Garret inside her mind, suppressing his rage at Kronos in order to help her. She grasped the mental lifeline he offered and shut out everything but Pericles's voice.

"Kronos said we could live as well as the lords in the Citadels," Pericles continued. "There were some mixed human-Opir colonies then, small and not very well protected. He said we should…" Pericles began to speak in a rush, as if fearing he would be cut off. "He said it wouldn't be wrong to take humans from the colonies, because we would only need them until we created a new society where all Opiri would be equal. Then we wouldn't keep running out of blood, and humans could have better lives in the Citadels." His eyes begged Artemis for understanding. "He *made* us believe him. We would raid the colonies and keep the humans for a while, but many of them couldn't survive in the wild. Then Angelus's agents drove us away, and we went north. We found more mixed colonies near Erebus and the San Francisco Enclave. Kronos tried to persuade the Opiri in the colonies to join us. Sometimes we fought them. Opiri and humans died."

"His memory is twisted," Kronos said. "The Master has warped his mind and would turn you against me."

"There was one colony where Kronos got to some of the Freebloods who were living peacefully with humans," Pericles went on, stumbling over his words. "They opened the gates to us. I tried to stay out of the way, but the others killed at least one high-ranked Opir before we got out." Pericles's eyes swam with misery. "After that, Kronos… couldn't control all the Freebloods who followed him. He decided to leave California, and a few of us went with him. He said he had to find a former vassal in Oceanus, and he sent us to find her. We found out she'd been exiled from the Citadel."

"Me," Artemis murmured. Garret moved up behind her, lending her his warmth as well as his emotional support.

"We split up and started searching the wilderness. But the group I was in broke up, and I…" He looked away. "I was too weak on my own. Chares took me in, and then they took Beth. I found out about other packs stealing children, carrying them north. And just before Chares decided to kill me, I heard a rumor about an exile in southern Washington who sounded a lot like Kronos. But after you saved me and I followed you to Chares's pack, I never thought I'd see Kronos again."

"I was looking for you when the Delosians captured me," Kronos said to Artemis, his voice beginning to rise. "These other things are fantasies, fruit from a poisoned tree."

"But it all makes sense," Garret said to Artemis. "He couldn't control the Freebloods in the south. He knew what *you* were capable of and believed he needed your help the next time he had to assert his dominance."

"Over the Master's followers," Artemis said. She stared at Kronos. "You allied yourself with him, always intending to take over when you found the means. But what were *you* doing for *him*, Kronos?"

"Nothing," Garret said, his aura sparking to brilliant life. "He isn't one of the Master's allies. He *is* the Master."

Chapter 24

Kronos sighed and sank into the throne-like chair. "Your vassal surprises me," he said to Artemis, "though it seems I underestimated *him* and overestimated *you*. All the time we spent together on the way here, all the many hints I gave you, and you never guessed."

"She believed in you," Garret said, somehow managing to put himself between her and Kronos again. "How much of that was your mind control?"

"I saw it not long ago," Artemis whispered, laying her hand on Garret's rigid back to keep from falling, "but I couldn't quite make myself believe. It seems so obvious now." She moved to stand beside Garret and met Kronos's gaze. "You sent me into the camp to look for traitors to the Master."

"And you found them for me," Kronos said, "though that was a small thing. I would far rather that you had continued to believe that I needed your help to dominate the Master and stop his 'evil' plans."

"Then you do admit to your own evil," Artemis said.

"Good and evil are limited human concepts," Kronos said.

"Why did you send Freebloods to steal half-blood children?" Garret asked, his voice very low.

"I assure you that they are safe," Kronos said.

"That isn't good enough."

"All will become clear in the future."

"But your army is defecting *now*. If you promised these Freebloods the same things you offered the ones in the south, it obviously wasn't enough to hold them when the 'Master' vanished."

"Yes," Kronos said. "I never should have left to find you, Artemis. But even that was not an irredeemable error on my part."

Garret's aura, no longer red like his hair but the color of old blood, seethed with dangerous anger. "You made a fatal error in thinking you could ever get Artemis to help you."

For the first time, Kronos let his anger show. "Surely you have more questions, Artemis, before we begin to quarrel in earnest," he said with biting sarcasm.

"Why did you change?" she asked, struggling to keep her voice level. "Why war and conquest instead of the separate, independent and peaceful existence you always wanted for our people in Oceanus?"

"After my supposed death," Kronos said, "I realized that what I had wanted would never be enough. There had to be redress for those who suffered at the hands of arrogant Bloodlords."

"So you plan to set your Freeblood hounds on the elite, steal their serfs and take over?" Garret said.

"A continuation of the old ways," Artemis said, "only with a new set of Bloodlords to replace the entrenched rulers. Do you truly think you can overthrow the Citadels with a few thousand troops?"

"It would not be difficult to rouse the disaffected Free-bloods within the Citadels," Kronos said. "It would only be a matter of recruiting them. A handful of spies would be enough. And I have not entirely discarded the philosophy you and I developed in Oceanus. I intended to offer the aristocracy a chance to surrender. Their capitulation to my demands would give us the opportunity to rebuild our society along more equitable lines."

"This isn't about your concern for Freebloods," Garret said. "There's no idealism in you, Kronos."

"Vengeance," Artemis asked. "Your answer to the Bloodlords and Bloodmasters who tried to kill you for turning against your own rank and challenging the status quo. You've become just like them."

"If I wanted revenge, I could have taken it long ago. There can be no new beginning without tearing the current system down to its foundation."

"And you think that after unleashing an army of Free-bloods to murder at will, you'll be able to control them afterward?"

"That is why I wanted your help, Artemis," Kronos said. "Why you *will* help me, because you know that without the proper guidance Freebloods are as savage as humans, and just as destructive."

Artemis's rib cage seemed to press in on her heart. "You will not stop with the Citadels. The violence will spread to the human settlements and Enclaves. Human troops were caught outside your camp. The abductions have already set the spark to the tinder."

Garret's strong hand found hers. "She isn't yours anymore, Kronos," he said. "She wouldn't help you even to save me or my son, so you can put that sick thought out of your mind."

"Such devotion," Kronos said, shaking his head. "But how strong is the edifice of your affection, Mr. Fox? You have every reason to hate her kind. Why did you let her turn you into one of us?"

"I knew I'd have a better chance of surviving to kill you," Garret said. "Where are the children?"

Kronos made a casual gesture, and one of his guards slipped away. Artemis turned to look for Pericles, but he had vanished.

"I believe you wanted to know what I planned for my little half-bloods," Kronos said to Garret.

Garret's aura burned so intensely that Artemis feared it might do him some physical damage. "It won't matter once you're dead," he said. He lunged toward Kronos but didn't get more than two steps before Kronos attacked him with such a focused blast of contempt that Garret was utterly unprepared to defend himself against it. Artemis was too slow to help him. He fell to his knees with a sharp exhalation, as if Kronos had kicked him in the belly.

But there was a sudden, vital flush of fierce exhilaration in the emotions Artemis shared with him, and she realized what he had done. Garret hadn't run at Kronos out of a reckless loss of restraint. He'd meant to give her a chance to assess Kronos while he was distracted. And he hadn't given her warning, knowing that Kronos might sense his intentions.

And for a few seconds, Kronos *had* been vulnerable. He had been so focused on punishing Garret that he'd briefly let down his mental shield, and Artemis had been able to look inside him.

There was a chink in Kronos's armor. He was capable of uncertainty. He believed that she was more powerful than even *he* had guessed, and he was also desperately afraid of Garret. Of what he and Artemis could be together.

Garret pushed himself to his feet, then stepped between

Artemis and Kronos, blocking the Bloodlord's line of sight. "Did you get what you needed?" he asked Artemis.

His dark maroon eyes narrowed in fury, Kronos shouted a command. Garret jerked, and Artemis felt another explosion of emotion from her lover, his aura reaching for someone she couldn't yet see.

Two soldiers walked around the corner with a red-haired child. A boy, dressed in a serf's tunic and pants, who walked with his smudged chin up and his eyes searching for the one he hoped to see.

"Timon," Garret said, his voice breaking.

"Dad!" the boy yelled. He started forward, and his aura, the color of a monarch butterfly's wing, stretched to meet Garret's.

"Let him see his father," Kronos said, as the guards restrained Timon. They released the boy, and Timon pelted straight toward Garret. Their auras mingled even before they touched, and Artemis was swept up in a vivid outpouring of love that obliterated all hate and anger with a single embrace. Garret lifted Timon off his feet and kissed his cheek, murmuring words of promise and comfort. Timon grinned, his slightly crooked teeth gleaming in a face less like Garret's than she had expected.

At last Garret set Timon down. The little boy examined his father's face, a deep line between his ginger eyebrows. "You're different," he said. "You're becoming like Mommy, aren't you?"

"Yes," Garret said, sobering quickly. "I'm sorry I couldn't tell you before I found you."

"That means you'll live a long time, like me," Timon said.

"Yes."

"And you won't go away, like Mommy."

Garret's throat worked. He turned Timon toward Artemis. "This is Artemis," he said. "She came here with me just to find you."

"And I am very glad to meet you," Artemis said.

Timon was wary. "Did *you* make Daddy this way?" he asked.

"Yes, she did," Garret said. "But I wanted her to."

"All right," Timon said, unfazed.

His resilience surprised Artemis, but she was profoundly grateful. He, like Garret, was a survivor, brave and strong. If the other children were like him...

"Mommy would be very proud of you," Garret said, his voice and aura thick with emotion. "Listen, Timon. I want you to stay with Artemis, no matter what happens. She's still stronger than I am. When we—"

"Did I give you the impression that I was letting you take the boy?" Kronos asked, leaning back in his chair. "I was simply curious to see if such a reunion would meet all my expectations." He smiled at Artemis. "Not at all like ours, was it, my child?"

"I was never your child," Artemis said, resting her hand on the crown of Timon's head.

The Master gestured at the Opiri who had brought Timon. "Bring eight of the children, the ones marked as of least value."

Artemis reached out with her free hand to grip Garret's arm, half-afraid that he might charge at Kronos again, and Timon grasped his father's fingers. It was as if a broken circle had suddenly been made complete, a circuit closed by the most powerful of emotions. Timon and Garret became one, and as *they* become one with *her*, a shifting aurora of red, orange and blue light enveloped them.

Timon's eyes grew very wide, and Garret froze. He was about to speak when a group of half-blood children, a mix of boys and girls, filed into the room. The guards pushed them to stand in front of Kronos's chair. Eight pairs of eyes, brown and blue and gray and black, fixed on Garret, Artemis and Timon without comprehension.

It was as if they had been placed in some kind of trance, made incapable of resistance, and this time Artemis thought *she* might be the one to fling herself at Kronos. She dropped her hand, and the glowing circle broke.

"Let them go," Garret said hoarsely. "If they're useless to you…"

"Of little use to my program, yes. But I think in terms of decades, not years as humans do. Everything you said of my little Freeblood army was correct. I know they will not be reliable soldiers over the long term. Once they have what they believe they want, they will falter, lose their discipline, turn their attention to selfish pursuits. That is in their nature.

"That is why I realized, even in the south, that I would need more malleable and adaptable troops for the future, after the initial work is done and the Citadels fall. Troops that can fight in daylight as well as in darkness, and who have absolute loyalty to me."

"My God," Garret said. He reached behind him to touch Timon again. "And you think you can mold these children so easily, make them forget their families and their lives?"

"I have no doubt of it. But that is only one aspect of my plan. Eventually, I will breed my own half-bloods from humans and Opiri captured in the first phase of my program."

"Decades," Artemis breathed. Her disgust and horror were building into a rage that might make even Garret recoil. "You have truly gone mad."

"I am not mad, Artemis. What I envision is a world dominated by those who are *both* human and Opiri. A world in which wars will eventually cease, because there won't be enough full-blood Opiri and humans to destroy each other, and this earth along with them. All I need to do is encourage each race's present fear of the other, and they will do most of the work for me."

"Not decades, but centuries," Garret said. "Unless you…"

There were no words, Artemis thought, to describe Garret's emotions then. They were so clear that she could see the images in his mind: terrible pictures of slaughter on a massive scale, people killing other people because they were of a different culture or appearance, or simply because it was convenient to get them out of the way.

"Genocide," Kronos said. "You humans tried it first. You have a long tradition of such cleansing. Your San Francisco Enclave developed a lethal virus that would have killed nearly every Opir who came in contact with infected blood."

"And good people stopped it," Garret said, his voice shaking.

"For the time being. The project can be revived."

"You cannot begin to implement your program without vast quantities of blood to support your troops," Artemis said. "You do not have enough humans to—"

"I am working on that, as well. I did say that I still saw value in some aspects of our original plan. Relieving Freebloods of their dependence on human blood is just the beginning, Artemis. There are dhampir half-breeds who do not require blood at all. I will have scientists working on this problem night and day, until we can extend those benefits to all Opiri."

"Will that matter to the Opiri and humans you have already slaughtered?"

Kronos leaned forward in his chair. "Just imagine, Artemis. A world of true peace. An earth permitted to heal. Is that not more important than the lives of a few thousand, even tens of thousands, of Opiri and humans?"

"You won't have peace," Garret said. "Eventually your

half-bloods will turn on each other, just as Opiri and humans have always done."

"But they have me," Kronos said, spreading his arms wide. "With Artemis's assistance, I will become their true father." He dropped his hands and signaled to the soldiers. The guards moved to stand behind the children, one Freeblood to each child.

"No," Garret said.

"There is a simple solution," Kronos said. "I will permit all of you to live, even to remain together. But only if Artemis agrees to stay with me."

"I can't," Artemis whispered. "I can't help you destroy—"

"I will be generous, my child. I will not expect you to work with me. I merely ask you to give your word that you will never use your abilities against me. If you were to break this agreement, then, of course, the boy and his father would die."

Garret looked down at Timon and then met Artemis's eyes. They both knew that Kronos was lying. He was still a powerful empath. If Artemis agreed to such a bargain, Kronos would find a way to coerce her into helping him. If she dropped her guard, and he got inside her mind…

Garret knelt before his son. "I'll need you to be very brave for a little while longer, Timon. Can you do that?"

"Yes, Daddy." Timon smiled and touched the tears on Garret's cheek. "I understand."

Garret rose and met Artemis's gaze. They didn't have to speak again.

"Do not harm the children," she said, bowing her head to Kronos. "I will do as you demand."

"Then come to me," Kronos said. "Release your vassal from your control, and he and the child will remain here as hostages, unharmed."

This, Artemis had not expected. Releasing Garret

meant breaking the newly formed bond between sire and vassal, and she had no idea what that would do to him. What it might do to *them*.

"Garret has not fully turned," she protested. "If I release him so soon…"

"You have made your choice," Kronos said. "Now do what must be done."

So he is counting on something going wrong, Artemis thought. Garret could become gravely ill or mentally unstable. She sent him a clear picture of the danger, unable to separate her fear from her warning. Timon was staring at her.

"It's all right," Garret said, as if he was reassuring her and Timon at the same time. But his gaze conveyed a far more complex message.

They would let Kronos think he had won.

"I must bite you again," she said softly. "But this time I will break the chemical bond that tethers you to me, and you will be free to do as you will."

"I understand," Garret said. He touched Timon's head. "Whatever you see, don't worry. Artemis is going to make me stronger."

"Okay," the boy said. But he grabbed Garret's hand again, and Artemis had to wait until Garret convinced his son to let go.

"Enough," Kronos said. "Artemis."

She expelled her breath and leaned toward Garret. "Listen to me," she said. "When it happens, drop all your mental barriers, even any you hold against Kronos. And give me all the strength you have."

It was obvious that he understood. He closed his eyes. She lowered her mouth to his throat and bit him quickly.

He stiffened. She tasted his blood and prepared to alter it yet again.

But more than merely his blood flowed into her. His

emotions—so complex, so familiar—mingled with hers and, as before, became so much a part of her that she could no longer separate his from her own. His belief in her buoyed her up above all fear and uncertainty.

Acting purely on the power of those emotions, Artemis shaped them into an arrow, nocked a bow crafted of unshakable conviction and let the missile fly.

Kronos began to rise from his chair, only beginning to guess at the danger when Garret and Artemis attacked. They made a single, surgical strike at the weakness Artemis had sensed before—the fear—and broke through. Kronos fought to restore his barriers, but Artemis and Garret were already flooding his mind, replacing greed and ambition and hatred with love and trust and hope.

Kronos tried to speak, to order his solders to strike at the children. His Freebloods stared at him, waiting for a command that never came.

"Return…the children to their quarters," Kronos whispered. "Leave me."

The guards escorted the children out of the room, and Kronos slumped in the chair like a discarded doll.

It is done, Artemis thought, still floating on the currents of two auras, two minds, two hearts joined in consummate harmony. *He cannot harm anyone now.*

Kronos croaked like a dying raven, gave a strangled laugh and shaped his mouth into a death's-head grin.

"Impressive," he said. "But where is…that admirable human quality…forgiveness?" His eyes fluttered closed. "What of…your wife, Mr. Fox?"

Chapter 25

The arrow rebounded and flew toward Artemis and Garret. Emotion become memory. Kronos's memory, of a time when his new ambitions had begun to take hold.

Garret bent almost double, and his pain battered Artemis like a fist.

"Pericles…didn't tell you," Kronos said. "It was when I was returning north, abandoning my first experiment. The Freebloods who remained with me…were beginning to starve. I sent them to raid a colony that…had the misfortune not to consider defense a priority." His voice hitched. "There was a Bloodlady. Very beautiful. I had heard of her. She…fought for her adopted humans with great courage."

Garret sobbed. Artemis fell to her knees beside him. He tried to push her away. Timon ran to him and put his small arms around his father's shoulders, tears streaking his face.

"I did not know…that you were her mate," Kronos said, "until Pericles said that Artemis had told him about your high-ranked Opir 'friend' who had died at the hands of rogue raiders. Artemis told me much about you and your origins, and I was able to deduce the rest." His chin dropped to his chest. "What have you won, Garret Fox?"

No, Artemis said silently. *No. No. No.*

Garret didn't hear her. His aura darkened until all traces of red were gone, until Garret himself was shrouded in shadows even Artemis couldn't penetrate.

He lifted his head. This time *he* nocked the arrow.

She fought the dark impulse the only way she knew how: with her love for Garret, with Garret's love for Timon and his unshakable belief in her. But he had created a wall impenetrable to every emotion but rage, and not even all her power and experience were enough to pierce it. Soon she found herself sucked in by the very love she felt for Garret…lost, ready to strike out, to obliterate Kronos's mind completely.

Daddy?

A small, warm hand clutched at hers. Suddenly she broke into two pieces—Artemis and Garret, with Timon between them.

Timon was the bridge.

"No, Garret," she said. *It will destroy you.*

"No, Daddy," Timon said, tugging on Garret's arm. "Stop!"

Garret blinked. His aura wavered, leaped again, guttered like a flame doused with water and then rose up greater than before. Hatred became a weapon deadly enough to destroy not only Kronos but every living being in the castle.

She had given him that weapon.

Artemis looked into Timon's eyes. "Can you help me again, Timon?" she asked. "Can we show him how much we love him?"

He hugged her tightly. "He loves us, too."

She was afraid to believe it, afraid to rely on emotions

that might not be real. But if she had to pretend in order to save Garret…

"Let's help him remember," she said.

If Garret had been in his right mind, he might have remembered that he had not always had this power. He might have realized that Artemis had given it to him when she changed him, when their minds and emotions had mingled and become indistinguishable from one another.

He might even have remembered that it was love that made it possible. But for him, now, there was no past, no future. Only the need to make *him* pay, the one who had taken Roxana and Timon from him.

Closing his eyes, Garret concentrated. The rage was a furnace inside him, a forge to create a weapon so powerful that nothing of his enemy would survive. And if the enemy's destruction reverberated outward, if it took the others of his kind down with him, there would be no one to mourn them.

The weapon took shape, red and black amid the seething flames. Garret seized it in his hands, but it did not burn him. It only grew larger, heavier, more potent. Its core began to hum with all the explosive energy of the world-killing bombs humanity had created during the War but never dared use.

Garret was not afraid to use *this* one. It began to vibrate, its shell no longer able to contain the energy of rage and hatred. He lifted it with his mind, positioned it, took aim.

We love you.

The words formed in his mind, distracting him from his purpose. He tried to brush them aside. They returned, more insistent than before.

We love you, Garret.

Love was a warm, soft light that wrapped around the

weapon, dulling its radiance, seeping into his soul. Again he tried to reject it, and again it refused to dissipate.

Love. Memory returned: of Roxana, and laughter, and Timon a babe in his arms. Love that even death could not destroy.

And then other memories: Artemis, when he had first met her…before he had realized how quickly his heart would accept her even when his mind could not. Artemis taking his blood, giving him a part of herself she shared with no other living being. Lying with her, joining with her, beginning to recognize the truth.

Love.

The weapon in his grip began to cool. He tried to hold on to it, but the memories were too thick now, and he was filled up with Artemis and Timon and the emotions that were everything his hatred was not. Emotions he couldn't fight, because the darkness he had harbored for so long could not endure the light.

But then the new images formed in his mind. Ugly, distorted, unbearable scenes of death at the hands of savages.

See how your Bloodlady suffered, the enemy said. *See how she died.*

Light collapsed in on itself. Garret grasped the weapon again. Timon vanished. Only Artemis remained, a small, blue point of radiance nearly overwhelmed by the shadows.

He tried to push her out, but she resisted. The blue began to spread. It crept into the dark corners, invaded the crevices, exposed the monsters. And as she advanced, she absorbed the bitterness and rage and need to destroy. She took them into herself. The blue became a crystal, ever-expanding, threatening to crack with the pressure building inside it.

Too late, Garret turned against his darkness. Too late, he reached for the blue, strove to hold the pieces together.

The crystal exploded, hurling shards toward the source

of pain. A roar deafened Garret, and he felt blindly for Timon. He wrapped his arms around the small body and curled himself over it.

Then the shadows were gone. He opened his eyes. Kronos lay on the ground before his throne, staring, mouth ajar. He was still breathing, but there was nothing behind his eyes. No emotion. No mind.

Artemis knelt a few feet away, rocking slowly, tremors working through her body. Garret swept Timon up and carried him to her side.

"Artemis?" he whispered.

Pericles ran into the room, panting heavily, and skidded to a stop when he saw Kronos. He leaned over his knees, catching his breath.

"I… Is he…?"

"He can't hurt anyone else now," Garret said, crouching beside Artemis and lifting her chin.

Pericles straightened. "I just found out…that there's an army on the other side of the ridge."

"An army?" Garret asked, tearing his gaze away from Artemis's face.

"Soldiers from three Enclaves are here looking for the children," Pericles said, "and they've trapped the Freebloods who've been escaping from the camp."

"Human soldiers?"

"Not only humans," Pericles said. "Some Opiri, too, from the colonies, but they've all come for the same thing. They blame all of us for the kidnappings."

"You *are* to blame," Garret said coldly. "How many Freebloods are trapped?"

"Hundreds. I don't know how many are still in the camp, but the ones who escaped were trying to get out of the valley when they were surrounded. Kronos sent most of his soldiers to deal with the deserters, but the soldiers and refugees are outnumbered fifty to one." He swallowed. "Daniel is down there, too. He's trying to keep the humans from attacking, but it's only working because some of the humans and Opiri don't want to cooperate with each other."

Daniel, Garret thought. Somehow, he wasn't surprised.

"Artemis," Pericles said, moving toward her, "I know you came here to get Timon and free the children. But you care about our people, too. You know they're not all bad. You believed in me. A lot of them were misled as I was. You were, too. You can help us."

Artemis didn't answer. Garret cradled her face in his hands.

"What's wrong with her?" Pericles asked.

"I don't know," Garret said, stroking Artemis's temples with his thumbs. "She doesn't seem to hear us." He stared at Pericles. "She can't help you now."

Pericles backed toward the tunnel. With a low moan, Artemis stirred. Garret's attention snapped back to her, and he tried to feel her mind.

It was as if they'd never had any empathic bond at all. He remembered how she had tried to absorb his fury and hatred. He remembered a blue crystal of pure emotion, remembered trying to hold it together as Artemis struggled to control the forces he had unleashed within himself.

He had not defeated Kronos. *She* had. And she had paid a terrible price for her victory.

He glanced at Timon, whose eyes were shining with tears. "She's very far away," Garret said. "We have to help her until she can find her way back."

Timon nodded, biting his lip. "What should we do?" he asked.

"I want you to stay with Artemis. Take care of her." He kissed Timon's forehead. "You were very brave. Now be brave for her."

He left his son with the woman his rage had nearly destroyed and went in search of the children. Around the corner he found a long corridor punctuated by cell doors that seemed to stretch far into the distance. All the soldiers were unconscious, sprawled across the floor like puppets with cut strings.

The doors were unlocked. One by one he opened them and released the children inside. Nearly a hundred half-bloods of all shapes and sizes emerged, most under ten years old, frightened and hungry and bewildered.

With a few words of comfort and a promise that no one would hurt them again, he ushered them to the main room. They hesitated when they saw Kronos, but Garret showed them that the Master was unable to move or speak, and they scurried past him. With all the natural resiliency of children they began to talk in low tones, staring around the room as if to confirm the bewildering fact that they were free.

Artemis was on her knees, Timon pressed close to her. They both looked up at Garret as he went to them.

"Artemis," Garret said, dropping beside her. "Are you all right?"

"The children…are well?" she asked, ignoring his question.

She can't feel them, Garret thought. He suppressed his despair and smiled.

"They will be," he said. "Like you."

Her smile was a mask over a hollow space. "The empathy…it's gone," she said. "For so long I lived without it. I pushed it away. But now that I don't have it…"

"You'll get it back," Garret said, holding her gently by the shoulders.

"I don't know what you're feeling," she said.

"Don't you?" He pulled her close to his chest with one arm and hugged Timon with the other. "You don't need to see into my thoughts, Artemis. You saved me and defeated Kronos. You need time to heal."

"Can you feel *me*?" she asked.

He realized that he still registered some of her emotions: anguish and fear and a tiny mote of hope buried deep underneath.

"I know you're hurting," he said, "and that I'm to blame. But you will heal. I promise."

She touched his face. "I heard Pericles," she said. "About the army. He wanted me to help."

"There's nothing you can do."

"But they *are* my people, whatever they have done," Artemis said. "Kronos would have given them an evil purpose. They must find a better one."

"But it's not your responsibility to find it for them," Garret said, mastering his anger.

"A war is about to begin," she said. "The war we never wanted to see happen again. If it starts here with slaughter, it will not end here."

"But I know what Pericles would have asked you to do…use your empathy to influence the soldiers threatening the Freebloods. It would have been wrong then, and it's impossible now." He lowered his voice. "We're taking the children someplace safe until their people can reach them. That's all that matters."

Supporting her weight against his body, Garret helped her to her feet. Timon huddled close, shyly reaching for Artemis's hand.

She half turned to stare at Kronos. "We can't leave him here," she said. "What if he wakes?"

"He won't," Garret said. "Your empathy was damaged because of my emotions, but what *he* suffered went far beyond that. If he recovers at all—"

He stopped, thinking about the children. They'd suffered enough horror without knowing that a powerful man's mind could be broken beyond repair.

"The children," Artemis murmured. "You're right. We must get them away."

Together, they gathered up the children again and moved among them, speaking personally to as many as possible. Artemis was as easy with them as she had been with Timon, but Garret knew she was relying on her own natural goodness and not on what their feelings told her.

They were discussing what to do with the children when Pericles returned.

Artemis went to him at once. "Has the war begun?" she asked.

"Artemis!" Pericles said, flashing a grin. "You're all right!"

"Has anyone been hurt?"

Pericles's smile faded. "No, but—"

"Find Daniel," Garret said, sensing Artemis's plan. "Tell him to keep talking to the humans and Opir who have come for the children. Tell them that we'll bring the children to them by sunset, but that they must not attack."

"You don't understand," Pericles said, panic rising in his voice. "They're already coming. They're outside the castle *now*!"

Chapter 26

Garret listened. He'd become something more than human, and now he could hear what he'd been too pre-occupied to notice earlier: many voices and hundreds of marching feet. He smelled the dust kicked up by their boots, their perspiration, their fear.

It wasn't only the invading army approaching the castle. The Freeblood deserters were with them.

"They have prisoners," Garret said to Artemis. "If you want to save the Freebloods, we have to show the humans and Opiri that the children are all right."

"Can we go?" a dhampir girl asked from among the crowd of half-blood children. "Is it safe?"

Safe, Garret thought. Anything might happen with passions burning hot and humans afraid for the abducted half-bloods.

"I still look pretty human," Garret said. "I'll go ahead and find Daniel." He touched Artemis's cheek. "I need you and Pericles to stay and take care of the kids until I give the signal."

"Garret—"

"If the humans see you, they may act before they think. You must stay here, Artemis."

She met his gaze. "You cannot protect me from everything."

"No," he said bitterly. "Not even from myself." He dropped his hand. "Please look after Timon. I promise I'll return as soon as I can."

He turned to go.

Artemis called after him. "I am sorry about your wife," she said. "So very sorry."

Unable to find his voice, Garret entered the tunnel and retraced the route back to the bailey. The covered courtyard was deserted, as were the battlements. He paused to listen to the increasingly agitated voices outside the high gates. Someone was demanding that the hostages be punished if the Master did not appear. Others were debating an assault on the gate or suggesting scaling the walls.

Garret found several daycoats hanging along the wall inside the gate, thought about the sunlight and what it might do to him, and decided to risk exposure. The less he looked like a Nightsider, the better.

He took a deep breath, thought of Artemis and the children, and threw all his strength into opening the castle gates. He stepped out into the sunlight, wincing at the sudden discomfort.

"Daniel!" he shouted.

The human soldiers surged forward, weapons bristling, threatening to trample Garret beneath their booted feet. The Freeblood prisoners, many of them trapped among the forward troops, faced the same danger.

"Stop!" someone shouted. Daniel emerged from the

packed line of men and women, and stood between them and Garret, a lone figure holding the wolves at bay.

"Garret," he said, gripping Garret's forearms and staring into his changing eyes. "Pericles told me what she'd done to you."

"Artemis did nothing but help me," Garret said. "We have the children."

"The Master—"

"—can't hurt anyone now."

"He's dead?"

"Even if he recovers, he'll never have the full use of his mind. Artemis made sure of that."

Daniel didn't ask any awkward questions. "Is Timon all right?"

"He's inside with Artemis and the other children." Garret peered over Daniel's head. "Get them to back off. I won't bring the kids out if there's any threat to them or Artemis." He met his old friend's gaze again. "Do you understand, Daniel? Whatever you may think Artemis has done, she's on our side. And she's not well."

"What's wrong with her?"

Garret closed his eyes. "She lost something," he said. "I'm not sure if it's permanent. But Timon and I will both be there for her."

"She was never your wife, was she?"

"Not yet."

Daniel nodded. "I'll get the human troops to back off so the children can come out."

"You'll need to do more than that," Garret said. "You have to persuade the armies to let the Freebloods go. They were under the influence of a Bloodlord who lied to them and backed up those lies with power you can't begin to imagine. Killing them will be murder, and there's still a chance they can change."

"How?" Daniel said. "No mixed colony will take them

in. They'll go back to scavenging and raiding, as they've always done."

"No," Artemis said, coming up beside Garret. "I will see that they do not."

Garret looked at Artemis in her heavy daycoat, knowing he'd been a fool for thinking she would stay inside just because he wanted to keep her safe.

But it was her words he found most alarming. He didn't get the chance to ask her what she meant, because there was a great heave in the crowd on the causeway as Daniel passed on Garret's message about the children. The human soldiers dragged the Freebloods back with them, leaving a clear space in front of the gate. A moment later the children emerged, Timon in the fore. He ran to Garret and put his arms around his waist. The other children, blinking in the sunlight, drifted out behind him.

There were cries of recognition and relief scattered among the troops, and currents of movement as parents tried to shove their way toward the gate. Running feet, happy cries, weeping. Joy.

But there was also fear. Kronos's deserters were still trapped, and not all the anger was gone, not from the parents and kin who wanted revenge.

Revenge that would destroy everything it touched.

"Timon," Garret said, touching his son's soft red hair. "You were too young to remember my friend Daniel, but he came to help the children. He would very much like to talk to you about them."

Timon subjected Daniel to a grave, assessing examination. "All right, Daddy," he said. "Will you take care of Artemis?"

"I'm going to talk to her now." Garret nodded to Daniel, who knelt to Timon's level, and then left them to guide Artemis back into the bailey.

"Artemis," he said softly, "you need to rest. You shouldn't have—"

"I am not ill," she said. Her eyes were focused, no longer shadowed or dazed with loss. "My mind is clearer than it has been in a very long time."

"You're temporarily disabled. No one expects—"

"Not disabled," she said. "Only different. Better able to serve my purpose."

"Your purpose is to live your life fully," he said. "Live it with me, with Timon."

"No. I have a duty, Garret." She looked out the gate at a group of cowering Freebloods. Terrified and angry, remorseful and defiant, women and men. Those who had been Opiri for many decades and others who had been changed only within the past year. They were, Garret thought, no more alike than any given set of humans.

"Look at them," Artemis said. "I searched for a way to help my people make a new life, and now that chance has been given to me. Kronos betrayed these Freebloods. They must have something to replace the false dreams he gave them. Peace is still possible, but only if they can truly learn another way. And now that I have lost my empathy, I will never be tempted to misuse it."

Suddenly Garret realized that he was truly on the verge of losing her. She had suffered a severe mental trauma with Kronos's defeat, and her convictions had been shattered by his betrayal of everything she had held dear.

If he couldn't make her see that they belonged together…

"Artemis," he said, "no matter how brave you are or how well you can lead, you're only one woman. You've done enough."

She met his gaze with deep sadness. "When you left your colony, did you truly believe that you would find Timon? Did you imagine that you would help free all the stolen children and destroy the Opir who caused so much suffering?"

"I didn't do any of it alone," he said. "You were there."

"But you would have fought to do those things even if you had never met me," she said. "If I let doubt stop me now, I will always know that I failed."

"No." He took her by the arms carefully, desperate to make her listen. "There are other ways you can make a difference. If you were to join a mixed colony, you could help Freebloods acclimate and understand how their lives will change as functional members of a peaceful society. Admittedly it would be on a smaller scale, but you would be contributing something truly valuable to our future."

"Our future," she said. "Kronos... *I* always believed that the only safe way for Opiri and humans to coexist is to live separately, apart from corrupting temptation."

"Kronos was wrong. Living apart isn't a lasting solution. We have to find a way to exist together, Opiri and humans. Free and equal. As you and I have been."

He didn't have to feel her emotions to know how much she was struggling, torn by conflicting desires. But one of those desires was to stay with him.

To love him.

"Think, Artemis," he said. "You saw how Timon responded to you. I haven't seen him this way since his mother died. He needs you now, as much as he needs me."

"I want only happiness for you and Timon."

"Then you'll have to help us find it, Artemis."

"I can never be what Roxana was to you." She gazed across over the massed humans and Opiri to the mountains. Snow began to fall, settling gently on her hood. "Accept what must be, Garret. Return to your people."

"And who *are* my people?" he asked. "I'm a Freeblood now. I won't go back to Avalon, and I can't accept Daniel's way. I certainly won't join a pack and hunt humans. Timon and I have to make a new home. We can't do it alone."

"Of course you can," she said. "You are one of the strongest men I have ever known."

"Daddy?" Timon ran up to Garret and hugged his legs, pressing his face into Garret's pants. "I want to go." He held out his hand to Artemis. "Come on, Artemis."

She looked away.

Timon's lip began to tremble. "What's wrong, Daddy?" he asked.

Garret bent and lifted Timon to his shoulder. "Artemis has a hard decision to make. She wants to help people who don't have any place to go. I want her to stay with us."

"Me, too," Timon said.

Artemis clenched her fists. "You cannot coerce me, Garret."

"But I can and will use every means to convince you."

"I have heard your arguments," she said in a low voice.

"But not the final one." He set Timon down and turned her face toward him. "I love you."

Her expression crumpled, and he thought he'd won. But she was still fighting him, and he could think of only one reason why.

"You don't feel the same way," he said, forcing the words around the knot in his throat.

She shook her head. "I know how much you loved Roxana. No one can take her place."

"That's right. No one can. But I don't want a replacement. I want you, for as long as we live."

"It is not in the nature of Opiri to mate for life."

"It's not in the nature of Nightsiders to give up on human blood, but that's what you expect them to do." He ran the pad of his thumb along her cheekbone. "What proof do you need, Artemis?"

She didn't answer. Her gaze turned inward, as if she were seeking refuge from the pull of too many obligations.

"She's so sad," Timon whispered.

"Very sad," Garret said. "Are you feeling well enough to stay with Daniel a little while longer?"

"Will you make Artemis feel better?"

"I hope so, Timon."

The boy hugged Garret again and went out the gate. Fighting the need to pull Artemis into his arms, Garret could think of only one other way to reach her. He closed off the outside world—all the smells, the noise, the feelings—and reached inside himself, digging beyond the surface of his emotions, into their core, and then deeper still, where he had gathered the fragments of a shattered blue crystal.

Then he released his hold on the physical plane completely. Like a diver plunging into a lightless ocean, he swam so far beneath the surface that he could no longer even sense the presence of land.

But he was Opir now. He could see in darkness. He glimpsed the crystal and stretched his hand to grasp it. His fingers slipped. He tried again.

And caught it.

Jagged edges cut into his palm. He hurled himself up, fighting for breath, searching for a surface that seemed to have disappeared completely.

Artemis, he said.

No answer. He held the crystal close to his heart, hardened his will and hurled it into darkness.

Catch it, Artemis, he said. *It's yours. And mine. And Timon's.*

It is life.

The crystal shot through the darkness and vanished. Garret's lungs filled with shadows as thick and choking as mud. He continued to fight, reaching for the one thing that could draw him home.

Her hand caught his. She pulled him up and up, and his body regained its strength. The water was suffused with blue light, shot through with streaks of orange.

He broke the surface. Artemis's lips were on his, breathing life back into him, her love around and inside him.

When she released him, her emotions were as crystal clear and vivid as the waters of a pristine lake.

"I *felt* them," she said. "Your feelings, your—"

"Love," he said, lacing his fingers through her hair. "And I feel yours, Artemis. You can't run from it."

"I cannot run from my people. But I—" She searched Garret's eyes. "I won't leave you now."

Her anguish almost undid him. He thought of the new life he and Timon would have to make. He thought with pride of his son's courage and resilience, his ability to see a woman just like his kidnappers as a person worthy of love.

But could Timon adapt to a life completely unlike the one he'd always known, a life with the very people who had taken his mother, then taken *him*?

"I need to talk to Timon," Garret said, touching Artemis's hand. "Don't go anywhere."

He walked out the gate to find Timon. He drew him aside and talked with him, not at all certain of what to expect.

When the conversation was finished, he took his son by the hand and led him back to Artemis. She smiled at Timon, though Garret could see how much it cost her.

"Timon and I have talked it over," Garret said. "We think that what you have to do is important for the whole world. That's why we're coming with you."

Her eyes widened. "Coming with me?"

"To teach the Freebloods how to live in peace with humans. I'm one of you now. We can make a difference."

"But you—" She broke off. "I can't let you give up everything you know to help those you have regarded as your enemies for so long."

"I have no hate left in me, Artemis," he said. "You leeched that poison. You took my humanity, but you gave me new eyes to see with. Let me use them. Let me help you."

"Me, too!" Timon said. He puffed out his chest. "*I'm* not afraid."

Artemis looked down at him. "He has been through so much. As brave as he is…"

"It's the children who will make the difference in the end," Garret said. "Timon is an ambassador to the future." He laid his hand on his son's head. "If he finds it too difficult, we'll do whatever we have to. Until then, let him try."

A voice Garret recognized carried over the murmur of shuffling feet, shifting bodies and low conversation. Pericles was speaking with Daniel. He glanced toward Garret and Artemis, turned and slipped away into the crowd.

"What about Pericles?" Artemis asked. "He is not an innocent."

"Kronos mocked us about forgiveness," Garret said, watching the young Nightsider disappear. "I can't forgive the Freebloods who killed Roxana, but eventually I'll have to accept the ones who took the children. I can try to start with Pericles."

"That is all any of us can do," she said. "Try to begin again." She looked into his eyes. "Thank you," she said. "Thank you for believing in me. For this sacrifice."

"Where is the sacrifice?" He gathered her into his arms.

"I love you." Their emotions mingled, and Artemis flung back her head and laughed.

"I love you," she said. "I *love* you."

"Me, too!" Timon said.

They pulled him close, and they all laughed together.

* * * * *

Debbie Herbert writes paranormal romance novels reflecting her belief that love, like magic, casts its own spell of enchantment. She's always been fascinated by magic, romance and gothic stories. Married and living in Alabama, she roots for the Crimson Tide football team. Her oldest son, like many of her characters, has autism. Her youngest son is in the US Army. A past MAGGIE® Award finalist in both young-adult and paranormal romance, she's a member of the Georgia Romance Writers of America. Visit her on the web at debbieherbert.com.

Books by Debbie Herbert

Harlequin Nocturne

Dark Seas

Siren's Secret
Siren's Treasure
Siren's Call
Bayou Shadow Hunter

Visit the Author Profile page
at Harlequin.com for more titles.

BAYOU SHADOW HUNTER

Debbie Herbert

This book is dedicated to my mother,
April Deanne Goodson Gainey,
who passed away while I wrote this book.
I thank her for her belief in me as a woman
and as a writer. Miss you, Mom.

Chapter 1

"Thunder Moon comin' tonight. Yer life is fixin' to change."

Grandma Tia called the August full moon "Thunder Moon" and proclaimed it a time of enchantment. Annie had to admit tonight *did* appear magical and mysterious. The forest beckoned with its thick canopy of trees draped in long tendrils of Spanish moss that fluttered in the sea breeze with a silver shimmer like a living veil of secrecy.

And so they had burned tiny scraps of paper where they'd written what they wanted purged from their lives. As she'd done every month for most of her life, Annie had written only one thing. The same thing. She held the paper to candle flame, watching it catch fire and curl in on itself before the wind carried it away. It splintered into tiny embers that flickered like fireflies before turning to ash.

Annie sat on the bed, hugging her knees to her chest and staring out the window, pondering her grandma's words. She could use some change. Lots of it. If only she could get rid of… No. No point agonizing over that, when she was so close to sleep.

A green glow skittered erratically in the swampy darkness.

Very pretty. Annie turned away from the bedroom window, yawned and slipped into bed, pulling a thin cotton sheet over her head like a cocoon.

Wait a minute… She jerked to a sitting position and peered out the window across the room. Each glass pane framed squares of refracted moonbeams piercing through tumbles of tree limbs. A patchwork quilt of the macabre.

But on second glance, no green, glowing orbs of light dotted the night's landscape. Must have been a trick of the eye or the flash of a dream. Perhaps it was merely that Grandma had planted the suggestion of something magical happening tonight when they had gone outside after dinner and held a brief lunar ritual. Full moons represented death and change, a time for powerful magic.

A ball of light again materialized at the tree line, not more than twenty feet from their cottage. It burned blue at the center and green at the edges. Annie instinctively touched the silver cross nestled in the hollow of her throat, palm flattening above the rapid thumping of her heart.

A teal stream of light broke away from the orb, forming a tail like a comet hurtling across the night sky. The pixilated specks of color were magical as fairy dust, coalescing into the shape of an arm, beckoning her closer.

Dare she?

Annie scrambled off the bed, feet touching the rough-hewn pine floorboard, still sun-warmed from the day's ferocious heat. She raced to the back door and slid into flip-flops she kept at the entry. Hand on the door, she paused and glanced to her left. Grandma's bedroom door was open, and her deep, labored breathing wafted across the cottage. Annie softly tiptoed to the room and peeked inside.

Grandma Tia's hair was wrapped in a satin cloth that nestled against a white pillowcase. Her lined face was relaxed in a way only produced by sweet dreams. The weight and worry of time and life's sorrows laid aside in a few hours of respite.

She wouldn't rouse her from slumber. Grandma Tia's heart condition meant she needed rest. Annie's eyes rested on the red flannel gris-gris bag hung on the bedpost. Which reminded her to grab her own mojo bag. She hurried back to her bedroom, retrieved it from beneath the pillow and tied it to the drawstring of her pajama bottoms. Just in case. A quick glance out the window confirmed the green light still hovered a few feet above ground.

Despite the late hour, humidity cocooned her body in a damp embrace the moment she stepped outside. To top it off, the light had disappeared again. She sat on the concrete porch steps and lifted her hair off the back of her sticky nape, waiting and watching.

Probably nothing but swamp gas. The night buzzed with a battalion of insects, and she cocked her head to one side, listening, actively expanding her energy outward to pick up even the subtlest of sound—the wind swirling clumps of sand, the hoot of an owl far away—all against the eternal ebb and flow of the distant ocean tide.

What was she doing out here? Normally, she wouldn't think of investigating something alone, but, like a cat, curiosity overrode her fear.

Something prickled her skin. The air danced with a faint tinkling—like the fading echo of tiny bells rung from deep within the forest. Annie closed her eyes, gathering the vibration of musical notes, assimilating a pattern: *one*, two, two, *three*, two, two, *five*, two, two.

Melodic patterns had called to her since kindergarten

when a teacher handed out metal triangles and wands. She'd pinged the base, and the ringing vibration had shivered down her spine. A living pulse that had been a first clue of her gift, her curse, her fate. Other kids had banged away on the triangles until the pureness of the music changed to an unbearable din, and she'd run out of the classroom.

She'd been running ever since.

But tonight's high-pitched bell notes made her feet itch to dance and throw her arms open to embrace the night. It had a certain symmetry and lyrical quality that charmed. It drew her, tugged at her soul...

Annie opened her eyes. More than a dozen orbs of light danced in the distant darkness. They were a rainbow of colors and sizes and varied in brightness.

That was where the music came from.

They called her, beckoned her to draw near. She rose unsteadily to her feet, light-headed with awe, and slowly stepped away from the cottage. The lights bobbed and darted behind and between the oaks. All at once, the orbs disappeared, as if someone had turned off a switch. Annie ran toward the woods. For once she ran *to* the music instead of *away* from its source.

Wait for me. Don't leave me behind.

As if hearing the unspoken words, a bluish-green orb flashed. A spectacular, southern aurora borealis. It was the first, lone light she'd seen from the bedroom window, as distinctive and individual as a human form. She ran across the yard, plunged into the woods, down a narrow trail littered with pinecones and broken twigs. Black night, thick with heat, pressed around her body, yet she stumbled forward, ever deeper. More lights bobbled ahead, just beyond reach. Mosquitoes buzzed her ears and nipped her arms and chest. The sulfur smell of swampland grew more pungent and sharp.

Annie didn't care. The blue light glowed like a lantern against the darkness, and the crystalline notes played from its burning core. Low-lying branches scraped her arms and face, and her legs grew wooden with exhaustion as on she walked, following ever deeper.

A clearing opened onto a muddy bank, and Annie pulled up short at the sight of a brackish pond. Mud gooshed over her sandals and between her toes. The slimy sensation worked like a face slap. Blackness shadowed the night as a cloud passed over the moon, and the glowing orbs vanished once more. The music stopped, and silence gathered, dense and foreboding.

"Umm…hello? Anybody out there?" She didn't know whether she felt more foolish or frightened. She lifted one foot out of the goo and almost lost a sandal. "Terrific. This is just great."

Screeching erupted—as if a parliament of enraged owls or a volt of vultures were descending on her for interloping on their territory. Annie clamped hands over ears and squeezed her fingertips over the ear canals, but the noise and pressure felt like a bomber plane taking off inside her brain. Turning blindly, she ran, desperate to escape the sound attack.

What the hell is this? Where is it coming from? It was like a combination of an animal screech, a howl of pain, shattering glass and a jarring, jumbled chorus of dissonant chords, as if someone were banging an untuned piano.

Silence crashed the darkness. Annie leaned her back against an oak tree and hunched down, panting. Relieved the noise had stopped but expecting it to return any moment, her body was coiled and tense. She grimaced at the stitch in her side and tried to regulate her breathing to a slower pace. *Calm down. Think.*

She tilted her head upward, rough bark grazing her scalp. The moon glowed, laced with a web of black thread from the treetops. The sky held a thin promise of dawn, evidenced only by a violet-hued line in the east that graduated to black by degrees.

Great. So she knew where east lay. But that was the extent of her internal compass. And it didn't help her figure out how to get back to the cottage. Best to stay right where she was and wait for daylight. If she was lucky, someone, maybe a hunter, would be along, or she would recognize some landmark once the sun emerged.

How could she have been so stupid as to trot off at night into the bayou after a will-o'-the-wisp or whatever that light was? She shuddered. Focus. Right now there were rattlers and water moccasins and gators to worry about. And who knew what other cursed creatures roamed the land.

She swatted at a mosquito nipping her arm. Hmm. Could snakes climb trees? A glance upward revealed that seeking higher ground was a non-option. The nearest limb was several feet above her standing height. When she recouped her strength, perhaps she should search for a stone or stick just in case...

"Help me!"

The deep baritone voice rumbled along her spine.

Annie scrambled to her feet and searched the shadows. "Who's there?"

Silence. Okay, she was going to be that person in the headline news who was lost in the woods and found days later, a nutcase raving about swamp monsters and Big Foot and saying she'd been carted away by aliens on their UFO.

Nothing's out there.

"Please."

The anguish in that word was too tortured not to be real. Annie shivered despite the heat and sweat coating her body. Ignoring someone else's pain went against all her healing instincts. "Where are you? *Who* are you?"

An orb manifested not ten feet from where she stood.

No warning, no gathering of light, no sound. One second before loomed a dark void, and in a clock's single tick, the orb absorbed the space.

The blue-green light swirled and pulsed like a breathing, living thing. The same orb she'd seen first from her bedroom window.

So the question was no longer where or who but "*What* are you?" she whispered.

"The shadows trapped me."

The voice rumbled in her gut, vibrating in her being. "You're…trapped in the light?" she asked haltingly.

"My heart beats within. Look."

At the core of the blue light shone a concentrated mass of teal that swelled and contracted. In, out, in, out, pulsing with the cosmic rhythm of life.

A heart.

Not the flowers-and-lace, cupid sort drawn by five-year-olds, but the it's-alive-and-it's-real-and-it-beats kind. Annie's breath hitched, and she took an unsteady step backward. She couldn't stop staring at the fist-sized gelatinous mass of muscle that pumped and wobbled.

"I need out," the low-timbered voice pleaded. "Help me get out."

She shook her head violently, her own heart pounding a song of fear. "I don't know how." And even if she did, no way was she freeing…whatever it was. Not until she knew its true nature.

"My name is Bo," it said. "Find Tombi and tell him I live. He's in grave danger. Trust no one within the circle. I was betrayed. And if he was ever my true friend, he needs to find that betrayer. I can't be released until then."

"I don't know this Tombi person," she protested.

"He's coming now. Tell him to beware."

Annie swung her head in all directions but saw and

sensed nothing in the shadows. "Why don't you tell him yourself?"

"He can't hear me, witch. No one ever has but you."

"Oh," she breathed. "That's why you brought me here." It... Bo...either knew her grandma or of her reputation. "I think you want my grandmother, not me. I'm only here on a visit and—"

"Warn him."

The light shifted, swirling in individuated sparkles and growing smaller, denser.

"Wait," she called out sharply. "Where are you going?"

But it had vanished.

A man slipped into her presence, silent as a windless sky. He leaned against a cypress, arms folded, face and body as unyielding and hard as the ancient tree. Eyes and hair were black as the night, and the only lightness on his figure was a golden sheen on his face and arms.

Friend or foe?

Silence blanketed her mind. A condition she normally welcomed, but not now. Where was her accursed ability when she needed it? Not the slightest syllable of sound surrounded the man.

"Who are you?" she asked, hoping her voice didn't portray fear.

He stepped closer, and she willed her feet to remain rooted to the ground, to cloak the fear.

"Who are *you*?" His voice was deep, sharp-edged with suspicion.

She'd been wrong. The golden sheen of his skin wasn't the only thing that stood out in the darkness. The man's eyes radiated a copper glint like an encapsulated sun with rays. His teeth were white and sharp.

He didn't wait for an answer. "Who were you talking to? There's no one else out here but us."

"I was talking to myself," she lied. No sense exposing herself to ridicule.

"Roaming the woods alone at night and talking to yourself?" He scowled. "You must be crazy."

Despite the scowl and rough tone, the icy touch of fear at the base of her spine thawed a bit. This stranger could think what he wanted about her mental health and lecture her ad nauseam about the idiotic decision to follow the wisp. At least he wasn't attacking her. If he meant harm, he could have lunged forward and grabbed her by now.

"Yes." Annie agreed. "I'm totally off my rocker." Wouldn't be the first time someone thought that. "How about being a good Boy Scout and help me find my way home?"

"First, tell me your name and why you're out here."

"Fine. My name's Annie Matthews, and I saw a strange light from my bedroom window. Like an idiot, I decided to check it out. Now, can you please get me out of here?"

He stared, those strange copper rays in his irises warming her insides. Abruptly, he turned his back and stepped away.

What a jerk. Annie's lips tightened to a pinched line. "Hey—wait a minute. Are you going to help me or not?"

The man didn't even look back but motioned with an arm for her to follow.

She let out a huge sigh. Jerk or not, her best bet was to follow him out of the swamp. Annie stumbled after him and onto the barest sliver of a trail. The narrow footpath was canopied by pines and oaks, obscuring the full-moon light. Her toe caught under a tree root, and she pitched forward, free-falling. She braced herself for the impact of packed dirt to face.

Strong arms grabbed the sides of her waist, and her chest bumped solid flesh. Annie raised her chin and stared deeply into the brown eyes. "Th-thank you," she whispered. His hands above her hips held fast, steadying her—burning her. Annie's hands rested lightly on his chest, and she couldn't move or speak.

A low, thudding bass note, a drumbeat, pounded in her ears. Was it from her heart beating faster, or was sound escaping his controlled aura?

"I forget you can't see like me." He took one of her hands in his. "Stay close."

Before she could object or ask what his remark meant, he pulled her forward.

She should be terrified alone in the woods with a stranger.

But for the first time since hearing the voice inside the wisp, Annie felt safe.

The narrow trail of dense shrubs and overarching tree limbs gave way to a wider, more open trail illuminated by the Thunder Moon. It was as if he were leading her down a silent passage that exited a nightmare.

At the edge of the tree line lay an open field. Weeds and brambles rippled, silver-tipped from moonbeams and glistening like drops of water dancing on waves. A glow flickered in Grandma Tia's cottage, a lighthouse beam signaling home.

Annie glanced at the man's chiseled profile. Harsh, fierce even. *Handsome* seemed too pretty a word to describe him. He was powerful, a force of the night.

"Beyond this field is a dirt road that leads to County Road 143. Know where you are now?"

She laughed, giddy with relief, and pointed to the cottage. "Of course. That's my grandma's house. Her name's Tia Henrietta. Maybe you've met her before?"

"The witch in the woods?" Surprise flickered in his eyes. "I should have guessed. Are you one, as well?"

She tugged her hand away from his. "No more than you."

His hand reached out and stroked the red flannel mojo pouch belted at her waist. "What magic is this?"

"Gris-gris bags. My grandma makes them. For protection."

"Didn't work, huh?"

"Sure it did. It brought you to me, and then you brought me home."

His lips curled. "I don't know what kind of magic your grandmother claims to have, but that pouch didn't help you when the will-o'-the-wisp conjured you into the woods."

"What do you know of them?" she asked, burning with curiosity now the danger had passed.

He ignored her question. "So you followed this light. What happened next?"

She bit her lip. "Looks like I'm the one doing all the talking. How about I tell you one thing, then you tell me one thing?"

He nodded. "Deal."

"Okay, then. The light disappeared a few minutes. When it came back, something inside it spoke." Annie took a deep breath. This wasn't easy to talk about. This was partly what alienated her from everyone. The crazy sticker on her forehead.

But the man didn't flinch. "What did it say?"

Annie hedged. Once again, she was doing most of the talking. "Tell me your name."

"Tombi. Tombi Silver."

She inhaled sharply, and his eyes narrowed.

"What is it?" he demanded.

"The voice. It mentioned you by name."

He leaned in and grabbed her arms, not bruising-hard, but enough so that she couldn't run away. "What. Did. It. Say?"

What the hell. This wouldn't be the first time she'd been used as a conduit for messages. Best to relay it and get on with her life. Otherwise, the wisp or spirit, or whatever that thing was, would keep appearing in some form or another until it had its way.

"It said you were in great danger and to trust no one, not even your inner circle. That there's a betrayer in your ranks, and if you were ever his true friend you need to find the betrayer, so he can be released."

She didn't think it possible the man—Tombi—could look fiercer, but he did. He let go of her and shook his head.

"No. I don't believe you."

Annie hitched her shoulders and raised her palms. "Fine. But that's what the thing told me."

"Did it have a name?"

"Bo."

Ringing flooded Tombi's ears. *There's worse things than witches. Much worse.*

"What did Bo say?"

Annie recoiled, and he realized he was shouting. With great effort, he lowered his voice. "Tell me what he said."

"He's trapped inside a wisp and wants you to free him."

Guilt and anger heaved in his stomach. "I've been trying to find him for weeks. Why didn't he come to me? I was his best friend."

Bo. His blood brother and childhood comrade. Always reliable. Always quick with the jokes and the laughter. And the only man who could make Tallulah laugh. His sister hadn't smiled in months. Not since Bo died. Sometimes he wondered if she ever would again.

"*Was* your best friend?" Annie's eyes rounded. "What happened to him?"

Tombi gritted his teeth. Oh, she looked innocent enough. Standing there in her flower-print T-shirt and drawstring pajama shorts. Brown hair tumbling in waves down to her hips. At first glance, she'd appeared a mere slip of a girl—skinny and all legs.

His eyes shifted to the fullness of her breasts and slight swelling of her hips. Definitely a woman. A very sexy woman. Not that it mattered. Evil spirits roamed in many guises.

"He died. Snakebite." He watched her closely, checking for signs of guilt or glee.

She shuddered. "That's horrible."

"Died right where I found you tonight."

Annie crossed her arms and looked downward apprehensively. "I hate snakes. Was it a rattler or a water moccasin?"

"Rattler. He died alone out there in the woods." How many times had he imagined Bo's horrible death? Imagined him feeling the rapid, burning spread of venom in his veins, knowing he was doomed.

Tombi drew a rasping breath. "He shouldn't have had to die alone."

"Nobody should," she agreed. "How—how did he get trapped in a wisp?"

"You really don't know?" he asked sharply.

"No." She squared her shoulders. "I've only been out here a few weeks visiting my grandma. Lots of weirdness down here, even more than usual this summer. Stuff I've never seen before. Or heard."

"About what you heard…what did Bo say exactly?"

"I told you. There's a betrayer in your ranks. He wanted me to warn you of danger."

A likely story. Wasn't that the way evil sank its fangs into people? It insinuated and manipulated fear and mistrust where none existed. Until you became paranoid and relied only on your own wits for survival. He'd seen it so many times over the past few years.

"I don't believe you."

She shrugged. "Suit yourself. Don't shoot me, I'm just the messenger."

"You always go around hearing voices?" he sneered.

"Yes."

Her quick, short response surprised him. "You do?"

"You already think I'm a witch, so—what the hell—yes, I hear things. Not voices usually. I hear music around people."

"Music?" He snorted. What kind of strange magic was this?

Her lips compressed in a thin line. "It's what drew me to the woods tonight. I heard the most beautiful music—it sounded like fairy bells."

Tombi considered Annie's words. "Did you smell anything?"

"Hmm? No. Not unless you count the constant smell of the ocean. Do the wisps have a certain smell?"

"They can. Will-o'-wisps appeal to different people differently." With him, they tried to mask their foul odor under the clean, sweet scent of balsam fir. He'd learned not to be drawn in by it.

"Your turn," she said, casting him a curious look. "What are *you* doing running around the woods in the middle of the night?"

"Chasing shadows." A half-truth.

Annie scowled. "Not fair. I answered your questions."

As if there were anything fair about life.

The silhouette of an old woman appeared at the cottage window. Impossible to see her facial expression from this distance, but the prickling of his forearm skin alerted Tombi that she watched. Somehow, through distance and darkness, the old lady's eyes clamped upon them.

Witch.

And this Annie girl was Tia Henrietta's direct descendant. She was a perfect target for the dark spirit ruler and his host of creatures, potentially more valuable than a normal human who possessed no sensory power whatsoever. Had she been tainted yet by evil? Despite her scowl and crossed arms, she looked as harmless as a kitten with her big, wide eyes and skinny arms and legs.

Don't be fooled by appearances. Tombi met her challenge with evasion. "There's evil and dark shadows in the bayou that you've never imagined. If you're not part of it, best you don't learn."

She cocked her head to one side and stilled, as if listening to something he couldn't hear.

"What is it?" Tombi asked sharply. "Do you hear something?"

She nodded. "It's faint, but distinct."

Could this girl really hear others' auras? Tombi shifted his feet and concentrated on containing his energy. The only sound in the night was the constant rolling of distant waves and the eternal screech of insects.

"It's gone now," Annie said. "But I heard your aura. Finally. I've never run across someone that I couldn't."

An undertow of intrigue tugged his mind. "Well? What do I sound like to you?"

"Drumming. A deep bass note. Steady as a heartbeat."

He studied the delicate features of her face, the heart-shaped chin, small nose and wide brown eyes beneath arched brows. Air charged between them, an unexpected sexual energy that rolled over him. The jackhammer beating of his heart exploded through his normal wall of self-control. The darkening of Annie's brown eyes said she heard it. Her gaze dropped to his lips, and Tombi leaned in...

"Annie?"

The old lady's voice cut through the night. It felt like ice water dousing his fevered skin. At the cottage, Annie's grandmother leaned her considerable girth half out of the window.

"Whatcha doin' out there? Who's that with ya?" she yelled.

Soft, moist heat brushed his left jaw. Startled, his gaze returned to Annie.

"Thank you for bringing me home." Her voice was breathless, and her hair was tousled and wild. She stretched up on tiptoes and planted another quick, chaste kiss on his cheek. "I have to go now."

Annie ran through the moon-silvered field, and he followed her slight figure until she entered the cottage. Bemused, he lifted a hand and traced his chin and jaw where her lips had momentarily caressed his skin. The memory of those quick kisses left him feeling anything but chaste. Why had she kissed him?

The light in the cottage blinked out, but Tombi lingered, reluctant to resume his hunt. For a small interlude, Annie had pricked through his armor, had touched something deep inside.

Bewitched him.

Chapter 2

Why had she kissed him?

True, he'd saved her from spending the night in the swamp, but he'd been evasive. Even accused her of being a witch.

But she'd been irresistibly pulled to his masculine strength, in a way she'd never experienced before. Kissing strangers was a novelty. Best to place the blame on the Thunder Moon and forget it ever happened. With a deep sigh, Annie shook off the question. It was done. Over. She might never see Tombi again. And she certainly would never go back into the night woods chasing will-o'-the-wisps.

Filled with resolve, she returned to preparing a new batch of mojo bags designed for attracting the opposite sex. Grandma Tia had awoken this morning declaring they would be in demand today, and supplies were getting low. Annie crushed lovage leaves with a mortar and pestle, releasing its unique lime and celery fragrance.

The cramped kitchen could almost be mistaken for one set in medieval times. Dried herbs from their garden hung from the ceiling. The countertops were wooden, as were the floors, table and cabinets. On the pine table, Annie had spread out over a dozen pink flannel mojo bags and mason jars filled with dried flowers and spices.

She emptied the freshly ground lovage into a new jar, humming contentedly. Next, she took a pinch of powdered substance from each jar and placed it in the bags, along with a sprinkle of salt and a tiny magnet. The base ingredients were set. Her grandma would personalize each bag as needed.

The murmur of conversation from the living room grew louder. Grandma Tia's voice was low and calm, in contrast to the other woman's high-pitched agitation.

"That hussy knew Jeb was my man, and it didn't make no bit a difference to her."

Every syllable of the woman's words buzzed like angry bees in Annie's ears. She hummed louder to block the buzzing and opened the pantry, which was lined with shelves of different-colored mojo bags, stones, nails, oils, graveyard dirt and hunks of dirt-dauber nests. A few murky jars were filled with liquid the color of swamp water, and she shuddered to think of what unsavory ingredients her grandma used in other kinds of spells.

Tia Henrietta popped her head in the door. "I need that there—"

Annie plucked two items from the shelf and held them out. "Here's twine and a vial of Stay Me oil. You need to add these to one of the pink bags for a Taking-Back-Yer-Man spell. Right?"

"You a quick learner, child." Grandma Tia gave a broad wink before closing the door behind her.

Annie shook her head in bemusement. It wasn't too hard to learn the hoodoo basics. Grandma Tia had explained there were certain common spells: one for getting back a lover (mostly female customers), another for gambling luck (mostly men) and another for revenge or blocking enemies (popular with both sexes). That was in addition to using the all-purpose good-luck charms and cleansing waters she concocted.

The front door slammed shut, and Annie watched the wronged woman march to her sedan, tightly clenching the mojo bag in her right fist. The hapless Jeb didn't stand a chance against her determination to cure him of his wandering ways. What a relief Grandma hadn't insisted she join them for the consultation. Lately, Grandma Tia had been making her meet customers, saying she needed to come out of her shell. But she'd given her a break today and let her putter about the kitchen, allowing her to get her bearings after last night.

The teakettle whistled, and Annie poured steaming water into two mugs and carried them on a tray into the living room.

Her grandma was sprawled on the sofa, head in her hands.

"What's wrong?" Annie hurried forward and set the mugs on the coffee table.

Tia brought her hands down and smiled wanly. "Nothing. I'll be just fine after tea."

"It's your heart, isn't it?" Annie asked, helping her sit up and placing a pillow behind her back.

"Cain't expect it to last forever." Grandma Tia mixed a dollop of honey into the hawthorn-berry tea. "This will revive me right nice."

But one day it wouldn't. Annie nervously adjusted the pillow.

As if reading her mind, Tia spoke again. "Don't you worry 'bout me. I'm ready to meet my maker anytime He calls."

What would she do without her grandma? Her real home was here in Bayou La Siryna, always had been. Here she wasn't surrounded by people and their constant cacophony of sound and music. Unwanted sounds she'd never learned to mute or tune out. And if Grandma Tia died, there went all hope of learning to control it.

Annie sat on the couch, legs crossed, and sipped coffee. None of that slimy grass-tasting herbal tea for her. Her right leg jittered in rhythm with the tumbled whirling of her brain.

"Ain't hard to guess what yer thinkin'."

Annie cursed the guilty flush that heated her face. No use denying her one-track wish. "I can't believe there's nothing you can do to help me. There must be something."

"Why would you be wantin' to block a gift?" Tia clicked her tongue in disapproval. "One day you gonna be thanking the blessed saints for that hearing of yers."

"It's ruining my life. Why can't you see that?" Annie set down her drink and stood, pacing the floorboards. This time guilt did more than stain her cheeks; it burned her heart. Grandma Tia probably wasn't long for this world, and Annie was impatient and snippy with the one person in the world who best understood and accepted her peculiarity.

"I'm going outside to cool off," she announced, using her last bit of self-control not to slam the door on the way out.

Cool off? What a joke. The humidity slapped her as soon as she stepped onto the porch. Annie sat down and stared at the gigantic live oaks draped with moss. Beautiful in a gothic, eerie kind of way. Burning cement cooked her butt, and she shifted her seating position.

Maybe it had been a mistake to come again this year after all. Still, she couldn't bear the thought of her grandma living alone. And Mama had wanted no part of traveling down here, saying she'd rather go to hell than come back to Alabama.

So she sent me instead. Dear mom had jumped at the chance to get her weird daughter out of the house and out of her hair.

It certainly was hot as Hades down here. And the gazillion buzzing, stinging insects in the bayou were the devil's own reward. Annie swiped at a mosquito sucking her forearm.

A whisper of song blew from the treetops and teased her ears. The plaintive, haunting beauty of it was unlike anything she'd ever heard. It was as pure as a dulcimer's plucking. The notes warbled like a bird's call and bubbled like water gurgling through rocks.

Annie half rose and then sat back down with a groan. This music was different from the will-o'-the-wisp's eerily luring tune, but she wasn't going to be fooled into returning to the woods. Tombi had claimed evil dwelled there. A dangerous place swarming with snakes and spirits. Just the thought of snakes was enough to keep her rooted to the porch.

The screen door creaked open on rusty hinges, and Grandma Tia framed the doorway.

"Somethin' calling ya to go in them woods again."

Annie narrowed her eyes. For all her savvy acumen in eking out an existence bartering mojo bags and spells for groceries and other necessities, her grandma really did have an unsettling sixth sense.

"I won't be drawn into the woods again," Annie assured her. "Once was bad enough."

"This time, you should go."

Annie snorted. "Tombi said there was evil out there. Besides, I hate snakes, and I imagine the woods are full of them."

"It's still daylight. Yer Tombi will protect ya."

"Why do you trust this stranger? You've never even met him."

Again, the fluting notes of music drifted and tempted. They chirruped and whistled like a bird in flight.

"You hear that?" Annie asked, looking toward the woods.

Tia shook her head. "Not a thing."

Annie stood and lightly brushed the rear of her jeans. Gritty sand and red clay dust permeated every surface outdoors. "You think Tombi's out there now?"

Tia's eyes danced. "He been out there most of the day, hoping to see ya."

She couldn't stop the delicious shiver that vibrated along her spine. Annie cocked her head to the side, studying Tia. "You sure he's trustworthy?"

"I have a good feelin' 'bout him."

Still, Annie hesitated. Grandma's sixth sense wasn't infallible. She often leaned on the side of reckless and trusting.

"You want everyone to come to you. Just like you search for answers to yer problems outside of yerself." Tia patted her ample chest. "Sometimes you gots to take heart and just rise up to yer problems."

Even her old grandma thought she was gutless. Annie straightened her shoulders. "Fine. If I don't make it home tonight, send out a search party."

She marched into the woods, her posture rigid as a stone column, knowing her grandma watched. "Might as well have called me a coward," she muttered, stomping through tall weeds and red dirt. Once inside the woods, Annie leaned against a tree, closed her eyes and fully opened her senses, straining to catch the pure music she'd heard on the porch steps.

Cascading trills floated through the swamp. The same pure melody that had captured her attention from the cottage. "Here I go again," she said with a sigh, carefully making her way along a thin trail almost eclipsed by dense shrubs on either side. But daylight, and Grandma Tia's urging to follow the music, gave her a measure of confidence.

The notes grew louder, more fluid and enchanting. Annie rounded a bend and recognized the water bank where she'd drifted last evening.

A man sat on a fallen tree limb, playing some sort of reed instrument. Although his naked, broad back faced her, Annie sensed it was Tombi. She wasn't Tia Henrietta's granddaughter for nothing.

Staring at his sleek, muscled torso made her throat and mouth dry. She licked her lips and swallowed hard. She'd bet her grandma's pantry full of hoodoo charms that Tombi had women follow him everywhere. The Pied Piper of Bayou La Siryna.

The music stopped. In one fluid motion, like a dance of danger, Tombi jumped to his feet and whirled around, a dagger gleaming in his right fist. The wooden instrument he played dangled loosely in his left hand. Warrior and musician melded into one. His face was taut, and his eyes instantly fixed on her.

Whoa. Annie threw up her hands and took an involuntary step backward. For all she knew, Tombi might have deliberately summoned her with the music, luring her to him against her better judgment. She'd done the same thing following the will-o'-the-wisps last night.

Tombi slowly lowered the dagger and secured it in the leather sheath belted at his waist, never breaking his gaze. "You came back," he said in a flat tone.

He didn't act like a man hoping to see her, as Grandma Tia had claimed.

"I had to. You never told me your story." Annie walked forward and nodded at the dagger. "You always this uptight?"

"These woods are full of danger."

"Really? Because even my grandma thinks it's perfectly safe out here during the day."

He frowned and crossed his arms. "It used to be."

A series of scars tattooed the smooth, muscular plane of his chest and shoulders, distracting her from his unsettling response. "Have you been in knife fights?" she blurted.

Tombi grabbed the T-shirt on the log and swiftly pulled it on.

"I'm sorry." Annie was horrified at her rudeness. "I shouldn't have asked."

"I'm not ashamed of them," he said gruffly. He nodded at the log. "Sit."

Her embarrassment faded. "I don't take commands like a dog," she said, lifting her chin.

A ghost of a smile flitted the corners of his lips, so fleeting she might have dreamed it had been there. He bowed his head a fraction before he sat down, but didn't apologize.

Annie gestured to the surrounding trees. "So, what's the danger? Are the wisps malicious or something? I mean, your friend sounded sad and desperate to me—not evil."

"In real life, Bo was all that was true and good."

"And now?" she prompted.

"Remains to be seen." He studied her, eyes narrowed and unflinching.

Annie smoothed the tumble of curls away from her face. "What do you mean?"

"It's hard to tell good from evil sometimes."

"Do you see everything so black-and-white? Surely there's a dozen shades of gray in between."

"No." His jaw muscles clenched. "You're either with me or you are with Nalusa."

"Nah-loosa?" she asked, testing the unfamiliar word.

"Nalusa Falaya—it means 'long black being' in Choctaw. He's a spirit that resembles a man, but he can shape-shift into different forms."

Annie drew a circle in the dirt with the toe of her sneaker. Root working—the conjure magick of her grandma—was one thing…but this? It sounded like an old Native American tale invented to keep children close to camp and away from the dark unknown.

"You don't believe me." Tombi picked up a large stick on the ground by their feet and flung it violently. It hit a tall oak and splintered with a crack as loud as gunfire.

Annie sidled away from the heat of his anger, not wanting to be singed by his sudden wrath. "I really should head back home," she offered in a small voice.

"It's real," Tombi said harshly. "Nalusa exists. And he can change into snake form. And I believe that wasn't any ordinary snake that killed Bo. It was Nalusa."

"So, now you're out here trying to hunt this Nalusa down. For revenge." She backed away slowly, not wanting to set him off again. "Got it."

Tombi also stood. "Not just me. There's a whole tribe of us."

More people who shared his delusion? She glanced around uneasily, hoping she wasn't about to be ambushed by a group of demented, make-believe warriors.

"I know it sounds crazy, but it's true. C'mon, you saw the will-o'-the-wisps last night with your own eyes. Remember?"

Annie rubbed her arms. He certainly had her there. "Okay," she reluctantly conceded. "I admit there are things I know nothing of. I'd rather keep it that way, too."

His brow furrowed. "Whether you ignore Nalusa or not, he still exists."

"Yeah, well, I'd rather not make his acquaintance. I have enough problems as it is."

Alarm flickered in his dark eyes. "But Bo spoke to you. You have to help us."

Annie shrugged and took a step backward. The last thing she needed was to get caught up in his personal crusade for revenge. "Come, see my grandma one day. She'll do a protection spell if you like." She plastered on a smile and waved. "Nice seeing you. Thanks again for helping me find my way home last night."

Two steps and her shoulders tensed at the heavy pressure of his palms bearing down, barring an easy exit. Damn. He wasn't going to make retreat easy. Tombi guided her back around to face him.

"We need you, Annie." He swallowed. "Please."

She could tell the plea wasn't easy for Tombi. Pride and dignity announced their presence in the strong jaw and stiff posture.

"But I doubt I'll ever hear Bo again," she protested. "I have no plans to be lured back into the woods by the wisps."

"The wisps are controlled by Nalusa. But as long as you're with me, I'll protect you. I promise."

His words were deep and solemn. No doubt he would do his best to protect those on his side.

"I believe you."

"Good. Then come with me and—"

She shook her head and backed away. This wasn't her battle. "No. Sorry. I don't want to get involved."

Tombi glared at her, and his full lips compressed to a tight line. Evidently, he was a man used to getting his own way.

Too bad.

Stubborn woman.

Tombi took a deep breath to calm his temper. Somehow, he had to convince this slip of a girl to help him. Maybe…

His gaze dropped to her lips. Those lips that had unexpectedly kissed him last night. Annie felt the attraction between them. He could use that to his advantage. Tombi slid his palms down her arms and urged her forward. So close their bodies almost touched.

Her brown eyes widened and darkened into black pools of desire. She raised her hands and placed them against his chest. Yes, this might be so easy. So pleasurable.

Later, he couldn't say who moved first. All he knew was that their lips met and their hands explored one another. Her fingers traced the bulge of his biceps, then kneaded the muscles along his spine.

Tombi stroked the thin shoulder blades on her back, ran his calloused fingers through her soft curls. She was so petite, so delicate. Fragile enough he wondered if it might hurt her should he release his full passion.

A tiny, whimpering moan cut through his reservations. She wanted him. Tombi lowered his hands until they cupped her ass. That cute ass that he'd watched walk away last night and that he'd pictured ever since. He squeezed, letting Annie feel his desire press against her core.

She moaned again. Or was that him this time? It didn't matter.

"Stop." Annie stepped out of his embrace and hugged her belly. "Sorry. It's just…this is too fast. I barely know you."

He stared at her, willing his heartbeat to slow and his brain to catch up to her words. "It's okay," he said, running a hand through his hair. "I understand."

"Thank you," she whispered, turning and making her way down the path.

Tombi shook his head to clear it. He was supposed to use their attraction to convince her to work with him. Somehow, he'd lost control, and Annie was slipping away from him once more. He couldn't let that happen. He—

rather, his people—needed her skill in communicating with the *shilup*, the human spirits that wandered the land of the ghosts. Bo's spirit had been captured by the wisps, and remembering the plight of his trapped friend cooled his fever.

"Wait," he called to Annie's retreating figure.

She turned and gazed at him expectantly.

What could he offer her? This was his fight. Not hers. She was right to not get involved. Yet, Nalusa grew stronger every day, and they were desperate to stop his spread of power in Bayou La Siryna. Just last week, Nalusa had gone farther away from the swamp and invaded the heart and mind of one of his hunters while he was asleep in his own bed. Marcus had even entertained thoughts of suicide but wisely had called Tombi for help, recognizing that Nalusa was at the root of his despair.

Tombi scrambled to recall the bits and pieces of conversation with Annie, searching for an angle. He remembered her troubled face as she mentioned hearing other people's auras.

"What if I could help you?"

Her lips twisted with suspicion. "Help me with what?"

He approached Annie, confident of victory. "You want to control your sense of hearing. Correct?"

Her body and eyes lit up. "Really? You can help with that?"

"Really. You told me how surprised you were when we first met because you couldn't detect any sound from my aura."

"I remember."

"That's because I control my energy field most of the time. I can teach you to do the same."

"And that will help me block unwanted sound?"

He had no idea. But it seemed logical. "Absolutely," he said with conviction.

"And if I help you, you promise to protect me?"

"I do."

Annie looked down to the ground, and Tombi held his breath, awaiting her answer.

"I'm in," she said in a rush.

Chapter 3

What had she gotten herself into? She wanted a normal life, but what good was that if she was killed in the process? But she had to try. She had to trust that Tombi would protect her.

Grandma Tia had been no help, and no matter how many spells and strips of paper she burned under the full moon, nothing changed. If anything, her hearing grew stronger, more disruptive.

Tombi nodded. "Great. We begin now."

Hope bubbled through her like uncorked champagne on New Year's Eve. She was about to start a new life. Do all those things she'd longed to do: get a real job, be around people and relate normally. Simple acts most people took for granted.

He turned and beckoned her to follow.

"Where are we going?" she asked happily. No waiting for the full moon this time. Hope had arisen right here in the midafternoon sunshine. "Is there a special place for a spell? Like an energy vortex or something?" She hurried along the path.

He shot an incredulous look over his shoulder. "What are you babbling about?"

"I'm curious how you're going to do this. I think Grandma Tia never helped me because she didn't know how, though she would never admit it."

"We aren't casting any spells."

"Are you taking me to a special healer, then? Like a shaman?"

He sighed loudly and planted his feet so abruptly she plowed into his back.

He turned and steadied her. "We're going to my camp, so you can meet the other hunters. I want to know who that betrayer is. If there is one."

Annie's eyes narrowed. "So, you won't help me until I help you first."

"That's right."

Worry quickly overcame her frustration. "But what if I can't pick up anything from them?"

"You will," he said confidently. "I'm the best in the group at controlling my energy, yet you picked up the drumming."

"But it was only a drumming sound. Nothing good or bad about it," she protested.

"True, but it picked up something of my nature. A primitive beat passed down through my ancestry."

"Don't get your hopes up," she muttered, picking her way carefully through the prickly saw palmettos and dense underbrush. Tombi kept a slower pace today, albeit still a brisk one. "Tell me about these other hunters."

The more she knew going in, the less nervous she would be. Annie hated meeting new people, especially in a group situation where each aura would jumble with the others into a confusing din.

"We're down to four in the inner circle since Bo died. Me, Chulah, Hanan and my sister, Tallulah."

"So, what is it you actually *do*? How do you fight Nalusa and his shadow spirits?"

Tombi didn't answer right away. "It's something you would have to see and be a part of to really understand."

Meaning he didn't want to say any more on the subject. Great. Fine by her. The less she knew, the fewer nightmares she'd dream. She'd help him find the betrayer, and he'd help her control hearing auras. Then she could have the normal life she craved, and he could…maybe win his battle. Get revenge for his friend's death. They could both move on.

They continued until the path widened, and she spotted over two dozen tents pitched in a field. They were arranged in a circle, and in the middle of it all was a thin stream of smoke that wafted upward from a modest fire. The acrid smell of burning oak stirred her with a sense of home and cozy evenings warming by the fireplace.

"You all must be great friends," she said, picturing them telling stories in the evening by campfire, sharing a bond of fighting evil. They were all part of something bigger than themselves. For a moment, it made her own dream seem small and selfish.

And he wanted her to come into this…this tight group of friends and point the finger at one of them? Annie rubbed the unexpected chill on her arms. She wasn't sure what she feared most: being unable to recognize the betrayer, or singling out someone and facing their collective wrath.

Nobody would thank her for disrupting their alliance, that was for sure. She peeked at Tombi's stern profile, took in his long, slightly hooked nose, pronounced jaws and cheekbones, and heavy brows. What was his role in this band of hunters?

"Your name's unusual. What does it mean?" she asked abruptly, hoping to learn more about him.

"Ray of light."

Annie snorted, and he raised a brow. "What?"

She couldn't help but giggle. "You're no ray of sunshine."

He stared at her blankly before a rusty rumble of laughter escaped his mouth, as if it had been years since one last escaped. "At one time, my people worshiped the sun, so to be named after its ray is a great honor."

"What about your friend Bo? Is that a good ole Southern name as in *B-e-a-u*, short for Beauregard?"

"No. It's *B-o*, short for Bohpoli. That's Choctaw for 'thrower.'"

Would she ever hear Bo again? She shivered, remembering his plaintive pleas for help.

Although their movements were quiet and their voices low, they had attracted attention. A woman and three men solemnly filed out of the tent circle and stood in the center, awaiting their approach with unsmiling faces.

Holy hoodoo, this was going to be even tougher than she imagined.

Annie tugged the back of Tombi's T-shirt, and he frowned down at her. "What?"

"Have you told them anything about me?"

"We tell each other everything."

She groaned. "Terrific. Bet they can't wait to meet me. I wish you hadn't told them."

"There should be no secrets among my hunters. No doubts or suspicions about the man—or woman—you have to depend on for your life."

Her shoulders slumped. She couldn't argue with his logic, although she resented the situation he'd put her in. They walked onward several minutes, not speaking.

Tombi abruptly halted and frowned her way. "You care so much what others think?"

"Of course I care." She thought of all the times people had skirted around her in school hallways or outright laughed in her face. She'd watched from the sidelines in the purgatory that was high school, unsure which she craved more—the huddling conspiracy of a group of girlfriends to share secrets and fun times with, or some cute guy to take her to dinner and a movie and whisper sweet seductions in the back of a car. "Everyone cares."

He shrugged. "Not me."

Easy for him to say—with his looks he probably had any woman he wanted. And he had a tribe of like-minded friends and family. Why should he give any thought to what was so easily granted to him?

Annie reluctantly walked beside him, trying to emulate his mask of calm. They came to a halt six feet in front of the group.

"This is Annie Matthews." Tombi gestured to the left with his hand. "This is Tallulah, Hanan and Chula."

The silence roared in her, air compressing and as stifling as a sealed coffin. They formed a firewall of mistrust and resentment, shutting her out of their circle. Annie sucked in her breath at the glittering hostility in Tallulah's obsidian eyes. Nearly as tall as her brother, she bore the same long face, chiseled features and strong chin. It shouldn't have worked for a female, and while she wasn't beautiful in a Miss America or girl-next-door kind of way, Tallulah was striking and commanded attention. Annie barely took in the stoic features of the other three men.

Tallulah put her hands on her hips. "Well?"

"W-well what?" Annie stammered. She glanced at Tombi in a silent plea for help.

"Go ahead," Tallulah challenged. "I dare you to point a finger at any one of us. You don't know—"

"Enough," Tombi cut in.

The man next to her—Chula—lightly touched Tallu-lah's forearm, and a whisper as tender as a lullaby brushed over Annie at the gesture.

"We already debated this last night and agreed to meet Annie. Let's get this over with." Hanan pinned Annie with a hard stare, and the whisper of sound vanished. "The sooner, the better."

Annie swallowed hard at their collective stare. Talk about being on the spot.

"It's not that easy. I have to be around you for a bit." She cast another look at Tombi. "Can we all sit together by the fire?"

Tombi nodded, and she followed him to the middle of the pitched tents, the others following in silence behind them.

In the center was a stack of firewood coated in ash. Colorful wool blankets were spread in a circle around the campfire. They each went to a blanket and sat, except Tombi. "You can have my blanket," he said, pointing to one. "I'll stand."

She sank down and crossed her feet beneath her. Annie tried to relax and open her senses, but it was difficult as the others stared at her expectantly. As if she was some kind of circus performer. She closed her eyes, more to shut out their stares than out of necessity.

The unnatural quiet unnerved her. How did they do it? They each had some type of guard up, some way of blocking their music. Her palms gripped her knees. Very well. She'd try to wait them out, see if any sound escaped.

The vibrations of a deep rumbling laugh iced down her spine. *Witch.* The word was an accusation, underlain with mirth. *Be gone, little girl.*

Annie opened her eyes and met their curious, blank stares. "Did you hear that laugh? That voice?"

No one spoke.

Tombi uncrossed his arms and sat beside her on the blanket. "What did you hear?"

She bit her lip. Had the laugh and the words come from one of the hunters, or was there something else out there? Something just beyond the ring of trees and the safety of the fire where shadows lengthened and danced?

Annie shook her head slightly and closed her eyes again. Silence blanketed her as thick and unrelenting as a stone wall. It was hopeless. Nothing else was coming through that wall.

She opened her eyes. "I don't know how y'all do it, but I'm impressed."

"Do what?" Chula asked.

"Close off your energy." Annie turned to Tombi. "Isn't that how you described it? Keeping everything closed in?"

Tallulah made an impatient *tsk* sound. "Why did you tell this girl our secrets? For all we know, she could be one of them."

"One of who?" Annie asked.

"Don't act so innocent," Tallulah snapped. "If there's someone controlled by the dark side, my guess is that it's you."

Annie rose to her feet and took in their hostile stares. "I didn't have to tell Tombi what I heard last night. I didn't ask Bo to seek me out. And I certainly don't have to take your attitude."

She stalked off. Screw them. She'd tried. Not her fault if they had some special power to resist her hearing.

Dry grass crunched in the parched soil behind her. Tombi stepped to her side and walked, matching her pace.

"I'm not going back there," she spat, "so don't try to talk me into it."

He said nothing but walked in front of her as they re-entered the narrow path. He held back branches to keep them from slapping her in the face. A snapping, crackling sound simmered in the air swirling around him, like dry brush catching fire.

"You're angry with me," Annie said. "I really did try. But your sister…" She tried to collect her temper. She still needed his help and insulting Tallulah wouldn't serve her cause. "You are going to help me. Right?"

She looked desperate, but Tombi hardened his heart. He wasn't about to give up. Not as long as Bo was trapped and not as long as Nalusa and the other shadow spirits grew and trespassed the ancient boundaries.

"Eventually," he promised. "What did you hear back there?"

"Nothing that can help you."

Tombi stopped in his tracks and folded his arms against his chest. "Might as well spit it out. I'll be out in these woods through the night anyhow."

"Do you live out here all the time?"

"Only one week out of the month, around the full moon."

Her dark eyes widened. "We believe in the power of the full moon, too."

"We?"

"My grandmother and I." She swallowed. "And others like us."

"Other witches?"

"Why must you put labels on people?" she countered. "We're known by many names, and we all have different practices—root workers, healers, pagans and, okay, witches."

"Do they all hear as you do?"

Her full lips twisted in a scowl. "No. I'm the lucky one."

Tombi shook off his fascination with Annie and her

kind. "You neatly skirted my question. What did you hear back there?"

She sighed, realizing he would interrogate until she answered his question. "A laugh. Not a funny one, but the laugh of the evil or crazy or demented. And then...the voice called me a witch and told me to go away."

Tombi considered her words. He hated knowing Nalusa knew of Annie and her gift and their connection, but Nalusa must be worried to warn her off. That was, if Annie wasn't in league with him to start with.

"So, just like that, you're giving up?"

She winced at the sharp edge of his tone. "The attitude of your sister and your friends didn't make me want to stay and try harder."

He grew hot thinking of Tallulah's antagonism. Annie didn't deserve to be treated that way. Even if he had his own suspicions, nothing would be gained by hostility.

"They can't help but be suspicious of strangers. Time and again, Nalusa has gained a foothold over people, even if only temporarily. Made them say and do things they wouldn't normally do."

Annie lifted her chin. "I can assure you that I'm in complete command of my own thoughts and actions."

"I'll help you, but you have to help me, too."

"Can't you just say some words and cure me?"

"Nothing's that easy. It's a process. It takes time to learn to control your energy."

"You say you don't trust me. That goes two ways. I think you're dragging out everything to suit your own purposes."

"You've barely spent five minutes among us. You'll have to gain their trust."

"Or catch them unawares," she muttered.

"That would be hard to do. Our hearing may not be as sharp as yours. But we can sense energy before it senses us."

"You have to sleep sometime."

Of course. He should have realized. Tombi laid a hand on her thin shoulder, noticing his palm engulfed the side of her neck and curve of her shoulder. "Come meet us tonight. Hunt with us and spend the night."

Her eyebrows drew up. "Spend the night with you in your tent?"

An image of Annie, naked and curled up beside him, flushed his body with desire. "I can spring for a new tent and sleeping bag," he said past the dryness at the back of his throat.

"I'll think—" She came to a dead halt and tilted her head to the side, listening to a faint sound.

"Wh—"

She raised a finger to her lips to silence him. Her forehead wrinkled, and her eyes grew distant. Suddenly, Annie grabbed his arm and looked around wildly. "Let's run!"

And then he sensed it, too. Dread enveloped him like a heavy blanket. The metallic scent of blood and a whisper of decay could alone mean only one thing. Nalusa was near.

Very near. Within striking range.

Not now. Not with Annie so close. "Go without me," he urged.

She stood still, as if paralyzed, staring at him with brown eyes full of fear. "But what about you?"

"I can take care of myself." He drew out the dagger from his side. "Go!"

She hesitated.

A rustling whipped through the underbrush, unnaturally loud, drowning out birds and insects and the rumble of the sea. A sibilant hiss sent a tingle across the skin of his back and arms. Another second and Nalusa would be upon them. Tombi looked over his shoulder and pointed at Annie with his dagger. "I said, go!"

Her dark eyes were like a well of smooth, black water. And in those pupils Tombi saw a triangular head arise, a long forked tongue slithering from its mouth. The snake's copper eyes appeared to hold Annie entranced. The Medusa of the bayou.

If Bo were still alive and with him, he'd throw a dagger accurate enough to strike the snake in between the eyes. Tombi didn't trust his aim to be as accurate. He needed to be a little closer. He slowly turned to directly face Nalusa, his body a shield to protect Annie behind him. Nalusa coiled his long snake form in upon itself, his muscles rippling beneath the gray-and-brown patchwork of scales.

The striking position. His tail rose up with its rings of rattles and shook. The sound was as loud as a tumbling steel barrel full of iron pellets.

Tombi deliberately stepped toward Nalusa, every nerve flooded with adrenaline. Warring instincts battled inside. His muscles twitched to take action, to strike the enemy, yet his mind urged caution. One miscalculation and his tribe would be further reduced and without its leader.

They were within a few feet of one another. Striking distance. Tombi willed Annie to leave, but he sensed her presence behind him.

Why hadn't she run? His jaw tightened. It could be the two were in league together. She drew him to just the right place at the right time. Tombi shrugged off the disquieting notion, trying to stay focused. If he lived, he would have his answer. If he didn't…the other hunters would guess at her treachery and the trap she had plotted.

But no matter. The death match was on. He had to kill this monster before Nalusa crept past his boundaries, past the deep swamp where his ancestors had bound him many years ago. Hurricane Katrina had unleashed something; her destruction and the resulting chaos in the Deep South had made it possible for Nalusa to escape his chains and increase his power.

Now he seemed ready to inflict his evil upon the world. Now he must die.

Tombi lunged forward, aiming for the eyes. His dagger sank into the thick, muscular skin of the snake, under its throat. It was as if he could feel the pain in his own body. A bolt of agony exploded a few inches under his collarbone, a needle sharpness that quickly radiated toward his chest, as if he'd been injected with poison.

Bitten. He'd been bitten. Moaning rent the space between man and beast, and Tombi couldn't say if it was his own or Nalusa's. Blood poured from the snake's throat where Tombi's silver dagger had sunk in deep. Its black tongue whipped out, ready to strike again.

Tiny white grains and bits of dirt rained down on Nalusa's coiled body, and he jerked backward, eyes fixed somewhere past Tombi's shoulder. What was happening?

Tombi took advantage of the distraction and scrambled to his knees, but pain exploded everywhere, and his vision filled with tiny black dots. His limbs felt numb and paralyzed, and with every breath the pain spread farther, deeper. He collapsed on the hard ground. *I'm joining you, Bo.*

The image of his parents arose as he last saw them. His father whittling his latest sculpture, his mom shucking corn. All that work, and the sculpture was taken out by the tide, by that bitch of a hurricane, Katrina.

I tried. I failed. You win, Nalusa. He could do no more.

Annie ran across the field to their cottage. Ran until her lungs burned and her chest heaved like fireplace billows. And still there wasn't enough oxygen to fuel her body's race against time. *Don't die don't die please don't die.*

She'd flung the salt and consecrated earth from her mojo bag at the attacker, but it may have been too little, too late.

Tombi's unconscious body, sprawled in the red clay dirt, was as clear to her as the door to the cottage. She couldn't, wouldn't think of that—thing, not a snake and not a man. The snake form had dissolved into a thin, tall column of a creature howling with pain. Tombi's dagger had dislodged, and the creature retreated to the darkness of the woods from which it had come.

But not Tombi. She'd felt his pulse, saw the slight rise and fall of his chest. So fragile.

The door opened, and Grandma Tia descended the steps, carrying the large straw bag that held her roots and herbs for her healing home visitations.

"Hurry." Annie tried to scream, but her voice was only a puff, as light as dandelion seeds that scattered in the briny breeze.

Tia hustled over with a speed and agility Annie hadn't observed in her for years.

"Where is he?" she asked without preamble.

Annie hastily removed the shoulder strap from her grandma's bag and hoisted it over her own shoulders. "This way. He's been bitten, Grandma." She felt six years old again and seeking her grandma's comfort after other kids made fun of her. She still needed her assurance and knowledge, wanted her grandma to tell her everything was going to be okay.

"Ole devil snake got 'em, eh?" They were only midway through the field, but Tia's breathing was already labored.

"Your heart," Annie said, drawing burning air into oxygen-starved lungs. She laid a hand on Tia's shoulder. "Tell me what to do, and you can stay here."

"Ain't goin' be that easy," Tia huffed. "Gonna take both of us to set this right." She nodded at the trail. "Best keep on. Sooner I start workin', better chance he lives."

They hurried on, and Annie resumed her frantic litany. *Don't die don't die don't die.*

There. His body lay in the same spot. Annie laid his head in her lap and swept his long hair out of his eyes. Only a supernatural force could have felled such a strong man. Such a warrior. His bronze skin stretched tightly across lean, compact muscles. She wondered what had drawn him into this fight with evil, what ancient curse haunted him and his people.

Grandma Tia began humming and chanting, calling upon her Jesus and the holy saints as she pulled out herbs and protection wards from the bag—graveyard dirt, hollowed-out dirt-dauber nests, chopped swamp-alder root, strings of Dixie John root, and other bits and pieces of unidentifiable objects.

"I call on thee, archangels most high," Tia said in her firmest voice. "I call on thee, King Solomon, and thou keys of wisdom, and I call on thee, Moses, for thy power and faith. By the spirit of the Great Black Hawk, I summon thee."

Annie kept her eyes fixed on Tombi's swollen chest with its mottled skin as her grandmother continued her petitions. It could have been ten seconds or ten minutes later—Annie couldn't say—but Tia stopped and turned grave eyes on her.

"It ain't working."

Annie's fingers sank tighter into Tombi's shoulder, and she squeezed, willing him to fight. "You can't quit. Keep going."

Tia drew a long, unsteady breath. "Ain't but one thing left to do." She unpacked a poultice, laid her hand directly over the open wound and prayed, then placed the poultice on the broken skin.

Annie gulped. "Aren't you worried about infection?"

"We way past that point, child. Now I need you to help

me. We goin' to draw that poison out of his body and into mine."

"But—we can't. What will the poison do to you? Your heart—"

Tia held up a hand, face stern. "My time on this here earth is almost up anyhows. We gots to try. Now. What I want you to do is find that gris-gris bag full of wormwood in my bag and sprinkle it all around us."

Annie hastily rummaged in the purse, pulled out a black satin drawstring pouch and held it to her nose. A pungent, bitter smell tickled her nostrils. "Is this the one?"

"That's it. Now you get to work and recite parts of Psalm 91. And don't interrupt me, no matter what. You hear me?"

Her upbringing left her no choice but to respond properly to the authority in that voice. "Yes, ma'am."

Tia's eyes softened, and the rigid set of her face melted. "You always been a good girl," she said. "My shining star with the gift. You hear music where the rest of us hear silence." She turned abruptly away. "Now get to work like I taught you."

It felt like a farewell.

Surely not. Grandma Tia was no voodoo hack. She was the real deal. Knew things, sensed things, felt things.

Annie circled around them, a few feet out, crumbling bits of wormwood petals and letting them fall onto her path. The words of the psalm were ingrained since childhood.

"Thou shalt not be afraid for the terror by night, nor for the arrow that flieth by day, nor for the pestilence that walketh in darkness, nor for the destruction that wasteth at noonday."

Heat singed upward from below where her grandmother knelt beside Tombi's body that was sprawled on the hard ground. The sweltering air battered Annie's temples with headache. The wormwood's bitter, camphoraceous scent deepened, and her fingers tingled with numbness—some toxic effect of the herb intensified by the spell. A golden light flowed between Tombi's chest and her grandma's hand.

Annie stopped her recitation, mesmerized by the etheric glow.

Tia cast her a sharp glance. "Don't stop."

She cleared her throat and continued circling. "No evil shall befall thee, neither shall any plague come nigh thy dwelling. For he shall give his angels care. They shalt tread upon the lion and adder."

The swelling and redness of his skin decreased. Tombi stirred and wet his lips. A low moan escaped.

"It's working," Annie exclaimed, wanting to tap-dance around the sacred circle. The golden, healing energy had wrought a remarkable change. There was still some swelling, but the angry red streaks of infection had disappeared. "You did it, Grandma—" She stopped abruptly.

Tia's olive skin had grayed and wrinkled even more, to the point it resembled elephant skin. Her eyes held an unhealthy glaze, as if she were burning with a fever.

Annie sank on her knees and hugged her grandma. "Don't leave me," she begged. "Tell me how to help you."

A laugh so faint that even she couldn't hear it—it could only be felt from the rumbling of Tia's chest and throat. "It's all in the good Lord's hands now, child."

Annie burrowed her head in her grandma's gray hair with its witchy, herbal smell. The smell of home and safety and love. Her grounding force in this world.

"I'm going to get help," she promised, mind whirling with the action she needed to take: get up, run to the cottage, find her cell phone and car keys. Call the ambulance, drive through the field, manage to get these two in the car and drive them to the cottage for the ambulance to transport them to the hospital.

Once at the hospital, the doctors would demand to know what happened…

"Hey," Tombi asked with a note of hoarse puzzlement. "What's going on here?"

A frisson of resentment washed over Annie. This had been *his* fight. Not hers. And certainly not her grandma's. If she'd never met him, her grandma wouldn't be hovering at death's portal for the afterlife.

She'd sacrificed her own safety and, worse, her grandma's health. All for a promise. One that Tombi didn't seem in any hurry to fill.

"My grandma absorbed the poison meant for you," she said, hot tears scalding her cheeks. "I wish I'd never met you."

Chapter 4

Tia's deep olive flesh turned ashy. The glaze of her eyes and burn of her skin indicated a dangerously high fever, as if a volcano had exploded inside her body.

How much longer for that ambulance? Seemed as if it had taken hours to get her grandma back to the cottage and make the call for help. Annie held Tia's hand and stroked her hot forehead. "Isn't there some kind of special tea or gris-gris bag I can get for you?"

"Fetch my crystal from the altar and light a candle." Tia's voice was weak and hoarse. She swallowed hard. "And say a quick prayer while you're at it."

Annie scurried to do her bidding, glad to take action. Seeing someone in pain, especially the rock of her universe, was to suffer alongside them.

Don't die. Sure, she'd known Tia's heart was winding down, but Annie had expected weeks, if not months, to share with her grandmother. Time to soak in her care and wisdom. Time also to be trained in root working and to, hopefully, cajole a reverse spell to banish the musical auras that assaulted her mind.

At the altar, Annie grasped the large chunk of polished carnelian that, despite its vivid orange-red color, was cooling and soothing to the touch. With shaking hands, Annie struck a match. It hissed loudly in the quiet and emitted a whisper of sulfur. She applied the flame to the white columnar candle that smelled strongly of patchouli and cloves. Beside the candle was a framed print of a stern angel with spread wings.

Annie collected her panicked thoughts and prayed. "Dear God…universe…angels…help my grandma," she whispered in a rush. "She's done nothing but help people all her life, and now she needs you. The time isn't right. I'm not ready." Annie drew a deep breath, ashamed she'd wandered into selfish territory. A groan from the next room, and she drew the prayer to a quick close. "Please and amen."

She hurried to the den, where Tombi leaned over the sofa toward Tia, as if drawing closer to hear her speak. Or check her breath for life.

A jab of fear wrung her gut. "Is she…?"

"She's alive," he said with grim authority. "But her pulse grows faint."

A siren sounded from far away.

Tombi straightened. "I'll wait out front for the ambulance. Make sure they don't have trouble finding this place." He brushed past, and Annie lifted her chin, turning her body to the side to avoid accidental contact. It might be unfair to blame him for Tia's condition, but she couldn't help resenting him, nonetheless.

Tombi raised a brow but said nothing.

The door shut behind him, and Annie let out a deep breath, resuming her place by Tia's side. She slipped the carnelian crystal into her grandma's weathered palm, and Tia curled her fingers over the rock.

"Does this help you?" Annie asked, hoping it eased the pain.

Tia nodded. "Helps me focus. To say what needs sayin'."

Her grandma took a long, raspy breath, and Annie winced at the rattle that sounded like oxygen was leaking and gurgling from her lungs. She eased down and sat beside Tia's sprawled body. "Take your time. I lit the candle and said a prayer like you asked."

"Ain't much time left."

"Don't say that," Annie scolded. "You're going to be fine."

"Listen." Tia struggled to rise on an elbow, but gave up and sank back into the cushions. "I know I been a disappointment to you this visit."

Annie started to deny it, but Tia cut her off.

"We ain't got time for nothin' but the truth between us. And the truth is, you need to help Tombi. He needs you. He needs your gift."

But what about me? It's not what I want.

Tia frowned, eyes sparking with reprimand.

No doubt she'd heard the selfish, unspoken thought. Guilt and shame washed over Annie in a heated flood of remorse.

"You listen here, Annie girl. You help that man. Now. Tonight."

Annie shook her head again. "No way. I'm staying with you."

"I'm goin' somewhere you cain't follow."

"You aren't going to die," Annie insisted.

"I mean it, missy. You go with Tombi. Promise me."

Her tone was fierce, insistent—one that Annie remembered as a child. A you-better-mind-me-this-is-your-last-warning kind of voice. The siren's wail grew distinct and piercing.

Annie crossed two fingers behind her back. "Okay."

Tia tugged Annie's right hand around to the front of her body. "You stop that childish nonsense, or I'll haunt you all yer living days."

"Yes, ma'am."

"Now, then. They fixin' to take me to that infernal hospital." Tia sniffed as if she'd smelled something unclean. She hated the hospital and always said they hurt more than helped. "Guess it's for the best in this case."

"They'll take good care of you. You'll be better in—"

"Hush. If you ever loved me, if you ever trusted my judgment…don't go to the hospital with me. Say you won't."

Annie's shoulders slumped. "Okay," she whispered in defeat, crushed at the mandate. "Is there at least some spell or working I can do while you're gone?"

"No. You be my good girl and help Tombi." Tia's eyes filled with tears that poured down her cheeks like trickles of rain.

Annie couldn't ever remember her grandma crying, except that one time when Annie's mama got in a huge argument with Tia and walked out, saying she would never come back to this backwater hell. That day, Tia's great shoulders had heaved in silent sobs.

Flashing red lights strobed through the window like a disco party from hell. Annie squeezed Tia's hand.

"You always were my special girl." Tia nodded. "But now it's time for my release. Tombi is your destiny now. Ya hear?"

The screen door burst open, and two men in dark blue uniforms entered with a stretcher, Tombi close at their heels.

The men hurried to Tia's side and took her pulse, listened to her heart, assessed for damages. Tombi explained what had happened, and Annie sank to her knees, hands covering her mouth. How could her grandma expect her to stay here while she went to the hospital?

Tia was transferred to the stretcher, and the men labored to the door with their heavy burden. She still clutched the carnelian in one hand, taking a piece of home with her to a foreign place bustling with antiseptic, modern doctors who prodded you with needles and probed your flesh and innards with an impersonal, impatient air.

It was about as far from hoodoo healing as you could get.

"We're taking her to Bayou La Siryna General Hospital," one of the young men said.

She couldn't speak past the clogged boulder in her throat, but Tombi responded. "Thank you. Family and friends will follow shortly." He walked the EMR staff to the door and shut it behind them.

Annie curled into the sofa. The cushions were still warm from her grandma's fever and smelled like her special scent of cinnamon and sandalwood. She punched a throw pillow, aching with the need to follow her grandma.

But she'd promised.

She gave in to her grief and sobbed into the battered pillow.

A warm hand touched her shoulder. "Annie?"

She jumped. She'd completely forgotten Tombi was present.

"You," she spat.

A flinch danced across the hard planes of his face, so fleeting that she wondered if she'd misread it. He withdrew his hand.

"I'm sorry about your grandmother." He stood erect and awkward, as if unsure what to do or say.

Annie swiped her eyes and edged away from his presence. She tucked her feet beneath her on the sofa and hugged her knees to her chest. "Why don't you go away and leave me alone?"

She didn't care if she looked or sounded childish. Grandma Tia was gone. And it was all his fault. If she'd never met him, never made the mistake of following the will-o'-the-wisps into the woods, her grandma would still be here.

I'm going where you can't follow. Was Tia talking about her death? Or something else?

"Is there someone I can call?" Tombi asked. "Family? A friend?"

Annie didn't want to call her mom. It would take her hours to drive down from the north Georgia mountains. That was, *if* she came. And she'd be impatient and cross that Annie hadn't gone to the hospital. No matter that she'd shirked her own daughterly duties. Best to wait a bit for some news on her grandma's condition before calling.

Annie nodded at the desk by the far wall. "Open up that middle drawer. There's a blue address book in it."

She watched as Tombi rummaged in the drawer. His green T-shirt was streaked with red clay dirt, as were his blue jeans. It reminded her that he'd been lying on the ground deathly ill less than an hour ago. She shouldn't care but…

"Hey, are you okay?" she asked reluctantly. "Maybe you should have gone to the ER, too."

He shut the desk drawer and came toward her. One side of his mouth twitched upward. "Nice to know you care."

He handed over the battered book, which was crammed with names and addresses scribbled in Tia's large, dramatic script. Grandma wasn't one to trust computers for storing information.

Annie found Verbena Holley's name and picked up her cell phone. Verbena was a longtime family friend who would drop everything and stay with Tia at the hospital. She also wouldn't question Annie about Tia's demand that she remain at home. Verbena was almost as eccentric as Tia and possessed absolute faith in Tia's wisdom.

That done, Annie hung up and let out a deep breath. She felt a fraction better that her grandma would have a familiar face by her side this evening. Outside, shadows lengthened, and twilight wouldn't be far behind.

Tombi paced their small den looking large and out of place. He belonged to the night and to the swampland, not here in this mystical room with its herbal sachets, saint statues and candles. His stride was cramped, his posture rigid. He kept his eyes to the ground, hands tightly interlaced behind his back.

"You don't have to stay," Annie said. "You should go back to your friends." After all, Grandma Tia hadn't said she had to help him immediately. It would be best if he left, and she could gather her wits and form a plan. "They probably wonder what's taking you so long to return." And no doubt would blame her for his injury.

He stopped pacing and gave her a ferocious stare. "I'm not going back without you."

Beneath the glare of his eyes, exhaustion and pain had left a faint trace. Annie wanted nothing more than to demand he leave, but she couldn't send out a man who had been so near death.

My destiny. Was her grandma just being fanciful?

Annie stood and pointed to the sofa. "Why don't you sit, and I'll fix some tea. Something to make sure the fever lessens."

He narrowed his eyes. "What kind of tea?"

"A little this, a little that." Realization struck. "What did you think I'd put in your drink?"

"Poison, perhaps." He arched a brow. "What do witches brew? Toadstool soup with dragon blood and gator claws?"

That was rich. The guy practically killed her grandma and then suggested *he* didn't trust *her*? "Don't forget magic mushrooms and bat whiskers," she drawled.

Too bad she didn't have access to something like truth serum to find out more about his background and intentions. Still, her healing nature couldn't ignore Tombi's underlying suffering. And keeping busy was her preferred method for dealing with sorrow and worry.

In the kitchen, her safe haven, Annie set the iron teakettle on the stove and mixed together a pinch of elderberry, angelica and feverfew for taking out any underlying fever, plus a dash of chamomile for relaxing. Not truth serum, but maybe if Tombi relaxed he would open up more. Couldn't hurt.

She reached up on tiptoes for the container of stevia.

"Interesting place."

Annie spun around like a ballerina *en pointe*. "I didn't hear you come in," she sputtered. "Sneaking up on me?"

"No. It's just my way. The way of most hunters. I came to see if I could help."

Annie leaned against the counter and folded her arms. "I think you wanted to keep an eye on me." She waved a hand around the kitchen. "Go on and look. We're fresh out of arsenic and eye of newt."

Tombi squinted at the jars of dried spices and roots lining the countertops, the basket of pink mojo bags she'd assembled earlier that morning and the bunches of dried herbs hanging above on the ceiling. "Unusual, but nothing overtly suspicious, like a box of rat poison."

Was he serious? Annie frowned. "Now, look here, you can't just—"

Tombi opened the pantry door, and she drew away from the counter, spine stiffening. "Who said you could go poking about everywhere?" she demanded.

"You said I could look around." He stepped in the pantry and ran a finger over the shelves. "Ah, now it's getting interesting. Graveyard dirt, coffin nails and—" he picked up a sealed jar and turned "—swamp juice?" His nose crinkled at the puke-green cloudiness. "Looks like it could kill someone. Bacterial infection would be a gruesome death."

"Put it back, and mind your own business."

He returned it to the shelf, and Annie poured steaming tea into two mugs. She lifted the silver ball that held the loose ingredients in the teapot and waggled it. "We're drinking from the same pot. Just so you know."

Tombi sank into one of the cane-backed kitchen chairs, and Annie sat across from him at the table. He filled the room with his strong presence, overpowered what was once her peaceful sanctuary. Made it disturbing.

Exciting.

Even the air she breathed reeked of masculinity and testosterone—forceful and heady.

Annie slid the ceramic bowl filled with packets of sugar to the middle of the table. "You'll want to sweeten up that brew. It's a bit bitter. If you'd rather use honey, we have some."

"This will do."

She couldn't meet his eyes, instead staring at his lean, muscled forearms and large hands as he ripped open a sugar packet and stirred his tea. What would it be like to have his hands touching her all over? A warm flush blossomed on her cheeks, and she gripped her mug with both hands to steady the turmoil Tombi awoke in her body.

Stop it. He can't be trusted. So far, he had brought nothing but empty promises and disaster.

Tombi swallowed a mouthful of the astringent tea and struggled to conceal his revulsion. But if it would help strengthen his aching limbs and exhaustion, he'd drink every drop.

Annie regarded him, lips curled sardonically. "That's right, my dearie," she crooned in a crackly, crone voice. "Drink every last drop or the poison is no good."

He set the mug down with a bang. "You wouldn't." A heartbeat. "Would you?"

She folded her arms. "What do you think?"

"You wouldn't."

Her eyes narrowed. "Don't be so sure about me. After all, you might have got my grandma killed today. Things like that tend to piss people off, you know."

"It's highly unusual for Nalusa to attack before nightfall. It's as if he were lying in wait for me. As if someone had tipped him off."

"What the hell is that supposed to mean?" She jumped up, hands gripping the table with white-knuckled anger. "You think I contacted a…a…snake? I never even heard of Nalusa until yesterday."

"So you say."

Tombi couldn't let it go. He'd become a jaded man, not by birth disposition, but because of the deaths and trapped spirits he'd witnessed over the past ten years. He and his tribe tried to release all the ensnared souls, but they kept growing in number. Secretly, he despaired there was no stopping Nalusa's increasing spread of misery. How was he supposed to trust this girl—this witch who mysteriously appeared in the dead of night in the swamp and claimed to speak to Bo?

Annie made a disgusted clucking noise and noisily set about tidying the kitchen. "Don't drink the tea, then. Suffer. Means nothing to me."

She dried some silverware and threw it in a drawer, where it clanged. "If anyone's scared, it should be me."

"Scared? I'm not scared." For spirit's sake, he faced creatures of the dark on a daily basis.

She stared pointedly at his half-filled mug and raised an eyebrow. "Really?"

Tombi lifted it to his lips and took another experimental sip. The liquid had cooled considerably. He raised the mug in a salutatory gesture. "To good health." He downed the whole mess in four gulps.

Great Spirits almighty, that was nasty stuff.

Annie threw the dish towel in the sink and stared at him. "Your skin is starting to get a little pale and clammy," she noted. "Perspiration's beading on your forehead. You sure you're okay? Maybe I poisoned you after all."

Tombi lifted his right arm a few inches, then dropped it by his side. He'd almost given her the satisfaction of touching his forehead to check.

"Your jaw is twitching, too."

"It tends to do that when I'm annoyed."

"Better annoyed than worried sick like I am." Annie glanced out the kitchen window, and her body slumped, as if the fight and anger had melted from her spine and left her in a pool of misery.

Damn. He fought the guilt that pestered his gut. He didn't ask that old lady to save him. "Look, Annie, I'm sorry about your grandma."

She waved a hand dismissively, back still toward him.

"Maybe you should go to the hospital," he drawled, reluctant to encourage her but compelled to show compassion. Tia Henrietta had saved his life; he owed her.

"She'd kill me. She specifically begged me not to."

"Did she say why?"

Annie sighed. "She seems to think you are some kind of hero or something."

"I wish she hadn't taken the poison," Tombi offered.

She faced him and tilted her head to one side. "Did she

say something to you right before the ambulance came? I saw you lean over the couch where she lay."

He shuffled in his seat and shrugged his shoulders. "She moaned, and I got closer to see if she was trying to talk. But she was mostly incoherent."

Mostly.

The word and its meaning seemed to slip by Annie. Thank the spirits.

"She has a weak heart. I don't see how she can recover from this." Her eyes were a reproach.

Tombi frowned, hardening his heart. He couldn't let his resolve to mistrust all strangers end. He had a mission. His people depended on him. Should he fail… No, he couldn't go down that dark corridor of possibility in his mind. Bad enough the worry haunted his dreams.

Her voice rose an octave. "And to top it off, you seem to believe I brought all this on myself and my grandma."

Tombi pursed his lips. "You could have set a trap, not knowing your grandmother would come swooping in to save me at the last possible second."

"Of all the ungrateful…" she sputtered. "If not for us, you'd be dead or ate up with fever."

He paused, struck by the fact that he was ready to return to the hunt, full of vigor. "That tea actually helped," he let slip in surprise.

"Of course it did. You…you…" Again, she was so angry that words failed. She planted her hands on her hip and glared.

He smiled, and she stepped close to him.

"Stop smirking." Annie pushed against his chest. She was so small, so petite, the top of her head hit him only chest-high.

Instinctively, he grabbed her arms and pulled her closer into him. She smelled mysterious—like herbs and musk and a touch of some flowery scent that was deliciously, dangerously feminine.

He remembered their kiss. Would she ever want to kiss him again—now that she held him responsible for Tia's illness? Loss and regret swept through him like an errant breeze.

If circumstances were different. If there wasn't so much at stake. If only… But it did no good to wallow in "ifs." It wasn't as if he'd had any choice in the matter of his destiny and duty. His hands still held her forearms, but they loosened—and she didn't pull away. He hardly dared move for fear of shattering the magic.

The only sound in the room was their joined breathing, hers lighter and more rapid than his. Her chest gently expanded and contracted. And then, oh-so-slowly, they eased their bodies together, and her cheek lay on his chest. Tombi leaned down and rested his chin on the cinnamon warmth of her dark hair.

Outside, the sky darkened. Leaves and moss would begin to rustle in the ancient oaks. Soon, birds of the night would swoop from branch to branch, screeching and spying and reporting back to Nalusa on the hunters' movements. *Ishkitini*, the horned owl, was the most ominous bird of prey, because his screech foretold a sudden death or murder. Will-o'-the-wisps would glow and skitter about with the energy of the trapped deceased.

The windowpane's reflection captured their joined silhouette like a flickering trick of the eye. Nebulous and passing, a fragile thing of impermanence. Tombi closed his eyes and stroked her arms. They were as soft and slender as a robin's wing.

The phone rang, and she jerked and wiggled out of his embrace, returning to the table to pick up her cell phone.

"How is she?" Annie asked, face set in tense worry. "Uh-huh. That's good…right?"

Reassured the call wasn't death news, Tombi let himself out the front door and stood on the porch. She'd appreciate her privacy. The heat and the night pressed down on him, cloying and heavy.

He had to return to the others. His duty was clear. Somehow, he must convince Annie to come with him. This cottage wasn't safe for a young woman alone. She'd been lured once by a will-o'-the-wisp. It could happen again. Their call was almost impossible to ignore.

And then there were Tia Henrietta's words. *Annie is your destiny. Without her, you fail.* And as he'd started to straighten, the old woman's hand had gripped his with surprising strength. *Take care of my granddaughter.*

Destiny? Destiny be damned. It was enough that the gods had placed this duty on him, this infernal battle with Nalusa and his shadows. No doubt Annie could prove useful with her extraordinary hearing. But that tiny woman wasn't a key to battling evil. She didn't stand a chance against dark forces she'd never before encountered. *If* she was an innocent, he reminded himself grimly. And as far as taking care of Annie…wasn't it enough that his fellow hunters depended on him as their leader? He didn't need another burden.

The door creaked open, and she stood beside him.

"How's your grandmother?"

"Miss Verbena says her vital signs are stabilized, but she's in a coma."

He tried to find comforting words. "Her brain just needs a rest while she battles the poison."

"I don't like it." Her voice was small, weak.

He should say something sweet, something comforting. But he didn't know how. Even his twin, Tallulah, wasn't much good at sweet-talking. If Hanan were here, he would know. His friend was always quick with the comebacks and the right, appropriate thing to say. A real asset in his job as the county sheriff. Tombi stiffened, feeling awkward. "Come with me. Stay with my people."

She shot him a sideways glance. "Why?"

"So you can help us."

She sniffed and turned for the door.

He'd said the wrong thing.

"And because we could use your gift. We…apparently, need you."

"Well, I don't need you. Grandma made me promise not to go to the hospital, but she can't make me leave this house. I'm staying here in case Miss Verbena calls with more news."

"You can take your phone with you."

"Coverage is spotty in the woods. I can't chance it."

"But even if there's news, good or bad, there's nothing you can do," he pointed out.

She gave him a look that would surely curdle even Nalusa's milky venom. "I want to know everything the moment it happens." Her words were slow and deliberate, as if she were talking to a not-so-bright child.

An unexpected warmth flushed Tombi's cheeks at her condescending tone. He scowled to cover his embarrassment. Time to show his ace in the hole. "Your grandmother asked me to take care of you."

"When?" Her eyes narrowed to suspicious slits.

"That time you saw me bending over her before the ambulance came."

"You said she was incoherent."

"I was trying to save your pride."

They glared at one another. In the distance, an owl screeched. A bad sign.

Very bad.

Chapter 5

Annie shivered, breaking the tension. "That owl sounds creepy."

"Ishkitini," Tombi grumbled. No good ever came of the horned owl's cry. It often foretold death. But no sense troubling Annie with that information. She'd assume it was an omen about her grandmother, and then she'd never agree to go with him. Plus, he had to admit, he didn't want to upset Annie.

"A dangerous night to be alone. You'd be safer on the hunt with me," he said.

Her eyes shifted to the woods and back to him.

She was weakening.

"Besides, you shouldn't be here alone tonight worrying about your grandmother. Go on the hunt with us. It will take your mind off your problems."

"Why should I go? It's obvious your friends don't want me around. At least at home, I won't be insulted."

Damn Tallulah and the others for their hostility. It had

been a mistake to tell them he'd brought Annie to possibly find a traitor. Nobody appreciated a messenger with bad news. "You'll be by my side during the hunt," Tombi promised. "The others follow their own path in the night darkness."

She glanced over to the woods again. "I have to admit I'm curious about your hunt." Her eyes met his. "Does what you do involve anything gruesome? You know, like, bloody stuff?"

"Not usually."

"Good." She pinned him with a hard look. "And in return for going tonight, you'll teach me how to control my hearing?"

"For one night's work?" The words tumbled out, unfiltered. Oh, hell. By the look on her face, he'd lost any chance of getting her cooperation.

Annie marched back into the cottage, slamming the door shut.

He opened it and followed her inside. At least she hadn't locked him out. "How about this? Spend time with us, and let me know if you have suspicions about anyone. In return, I'll teach you what I can."

Anger twisted her delicate features. "Teach me? I didn't think I'd need lessons."

"How else did you expect to learn to control your gift?"

"I thought… I thought…" She sputtered to a stop.

"I never said it would be easy."

"You never said it would be hard, either." She rubbed her temples. "Just how long will these lessons take?"

"Hard to say." He folded his arms and considered. "Could take weeks, could take months. That is, if you can follow my teachings. Not everyone can control their energy."

Annie sat on the sofa and took a deep breath. "Okay, there are a couple of things troubling me about what you just said." She held up an index finger. "One, your people can guard against leaking their energy, making it difficult for me to hear their auras. So I can't guarantee I'll be able to pinpoint this person."

She held up a second finger, but Tombi interrupted, "Let me take your objections one at a time." He sat across from Annie, their knees almost touching. Warmth radiated from her slight body, and he clamped down the passion she aroused as he cleared his throat. "After a night chasing shadows, we gather back at the campsite and fill each other in on the night's events. We'll eat a light meal and then go to our tents and sleep until the heat of the day drives us out. Usually about noon."

"I don't see what this has to do with—"

"I'm getting to that," Tombi promised. "Stay alert while they sleep and walk around the camp. See if you hear anything suspicious then."

Her brow creased and then cleared. She nodded. "They must let down their guard during sleep."

"Exactly. Now what's your next objection?"

"You said you would teach me *what you could*. What the hell does that mean exactly? First you claimed you could cure me of this gift. Now it sounds like you're waffling."

"No waffling."

"Then are you saying I'm unteachable? I can assure you, that's not true. Not at all. There's nothing wrong with my intelligence."

Tombi raised a brow and regarded her silently.

She had the grace to look sheepish. "Sorry. Touchy point with me. I was teased unmercifully in grade school because I had to be taught in a separate room one-on-one with a teacher's aide. The music from all the other students made it impossible for me to concentrate in a regular classroom." She took a shuddering breath. "They used to call me Crazy Annie."

That must have been tough for a sensitive girl. "Kids can be cruel. I promise I wasn't making a comment on your intelligence. What I meant was that I'll show you how I block my energy. It's a skill my parents taught me, so it stands to reason that, with the right training, you can do the same."

A wistful sadness shadowed her eyes.

"You don't think you can do it?" he asked gently.

She bit her lip. "Oh, it's silly. But what I was really hoping is that you'd arrange for a shaman to remove it. You know, something quick and easy."

He fixed her with a hard stare.

Annie flushed. "I know. That's awful of me. I just want to get on with my life."

"Meaning what? What would you do without your special hearing ability that you can't do now?" Annie was hard to understand. He could control his senses to some degree, yet it didn't change who he was, or his purpose in life.

She threw up her hands. "You can't laugh."

At his steady wait, Annie admitted, "I want to be a librarian."

"Then do it." He shrugged. "Now. No one's stopping you."

"Even in a library, the noise gets to be too much after a while. There's more peace and quiet there than any other public place, but it still grates. I can't see me working as a librarian forty hours a week."

Annie stood and walked around the small den, picking up stray items and straightening stacks of books and magazines. "And it's more than wanting to work a full-time job. I'd like to have friends, a family, a social life."

"The music is that disruptive for you?" It might be hell

for Annie, but this extraordinary ability could only be good for his hunters. And he would try to help her control her gift.

Eventually.

Once he'd gotten all he could from her. Duty first, always.

For the first time in days, a surge of hope fueled a fire within him. "Then what do you have to lose by helping me?" he asked. "I'll make sure no harm comes to you."

She carefully placed a book back down on a coffee table. "I really, really, really hate snakes," she said, dead serious. "So you'd better protect me like you promised."

"I will," he vowed. "With my life." This he could say with no guilt or deception.

Annie picked up a picture of her grandma and bent her head over it. Her long, wavy hair covered her face, but her shoulders shook, and he knew she wept. Surprisingly, it made him long to put his arms around her and kiss away her tears. He hardened his heart—this wouldn't do at all.

"It's what your grandma wanted, too," he reminded her, pushing Annie to make a commitment.

She nodded, slowly putting down the picture. "I'm ready."

He tamped down a satisfied smile. What the hell was wrong with him? Her grandmother was probably dying. A familiar fear flickered along his nerves. He was turning into the shadows he hunted, losing his humanity and compassion.

"Should I bring anything?" she asked.

"No, I have all the provisions we'll need."

She set about blowing out the scattered candles flickering in the room, grief making each act seem like a small goodbye.

"You'll be back tomorrow afternoon," he said.

"I wonder when—or if—Grandma Tia will ever come back. This place may not be much, but she loved it."

He considered his surroundings more carefully. The worn furniture, the framed pictures, saint paintings and jars full of wildflowers strewn everywhere. It was an unexpected blow to his heart, reminding him of a similar modest place filled with colorful wool rugs and books and carved statues his father had whittled. A home that always smelled faintly of corn bread and wood shavings. A place swept away by Hurricane Katrina, along with a peace he never expected to find again.

"It's her home. Your home," he said simply.

"Yes. I only lived here during the summers, but it felt like my true home. The one place where I was wanted." Annie cleared her throat and set her shoulders back. "Let's go."

She didn't need to tell him a third time. "Okay. I'll wait for you outside."

He left, sensing she needed to collect her emotions before leaving. Night had come once again, bringing with it danger and whispers in the wind. But it was also beautiful in its own dark, mysterious way. The full moon shone bloodred, and the tall trees stood like sinister sentinels of doom.

Annie popped her head out the door. "Do we need flashlights?"

"Not necessary."

She gave him a quizzical look as she shut the door and locked up. "How about you explain a few things to me before we get to the campsite?" She pocketed her keys in a small, crocheted purse and joined him.

"What questions do you have?" he asked reluctantly. Tombi set off in long strides toward the trail. Normally, he evaded questions from outsiders, but Annie would be part of the hunt tonight, and she had a right to ask.

"For starters, how do you see so well in the dark? And slow down before I trip on a tree root or run into a tree."

He slowed. "Sorry. I'm not used to being with an outsider."

"I'm always an outsider," she mumbled.

"No offense. It's just a word we use for those not of our nation." He took hold of her hand. "It will be safer this way."

To hell with that. It was electric. He guessed from Annie's sharp inhale that she felt the same current buzzing through her body. He forced himself to focus on the path. This was no time to indulge in lustful distractions. Mistakes out here got a man killed.

"Lesson one. I have unnatural night vision, as do the rest of the hunters. It's how we were first identified by our ancestors. And since all natural gifts have a purpose—" he squeezed her hand "—they soon found why. It was one of the gifts from the spirits for us to fight and protect ourselves from the evil ones."

Annie snorted. "I don't believe all so-called gifts are for a reason. Sometimes things just are. Like genetic mutations. And why does evil exist in the first place? The spirits didn't have to allow Nalusa power."

"Why does your God allow the devil to live?" he countered. "It's impossible to question such things. We have to deal with what is instead of trying to pry into the intelligence of our creators."

"You have a point," she admitted grudgingly. "But go on—what other abilities do you have as a shadow hunter?"

He continued, glad Annie's questions seemed to keep her distracted from her anger against him. "As you guessed, we can control our energies. Which usually means creatures don't sense us until we are very close."

She stumbled slightly, and he steadied her. "I can see how that's useful. What powers do your enemies have?"

His enemies. Tombi searched the gathering twilight. "They can't sense energy as well as we can, but they have their own elements of surprise. Nalusa can shape-shift to other forms. You saw him as a snake."

Her tiny hand trembled in his own.

"Sometimes he appears as a tall, dark being with small eyes and pointed ears. And there are the will-o'-the-wisps he controls. They can take you alive or steal a soul that's not yet crossed over to the land of the dead."

"But why? What does he gain?"

"Evil doesn't always need a reason to exist. It's the nature of the universe, the duality of our world. But in Nalusa's case, any kind of death or destruction, any human suffering, contributes to his power. He feeds off our misery."

"He sounds like the very devil," she whispered. "Sorry, but I hope we don't run into him tonight." Annie shivered but continued to pick her way through the woods with his guidance, carefully stepping forward and trying to avoid the large, gnarly tree roots that erupted from the soil.

Even with his heightened senses, Tombi's night vision was limited. He could see enough to break the dark into lighter and darker shadows and to be sensitive, like a cat, to any kind of movement, even from a considerable distance.

They would arrive at camp in minutes. Would she find any of his people were really betrayers, working against them and for the dark side? That was the worst part of the shadow world; they could insidiously invade your mind and heart. You had to be constantly on guard against their influence.

"What, exactly, do you do when you find Nalusa or a wisp?" Annie asked, breaking his melancholy thoughts.

"I'll tell you when we get to camp. It's not wise to speak of such things out here in the woods."

Her eyes darted around the path, as if expecting Nalusa to grab her any second, but she kept moving forward.

He silently kept watch over her as she stumbled along,
wondering at her story. He couldn't afford to discount Annie's claim of speaking with Bo. His friend—so powerful
and so close to the tribe—might have found a way to do
what no other trapped soul had done before: break through
a wisp's barrier and speak a warning.

That was, if Annie wasn't lying, if she wasn't under
any shadow influence. There was no way to judge. He'd
observe her closely for any inconsistencies or suspicious
moves.

Because that was the worst power his enemy possessed,
the most dangerous. He could rot your soul on the inside,
could find purchase in the flimsiest of your sins and make
them into something larger, until they became a wicked
cancer that contaminated your mind. All the while, on the
outside, your friends and family couldn't tell the invisible
transformation beneath skin and bones.

The worst evil was the one that lived in your own heart,
waiting to be fed and exploited by the shadows.

As always, Annie heard before she saw: a low murmur
of voices, a rustling of feet against earth and a thrum of
excitement like the muted power and hum of an ocean
undertow.

And she was about to be dragged down into the strong
current.

The closer to camp, the stronger the pull. At last the
other hunters came into view, dark shadows with eyes
that occasionally glowed like a cat's with refracted moonbeams. Those pinpricks of light focused on her and Tombi,
but mostly her.

"How come your eyes don't glow like that?" she whispered.

"Those of us who are masters at containing our energy are able to suppress any sign that gives away our location."

"There's more people tonight than the group I met earlier."

"You only met my inner circle this morning."

One of the shadows moved closer. "We wondered where you were," said a low voice.

Annie recognized that voice. Hanan. Some people never forgot a face; but she never forgot a voice.

"So you brought her again." His voice was flat, neutral as Switzerland, but Annie registered the dig.

Tombi's hand rested on her shoulder. Possessive, comforting. Her insides warmed from the contact.

"Annie might help us turn the tide against Nalusa."

She silently berated herself. She was only important to him if she suited his purposes. Best to remember that.

Hanan nodded. "Barrett needs to speak with you before he sets out."

Tombi released her shoulder. "Be back in a minute."

The two men walked off together beyond her sight and sound. Annie marveled at their self-containment. She was in a group of over twenty people, yet the music was subdued and manageable.

A sharp pinch at her elbow caught Annie completely by surprise.

"You may have my brother fooled, but not me," Tallulah said in a fierce whisper. Her eyes glinted with suspicion. A jangle of minor keys plunked the air surrounding her tall, lithe figure. "You never talked to my Bo. If he could talk, his spirit would have come to *me*, not you, witch."

Her Bo. So that was how it had been between them. Tombi should have mentioned that the two of them were lovers. Still, it was hard to find sympathy for the malicious Tallulah.

"I didn't seek him out," Annie protested. "I can't help it."

"I can't help it," Tallulah mocked in a high-pitched trembly voice. "What's your real game? Who sent you here?"

Where was Tombi? Annie scanned the campground, where hunters' shadows moved into the woods and disappeared into darkness. They moved alone or sometimes in groups of two. Loners. Instead of talking, they used a series of hand signals to communicate. A few she could understand—wait, this way, goodbye—but most she couldn't decipher.

Tombi appeared suddenly from behind. "Go," he told Tallulah in a low, harsh voice.

Chulah materialized by Tallulah's side and motioned for her to join him.

But Tallulah wasn't finished. She edged closer, and her harsh breath was in Annie's ear. "I'll be watching you." With that, Tallulah spun around and sauntered into the woods, Chulah close at hand.

"She's had a hard time since Bo's death," said Tombi.

Of course he'd defend his sister. But Annie found it hard to muster understanding for that Amazon. Tombi's twin possessed a black panther's stealthiness, a feline wildness marked by sharp claws and growls and hisses.

Annie would come out on the losing end of that catfight.

"We need to talk." Tombi motioned, and she followed him into his tent. The darkness was utter under the canopy. She sat down on a pallet made of blankets. A low, throbbing drumbeat suffused the tight space between their bodies.

She wanted to sink into that sound, to lie down and fold into the steady, pulsating notes. Feel its vibration stroke her naked skin.

"The tent will muffle our voices a bit. I'm laying down a few rules before we start."

The baritone filled the cramped space with its power. Too bad his words tempered the sexy effect of his music.

"I won't cause trouble," she whispered, curtailing the teenaged desire to roll her eyes. "I'll stick close and keep quiet."

"Good." He leaned over, and she felt the hot skin of an arm and the side of his waist brush against her chest and face. Her breath quickened. His scent, his aura, drew her to him, and she was helpless to fight the pull. Being near him was sexually hypnotic. How easy it would be to reach out and pull him closer. Feel the weight of his body on top of her own. Despite the sadness of the evening and her chaotic thoughts, she was drawn to his music, as if her were the Pied Piper of the bayou.

The tent was intimate. She didn't want to hunt, she wanted to stay here, with Tombi. Safe and protected and exploring the pleasure of his body.

Crazy.

Wrong time, and possibly the wrong man.

But as if her arms weren't controlled by her brain, Annie reached around his back and drew him to her.

His back muscles tightened beneath her touch, and he drew in a ragged breath. Tombi stilled, as if warring with his sexual desire and his duty in the world outside the tent.

Annie wanted him desperately, just for a few minutes, a little slice of time. She saw how much he gave to the others, how they looked up to him. She saw how he defended his sister. In spite of Tallulah's nastiness, he made allowances for her grief. Didn't he deserve a few minutes of happiness for himself?

Didn't she?

Who knew what dangers the night and the hunt might bring?

In the hushed darkness, their breathing forged wisps of desire that swirled in the confined area.

Tombi groaned, as if admitting defeat, and his weight slammed into her, sending them both down, bodies pressed hard against the earth. His lips and tongue were on her, in her, warm and electric.

He moaned again—no, wait, that was *her* this time. Her body was in a fever of longing. Annie couldn't remember the last time—if ever—she had been so desperate with desire. Need curled and twisted her gut.

"You're so damn sexy," Tombi ground out.

Passion flamed hotter in her veins, along with triumph and humble gratitude that she, misfit Annie Mathews, could affect him so much. She arched against him, and his mouth tracked kisses down her neck and past the hollow at the base of her throat. He pushed up her T-shirt and unhooked her bra. One of his hands glided to her breasts and palmed her rounded flesh. His mouth lowered and covered a nipple, his tongue flicking the bud, sending unbearable need to her core. Tombi's full manhood ground against her, hard and insistent.

"Tombi? Tombi? You there?"

The insistent whisper outside the tent flap exploded on their private ecstasy.

"Damn it," Tombi muttered. In a heartbeat, he pulled away and ran a hand through his long hair.

Annie watched him scramble out the tent and hugged her arms to her waist, missing his heat and touch. Quickly, she hooked her bra and pulled down her shirt. She felt disoriented. Seconds ago her mind and body had been united and focused on physical release. Now her thoughts were chaos.

Low murmurs sounded nearby. Was there some kind of trouble? Annie silently crawled to the tent's front and poked her head out the slotted opening. Tombi and Hanan were several feet away, and they immediately turned as one to stare at her.

Not much, if anything, would get past these men. They could probably pick up a frog's croak from a hundred yards out. She ducked her head back inside, as if she'd been caught eavesdropping.

Tombi crawled into the tent and sat as far from her as he could in the small space.

The passion party was definitely over.

"So here are the simple rules," he said, as if nothing had happened between them. "Stay within arm's reach of me and avoid talking unless it's an emergency. I'll be searching for will-o'-the-wisps, and when I come within range, I'll shoot it with a slingshot. We aim for the glowing heart in the middle. If we hit it dead-on, the wisp will release the spirit and lose its power."

"And the trapped spirit will be freed?"

"Exactly." He hesitated. "I've been searching for one wisp in particular."

"Bo," she guessed. "You want to help your friend."

He nodded. "If you hear Bo again or sense he's near, point me in the right direction. Other sounds to beware of are snake rattles or music from the wisps. You might hear them before me. If you do, tap my arm."

She cringed at the thought of snakes. "Seems like the wisps would be easy targets with the way they glow and the music they make."

"But nature's provided them with speed and the ability to momentarily lose their light. Makes it hard to zero in on them."

"And what has nature granted you? What does it mean when you say you can control your energy?"

His eyes shifted to the opening, as if impatient to be on the move. "The quick and dirty version is this—we can create a field around our bodies that makes it hard for Nalusa and his wisps to see, smell or hear us in the dark."

He reached behind her, pulled out a camouflage duffel bag and slung it over his right shoulder.

So that was what he'd been looking for earlier when he'd leaned across her body. And she'd grabbed at him like an out-of-control hormonal teenager. Annie winced inwardly. But she consoled herself, knowing that he had obviously enjoyed their kiss.

"Let's go."

His command cut through her musings. She followed him out, and they walked across the open field. Annie took care to stay close and stay silent.

It was like another world at night. Although it was still hot, the humidity was at a bearable level, and she became even more hyperaware of sound and smell—the gentle lap of the Gulf water, the crickets, the unnerving screech of an owl. The breeze smelled of pine and moss and sea salt that invigorated. It was the smell of childhood summers and freedom.

Tombi kept a slow pace, most likely for her ease, and managed to avoid most twigs and dry leaves. Annie winced at the first few crunches her footfalls produced. Somehow, though he weighed twice as much and his foot size was a great deal larger, Tombi walked almost soundlessly.

To his credit, he didn't utter a word or give a disapproving warning look. *Because you are doing just what he wants you to do. He needs you to find Bo again.* Tombi didn't care so much about stalking prey as he did about finding his friend. And she was his key.

Her legs tired, and her arms burned from scratches and brushes with foliage and bark. On and on and on they walked until she'd lost all sense of time. Her jeans were hot, but at least her legs weren't getting sliced and battered like her arms. How long would this go on? She'd assumed it would only be a couple of hours, but now she feared he would keep hunting until dawn.

Every few minutes he would turn and look at her, an eyebrow raised in question. *Have you heard anything?*

And each time she'd had to shake her head "no."

Annie kept her senses fully opened, a rare event. She heard more intricate, softer sounds now, rustling leaves, a lone car passing by from a great distance. The other noises she'd heard earlier deepened, and she awakened to the more subtle tones like tree roots pulsing and pushing the earth, inch by inch, mining for nutrients. The ocean lapped the shore with a splash, announcing the end of its journey until the undertow pulled it back to start a new one. Insects droned and squeaked in their thirst for survival. Small critters like squirrels or rabbits or foxes skittered amongst dense underbrush.

Eat or be eaten. Perish or thrive. The cadence of survival was a constant dance of retreat and attack, a crescendo and decrescendo of noise.

Tombi unexpectedly pulled her close to his side. His mouth covered one of her ears. "Do you need to rest?" he breathed. Her skin and insides vibrated with arousal.

She nodded, and he led her to a fallen limb where they could sit. Annie sank on to the rough bark and fought the urge to break into a loud sigh of relief. Tombi removed the camo bag from his back and produced a water bottle. Wordlessly, he handed it to her.

Annie gulped the cold water. She lifted it to her lips for another draught, pausing at the faint, floating notes wafting in the breeze. Bewitching, evocative notes that pulled her inside, urging her to come forward, to more clearly enjoy the exquisite melody. She dropped the water bottle and rose to her feet, circling to catch the direction of the music.

The music grew more distinct. And even though she

knew its charm held an ugly underside, the need to follow the sound twisted her gut with longing to be closer,
to bask in its loveliness.

Tombi's touch on the middle of her back steadied her.
Again, he whispered in her ear. "Is it Bo?"

She considered. "I don't think so," she said, keeping
her voice barely above a breath.

Disappointment tightened his face.

"But there's more than one," she added. "It's a blended
sound. I'd guess at least five or six separate voices."

"Damn. How far away?"

"About fifty yards." She pointed toward the east. "In
that direction."

Tombi pulled out his slingshot and palmed several
rocks. "Can't wait here and let them circle us in an ambush."

"What would happen if they did?"

"Your soul would be in jeopardy. They invade your
mind like a cold smoke. A vapor that seeps in by any crack
in your mental armor."

"I'll go with you," she said hurriedly. "I can help throw
stones."

"No," he said, cutting her off at once. "You'll be safer
here. Stay put and don't go anywhere."

He placed a couple of stones in her hand and left, disappearing in sudden, silent movements.

Jerk. He'd promised to stay close by her side, yet at the
first whiff of a fight, he'd abandoned her. Annie sat back
down on the log, put the stones in her lap and pressed her
fingers to her ears, trying to at least partially block the
will-o'-the-wisps' alluring call. It helped, but it wasn't perfect. Annie resorted to her second round of defense; she
sang silently inside, blocking outside sound from over-
powering her emotions.

Much better. Not perfect, but better. It was tolerable.

Good thing, because her last defense was running away, and right now that wasn't an option.

The relief was short-lived.

A stealthy note of caution and cunning crept over her flesh like sticky syrup. Something or someone was at the edge of her awareness. Annie dropped her hands in her lap and stared into the inky void.

A rumble vibrated in her mind, like she'd imagine an earthquake would produce. But the ground wasn't trembling. Where the hell did it come from? Even the wisps had fallen silent. Did this mean Tombi had been hurt or captured? Dread prickled her scalp.

A harsh noise like grating metal erupted. Annie jumped up, nerves jangling with adrenaline.

The rumbling and grating ceased, and a small childlike voice whispered in the night.

"Help me. Please."

Annie's breath was so loud and ragged she might as well have had a beacon of light shining on her, telegraphing her location.

"I'm trapped," the voice said plaintively, louder this time.

It called to the healer in her even more than the wisp's enchanting songs.

She had to help.

Chapter 6

"Over here."

Annie squeezed the rocks fisted in both her palms and took a couple of steps forward. She held her hands out in front of her to avoid slamming into anything and carefully followed the voice.

The exquisite music returned, and she realized the voice was a soul trapped in a wisp. Thankfully, it appeared to be solitary in its flittering about the swamp. If only Tombi were here, he could help this poor soul. As for herself, she was always the last one picked for any kind of sport at school, including softball. So her strength and her aim were highly suspect. She'd be lucky to hit a large target even at the mere distance of ten feet.

Forward progress was painfully slow, but the volume of the music increased, and Annie knew she was close. She leaned against a tree and took a deep breath. Might as well speak up; the wisp already knew she was present. "If you want my help, come to me."

A swirl of pink and purple shone through a patch of brambles a few yards ahead.

"That was quick," she muttered.

Symphonic music emanated from the wisp, soothing her fear.

Be careful. Annie focused on the rocks balled in her hand, their sharp edges scratching into her flesh. *Focus on the soul who wants freedom.*

In the span of time it took for a struck match to catch flame, the wisp floated to within six feet of where she stood with her back pressed into the jagged bark. Its brightness lit the woods stronger than any lantern. At its center, a heart shone violet blue like the color at the base of a candle flame. That was her target. Her mouth grew dry. Could she really do it? Tombi never said what would happen once the spirit left a will-o'-the-wisp.

"Whoever, whatever you are inside there, you better help me if I free you." Annie stepped away from the tree, raised her arm and threw the stone in her right hand.

It landed several inches above the heart, harmlessly passing through the wisp's pink-and-purple vapor. The beautiful music stopped, and a growl rumbled in warning. Quickly, she transferred the rock from her left hand to her right and whirled it again at the glowing heart.

Dead-on.

A high-pitched screech wailed, and gray smoke shot out of the wisp's center. The rest of its glowing form collapsed upon itself, as if it had lost its skeletal base. Its shine dimmed and grew smaller, until it was about the size of a basketball. Would it retaliate? The need to run fueled her body, and her veins pulsed with adrenaline, but how could she run in this darkness?

"Follow me," said a tiny voice from below.

Annie looked down, and floating only a few inches from the ground was a swirling ball of gray-yellow smoke.

"You have only a few minutes before either the wisp regenerates or other wisps hunt you down."

Chills chased up and down her spine. "But how—"

The light wobbled in the air. "There's enough light that you can see a few feet ahead of you at a time. I'll take you down a path that leads to a paved road. Hurry!"

A faint rumble near the wounded wisp was all the encouragement she needed. Annie picked her way along the dirt path, frustrated with her slow pace.

"Hurry," the light urged again.

"I can't go any faster."

"Try."

The light streaked ahead, and she quickened her step to keep up. "Don't leave me, you ungrateful little…" Annie bit her lip to stop the insulting words. It would be foolish to anger the tiny soul helping as best it could. Tombi was nowhere around, for damn sure. Some protection he turned out to be.

She plunged on, her focus on the small soul she'd rescued and the lucent beam it cast. Red clay, pine needles and twisted tree roots had never appeared so beautiful. Nothing mattered except continuing, one foot, then another, doing what was necessary for survival. Her breathing was labored and unnaturally loud, a roar in her ears.

"You're almost to the road," the soul squeaked in its small voice. "You're on your own from there."

"Where are you going?"

"I'm crossing over."

"You're entering the afterlife? Is that a good thing?"

"The best."

At least one lovely incident occurred this evening. A soul's passage from Earth was a solemn, miraculous rite. "What's your name?" Annie asked.

"Not important. All that matters is that you make it home."

The soul surged to Annie's eye level, the swirling ball of color changing from its original grayish yellow to a blazing orange.

Her feet hit pavement, and she wanted to weep with relief at the sight of the open road.

"Keep going," the soul warned.

Panic returned. Annie looked up and down the road, but nothing appeared familiar. "At least tell me where I am."

The light whooshed away at a dazzling speed, pitching her into sudden darkness. It was leaving her, after all she'd done, all she'd...

The soul returned. "Another mile ahead is the intersection of County Roads 82 and 40."

Not far from home after all. "Thank you," she said, exhaling deeply with relief.

"Go." The soul slowly floated upward.

"Wait! I still can't see much without you."

It kept floating until it became one with the night. "You could have at least said thank-you," Annie complained, her face tilted skyward.

The grating metal noise sounded again from the edge of the woods. Annie took off on a brisk walk. There was a sliver of light from the moon now, but not much. It would be a miracle if she didn't trip and bash her head a dozen times on the blacktop surface before she even came to the four-way stop.

Damn Tombi. He should never have left her alone.

A captivating song unexpectedly entered her mind. One she'd never heard before. But how? This never happened unless she was near someone. And right now she was utterly alone. The song continued, like a balm easing soreness, a lullaby for frayed nerves. It wasn't the enchanting music of the wisps; this was more...relaxing and peaceful.

Annie's breath slowed while her feet continued their ceaseless march forward. If she had to run at some point, she would. She'd faced and defeated one wisp; she could do it again if needed.

"Thank you." The words were a brushed whisper in her mind. The rescued soul hadn't abandoned her at all. It had come back and provided comfort for the long journey home.

It was one of the sweetest acts of kindness she'd ever experienced. Annie's throat tightened. "You're welcome," she said aloud, past the aching lump.

The music played on. The sweet notes kept her steady, kept her from stumbling on legs burning with exhaustion. A side stitch smarted, like a surgeon's knife had sliced through half of her torso, and dehydration left her parched and with a headache. But the music kept playing until she'd arrived at her grandma's cottage. A long, cool glass of water, and she was falling into bed. A shower could wait.

Where the hell was Annie?

Tombi paced back and forth by the log where he'd last seen her.

"We've searched everywhere." Chulah arrived with two others. "I checked in with all the hunters. No one has seen or heard her."

"Keep looking," he snapped. Worry racked his mind until he thought he would go mad. He'd said he'd protect Annie. And now she had vanished.

His fault.

He should never have left her alone. Not even for a shot at capturing Nalusa.

His brain froze in horror. Did Nalusa get to Annie?

For the hundredth time, Tombi walked around the log, hoping to track a smell or visual sign for a clue. He slowly tracked in ever-widening circles. This time, a faint sulfur odor, mixed with balsam fir, drifted up from the ground.

Tombi knelt down and found a sprinkling of ash dusted on pine needles.

"Hey," he said, looking over his shoulder. "We have burnout."

Chulah knelt beside him, picked up a powdered needle and held it beneath his nose. "Happened well over an hour ago."

"Has anyone else hunted in this area tonight?"

"I already told you—no. The girl must have done it."

Tombi kept searching until he found two small, round rocks several feet nearby. The ones he'd given her for protection. "I shouldn't have left her side."

"How were you supposed to know it was a trap?" Chulah asked. "You thought a band of wisps might encircle the two of you."

"Better that than to leave her defenseless."

"You left her the rocks, and she defended herself," Chulah said, standing. "There's enough light now that it's possible she walked home. She's probably in bed asleep."

His friend lied to reassure him. Tombi stood as well, dread slowing his movements. He'd promised to protect her. What if another wisp had heard the burnout when the soul was released and made its way to Annie, bent on retaliation? His gut clenched.

"Why are you so worried about that girl?" Chulah frowned. "One explanation is that she defended herself and got either bored or tired of waiting on you to return and went home."

"*That* girl?" Tombi said, crossing his arms. "She's a woman, not a girl, and you know damn well she must be in trouble." He remembered the press of her body against his, the warm feel of her skin against his own. Annie Matthews was a woman. A passionate woman.

Twigs snapped, and leaves crackled beneath a careless foot. Tallulah burst through the underbrush to his side.

Her eyes were fierce and focused as she strode to where he and Chulah stood.

"We've wasted enough time searching for that foolish woman," she snapped. "Let's get back to camp."

"She's not foolish. Why the hostility? She's offered to help us."

Tallulah tossed back her long hair and lifted her chin. "Because she's under Nalusa's influence. He sent her here to spy on us and make us mistrustful of each other. There's no traitor."

His sister voiced his own misgivings, yet he found it increasingly difficult to believe the worst of Annie.

"Her grandmother is critically ill, maybe even dead, because she absorbed the poison Nalusa meant for me," Tombi reminded them.

"And Annie could have set you up to be bitten," Tallulah said. "Her grandmother might not have known what was going on. Why are you so blind?"

If she wasn't his sister, if he didn't know how grief-stricken she'd been after Bo's death, he wouldn't be able to control the temper heating his veins. "I've been leading this group for ten years. You've never questioned my judgment before."

The fierceness in her eyes faded, and her shoulders slumped. "I don't want you to get hurt, Tom-Tom."

She hadn't called him by that childhood name in years. His heart softened, remembering everything they'd been through together—the death of their parents and a new lifestyle with a host of duties thrust upon them at a young age. For spirit's sake, they'd only been nineteen when Hurricane Katrina had washed away the solid foundation of their world.

"Don't worry about me," he said softly.

Chulah stepped in and placed an arm over Tallulah's

shoulder. "Let's get back to camp and eat breakfast. We're all tired and hungry. You, too, Tombi."

"Not until I find out what's happened to Annie. Go if you want, but I'm going to keep tracking." He had to see her, had to know she was safe. The need to touch Annie, to hold her and apologize for leaving, was an ache deep in his soul.

Sleep was impossible.

Annie drank the tall glass of water she'd craved and collapsed on her bed, but an unease settled over her, a conviction that something bad had happened. She got up and went to the altar in the den, intent on lighting a candle to pray for Grandma Tia. A note from Miss Verbena had been propped on the mortar-and-pestle bowl, informing Annie that her grandmother had suffered a stroke.

A punch in the gut.

Sooner or later lack of sleep would catch up to her, but for now Annie was fueled with adrenaline and the need to check on her grandma. She showered, put on a clean pair of jeans and a T-shirt, and drove to the Bayou La Siryna hospital.

To hell with that coerced promise to stay away.

Annie's resolution stayed strong until she walked down the long hallway of the critical-care unit. From every door she passed, she heard a funereal fugue with its long, melancholy strains, as gloomy as Baroque organ music. Worse were the open doors to rooms housing patients in intense pain. Their aural music was sharp as glass shards, slicing through her consciousness. *Deep breaths. One step at a time.* Only her love for Tia was worth suffering these symphonies of agony.

Room 3182. She'd made it.

Annie pushed the cool metal door open and entered.

All was quiet. The sweet scent of violets triumphed over antiseptic's odor. Which meant Miss Verbena had recently been here, had been in vigil by the bed when *she* should have been the one doing so.

Tia's eyes were closed and her breathing steady, as if in peaceful slumber. As if her physical agonies were in a state of suspension.

Annie took her grandma's right hand in her own. Tia's fingers were cold and rough. Her grandma would hate that. She always said that if she were meant to tolerate the cold, she'd have been born a Yankee.

She found some lotion in the hospital toiletry bin and rubbed the balm into her grandma's cold flesh, pressing and kneading the rough skin, massaging in healing warmth. All Tia's flashy rings were gone. She looked bare without them, oddly lonely and vulnerable.

Tia's hands should be active—mixing potions, dealing tarot cards, lighting candles. Even saddled with a bad heart, her grandma would sit on the sofa in the evenings and read through old magic books, an index finger gliding down the page like a third eye, absorbing words. Or she would shuffle the cards and lay out spreads, searching for messages from the beyond.

Inside a metal locker was a blanket, and Annie tucked it over Tia's unmoving body, remembering all the times her grandma had tucked her in bed as a child. She'd never felt so loved nor as safe as when Grandma Tia chanted and hummed, asking for the saints' protection over "the young'un" while she slept. Tia would slide the sheets up to Annie's neck and pat her large, warm hands on Annie's slender shoulders, as if to seal in a prayer.

"Rest well, Grandma. I'll watch over you now." Annie pressed her palms into Tia's broad shoulders. "Saints be with us."

The air pressed down, and a humming rang in her ears,

as if she'd been submerged in a cave. What was happening? The contact with Grandma Tia had set something in motion. Every sound magnified: the grind of tires on the distant highway, a clock ticking. Down the hall, a voice called for a nurse. The sounds were distinct yet muted and slowed down. Annie sank into the chair by the side of the bed and squeezed Tia's hand.

"Are you there, Grandma? It's me, Annie."

Tia's chilled, lifeless hand suddenly warmed, then burned into Annie's palm and fingers. Instinctively, Annie started to pull back but stopped, afraid she'd lose this connection. Possibly the last she'd ever have with her grandma. She closed her eyes and concentrated. *I'm here. Don't be mad. I had to see you.*

A pinprick of light danced behind Annie's closed eyelids. With each flicker, a tiny note pinged…sounding like the metal triangles of elementary school. No, wait, that wasn't right. The notes were more like the Native American flute Tombi had played in the woods.

She didn't want to think about him. Yet, she couldn't escape the feeling that he was calling her somehow, that he needed her. Why was Grandma Tia always pushing him toward her, even while unconscious? An image of a flute pressed into her thoughts. It was more decorated than the one Tombi had played, as if it were used in ceremonies and rituals.

She'd never seen it before. But Tia had.

"What are you trying to tell me?" Annie asked.

The image, and the music, faded to a black void. Tia's hand cooled to a normal temperature.

The moment had passed.

Annie's eyes flew open, but Tia's calm mask of sleep was undisturbed. Profound relief washed over her body, and with it came a great weariness. She sank into the chair and slept.

* * *

Violets…the scent tickled her nose. Miss Verbena's lined face came into view.

"Annie, are you okay, dear?"

She jerked to an upright position and looked out the window. How long had she been asleep? The late-afternoon sun washed the air with bright power.

My name means ray of light in Choctaw, Tombi had told her. *We once revered the sun's power.* At the time, she'd laughed over his not-so-sunny personality, but his name fit. He was powerful and strong and important to his people, a central figure in a fight against shadow beings who wanted to block the light.

Her anger melted like butter in the heat. If Tombi hadn't ever returned to find her, he'd had a good reason. A chill settled in the pit of her stomach. What if he'd been injured last night?

She had to find him at once.

"You're so pale," Miss Verbena said. "I'll fetch you a glass of water. Have you eaten today?"

Her mouth tingled at the mention of food. "No. I guess I forgot."

"Lord a-mercy, I wish I'd forget to eat a meal." Miss Verbena patted her ample belly and dug a pack of peanut-butter crackers out of her straw bag. "This should tide you over until dinner."

Annie scarfed them down greedily as she gathered her pocketbook and car keys. "I have to run," she apologized. She hugged her grandma's dear friend. "Thank you for staying with Grandma Tia. I'll be back as soon as I can."

"'Course you will. You've always been a good girl, unlike your…" She clamped her mouth shut in a tight line.

"Unlike my mom," Annie said. "Have you called her? I know I should but…"

Miss Verbena shook her head. "That's your business.

Doubt she'd come, though. Always swore she never wanted to come back here again after they had that big blowout years ago." The scowl on her face softened. "Don't you worry, honey. I have a feeling ole Tia's gonna pull through this just fine. You go on and do what you got to do."

She carefully hugged the old woman, throat constricted with tears. "Thanks for understanding."

Annie hurried out, knowing that she had to find Tombi.

Chapter 7

Tombi kicked at the campfire ashes, placed his elbows on his knees and rested his head in his hands. He should be sleeping like the others in preparation for the last night of the hunt. Instead, his mind kept asking the same question over and over. *Where is Annie?* He'd checked her cottage, of course, but she wasn't home. Neither was her car, which meant she could be anywhere. He'd called and left messages on her cell phone, but she couldn't, or wouldn't, answer.

The air's vibration shifted, and the soles of his bare feet prickled from a subtle tremor. Someone was approaching. Tombi raised his head, and his eyes went immediately across the clearing to where a woman entered from a wooded path.

Annie.

Others might have mistaken her for a girl, but he knew better, had explored the rounded curves of her breasts and the slight swell of her hips. He rose slowly to his feet, his mind churning with passion, anger and relief. Mostly relief.

Graceful as a woodland sprite, she walked across the field, her brown wavy hair tossing in the breeze. She seemed to draw energy to her, as if the natural world became more animated in her presence. A dark angel, a whimsical witch who heard music where others experienced only silence.

Tombi went quickly toward her, away from the tents of sleeping hunters. A few were already stirring, preparing for various camp duties before the night's hunt.

"Where have you—" he started.

"You're okay. I thought maybe—"

They both stopped. Tombi reached for her, and she willingly walked into his arms. All the worry and anxiety of the past few hours vanished under the solid feel of her body pressed against his. He kissed the top of her head, inhaling the scent of flowers and musk. But he was conscious that the others would soon be stirring from their tents. Now wasn't the time to kiss again—they would be certain she'd bewitched him. He stepped back and scanned her body, checking for injuries.

"The wisp didn't hurt you?"

Annie blinked. "How did you know I was attacked?"

"We found the stones you threw and ashes from a released spirit." He had to know, dared to hope. "Was it Bo?"

"No, sorry. I had the impression the soul was a girl. And she never told me her name."

Tombi shook off the disappointment. It had been a longshot chance at best. "I tried to find you. Even went to your grandma's cottage, but your car was gone. I've been worried."

She shrank into herself. "I went to the hospital to see my grandma," she said shortly.

Did she still blame him for her grandmother's illness?

Hell, it wouldn't be any worse than the guilt that nagged at him over what had happened. "How is she?"

"She's still in a coma. The doctors said she had a stroke but they never mentioned poison, which I find strange."

"There never is. Nalusa's venom won't register on medical tests. People he's bitten were diagnosed with other conditions like heart attacks or allergic reactions."

"Has anyone been bitten and lived?"

Her eyes were so sad, so anxious, he couldn't tell her the truth. "Maybe," he hedged. "I can't be aware of every instance he's attacked or bitten."

"What happened out there in the woods? You never came back to me."

"I was drawn away. I'll explain later. But first, I need your help. Quick." He looked back over his shoulder at the campsite. "While everyone is still asleep."

She nodded. "That's why I'm here. I did promise."

Annie brushed past him and strode purposefully toward the tents. He followed a few yards after, hands clasped behind his back. None of his people would betray him; he was almost 100 percent certain of their loyalty.

Almost.

If Annie heard nothing incriminating, he'd report her finding to the others, and they could continue on as before, without the worm of mistrust wiggling in some dark recess of their minds.

She walked carefully among the tents and paused at one. A large moan erupted from inside, and she blushed. Even he recognized the music of passion. Annie scurried away, and he laughed.

She circled around a tent on the outside of the ring, her head cocked to the side. He raised an eyebrow at her, but she shook her head and moved on, tapping her lips and chin as she concentrated.

Only one more round of tents, and she would be finished. He silently willed her to hurry and be done with it. Before the last tent, the one closest to his own, she stopped. Her brows creased as she listened.

Tombi couldn't move, couldn't breathe. *No.* Not this tent. *Move on*, he wanted to scream.

But she didn't. She faced him and extended her right arm at the tent, pointing her finger. Quickly, he walked to her side and guided Annie away by an elbow.

"There's your man," she said.

"Not possible. You're mistaken."

Her eyes widened. "What's wrong with you? You've begged me for two days, and now you act like *this*? Sounds like you're making excuses for somebody." Her voice rose. "Who are you protecting?"

"No one," he denied, his own voice rising in anger. "Forget about it."

Annie put her hands on her hip. "Bo spoke to me. He said to warn you about a betrayer. Well, I've done my duty. If you don't want to listen to me, that's your problem."

Bo. Even now, hearing the name of his best friend pinched his heart.

Annie turned her back on him and stalked away from the center of the campsite. Already, hunters were stepping out of their tents to see the commotion. He hated public displays. He was a tracker, damn it. Controlled, in charge and rational.

Tombi caught up to her. "Where are you going?" he whispered harshly, not wanting everyone to hear their conversation.

"Home."

He grabbed her hand. "Wait. I want—"

She jerked out of his grasp and kept walking. "I don't care what you want anymore."

Annie couldn't leave. Not like this. He could still use her help. And she was his last living link to Bo. "I'm your only hope of learning to control your gift," he reminded her.

She stopped, and Tombi scrambled in front of her.

"When do the lessons start?" she asked through tight lips.

"Tomorrow morning."

"What kind of lessons are you giving her?" Hanan asked, arms crossed. He stood in front of his tent.

The tent that Annie had fingered.

Annie looked from Tombi to Hanan, eyebrows raised.

"He's my right-hand man, my closest friend since Bo died," Tombi explained in a low voice. "I trust him."

"Believe what you want." Her posture was stiff and her words clipped.

He'd hurt her feelings. Tombi tried to consider their argument from her perspective. She found his rejection of her findings as a rejection of *her*. Which wasn't the same thing at all.

Hanan ambled over and nodded pleasantly at Annie before speaking to Tombi. "Is it something I can help you with? I know you're pressed for time finishing the Anderson project."

"Maybe. I'll let you know." It was true he was behind on his carpentry jobs, but Tombi doubted Annie would want Hanan as a teacher. Not now.

"Sure, if you can help teach me to guard my energy like the rest of the hunters." Annie smiled sweetly and held out her hand.

All the frosty stiffness had melted. What was her game?

Hanan accepted the outstretched hand, covering Annie's small hand with both of his own.

Tombi frowned at the sight. The touch was held a moment longer than necessary. Hanan broke contact first.

"Chulah and I need to talk with you when you get a minute."

"Be with y'all shortly."

Hanan sauntered off, joining the other men in preparing a meal.

"You would really take lessons from Hanan?" Tombi asked.

"Someone needs to keep an eye on him." The lemon-tart tone returned. "What time should I come back tomorrow for a lesson?"

"Tomorrow?" he sputtered. "I thought you would stay the night."

"And go on another hunt? No, thank you."

Incredulity and frustration battled in his gut. He was used to directing everyone's moves. But Annie? She had her own life, separate from his people, and she had her own secret agendas.

Annie bit her lip to keep from smiling at Tombi's discomfort. He liked to wield power and expected others to fall in line with his wishes. But she was afraid if she allowed him to exert that same power over her, he'd stretch out the lessons and string her along until he got what he needed.

He took a deep breath. "Please, stay."

"Why do you want me to?" she asked, confused at his insistence. "I mean, it's not like you listen when I tell you what I hear."

"I do listen," he argued. "It's just, in this case, you're wrong. You heard thoughts about a dream he was having. Hanan isn't conspiring with Nalusa."

Self-doubt, her constant companion, crept in. It was possible he was right. Although, usually when she picked up dream music, it had an otherworldly, faint kind of vibe. Not the distinct, ominous tone that had emanated from Hanan's tent. The only way to know for sure if Hanan was a traitor was to spend more time with him, to catch him unawares.

No one could keep their energy contained all day, every day. Even Tombi couldn't. At unguarded moments, or at times of high emotion like when he kissed her, she heard the pounding of his heart like a snare drum vibrating in her gut. Still, other times, when he was wrapped up in his thoughts, she'd hear the notes of the Native American flute he was so adept at playing.

"Look, Tombi, I didn't get much rest last night. Let me sleep in my own bed tonight, and I'll stay for the hunt tomorrow night."

He shook his head. "That's no good. The week of the full moon ends tonight."

"Meaning what?"

"We all return to our real lives. The hunt won't resume again until the next full moon."

"You don't need me for hunting. You've done it for years on your own." She studied him closely. "I think what you really want is to see if I can speak with Bo again."

Tombi looked over her head, across the field to the woods. His face was hard and set. "He's out there, trapped. I'll do anything to release his spirit. I owe him at least that much."

Annie felt his pain like a lump in her own chest. "And he would do the same for you if the situation were reversed," she said gently.

"Tombi." Hanan waved him over to his group of four hunters.

"I have to go." He faced her at last. "I can't make you stay. As you've said, this isn't your fight."

How could she rest tonight leaving Tombi with such sadness? And Grandma Tia had fought hard to communicate with her at the hospital—to tell her that Tombi needed her. "Since you put it that way... I'll hang around."

His shoulders relaxed, as if a weight had rolled off. "Thank you. I guarantee to not leave your side this time."

"Go ahead and see your friends," she said.

"My tent is yours. Go take a nap until night falls."

"More orders?"

A smile broke across the grave landscape of his face. "Just a suggestion. Up to you."

Annie watched as he left her side, her heart lightened that she'd made the right decision in staying. And he was right. A nap would help keep her strengthened for the night ahead. She turned to walk to his tent and then froze.

Tallulah slipped out of Hanan's tent flap, as silent and fluid as a cat with her long, thin body. She stood and ran a hand through her tangled, mussed hair.

Her face was relaxed and peaceful in a way Annie had never seen. It transformed her stark, aggressive features into something lovely. Tallulah's gaze swept the area, then zeroed in on Annie. Her dark eyes tightened to suspicious slits.

She wasn't up for this. Not after seeing her grandma in a coma, not after the fight with Tombi. And not in a sleep-deprived fog. Annie went to Tombi's tent.

"Hey. Where are you going?"

Annie ignored Tallulah's strident demand. Everyone stopped what they were doing and stared; their eyes burned into her skin. She walked quickly, but lifted her chin and didn't glance right or left. Straight ahead lay safety. A few more feet and she could enter Tombi's tent and zip out the rest of the world a few hours.

Hot breath brushed the fine hairs at the nape of her neck. "Nobody wants you here. You don't belong."

Annie's skin prickled at the hostility, and her lips trembled. Stupid to let Tallulah's anger cut her to the quick. She pressed her mouth into a thin line. She wouldn't cry in front of everyone watching. Three more steps and she would be rid of the woman. Quickly, she reached the tent flap and knelt to enter.

Tallulah dropped to her knees alongside her. "What does my brother see in you?" she continued in that same dark whisper. "You're a coward. A lying coward."

Annie's hands fumbled at the zipper, and she tugged at it, eyes burning with tears.

I will not cry in front of them. Yes, it was true. She'd rather curl up in a little ball all alone than face Tombi's pit viper of a twin. Metal grated on metal, and nirvana opened. Annie ducked inside and battened down the hatch, allowing the salty tears to spill from her eyes.

Low-pitched laughter rang out inches away from the thin canvas lining. "Coward," Tallulah seethed again.

"Tallulah!" Tombi's commanding voice cut through the air.

How much had he heard? Despite the smothering heat, Annie curled up in the corner and pulled a sheet over herself, a turtle retreating into its shell. Shame smothered her as thick as the Alabama humidity. *You don't belong.* The words ricocheted in her brain, fast and deadly. She never belonged, and she never would. Even with a band of supernatural shadow hunters, she was branded as a misfit.

Hysterical laughter bubbled up, and she covered her mouth with the sheet to keep anyone from overhearing.

The sound of a zipper unfastening had her hastily rolling onto her side, back to the entrance. She didn't want Tombi to see her like this. Couldn't bear to see either pity or disgust on his stoic face.

"Annie?" he called out softly. "You okay?"

She feigned sleep, keeping her breathing deep and rhythmic. The air crackled with his scent, with his strong, commanding aura. Her heart pounded in time to the drumming that was his unique music.

A heavy warmth brushed against the back of her scalp

as Tombi's fingers stroked her hair. The tenderness almost undid her. She'd experienced passion before, but gentle gestures like this were foreign territory. Annie relaxed and stilled under his touch.

Tombi left in his quick, silent way, and she rolled onto her back. The smell of bacon and biscuits permeated the air. People shuffled around the campfire, speaking in low murmurs.

She longed to be a part of community like this. Mom and her string of stepfathers and stepsiblings merely tolerated her, and no one wanted to be friends with Crazy Annie.

Enough of the self-pity. Tallulah had hit a soft spot, and she'd overreacted. With any luck, no one had seen her tears. Her cheeks burned that everyone had witnessed her hasty scamper to Tombi's tent. Bet none of them had ever disgraced themselves by running away. The warrior spirit in them probably never backed away from a confrontation. Annie sighed and closed her eyes, imagining herself as one of them, eating and laughing together instead of lying in the hot, stifling tent alone.

She indulged in a familiar fantasy. She'd find a way to get rid of her supernatural hearing and go about her life doing all the ordinary things others took for granted. A job, a family, or even simple things like shopping at the mall or going to a concert. Maybe she'd even go back to school and get a college degree.

A smile tugged her lips, and she curled up, sleepy at last.

"Annie? Wake up. Time to eat."

She bolted to a seated position and inhaled sharply at the intimacy of Tombi's nearness. Memories of their previous kiss in the tent made her skin heat and her body yearn for more of the same.

Tombi retreated, even as his breath grew raspy and his eyes darkened. "A quick bite and we need to get a move on."

He was in full warrior mode, ready to hunt once more. Damn her traitorous body. She needed to remind herself that his focus was on defeating the shadows, and she was merely a tool in helping him win the battle.

Annie clambered out of the tent and followed him to the center of the campsite. The fire was long gone, but white-hot firewood gave off heat. Tombi piled an aluminum pie plate with several bacon slices and a couple of biscuits and handed it to her.

The smell set her mouth salivating, and she dug in. She hadn't eaten since the crackers at the hospital. Tombi silently poured her a glass of sweet tea, and she washed down the food with the sugared brew. Perfect. Food always tasted better when eaten outdoors. Either that, or she was really hungry.

Tombi sat across from her and leaned forward; his skin shone like bronze in the night. "Let's do something different tonight. Something a little safer."

Safer sounded great. "What?" she asked, setting aside her plate.

"We're going back to the spot where I first met you. Where Bo appeared and spoke."

She sighed.

"Thought you would like that."

"I feel like I'm damned no matter what happens tonight. Either you'll be disappointed he doesn't appear, or he'll talk and you might not like what he has to say." She couldn't help the bitterness that crept in her voice. "Like today."

"I don't discount what you heard. You just caught me by surprise. I didn't consider the possibility of you picking up on dreams." He stood, signaling the discussion was over.

She stood as well, determined to hold her ground. "I know Hanan's your friend. But you never know what's hidden in others' hearts." *Like your sister.* But she would keep her lips locked on that possible deception. If Tombi couldn't entertain the idea of a friend as betrayer, how would he react over a sister? A twin at that. Two hearts that once beat within the same mother.

From this point on, she would filter whatever messages the music or spirits revealed. Tombi and his people might have supernatural gifts, but they were no more accepting than anyone else in the non-gifted world.

Tombi held out his hand. "Whatever happens tonight, I won't be disappointed in *you.* Always tell me the truth, and we're good."

His words soothed Annie's hurt pride, and she placed her hand in his. The electrical charge that flowed between them gave her courage to face the long, uncertain hours ahead. Under coral beams shining from the Thunder Moon, she followed Tombi across the field and into the swampy woods. The constant chirp of cicadas and the eternal echo of the Gulf waters was a comfortable white noise in the background of her mind.

The stagnant smell of the bayou was more tolerable in the cooler nighttime temperature, and the occasional whiff of pine and brine was refreshing. Excitement unexpectedly rose within her. Whenever she was with Tombi, something exhilarating was bound to happen. Just being near him, touching him, made her feel alive. So different from the nights she had spent quietly at her grandma's cottage, grinding herbs and withdrawing from any human contact.

All this prowling about the bayou must have opened her senses in new ways, because Annie was able to recognize a few landmarks in the shadows. A familiar bend in the path here, a certain clump of saw palmetto there, a particular pattern of trees and moss…and they had returned to the place where Bo had spoken.

"This is it," she said softly.

Tombi led her to the fallen tree where she'd once heard him playing the flute. They settled down together, thigh touching thigh. Her skin tingled, and she was unsure if it was from the proximity of Tombi or the expectation of Bo reappearing inside a wisp.

Tombi's breath whispered against her ear. "Can't you conjure him? Use some of your hoodoo stuff?"

She started to roll her eyes, then paused. Not a bad idea. She didn't practice hoodoo spells much. Grandma Tia was so gifted and took care of everything, so she seldom needed to do a root work on her own. She'd have to rifle through her grandma's old grimoires and see what she could dig up.

"I'll do some research tomorrow. There must be—"

He placed a finger on her lip, and she realized her voice had grown too loud in the dark stillness of night. She stopped talking, and yet Tombi didn't move his finger. The pressure lightened, and his hand palmed her chin. Annie leaned into the caress and kissed his fingers, at last drawing one of them into her mouth and sucking the end of it.

In a swift move, Tombi had whisked her onto his lap. She straddled him and eagerly returned his deep kisses. Hot, wet, blistering kisses that she never wanted to end. The raw, honest need between them was unlike anything she'd ever experienced, not that she had that much experience. Just a couple of boyfriends who had found her convenient as an in-between kind of girlfriend until something better than Crazy Annie came along. She'd learned not to expect anything more. How could she, when she could barely tolerate their unceasing jumble of music every day and night? But Tombi kept his energy in check, and when it did pierce his aura, it was a drumbeat that matched her own heart.

He could be trouble for her heart. Big trouble.

But for now, she didn't care. The night was magical, and his kisses shattered her normal reserve. The barriers guarding her mind and spirit slipped away, and she immersed herself in the feel of his naked skin against her own, the silk of his hair, the calluses of his hands as he stroked her face, her neck, her arms, her back.

Ethereal music penetrated Annie's passion-fogged brain. She pulled back from Tombi and strained to hear better. Oh yes, she'd heard this tune before. Somewhere in the dark shadows, Bo had returned.

"What is it?" Tombi asked, his breath sharp with anticipation. "Is it Bo? Tell him I need to talk to him."

Don't tell Tombi I am near, Bo warned. *If I draw his attention, other wisps or Nalusa himself will pick up on it.*

Annie nodded. What did he want?

Find the music contained in the wind. Find it before Nalusa does, or all is lost.

She frowned. What was he talking about?

Tombi set her aside on the fallen tree and stood, peering into the shadows. "Bo? I'm still your friend. Talk to me." He turned to Annie. "What did he say?"

"To find the music contained in the wind. Or all is lost. Do you have any idea what he meant?"

He shook his head and gazed at the shadows. But the music had faded. Bo had vanished.

Chapter 8

Pink-and-purple light washed the sky. Annie yawned and stretched her arms. Her legs were stiff from sitting so long on the fallen tree, and her ankles were numb. Tombi was only a few yards away, pacing soundlessly, one hand to his chin as if deep in thought.

She walked to him, the crunch of twigs detonating like mini-explosions.

"We're done for the night, aren't we?" She pointed at the rising sunbeams. "And today you promised to start teaching me."

"I haven't forgotten."

Curiosity tripped along her nerves. "What's your secret? Why can't I hear your aura?"

"The spirit world assists us in blocking the energy we project. Let's go back to camp and have some coffee. I'll explain more."

She buried the scowl that wanted to break. More hostility from Tallulah and company? No, thanks. Besides, she was in dire need of using modern plumbing. "We're close to my cottage. We can have coffee there."

He nodded, and they made quick time, arriving at the cottage just as the sun rose over the horizon. To hell with dignity. Annie practically sprinted up the driveway and rushed to open the door. When she exited the bathroom, she found Tombi leaning in the doorway, lips twitching in amusement. Her bladder was too relieved to take offense.

"Go ahead and have a seat while I make coffee."

He dropped into a chair and crossed his legs at the ankle. Annie cast surreptitious glances his way as she went about brewing coffee. She cut two slices of coconut pound cake and set them on their best china.

"Dig in," she said, sitting across from him at the kitchen table.

He took a bite, and she waited expectantly.

Tombi didn't disappoint. "Wow."

"Grandma Tia grates real coconut and uses, like, a pound of butter in that cake. It's always a big hit." Annie sipped and set her cup down. "Now explain how the spirits help you."

Tombi took a long swallow. "Those of us who show paranormal ability during our teen years are given lessons by tribal elders on how to connect with spirits and seek their guidance. It takes concentration and a certain amount of dedication. For some, it's easier than for others."

"Bet you took right to it."

"Tallulah and I both did. Our father was very gifted himself—it seems to be passed down."

He made short work of the cake. Annie felt almost light-headed with hope and excitement. The life she'd always wanted was getting a step closer. She interlaced her hands and squeezed her fingers. "Keep going. I want details. Who are these spirits?"

"It's different for everyone. The spirits can be in animal form, or it can be your ancestors."

She nodded. "In hoodoo, we petition our ancestors for help."

"Do you have a particular ancestor who serves as a guardian spirit?"

"No." Some of her hope wilted. "I've tried to connect with my ancestors, but I don't have the skill of my grandma. I've asked them to remove my gift, but they don't respond."

"Could be you're asking the wrong questions."

"Now you're sounding like Grandma Tia. Next, you'll tell me to thank my ancestors for this gift that's brought me so much pain."

"Not necessary. But you can ask them why you've been granted your ability and how to manage it."

The coffee soured in her stomach. "Is that the best I can do? Learn to control it? I want to be rid of it completely."

"I don't know if that's possible. Could be that you've been granted this hearing for a special purpose, and once your mission is done, the gift will disappear."

"You mean, help you fight Nalusa."

"You said yourself that Tia felt we were somehow linked together. Maybe she never helped you not because she didn't want to or didn't have the necessary skill, but because she realized it would help you or others one day."

She pondered his words. "Maybe. But you aren't getting off the hook that easy. I want my lesson, not a philosophical discussion."

His jaw tightened. "We're getting there. First, you need to know how energy control works."

"Okay," she conceded. "You mentioned animal spirits. Do I have one?"

"Everybody does. We all have animal guides that come and go in our lives—depending on what we need. But a totem is an animal spirit that stays with you your entire life."

The idea rekindled hope. "Great. What's mine?"

"You'll have to figure that out on your own." He held up a hand to forestall her next question. "You invite them to introduce themselves, much like you pray to your ancestors for their assistance. Ask them to appear in your dreams. Pay attention to animals that you're drawn to or that show up over and over in your life."

"I like cats," she said hesitantly. "Maybe a cat is my totem?"

Tombi shrugged.

Some help he turned out to be. Figured he'd give her homework to do on her own. "Okay, once I discover my totem or find an ancestor willing to work with me, what comes next?"

"The way it works for me is that I connect with my great-grandfather. I quiet my mind and ask for his help. He comes to me, and I'm able to see the world through his other-realm eyes."

"A veil between the realms. Hoodoo has similar beliefs." Grandma Tia often spoke of it. "So that's how you and the others see at night. It explains a supernatural ability you have, but it doesn't explain how you block others from sensing you."

"While we're in a semi-present state between shadows and earth, our guides cloak our energy—others' perceptions of us are dimmed. It allows for total focus on the hunt."

"So I need a guide that will cloak my supernatural hearing, not so that I can be invisible to others, but to prevent my picking up their auras." She smiled. "I'm ready to meet mine." Problem solved.

Tombi snorted. "Not many are able to connect on their first attempt."

"Then I'll keep trying until I meet him or her…or it, if my guide turns out to be an animal instead of an ancestor. Can we do it now?"

"Try it tonight at dusk. It is said that's the most opportune time, when the sun descends from the sky and gives way to the mysterious moon. When all around supernatural forces awaken and lengthen the shadows of men."

Which meant a wait time of several hours. "Will you be with me when I try?"

He shook his head. "It's something you need to do alone, in your own way. I'm sure you and your grandmother already have rituals for this."

"Hmm." Annie tapped a finger to her lips. She'd pore over her grandma's grimoire today and find a root working.

"For novices, most guides will appear in dreams. As you lie in bed tonight, concentrate on your intent to meet your guide in dreamland." He cocked his head to one side. "I'll sort of be with you, after all."

"Come again?"

"I want you to spend the night with me."

Annie's face flamed with heat.

"Not in the same bed," he hastened to explain. A slow, sexy smile carved his face. "Unless you want to."

Oh, she wanted. She spoke quickly, hoping he wouldn't sense her flustered nerves. "I'm sleeping here tonight, in my own bed, with only fifteen steps to a working toilet— thank you very much."

"We wouldn't be sharing a tent in the woods. The hunt is over for this month, remember? You could stay with me at my cabin."

"I think I'll do better here at my own home, working at my own altar." Here, she felt closer to her grandma's presence, could perhaps draw on Tia's energy for help.

"Besides, I've got a ton of stuff I need to get caught up on—groceries, bills, the usual."

"And I'm sure you want to visit your grandmother again. How is she doing?"

"Still in a coma."

He swore under his breath. "I'm responsible."

She should argue he wasn't, because it was obvious he felt guilty. But Annie still harbored resentment. He had brought Nalusa to them; they would never have drawn that spirit's attention otherwise.

"Time apart will do us good," she said, picking up their empty plates and putting them in the sink. She needed time to do some research. Visit Tia again and see if her grandma had any more messages or could help her in her quest. "Hanan said you were behind at work, anyway."

He opened his mouth, and she kept talking, to forestall more objections. "What kind of work do you do?"

"I'm a carpenter," he answered tersely. "There's no reason we can't both do our own thing during the day and then be together tonight."

Annie dropped the forks she was rinsing, and they clanged in the sink.

A chair scraped, and Tombi stood behind her, placing his hands on her shoulders. "I don't expect anything from you. We won't share the same bed."

"Why are you so insistent I spend the night at your cabin?"

He hesitated, as if not wanting to tell her his reason.

"Well?"

"It's no longer safe for you to stay alone," he admitted. "Nalusa knows where you live."

Astonished, she turned around to face him, not realizing how close he stood. The nearness of their lips made her throat dry. Annie jerked back toward the sink. "I won't open the door for anyone. I'll be fine."

"I won't take no for an answer."

"I don't care what you do, but I want to stay here to-night, and that's the end of that."

Tense silence settled around them in the tiny kitchen.

"I'll leave you alone, then. For now," he said.

It sounded like a promise to return. She kept her eyes glued to the window and didn't see him leave, only heard the creak of the door as he exited. The door reopened.

"Lock up behind me," he ordered.

Before she could reply, the door shut again, and she obediently locked up. She watched as he strode down the driveway. His golden skin gleamed, kissed by the sun, and his black hair hung past his shoulders, as dark as if it carried the energy of the night.

Day and night. Sun and moon. Hunter and hunted. Tombi was a living veil between this world and the spirit world that he entered into at will.

A dangerous protector. He'd brought her and Grandma Tia danger, but he'd also offered his protection. She sensed he was an honorable man who took his word seriously.

Could he really be the key to her escape from this personal auditory hell, or did he plan on using her? He might be honorable, but he'd set his own code as to what was right and where his duties lay.

Lesson One hadn't gone the way she'd anticipated, but at least it was a start. Annie set about rummaging through Tia's books and papers, gathering them into a pile on the kitchen table. The stack was over a foot high. With a sigh, she opened a grimoire and began leafing through the yellowed paper filled with her grandma's bold handwriting, with its fat loops and exaggerated serifs. An acrid, licorice smell of myrrh and camphor wafted through the old tome. Bits of dried leaves and herbs crumbled into the binding and spilled on to the open pages.

Annie's heart spasmed painfully beneath her ribs. She

missed Tia with an ache that tightened her throat. Was her grandma faring any better today? She had to know.

For such a little bit of a woman, Annie sure had a huge stubborn streak. How could she possibly think she could defend herself against Nalusa and the shadow world? And what if she was part of that world, and that was why she was unafraid? He had to make her willing to stay with him in the evenings.

Tombi entered the restored antebellum home. It served as a visitor's center for those interested in touring the bayou for either bird hunting or walking the scenic hiking trail that featured a pier and pavilion where alligators were daily fed. Tallulah was cleaning a glass counter in the museum area that housed a collection of arrowheads, pottery and other Choctaw artifacts from bygone days. Her long hair was severely pulled back and braided, and she wore a red smock over jeans.

A familiar jolt of guilt and sadness pinched his heart. Tallulah should be managing the center instead of working as a combination cashier and cleaner. She'd been studying anthropology in college when Katrina crashed into their worlds.

She leaned against the counter and rubbed a hand along the small of her back. It had to be tough on her when she hunted at night and then had to come work the day job. A job that barely enabled her to eke out a threadbare existence. If he hadn't built her a small cabin on their family's land, she wouldn't be able to eke out any existence at all.

"Backache?" he asked.

She stiffened and returned to wiping the counters. "It doesn't matter." Tallulah slanted him a suspicious glance. "Don't tell me you're here to scold me about that girl again."

Scold? "I'm your brother, not your father."

"Good. I'm glad you remember. Because sometimes I think you forget." She set the bottle of window cleaner so hard on the glass, he expected cracks to fissure the surface.

Tombi inwardly sighed at the chip-on-her-shoulder attitude. Bo's death had made her bitter, as if it were the last straw in a string of tragedies. Something inside her had broken. As twins, they'd had a close camaraderie growing up, but in the past year they had been more like strangers. Worse than strangers, as they each knew just how to push each other's hot buttons.

A phone rang, and Tallulah stalked across the room to answer it.

He leaned his elbows on the counter and idly surveyed the ancestral artifacts while he cooled his infamous temper. *You're as fiery as the sun you're named after*, Mom used to say. Tombi liked to think he'd learned to control it, even if the flames of his anger still blistered his soul and tongue. But Tallulah tried his patience.

A wooden flute caught his eye. It was about twelve inches long and made of river cane. A snake-head design was burned into the tip with its sinewy body wrapped around the barrel. That was a new addition to this collection. It was so well preserved, somebody must have donated it. He shook his head. Too bad it wasn't for sale. He would love to add this to his own private collection. Instruments that harnessed the magical power of the wind held his respect and awe.

His twin returned. "What brings you here?" she asked bluntly.

"I did come to talk about Annie," he admitted. "Can't you cut her a little break? She's been drawn into this whole mess, just as we were years ago."

"Drawn in? What if she was recruited in by Nalusa? We've no reason to trust her."

"Trust or not, we need her. Her aura-hearing can be

used to track wisps and to prevent Nalusa attacking us unawares."

"We've done fine without her up till now."

"Not true and you know it. Nalusa's gaining ground, has been for a couple of years. The number of wisps multiplies faster than we can kill them. If this keeps up, he'll soon wander past the bayou boundaries and wreak havoc everywhere."

Tallulah pinched her lips. "So you say."

"You know I speak the truth. Once he slips past us, there will be no hope of containing the evil. He'll blaze a trail of death and misery on a national scale."

"So be it. We've done all we can." Her hands gripped the wash rag like a lifeline.

"That's my point. Now it's time to get outside help."

"What do you want me to do? Bake her a cheesecake and welcome her into the fold? Not happening."

He ran a hand through his hair and sighed. "All I ask is that you be civil. Don't attack her."

"You can't keep me from telling the truth."

"You don't know the truth," he exploded. "Just stay away from her, that's all I ask." He turned and started for the door. The long walk home would do much to cool his anger.

Tallulah ran in front of him, blocking his exit. "Don't be an idiot. Think with your brain and not your dick. This girl could be trouble."

"Her name's Annie, and she could be our salvation. You're the one not thinking straight," he snapped. Tombi took a deep breath. "I don't know who you are these days, Talli girl. And neither would Bo if he were still alive."

Raw pain bruised her eyes, and she sucked in a breath.

He laid a hand on her shoulder. "Sorry. But you needed to hear that. Consider what I said. If you can't treat Annie with any decency, it might be best if you stopped hunting altogether."

"You can't be serious," she said in a strangled voice. "You've known this girl only a few days. Are you completely under her spell?"

He withdrew his hand. "Leave Annie alone, or I'll exile you from the hunters."

Grandma Tia had been unchanged from yesterday's visit, as if any moment her eyes would flutter open. Annie could picture that moment. Her grandma would blink in confusion at the sterile, strange surroundings and then jolt out of bed, demanding to go home.

She had to believe that would happen. Had to believe that, despite her bad heart, her grandma had many months left. Peaceful months that would allow her to approach the end of life among her altars and herb garden and where she could sleep in her own bed at night. Months of entertaining friends and helping customers with her root workings.

Despite all reason, Annie had hoped her mother would come down for a visit after informing her of the stroke, even though she swore she'd never set foot in Bayou La Siryna again. But even with Tia hospitalized, Annie's mom was still being stubborn and heartless about not coming down. Grandma Tia never talked about it, but Annie knew the rift between them hurt her deeply.

She lit candles everywhere, and the glow was comforting. Although only late afternoon, the sky was a pewter gray and the sun hidden behind dark clouds. She hadn't paid attention to the news, but no doubt a hurricane brewed somewhere over the Atlantic Ocean. That or tropical storms always resulted in the Gulf area darkening and churning, making normally stagnant air whip with a briny bite, and the birds, even noisy seagulls, retreated in silence and out of sight.

The candles weren't just for atmosphere. If the upcoming storm were severe enough, the power would likely cut off.

Annie sat at the kitchen table and gripped her hands together. Excitement and fear chased in circles in her gut, percolating like a storm of their own.

Magical Musings, page forty-three.

The title and page number had flashed in her mind when she visited Grandma Tia earlier today. Annie sorted through the papers. She even knew what the book would look like: a brownish-yellow bundle of papers tied up with raffia, a sprig of marjoram in the bow.

At last she began going through the stack of books until she found *Magical Musings*. The aged, frail papers trembled in her fingers like bedsheets flapping on a clothesline. Page forty-one…forty-two…page forty-three. There. *Communing with the Dead or with Animal Spirits*.

Eagerly, she ran a finger down the ingredient list and began gathering the needed items, grateful for Tia's well-stocked pantry and hoodoo supplies. Lightning cracked, and the air sizzled with the smell of ozone. One Mississippi. Two Mississippi. Three Missis—

Thunder crashed. The lightning had struck only three miles away.

A frisson of unease chased down the nape of her neck to the base of her spine. Which was ridiculous. Grandma Tia wouldn't have sent such a specific message if she hadn't meant for her granddaughter to try the spell. Still, Annie wavered and shifted on her seat. *Maybe the timing is wrong?*

No. She wasn't going to let a thunderstorm give her the heebie-jeebies. They were a dime a dozen during the Alabama summers. She'd been seeking an answer for years to stop the music, and now she couldn't stand to wait another evening. With great care, Annie dressed the candles, lit the incense and began her petition. And waited.

And waited.

A great swell of silence numbed her brain. A silence so utter and profound it might as well have been a banshee screaming in her ears. A single word over and over: *no.* Disappointment sliced through the numbness. Surely, after all the signs, there had to be something. *Try harder.* Annie squeezed her eyes shut and strained to hear something—anything.

A great flapping beat the air, a stir of energy swooshed by like a freight train. She gasped and opened her eyes.

Whatever connection she'd made was instantly severed. Outside, the rustle of leaves in the wind and a scrape of limbs clawing the windows. A distant rumble of thunder. Whatever had made itself known had vanished.

Not fair. She stood and paced the room, hands fisted by her side in frustration. She'd try again before bedtime. And she'd keep trying the spell until spirits in the Great Beyond responded—if only to get rid of her and her constant petitions.

The lights died.

Gee, thanks, Alabama Power. This night just keeps getting better. Best thing to do with the little light that still oozed through the windows was to fix something to eat and get a bath.

Twin blazes of light pierced the den. Tombi? She hurried to the front door and opened it. Rain soaked his long black hair, and his jeans and T-shirt were soaked.

"Where's your umbrella?" she called out as he rushed up the porch steps.

He lifted his head and stared her dead in the face.

That wasn't Tombi.

Numbness froze her lips and limbs. "Hanan?" she asked

dazedly, leaning against the door frame for support. "What are you doing here?"

He smiled, but the severe angles of his face and the sharp beak of a nose failed to lighten the overall impression of harsh cunning. "I came to clear the air between us. Tombi told me what you heard. What you *imagined* you heard."

Annie calculated the viability of how swiftly she could shut the door and lock him out versus Hanan's speed and agility to block the move.

She wasn't optimistic. *Play along. Play it off. Play it cool.*

She returned his smile, smoothing her features to betray no concern. "We're good. Tombi explained you must have been dreaming. A nightmare, maybe."

Or maybe the sneaky Tallulah was the betrayer. She could only imagine how Tombi would take that news, seeing as how he got all defensive about a friend.

She tried to be fair. Tombi's explanation was rational.

A couple of beats of awkward silence passed. She raised a hand and gestured at the open doorway. "Come in, if you'd like."

He swooped in at once, and she tried not to wince as he brushed by her side and into the cottage. Annie listened intently, but not a single note escaped his tightly controlled body and mind.

She looked longingly at the yard. Her car was in the driveway, mocking. It might as well have been a mile away. She had a wild idea of grabbing her car keys and making a run for it. Just leave Hanan alone in the cottage.

And look like a complete fool for running off. Tallulah would have a field day. Reluctantly, Annie shut the door and faced Hanan. "Would you like something to drink?"

"No. I won't be long." He went to the sofa and sat, one leg bent, resting an ankle on the opposite knee. "That's some special ability you have," he said, getting straight to the point. "As a hunter, my senses are enhanced. I can see, hear and smell better than other humans. But I've never heard of anyone able to judge a person by hearing their energy."

Was there skepticism in his tone? Hard to tell with his poker face and silent aura. Annie never realized before how much she used her extraordinary hearing to glide through interacting with people—anticipating another's thoughts and motives before engaging in conversation. And always working on an exit strategy if the music became too disturbing or uncomfortable. She nodded slowly, unsure how to respond.

His gaze moved deliberately around the room, taking in the candles and altars and saint statues. The air smelled of patchouli and frankincense. "Feels like I'm in church. I expected Hoodoo Henrietta's place to have the opposite atmosphere."

Annie found her voice. He could put her down but not her grandma. "What did you expect? Broomsticks and skeleton skulls everywhere? A simmering cauldron? A black cat?"

He shrugged, seemingly unfazed at her anger. "Anybody would. Easy to judge someone on little to no evidence. Right?"

A clever trap. She'd fallen right into it. Heat scalded the back of her neck. "Point taken," she conceded. She'd been willing to condemn him on what may have only been a dream.

A loud, staccato hammering erupted at the door. Annie jumped.

Hanan smiled slyly. "I know who that is."

Chapter 9

Tombi didn't wait for permission to enter. He burst into the room. The only light came from candles lit everywhere. A romantic tableau if he'd ever seen one. His veins throbbed with anger. Some friend Hanan proved to be. Bo would never have gone behind his back and visited his girlfriend.

Girlfriend.

The word was like throwing ice on fire. His hot anger melted. Annie was *not* his girlfriend. Not his lover, either.

And he still didn't like her being alone with Hanan. "What are you doing here?" he demanded.

Hanan slowly stood. "Just saying goodbye." He offered his hand to Annie. "Are we cool?"

"Sure." She stood as well and shook his hand.

Her eyes were downcast, and Tombi couldn't decipher her mood. Embarrassed? Distressed?

"Why is it so dark in here?" Tombi asked, ever suspicious.

"Power's out." Hanan nodded at him and swept past.

"Be back in a minute," Tombi said curtly to Annie.

He followed Hanan onto the porch. "What did you say to upset her? Did you confront her about what she heard?"

"*Confront* isn't the word I'd use," Hanan drawled. "I pointed out that I shouldn't be condemned on so little."

"Nobody condemned you. If I believed you were a traitor I wouldn't have told you she pointed a finger your way. You had no right to come over here and upset Annie." The anger boiled up again. He shouldn't have left her alone—not even during the day. His rush to finish the Anderson carpentry job on deadline had tainted his judgment.

"You would have done the same had the positions been reversed. Both of us hate to have our integrity questioned."

True. He couldn't argue against that.

Hanan pushed off from the porch and started down the steps. "See you later," he called over his shoulder, with no rankle in his voice.

Tombi watched his friend drive off in the rain. He'd just acted like a complete ass, bursting into Annie's cottage and demanding explanations. As if she owed him one. He stuffed his hands into his pockets and returned inside. An unfamiliar feeling of sheepishness weighted his shoulders.

Annie stood at the rear window, back to him.

"Sorry about that," he mumbled.

"Don't be." She turned and walked to him with a shy smile. "I'm glad you came when you did. He chastised me." She hurried on at the sight of his frown. "But in a gentle way."

"He did the same with me outside," Tombi admitted.

"You're all wet." She ran her fingers down his hair, and his breath caught. "I'll go get you a towel."

Her ass swayed in her tight cutoff jeans, and he'd never seen anything hotter. Just being in the same room with the woman had him knotted up in sexual tension. Tombi peeled off his wet T-shirt and ran a hand over his wet locks.

"Here ya—" Her voice faltered. She stood in the darkened doorway, holding a towel and staring at his chest, as if mesmerized.

Tombi shifted uncomfortably in his suddenly tight jeans. He wanted to peel out of them, undress her and make passionate love. But he didn't want to scare her. Wasn't sure if she had any experience in lovemaking.

"Bring the towel to me," he said huskily.

She obeyed, as if in a trance. She walked so slowly to him that he was conscious of the rain beating against the windows and the smell of something earthy in the air. A cozy intimacy of the two of them against the rain-sloshed world outside.

Annie lifted the towel and began rubbing his skin. He wished it were her hands instead of fabric. Satisfied with her work there, she ran the towel through his hair.

Tombi abruptly pulled her to him and kissed her thoroughly, smothering her gasp of surprise. Her arms went around his bare back, and her hands traveled the length of his spine. He pressed his manhood against her core, and she arched into him, silently asking for more.

"Annie?" he asked hoarsely.

She gazed up at him with hooded eyes. And then blinked and took a step backward. Tombi swallowed down a groan of frustration.

"Not yet," she whispered. "I'm sorry. It's too soon for me."

He ran a finger down the side of her delicate, heart-shaped face. "Never apologize. A lady has every right to say no."

Annie nodded and cast her head down, her dark wavy hair obscuring her face. "Thank you," she mumbled.

He needed space. Space to cool his lust and dispel the

awkwardness. He strode to a window. Rain washed against the panes in sheets, but at least the thunder and lightning had grown distant. With any luck, the storm would pass within the hour.

"Why did you come back?" Annie asked from behind.

"I felt uneasy leaving you alone. Especially now that the power's out." He faced her. "Come back to the cabin with me. I'm not asking you to sleep with me. I have an extra bedroom."

"Or you could stay here tonight. No sense in you driving home in this weather. I can't offer much in terms of dinner, but I can always scrape something together."

He'd rather be at his own place, in his own bed, but he'd take what he could. Staying in the cottage beat camping out in her backyard or sleeping in his truck to keep an eye on things. "Deal."

She smiled, the awkward shyness dispensed. "Have a seat and I'll be back with food."

Tombi sank into the sofa, listening to Annie bustling about the kitchen. The domesticity of it settled warmly in his gut. How long had it been since someone fixed him a meal? Too long. Strange, he'd never noticed before how solitary, how lonely and stark his existence was at the cabin. He devoted his life to hunting during the full moon and the rest of his days to running his carpentry business. Always focused, always doing everything with a purpose and sinking into bed at night, exhausted.

He propped his legs on the coffee table and crossed his arms behind him, head relaxing into his palms. Inside was soft candle illumination, and outside the rain and storm were contained. He closed his eyes. Relaxed. He was exactly where he needed to be, and all was well in this moment. Tension drained from his body and flowed down to the ground, where it was absorbed.

A soft touch jiggled his shoulder.

He bolted upright and took in the unfamiliar surroundings.

"It's okay. You've been asleep." Annie's face was calm and a soft smile lit her eyes. "You've been out a couple of hours at least. But I couldn't wait to eat any longer and didn't want to dine alone."

She sat across from him, and he set his feet down. A tray on the coffee table was filled with apples, grapes, cheese and bread. He was starving. Even though it was late in the day, the pewter clouds had been rinsed clean by rain, and it was lighter now than before he'd fallen asleep.

"Sorry I couldn't do better. Power's still out."

"This is perfect. I can't believe I slept so soundly." Highly unusual. If he'd eaten before falling asleep, it would have made him wonder what Annie had slipped into his food unawares. Instead, he'd completely let down his guard. Was he a fool as Tallulah accused? He watched as Annie poured iced tea from a pitcher and handed him a glass.

She pointed to the dishes and silverware. "Help yourself."

He dug in and bit into a sweet, crisp apple, quickly downing fruit with slices of tangy cheddar cheese. She nudged over a wicker basket full of biscuits. Even cold, they were delicious smothered in real butter.

"Thank you," he said at last, fully sated. He leaned back in the sofa and crossed his arms against his chest, studying Annie.

"For what? Dinner wasn't much of anything."

She might not think so, but Tombi hadn't been so relaxed in weeks. And to have someone else fix and serve a meal, no matter how simple, was a novelty. His loins stirred. It had been a long time since that, too. He wondered if it was the same for Annie. "Have you been seeing anyone in Bayou La Siryna?" he asked. Subtlety was not his strong suit.

"As in…a man? No." She shook her head, dark hair spilling over her shoulders. Her eyes shuttered. "Not interested," she added in a flat voice.

Somebody had been burned. Fairly recently, judging from Annie's expression. "So, how long ago did you break up?"

She opened her mouth, as if to deny it, but then shrugged. "Four months."

He raised his eyebrows in an unspoken question.

"His name was Evan." Annie tapped a knife against the edge of her plate. "He's from North Georgia, where my mom and stepdad live. We dated over a year. Until he decided I was too weird…and someone better came along."

"He's an idiot." The words slipped out, unbidden. But at Annie's sudden smile, he didn't care.

"What about you?" she said.

That was the trouble with asking direct questions. Now she felt free to interrogate him on his past love life. He'd set himself up for it. But fair was fair.

"It's been over a year since I've seen anyone seriously. Her name was Courtney."

Annie raised her brows in a parody of his earlier gesture.

"She broke it off, complaining that my priorities were screwed up and that I cared more about the hunt than I did her."

"So she knew about you. About your supernatural tracking."

"No. I saw no need to tell her. She just thought I was into hunting with friends. But it didn't sit well with her. Courtney accused me of being secretive."

"You should have told her the truth. If you really loved her, that is."

"That's what she said." He'd thought about it and come close a few times, but something had always held him back.

"At least we're honest with each other," Annie blurted. "About what makes us different. Not that we're in a relationship or anything," she added quickly.

"No way." Relationship? It hadn't worked before, and it certainly wouldn't work now, not with Nalusa gaining power. He didn't have time for a relationship. Especially not with a woman like Annie. Sex? Sure. But her hesitation made him realize she wouldn't view it casually. He shifted uncomfortably, aware she looked offended.

"What I mean is, I don't have time for a real relationship."

"Just some sex on the side with a woman who's convenient? Hmm? Someone always underfoot anyway because you watch her closely to see if she's in league with your enemy?"

He wasn't fooled by her deceptively sweet voice. Annie was furious. "When you put it like that…"

"I put it truthfully. Praise the saints I turned you down earlier." She jerked to her feet and gathered up the uneaten food on to a tray.

"Annie, wait. I didn't mean that the way it sounded. I wouldn't sleep with a woman I didn't care for."

"I no longer give a damn." Her chin lifted, and she refused to meet his eye.

He stood beside her. "I can't think of having a serious relationship now. All my energy and focus need to be on Nalusa and doing the things I must to keep up the cabin and put food on the table."

"Your life sounds as miserable as mine." The anger melted, replaced with tears brimming her eyes.

He'd take her wrath any day over this. "I'm not miserable, and you shouldn't be, either."

"Really? Sounds to me like you have no life. All work, all grim responsibility, with no room for love and happiness."

Strange, he'd never given it much thought. Maybe at first, when he began hunting all those years ago. Somehow over the years, the hunting had taken over everything. But it wasn't as if he had a choice. To quit wasn't an option. "I do what I must."

"What are you—a machine or a man?"

Her words cut deep, and he struck back. "Are you saying I should be more like you and run away from everything? Close my eyes and stick my fingers in my ears?"

"I don't..." She clamped her lips into a thin line.

He'd gone too far. "I'm sorry."

She stepped backward and regarded him stonily, the food tray a fortress between them. "Go away and leave me alone."

Damn. He'd really made a mess of everything. "You're upset. Just let me sleep on the couch tonight to make sure you're okay. We'll talk in the morning when you've calmed down."

"Don't you dare tell me to calm down or how I'm supposed to feel."

He sighed. It was going to be a long night sleeping in his parked truck.

The sizzle of a rising sun, the pure notes of a Native American flute and an unidentifiable whooshing.

Annie squeezed her grandma's hand. "Are these sounds connected?"

Tia Henrietta remained immobile, her olive skin tinged with gray. The faintest vibration passed through Annie's fingertips where they rested in her grandma's palm.

Yes, a sign.

Somehow, everything was linked, connected by a thin gossamer thread she couldn't see.

The first two noises she associated with Tombi. The whooshing only started once she'd cast a spell to find a spirit or animal guide. So it might have been an ancestor spirit or an animal passing nearby, stirring the air.

Micro pressure tingled in her hand. Annie hardly dared breathe, awaiting a new message. She stared intently at Tia. A flutter of the eyelids and a twitch at the corners of the mouth passed over the remote, beloved face, a sign of presence.

"I'm here, Grandma. Squeeze my hand if you can hear me."

A gentle press upon her fingers, and Annie gasped, suffused with hope. She lifted Tia's frail, weathered hand and brushed her cheek against the arthritic knuckles. If tears could heal flesh, Tia's hand would be rejuvenated.

Should she call a nurse? Annie pushed the call button on the side of the hospital cot. "You're going to be all right, Grandma. We need to get you home soon. Would you like that?"

Again, a slight twitch at the corners of her mouth. And this time her eyes opened a fraction, revealing nothing but white. Her mouth soundlessly opened and closed.

"You're trying to speak." Annie stood and leaned over the hospital bed, bending over until her ear was inches from her grandma's mouth.

"Go to him." The whispered command was no less authoritative than when Grandma Tia was up and about, issuing orders.

"I can't leave you. Not now. You need me."

"She said go."

Startled, Annie whipped her head around. Miss Verbena stood in the doorway, frowning. "You heard Grandma way over there?"

"I heard you arguing and guessed the rest." She stepped forward and rubbed Annie's shoulder. "What's happened today? She talking?" Miss Verbena pulled out a chair and sat next to Annie. She withdrew a skein of yarn and knitting needles from her basket and took up her usual knitting. The needles clicked over the monotonous, background buzz of hospital machinery.

"You're not surprised?"

"Not a bit. Last night I dreamed that Tia would be a walkin' outta here by the end of the week."

"I never guessed that—"

A nurse bustled into the room. "What do you need?"

"My grandma just spoke." Annie grinned. "She's coming out of the coma."

The nurse frowned and stared at Tia's inert form. "You sure about that?" she asked suspiciously.

Miss Verbena winked at Annie. "She'll speak again when she gets a mind to. Meanwhile, I think it's time for you to skedaddle, young lady."

Annie shook her head and pinched her lips together. She wanted to be here when Grandma Tia opened her eyes again.

"I'll be right here," Miss Verbena promised. "You mind your Grandma, now. She ain't gonna rest comfortable until you do like she said."

The nurse shot Annie a curious look. "I'll get the doctor." She exited with the same bustle as when she entered.

Miss Verbena made a shooing motion with her hands. "Go on, now."

Reluctantly, Annie left, moving down the corridor as if her feet were mired in quicksand. She didn't want to leave Grandma Tia, and she certainly didn't want to see Tombi. *Go to him.* As if Tombi needed anyone, especially her. He'd as much as called her a coward. *Always running away from everything*, he'd said. The man acted as if he had no feelings outside a bloodthirsty need for revenge.

Last night, she'd scarcely slept, peeking out the window and seeing his truck in the driveway. She hoped his night was as miserable and sleepless as her own. In the morning, she'd gotten into her old car and left, deliberately ignoring Tombi and his truck as she drove for the hospital.

Shattering chords of pain assaulted her ears from opened patient doors. Annie quickened her step, skipping the elevator and opting for the stairs—less chance of running into others and their leaking auras.

She skipped along, heartened at Grandma Tia's minuscule awakening. Not only that, but Miss Verbena had dreamed she'd come out of the darkness, and her dreams always came true.

As far as Tombi, she'd show him she was no coward. At least, she'd try to. Annie bit her lip, picturing Nalusa in snake form. But Tombi had promised to stay by her side. She'd cling to him so tight, he wouldn't have an opportunity to escape her if he tried. Strengthened by her decision, and comforted at the thought of lunch and some downtime alone at home before she contacted Tombi, Annie prepared for a quick exit past the ER waiting lounge.

She took a deep breath and pushed open the door from the stairwell to the ER area. Misery wailed like a herd of banshees while an ambulance's real wail reverberated in her brain like a shotgun blast in a canyon. The trick was nonresistance, to let the sound flow in and out and not let it get trapped deep within. Annie focused on her breathing and kept her eyes on the lobby door leading to freedom. The siren echoes decreased in decibels. Another dozen steps and she opened the door to fresh air.

Oomph. Her elbow hit something hard.

"Hey, watch it, lady." An ambulance driver in an all-blue uniform scowled and jerked the gurney away.

Annie shrank back. "Sorry," she mumbled. "I didn't see—" Wait. She knew this man lying on the gurney with blood seeping down the side of his scalp from a head wound. Where had she met him before?

Two more EMR workers started past, with more patients. One of the men on the cot stared at her, recognition lighting his face.

"Hey, you're that Annie woman Tombi brought to camp." The man struggled to an upright position, pushing his dark hair from his face. He held his right arm in his left, and Annie fought nausea at the crooked, unnatural bent of his injured arm.

She recognized him now. Her gaze shifted to the other cot, to an unconscious, bleeding man.

"What happened?" she asked.

The EMR started to wheel him away.

"Hold on a sec," he told the guy. He grabbed her arm and pulled until she was eye level with him.

"We were attacked in the woods," he said in a low, fierce voice. "Ambushed."

"In broad daylight?" she asked. Horror weighted her down. "Where's Tombi?"

"Gone. Kidnapped. The wisps are delivering him to Nalusa as we speak."

Chapter 10

The shadows expanded and contracted into phantasma-
goric shapes as Tombi stumbled along the path, squinting at the images. *Something is very wrong.* The miasma
of evil was thick as clam chowder and as stifling as the
Southern sun. He tugged at his bound hands, staring stu-
pidly at the black cloth tied and knotted at his wrists. How
had this happened?

The last thing he remembered was screams and rushing, colored orbs surrounding him and the other hunters.
They had surged forward and converged upon him, their
colored, swirling forms cloying and pouring acrid smoke
into his nose and mouth. Through the smoke, he had made
out the figure of a short, bowlegged man with a weathered, gnomelike face.

Hoklonote, no doubt. A bad spirit capable of temporarily shape-shifting to human form. Tombi had glimpsed
him over the years, seen his face peeking out from the underbrush or gazing down from a tall tree, ready to pounce.

He'd seen him run away on occasion with a queer, wobbly gate that led Tombi to suspect his feet were misshapen, ill-equipped to give chase.

Hoklonote must have been the one to bind his hands. The wisps were formless vapors surrounding the heart of their dead, entrapped victims. But they all were in league together with Nalusa.

When he was a young boy, his parents used to tell him if he didn't stay close to home or if he stayed out too late at night, the evil spirits would get him. Growing up, he'd made sure to be home before dark. As he grew into a teenager, he'd scoffed at the old tales and believed them merely a ploy to keep children from straying too far in the woods and to coerce them into minding their elders.

The Choctaw version of the boogeyman.

Much later, he'd learned there was more than one boogeyman, that they were real and that they had names and roamed the bayou grounds at night in search of prey.

A sharp poke on his lower back startled him out of his stupor. Tombi reined in his wandering thoughts and concentrated on Hoklonote. He sniffed experimentally and smelled an odor of damp and decay, like rotting leaves or globs of worms surfacing above ground after it was saturated by heavy rains. He sensed Hoklonote's physical form only rose to the midpoint of his back.

Tombi took a deep breath. No point being led like the lamb to the slaughter. Even drugged, he should prove a match for the stunted spirit. Pride stiffened his spine. The least he could do was leave the world fighting like a warrior, same as Bo. Tombi screwed up his fists.

"You forget the wisps," the voice from behind cackled. "You're outnumbered."

"So the old tale is true, then?" His voice was slurred, his throat dry. Yet he pushed on. "You can read people's minds?"

"Sure can." The spirit's voice was high-pitched and tinged with glee. "Won't be taking me by surprise."

Damn. But he could still die trying.

"Quit them death thoughts," Hoklonote said. "Could be you can work out some kind of deal with Nalusa. Same as me, same as the wisps and same as other hunters over the years."

To hell with that, you little, stunted pygmy—

"Stunted, huh?" Hoklonote kicked him in the ass. "Better guard your thoughts."

Tombi gritted his teeth against the crack of pain at the base of his tailbone and continued the labored trek in the woods. He wanted to see Nalusa, face-to-face. If nothing else, he'd like to get a lick in on the beast, whatever form Nalusa chose to assume for their meeting.

"Foolish, foolish thoughts," Hoklonote grunted.

Tombi tried, yet he couldn't sense anyone else's presence but Hoklonote and the wisps. But that could be due to his drugged state dulling his tracking skills. Not that he expected an answer, but the question burned in his mind. "Has anyone else been drugged or hurt?"

Hoklonote didn't bother responding, but again prodded him with a sharp object, probably a stick, that pricked the base of his spine. With every step forward, Tombi felt more disoriented. His skin crawled and itched, and his tongue lay swollen and heavy in his dry mouth, as if he'd suffered a severe allergic reaction. His head was fuzzy, and he wanted nothing more than to curl into a little ball and sleep forever.

The wisps skittering around him were having none of that. Tombi's leaden legs managed to plod along. Again, he worried for his friends' safety. Where had everyone disappeared to? Distress sharpened his mind, which brought a new flood of anguish. Nalusa could kill in so many ways: snakebite, suffocation and entrapment in a will-o'-the-wisp body, or worst of all, a slow, debilitating despair of the mind that led to madness or suicide.

Annie had been absolutely correct. There was a betrayer in their group.

Annie. Her image arose so sharp and clear it felt as if she was within him, alongside him as he struggled to continue. Her hair was soft and brushing against him; he could smell her herbal, floral scent. Her mysterious hoodoo eyes penetrated all his defenses, saw through all his guards into the walled, hardened heart that was scarred and calloused from death and loss.

I'm coming, Tombi.

He could have sworn he felt the whisper of her breath in his ear. He stopped and glanced about, the sharp object in his back pushed deeper, puncturing flesh.

"What the hell was that?" Hoklonote ground out in surprise and outrage. "Ain't never heard the likes of that before."

It wasn't the drugs, then; Hoklonote heard the voice, as well. *Go away*, he urged silently, not sure if she could hear his thoughts like he heard hers.

"Speed it up there," Hoklonote demanded, unease sharpening his tone.

Tombi kept going, knowing that each step brought him closer to Nalusa, closer to death. Best to focus on that fact and block out Annie. He considered the confrontation awaiting him. No way he could win a fight in this weakened, hallucinogenic state. Whoever had betrayed him had won.

He was too drugged to despair. Too drugged to be afraid. Instead, body and brain felt numbed. A sense of fatalism spread through him. He'd tried his best and failed. He'd lost his parents and his best friend. His sister was like a stranger these days. He remembered the destroyed family home, his parents' tombstones, Bo's dead body and Tallulah's angry and shuttered face that masked a grieving heart.

Don't give up. I'm near. Again, Annie's whisper echoed in his ear and filled his body with her warm vibration.

"What's that?" Hoklonote asked. "Who's there?"

As much as it comforted him, Tombi scrabbled to again warn her off. It was too dangerous. *If you can hear me, go away.* Nalusa would love to get his hands on Annie. He could use her gift of hearing to his own advantage. He'd trap her in a wisp and never, ever let her go.

No. Annie's voice was firm. Why did she have to fight him at every turn?

Screams saturated his brain. Something new or a memory of what occurred prior to his being drugged? The painful prodding at his back ceased, and the wisps scattered. Tombi sank to his knees and rested his face in his hands, riding out the waves of screams assaulting his ears. Was this what it was like for Annie every day? And he'd accused her of being a coward, of running away from situations when it got tough. Remorse burned his gut.

And now he'd never have the chance to tell her he was sorry.

Never, ever.

Annie crouched behind a saw palmetto and watched as Tombi fell to his knees, clutching his head. She winced as if experiencing the scraped knees on her own body. A withered, strange-looking man standing behind Tombi raised a stick, poised to deliver a blow.

Hanan, Tallulah, Chulah and several other hunters continued their screaming advance toward the wisps surrounding Tombi. A volley of rocks unfurled and the wisps scattered, but not before a few were struck and disintegrated to ash. The strange man released his stick and ran into a thicket of trees, disappearing from sight.

Chulah dropped to a knee, withdrew a dagger and slit the cloth binding Tombi's hands. Annie scrambled to them and sat beside Tombi, running her fingers through his hair, matted with blood and sweat.

He looked up, eyes as blank and dark as an erased blackboard.

"What have they done to you?" she whispered past the tightness at the back of her throat.

Chulah shot her an impatient look. "The wisps' smoke is a hallucinogenic drug, deadly in a large enough dose."

Hanan emerged by Tombi's other side, and between them, the two men got Tombi to stand, placing an arm over each of their shoulders.

"Going to be a long walk home," Hanan mumbled. "Might not make it back before nightfall."

"I'm joining you, Bo."

Tombi's slurred pronouncement chilled Annie. "Not if I can help it."

"Get out of our way." Chulah scowled as they moved slowly, painfully toward the open field, where a four-wheeler waited.

Annie nervously scooted to the side and followed behind them. Tallulah walked beside her, shooting her dagger glares. As if she had anything to do with what happened.

Annie clutched her mojo bag and purse full of hoodoo supplies close to her chest. She had no idea if any of it worked, but she could try. After seeing the injured hunters at the hospital, she'd rushed home and gathered everything together and then arrived at the hunters' campsite in time to see the inner circle leaving to search for Tombi. They'd reluctantly allowed her to tag along when she promised she could help with any injuries.

She should have done more hoodoo work, and sooner, when her grandma was infected by Nalusa, but it had happened so quickly and she'd been unprepared. This time, she had everything needed for an uncrossing and good-health spell. She had prayed Tombi was unharmed but was determined that if he was injured, she'd go to the hospital and sneak into his room to perform healing rites.

But it might already be too late. Grandma Tia didn't specify how quickly it had to be performed once harm had been inflicted by an enemy.

Hanan and Chulah helped Tombi on to the four-wheeler, and Tallulah and Annie squeezed into the back, Tombi between them.

Hold on, Annie willed him.

He leaned his head against her shoulder, and she began whispering in his ear. "I beseech thee, Archangel Raphael, Healer, Angel of the Son, come now and heal—"

"What's that?" Tallulah cut in sharply.

Annie ignored her. "—Tombi from his enemy's poison. Deliver—"

"Stop that witchy stuff," she demanded, tugging at Annie's sleeve.

"—him and restore his health." Annie withdrew a mojo bag from her back pocket and opened the drawstring. "Provide the breath of life and healing energy." She blew into the mojo bag, infusing its contents with power and intent.

Tallulah jerked her arm. "Stop it!" Bits of dried herbs and crushed plant roots from the mojo bag scattered over their laps and the floorboard. Tallulah pick up the parchment paper and frowned. "What's this? A pentagram?"

"It's a drawing of Solomon's Seal." Annie gathered up the spilled contents.

"Leave her alone," Chulah said, glancing back at the commotion.

Annie shot him a grateful smile.

"All that mumbo jumbo can't hurt anything," he added.

Her smile faded. "It's not…" She sighed. What they

thought about her and her root work wasn't important. Only Tombi mattered.

Tallulah handed over the parchment, rolling her eyes.

Annie returned it to the bag, breathed into it once again and drew the string together. "Saints be with us," she muttered, stuffing the bag into the side waistband of Tombi's jeans.

He stirred and opened his eyes. His dilated pupils stared unfocused at the group, then narrowed and sharpened as he turned to his side. "Annie. I heard you."

"I've been right here, talking to you."

His hand claimed one of her own. "Not just now. But before, when I was captured and walking through the woods."

The copper rays in his eyes warmed the sudden chill bumps on her arms. "You heard my thoughts? That's never happened before."

Hanan frowned and peered at them from the overhead mirror. "Impossible. She was hiding behind the bushes, way out of your hearing range."

"How are you doing, buddy?" Chulah asked. "We'll be at the cabin in a few minutes, the hospital in fifteen."

Tombi shook his head. "No hospital."

Tallulah leaned over Annie and thrust her face close to her twin. "Don't be an idiot. Witch spells are bullshit. You need a doctor."

"You should see one," Annie agreed. She lifted his hair away from his forehead and saw swelling with a gash oozing blood. "You might have a concussion."

Tombi winced and jerked away from her touch. "My head is clearing. I'll be fine." He straightened and frowned at Chulah and Hanan. "What the hell happened out there?"

"We were ambushed," Chulah said, a grim set to his jaw. "The wisps were waiting on us as soon as we arrived."

"Betrayed," Tallulah ground out.

They hit a bump, and Annie's insides jostled. She cast a worried glance at Tombi, but his face wore the usual stoic mask. At least he was alert and coming out of whatever fog he'd suffered. A selfish, tiny jab of loneliness pricked her. When he was like this, he seemed so remote and removed—as if he didn't notice or need her.

Tombi kept his eyes peeled on the road ahead but grasped Annie's hand and held tight. Heat diffused over her body. Not even Tallulah's grimace of disapproval could dispel her glow inside. She sucked in her breath, relief and happiness unloosening the tense muscles in her shoulders and neck.

Annie closed her eyes and let the welcoming wind, from riding in the four-wheeler, brush over her face as the others discussed the attack and injuries. No death casualties, although three men were hospitalized and listed in serious condition.

"They weren't there to kill everyone," Hanan said. "Their objective was to capture you." He pulled up to a small cabin and brought the vehicle to an abrupt halt. "I wonder what Nalusa wants with you."

Annie shivered at the mention of Nalusa facing Tombi again. He couldn't be lucky enough to escape with his life on two different occasions.

"He hopes to cut a deal or truce." Tallulah scrambled out of the vehicle. "Either that or kill Tombi, thinking it will weaken all the hunters."

Typical Tallulah. The facts were laid bare with no emotion. You'd never know Tombi was her twin, that they had once heard one another's heartbeat in the womb.

Tombi stepped out onto the ground with only a slight wobble. He shook off Chulah and Hanan's offer of assistance and carefully made his way up the porch steps, hand gripping the railing.

Annie fell in behind everyone, uncertain of her welcome. Too bad, she'd do what needed to be done. Tombi wasn't out of the woods yet, and she wasn't finished with her healing ritual. That was—if he allowed her to proceed. The thought that she still might not have his full trust slowed her steps and weighed on her chest.

Inside, the spaciousness of the cabin surprised Annie. She saw now that the cabin was a deep, rectangular shape. The open den was large, and huge windows on the back wall framed nature's artwork of oaks and pines. Custom bookcases lined the side walls, and, ignored by all, she wandered over to glance at the titles: Choctaw history, animal spirit guides and archaeology magazines. Interspersed among the books were arrowheads and bits of pottery. There were also a few corncob pipes and Native American flutes decorated with feathers. Her mind tickled with faint piping notes. Could she hear his ancestors from the past? Instead of the normal dread of her supernatural sense, the sound filled Annie with awe and appreciation.

She ambled to the opposite wall, ignoring the buzz of conversation from another room where the others had disappeared. In the center of the largest bookcase was a Native American headdress decorated with colorful beads and feathers and shells attached with leather cords. A feeling of pride and majesty settled on her with a formal solemnity.

There were also several framed pieces of art featuring elaborate, beaded necklaces and collars. The need to create art in even a simpler, more natural past existence revealed a deep-felt human desire to express beauty, one that touched Annie. She fancied she could hear the lighthearted, higher-pitched voices of women talking and laughing together, beautifying the life of their community.

Being here was like walking through a time portal in a museum. It felt warm and right, like a secret home, a feeling of belonging and acceptance.

Wishful thinking. She pictured her mother's home in North Georgia, a shotgun-style house that was always cold in winter and stifling hot in summer. Everything in it was worn and shoddy and contained a past history of carelessness—just like the family who lived in it. Careless and hot and cold with their love.

Mostly cold.

Instinctively, Annie wrapped her arms across her chest. She didn't ever have to go back there again. She was done trying to earn their love. If her mom could shake off Grandma Tia and wash her hands of her own mother and hometown, Annie could do the same. *It's the last time I'll let history repeat itself,* she vowed. Crazy Annie was in the past.

She strode down the oak floorboard, taking in more of Tombi's belongings. It was obvious he was a man who took pride in his heritage and loved family and friends. Near the end of the bookcase was a shelf of framed pictures. Square in the middle was a small, faded three-by-five photo of a man and woman holding a pair of toddlers in their arms. She picked it up and examined it closely. Tombi and Tallulah. Tombi regarded the camera with wide, solemn eyes, while Tallulah's mouth parted in a huge laughing grin, a chubby finger pointed at the photographer.

Times had sure changed. Annie carefully set it down and retraced her steps to the headdress. She lifted her hand and touched one of the white feathers, startled to hear the slight swish sound of a bird in flight.

"Don't touch that."

Annie swirled around at the abrupt command, guiltily clutching her hands behind her back. "Sorry."

"Do you need a lift home?" Tallulah asked, scowling.

The message was clear. She wasn't welcome. "I can walk." Despite the heat in her cheeks, Annie lifted her chin and made for the front door.

"Suit yourself."

Annie refused to look at Tallulah as she left the cabin and fled down the steps.

"Hey! Where are you going?"

Tombi leaned on the door frame, swaying slightly. "I can't chase after you today. Come back."

Of course. How could she have allowed Tallulah to so completely sidetrack her? Tombi needed her. She'd come to do a job, and it was only half-complete. The first whiff of rejection had lanced the sensitive sore in her heart, and she'd run away, mortified.

Again.

Annie straightened her shoulders and went to Tombi.

Tallulah stepped onto the porch beside her brother. "You sure you want her with us?"

Tombi shot her a warning look, and she backed to the door. "Your call," she said, shrugging her shoulders.

"Don't you have some hoodoo juice or herb tea or something for me to drink?"

His smile was crooked, and the unexpected humor lightened the weight in her chest. She lifted her purse. "In here. The tea won't taste any better than the last brew you drank, but it will draw out any poison or toxins in your system."

Tombi held the door open, and she swept past him, back into the cool tranquility of his cabin.

Hanan, Tallulah and Chulah exited the kitchen, ready to leave.

"We'll check out who sent those texts," Chulah promised. "Pisa's a cop and has access to phone records."

Hanan fished the four-wheeler keys from his jean pockets. "And I'll notify everyone to meet here tomorrow. We'll figure out who sent it."

Tallulah stood behind her brother and flashed Annie a slash mark at the throat.

Annie paled. "It wasn't me."

Tombi faced his twin, hands on his hips. "What did you just do?"

"Nothing." Tallulah lifted her chin and smiled sweetly, sweeping past everyone. "Let's go. We all have lots to do before the gathering."

Annie watched them leave with relief. "Point me to the kitchen, and I'll make that tea."

He nodded and made his way out of the room. His gate was stiff and unnaturally slow. Tombi was hurt more than he wanted anyone to know. "Why don't you lie on the couch, and I'll bring it to you when I'm finished."

"I need to show you where everything is."

Stubborn man. Annie followed behind him. The kitchen had gleaming walnut cabinets with a matching island at the center. "Did you make these?"

He nodded, sinking into a chair at the small table in the corner. "Pots and pans are in the cabinet below the oven."

Quickly she set about brewing the tea. Outside the window, the sinking sun was a striking coral. She realized she was ravenous. "Are you hungry? What can I fix for supper?"

"Now that you mention it, I'm starving. You don't have to cook anything. I've got leftover spaghetti in the freezer."

With his directions, Annie got dinner going. She served him the herbal tea and returned to the stove, warming the spaghetti and buttering French bread. She found a pitcher of iced tea in the fridge and set the table.

The cozy intimacy of the meal restored her good spirits, as well as the sight of Tombi's skin turning from its former ashy color to its normal cinnamon glow. They settled into a comfortable silence. At last, Tombi set down his fork and pushed back his chair. "I feel like a new man." He held her eyes. "Thank you."

The simple compliment had her own skin glowing. "I just warmed up leftovers." She stood.

Tombi clamped his warm hand over her own. "You did more than that."

She screwed up her courage. "There's something else I'd like to do. If you'll let me."

He raised an eyebrow. "What do you have in mind?"

She so didn't want to do this. If only Grandma Tia were here, everything would be so much easier. Her grandma was the one with the real healing touch, the real magic. Her own attempts were weak, more hesitant. But she was on her own. She had to try. Annie took a deep breath, suppressing her inhibitions. If he refused or mocked her, at least she tried.

"I want to do a healing ritual."

Tombi strummed his fingers on the table. "And what would your ritual entail? Because we have our own purification rituals. Unfortunately, I don't have days to seek solitude and stay in a steam tent to purify my blood."

"I don't know that mine's as effective, but it's simpler and quicker. All that's involved is a prayer, lighting a candle and—" she stammered a heartbeat "—an anointing with healing oil."

"Who gets this anointing? Me or the candle?" He was as still and tense as a crouching jaguar, eyes intent and assessing.

"You." Annie cursed the burn in her cheeks. This was a sacred ritual, purely performed for medicinal and spiritual purposes.

Tombi slowly rose and came to her side, guiding her up by the elbow, until her body faced his, only inches apart. His aura melted into hers with the vibration of a base drum pounding in her ears and in her gut and in the womanly core between her thighs.

"Let's do it."

The deep, hoarse words implied more than an anointing. Tombi cocked his head toward the door. "This way."

Quickly, she grabbed her purse and followed him down a hall into a bedroom.

It was sparse and utilitarian. A large four-poster bed dominated the room, neatly made with green sheets and colorful Native American blankets folded at the foot. A matching wooden dresser and two nightstands. A brightly colored braided wool rug was in the center of the room. The windows were curtainless. Despite the barrenness of the room, Annie appreciated the minimalistic masculine atmosphere.

"We don't have to use your bedroom for the ritual." She stood by the door, clutching her purse.

"I'm going to take a quick shower. Just relax and set up everything."

Relax. Hah, fat chance. As soon as she was alone in the room, Annie walked to the dresser and pulled from her purse all she needed to arrange an altar. She placed a blue candle and a white candle on the table between a small, wooden statue of Black Hawk, a Native American spirit guide called upon in hoodoo as much as the saints.

The sounds of a water spray from the shower, and she pictured Tombi naked, the rivulets running down that silky black hair, onto his chest, down the lean abs and… Annie swallowed hard and returned to her task.

Carefully, she set out a stick of incense and a vial of sand from the Gulf Coast. She dressed the candles with Van Van oil and lit them with unsteady fingers, the tiny flame dancing between her fingers. Again she struck another match and applied it to the tip of the sage incense stick until it turned ashen, and curls of smoke saturated the air. She inhaled the pungent herbal scent and focused on the coming ritual.

Don't think about his naked body. Don't think about his wet flesh being lathered by soap. Don't think... As if.

She could think of nothing else. Sighing, she withdrew the last ritual item from her purse, a small glass bottle of healing oil. How would she be able to rub it across his chest without molding herself into his arms and kissing the strong plane of his jawline? From there she would be a hairbreadth from his lips, from his chest...and then she would be lost.

Well, it wouldn't be a crime if they made love. They were both single, consenting adults. Annie couldn't deny how drawn she was to his power and strength. Only— she wasn't the kind of woman who had casual sex. Oh, she wished she was. Very much. But for her, it went so much deeper.

Annie sat on the edge of the bed and closed her eyes. What did she really want? Her body yearned to feel Tombi inside her; it had been so long since a man had touched her. And emotionally, she had to admit, she was equally drawn to Tombi. The problem was she had no clue how he felt about her. He wanted her body, that was plain. And he wanted to use her gift to fight Nalusa. He was kind in trying to shield her from his sister and the other hunters' mistrust.

But did he love her?

The question drew her up sharp. Equally important, did she love him? If she didn't, she was close. So very close.

The shower spray ceased, and Annie paced, fighting a desire to flee the room and return home. The urge was strong. She went to the dresser, picked up her purse and flung it over her shoulder.

"Annie." Tombi lounged by the bathroom door, wearing only a white towel knotted at his hips. His long hair was sleek and plastered back from his temples, making his already severe face look harsher, more intense. "Running away again?"

Chapter 11

She was doing it again. Running. Over the years, it had become her go-to method for dealing with difficulty, ingrained since that disastrous kindergarten class with the unbearable, discordant triangle music. *You need to stop running away*, Grandma Tia had warned. *Stand up fo' yerself, girl.*

Grandma Tia was right. Tombi was right. She was sick of the cowardly acts.

No more.

Slowly, Annie pulled the purse strap from her shoulder and set it on the dresser. "I'm not leaving. I came here to do a job, and I intend to do it."

Tombi nodded. "Glad to hear that." He sniffed the air and pointed to the altar. "I smell sage. We burn it, too, for cleansing. Tell me how the rest of this works."

The matter-of-fact voice dispelled some of Annie's nervousness. He wasn't mocking her beliefs. "Sure. We traditionally use blue-and-white candles…" She inhaled sharply as he drew next to her. She smelled soap and some secret pheromone that was unique to him. And so utterly sexy and irresistible.

Tombi picked up the carved statue and examined it, frowning. "What's this?"

Would he take offense? "It's a statue of Black Hawk, an old war chief and spiritual guide we petition for help in battle. In this case, the battle is for your health. I'm worried that when the wisps attacked you, you inhaled some of their form or absorbed it through your skin. The earlier prayer to the saints helped in the emergency, and the fig-tree-bark tea helped revive your strength, but to really get rid of any lingering toxins, I think this ritual is needed. It's what I know Grandma Tia would recommend."

"Your recommendation is good enough for me." He put the statue back on the dresser. "Anything else?" Amusement lit his eyes. "I seem to remember you mentioning an oil rub."

Annie strove to keep her face and voice controlled and smooth. "If you'll sit on the edge of the bed, I'll get to work. I'll invoke Black Hawk in my thoughts while I rub your chest, above your heart, with healing oil."

"Time for the oil massage?" He gave a slow, sexy smile. "I like your witchy ways."

Annie pointed to the bed. "Just sit. And please don't talk while I rub you, because I'll be silently invoking Black Hawk while I do it."

Surprisingly, Tombi obeyed without a word. He sat on the bed and winked. "I'm ready. Actually, I'm a little tired, so I'll lie down instead of sit."

He swung his legs up on the mattress, and Annie blushed at the part in the towel that exposed him for a second.

Did he mean to do that? Sure he did. She should be angry. But instead, her thighs tightened in response. This would be the hardest ritual she'd ever performed. Annie licked her dry lips and went to the dresser again and retrieved the bottle of healing oil, spreading a generous amount in her palm. She rubbed her hands together, releasing the purifying medicinal smell of eucalyptus, allspice, myrrh and thyme.

Annie eased on the bed beside him and placed both her hands on his bare chest. At Tombi's dark look of desire, she closed her eyes, fighting the draw of attraction. The heat of contact was intensified by the slippery oil. Annie rubbed clockwise over his heart, determined to do her duty.

Inwardly chanting the familiar words of the petition eased her nervousness, and a deep calm settled through her body. A drowsing numbness crept into her fingers and palms, spreading upward, tingling unpleasantly.

So this was how Grandma Tia must have felt when she'd absorbed the toxins from Tombi after he'd been bitten by Nalusa in snake form, only it had to have been much more dangerous and intense.

It is done. All is well. The thought whispered through her consciousness, and she withdrew her hands and placed them in her lap.

Thank you, Black Hawk. She took a few deep breaths and opened her eyes, catching Tombi's frowning stare.

"Are you all right?" he asked, rising up on an elbow. "You look funny."

"I'm fine. Only a little tired."

"Damn." Tombi scooted over and patted the mattress. "Lie down and rest."

"Good idea." Lethargy weighted her bones, and she sank down on the bed. "Just a little nap," she murmured.

A large calloused hand gently brushed the hair from her face. "Are you going to be okay? I couldn't stand it if something happened to you."

He cared. Annie smiled with a secret happiness and

curled her knees into her chest. "I'm fine. Just hold me for a little while."

A warm, strong arm planted on the side of her hip. Nice. Passion warred against drowsiness. Sleep won. At last, she became aware that the pressure of his hands against her had vanished. Annie opened her eyes. "Where are you going?"

Darkness had settled in the room, and in the candle glow she watched as Tombi picked up the glass bottle of healing oil and returned to her side.

"Time for me to return the favor. Looks like you need this stuff."

"I'm okay." Black Hawk had reassured her on that point.

"Maybe. But this couldn't hurt." He emptied a dollop of oil into his palms and rubbed them together before sinking into the mattress beside her.

Annie's heart thudded with anticipation at the dark intent in Tombi's obsidian eyes. With great deliberation, he placed his hands on either side of the nape of her neck and rubbed the tight pressure points where skull joined spine. She rolled onto her back and sighed at the pain/pleasure cocktail as he worked his fingers and loosened the tight knots of tension.

The caress lowered to her shoulders, and Annie closed her eyes, relaxing into sensation. Bliss. If only this moment could last forever. A tug at the neckline of her T-shirt snagged her attention.

"This needs to come off," Tombi rasped.

She offered no resistance as he pulled her shirt over her head. One deft movement, and he'd unsnapped her bra and removed it, as well. Annie quickly pulled the bedsheet over her exposed breasts.

Tombi didn't remark on it, but resumed his ministrations on the curve of her shoulders. The oil glided like the liquid, healing caress of warm water. It spread from her shoulder to her collarbone and inched farther down to the round swells of her breasts. Her nipples tightened underneath the cotton sheet, and the friction made her core ache. She kept her eyes squeezed shut, unwilling to break the magic spell of passion.

A tug of the sheet, and she was exposed. Annie instinctively crossed her arms in front of her chest.

"What's wrong?" Tombi asked.

"N-nothing," she lied.

Evan's face filled her mind. She didn't want to think of him, didn't want to remember the feel of his rough hands and the quick thrust of his lovemaking. Or his jeer when it was over, complaining that she was frigid and should be grateful that he put up with her crazy ass.

"Relax," Tombi commanded. He reached across her and poured more oil into his palms.

Right. Relax. She calmed her quick, shallow breathing and concentrated on the cozy candle flames flickering on the walls and ceiling and the uplifting scent of the herbal oil.

Heated hands settled back on her breasts. "Am I supposed to say something special for healing?" he asked.

"Not necessary," she squeaked.

One hand palmed the skin above her heart on her left breast. "I'll pray to my own spirit guides," he murmured.

Peace engulfed Annie like a balm, soothing her skittish mind. Tombi's hands roamed lower, cupping her and teasing her nipples. She moaned and arched into his touch.

"You're so beautiful," Tombi breathed, his hot breath suddenly against her lips. "I love your body."

Surprise and relief bubbled inside. Annie kissed him, wanting to feel his lips, his mouth, his tongue. He kissed her back, settling his weight on top of her, pressing his erection against the apex of her thighs. *More, deeper, quicker.* Annie wiggled impatiently beneath him, inhibitions be damned.

Tombi rolled to his side and cradled her body against his own. The sexual tension between them grew and he pulled off what remained of her clothes. His mouth suckled her breasts and one hand lowered until his fingers probed the opening of her womanhood, and he inserted a finger.

Yes. She moved against it, delighting in the ripples of pleasure spreading all through her body, like a pebble dropped in smooth water.

Tombi moaned. "So damn sexy."

"You really think so?" she asked, seeking reassurance.

He took one of her hands and placed it on his erection. "There's your answer."

Her fingers curled over his long length, and she stroked him up and down, luxuriating in the smooth flesh. She did this to him, turned him on.

"I want you," she whispered, emboldened by the evidence of his desire.

His mouth lowered over a nipple. "There's no rush."

His tongue flicked her sensitive bud and need shot through her like an electrical shock. Annie gasped. "I don't want to wait."

Damn. Why did she say anything? Evan would have been annoyed; he'd taught her to shut up and go along with his tempo and desire.

Tombi raised his head and stared at her. "If you're sure that's what you want?"

His weight again pressed against her as he rolled on top. His eyes scorched her, the planes of his face were harsher and fiercer than she'd ever seen, even at that first encounter in the swamp. The candlelight behind him highlighted the golden undertone of his olive skin, and his long black hair hung loose about his broad shoulders.

She'd never been so sure about anything in her life. "Yes. Now." *Hurry.*

He took his sweet time, teasing his length along the wet folds of her core. Annie arched her hips, and he entered in one deep plunge, filling and stretching her completely. Her breath caught.

"You okay?"

She moved against him in answer.

Still, Tombi proceeded ever so slowly, deliberately, heightening the tension until Annie wanted to scream with passion. The ebb and flow of his advances were as powerful and deep as an ocean's tide. It consumed her, became the epicenter of her world.

"Please," she whispered brokenly.

He thrust deeper, quicker, and their bodies worked in harmony, a dance of desire as old as mankind. Annie was swept up in a thunder of need. Her muscles tightened, and release came, sending her free-falling back to reality. She sank into the mattress, exhausted and stunned. It had never been this way. Ever. She almost wanted to weep for the old Annie who had never climaxed, who'd always been told she was cold, who'd always been just a girlfriend of convenience.

What had he done?

Tombi stood at the window and surveyed the waning moon. The next time the celestial orb revealed its peak would be at the appearance of the Full Corn Moon. A time that had been a critical one for his ancestors as they harvested their maze and other crops for the barren winter ahead.

And he knew that in the weeks leading up to Full Corn Moon, he was preparing for a final battle. The bite from Nalusa, a betrayer revealing information that almost decimated the hunting band, and the gathering power and boundaries of Nalusa and the wisps convinced him that the scales had tipped in Nalusa's favor.

And the Old Shadow well knew it.

Nalusa would strike against them once and for all; Tombi could feel it in every cell of his body. He had only one hope at turning the tide in his favor.

He glanced back at the bed, where Annie lay sleeping. The white bedsheet was bunched up near the slight curve of her hip, leaving her shapely breasts exposed. Her hair fell against the linen in dark waves. She looked so womanly—yet still so young. A woman-child, a healer, a witch, a sound sorcerer—all wrapped up into one extraordinary person who didn't realize how incredible she really was.

Especially in bed.

His blood heated as he remembered Annie's shy but passionate response during their lovemaking. And he frowned as he recalled the drowsy happiness in her eyes afterward, the tender way she brushed his hair from his forehead and kissed his temples.

He couldn't allow himself to fall into her tender mercies, and he hoped she would be a sensible, modern woman about what had taken place between them tonight. He needed her gift of hearing, not her love. An unfamiliar, uncomfortable tug pulled at his conscience—had he used her tonight to further his own cause and get her cooperation in the fight against the shadows?

Tombi hoped he wasn't that kind of man.

As if hearing his unsavory thoughts, Annie thrashed against the sheets and bolted upright. Her eyes were wide and wild, and she clutched the sheet up to her neck.

"What's wrong? Did you have a bad dream?"

"I'm not sure." Her brows knitted. "I heard a flapping noise. Like a large bird did a flyby near my head."

"Must be your animal spirit guide trying to get your attention."

"A bird?"

He laughed at the disappointment in her voice. "Nothing wrong with that. Makes perfect sense, actually. Birds are messengers, just as you have been with Bo."

"I suppose. Secretly, I was hoping it would be a cat. A long, lean jaguar or panther."

"Cats that eat birds for breakfast, huh? Think of it this way—in our culture some of the most revered guides are eagles. They represent freedom, strength and victory."

"I could use some of that. Especially victory. How will I know for sure if the eagle is my guide? How do I communicate with it?"

"Watch when you're outside for a particular bird, or if feathers of a particular bird appear. If you keep looking, it will make itself known."

But he'd lost Annie's attention. Her gaze kept drawing up and down his body. "You're already dressed," she noted, picking at the sheet bunched in her hands. "Don't you want to...you know...come back to bed?"

Did he ever. Yet, Tombi hesitated. If she stayed with him indefinitely here in his cabin, shared his bed, Annie might have...expectations. Best to establish boundaries now. He sat on the edge of the bed. "About last night—"

The happiness in her face melted, the soft, vulnerable shine in her eyes hardened. "Don't worry. I expect nothing."

The reasons why she should do just that—expect nothing—died on his lips. Someone had hurt her badly. "Damn. Who made you so bitter? Evan?"

"He made it clear that a girl like me should be grateful for any attention thrown her way. That sex is just sex. Not to be confused with love." She turned her face to the side, stiff and brittle.

Tombi gently placed a finger on her uplifted chin and

drew her face toward him. "A girl like you? What the hell is that supposed to mean?"

"I've told you before, I'm known as Crazy Annie in my hometown."

"You're a beautiful, exceptional woman," he argued.

"Then why—" Her voice trembled, and she took a shaky breath. "Go on and say what you have to say."

"It's not you, it's me." Damn, that sounded lame even to his own ears. Tombi dropped his hand and paced the room, needing his space, needing to find the words that were impossible to formulate while staring into her disappointed eyes.

"It's like this," he began. "My life is dedicated to stopping Nalusa and the wisps and all the dark creatures of the night from taking control of the light, of all that's good in the world. It's been my mission since I was nineteen years old. It's what I was born to do."

"I wouldn't stop you," she said softly.

"You say that now. But when it comes time for me to face Nalusa, you might try to stop me from what I have to do. Guilt me into turning away." He'd seen it with a few hunters, the ones who'd chosen to marry and raise families. Priorities changed.

"No one's ever put me first. Don't worry, I won't expect it now."

The hard edge was back in her tone, in the pinched set of her lips.

"You deserve better than that." Tombi strode to the window, where the first sun rays peeped through the horizon, casting shadows that broke up the darkness. But for him, there was no ameliorating the darkness. He faced the truth, the secret fear he'd lived with for so long.

He was afraid that the darkness would win. Not just in the real, bayou backwaters and beyond, but deep in his soul. Ever since his parents had died, a wound had festered inside that had been fed through a series of subsequent blows—the death of his best friend, the loss of kinship with his twin sister, the growing realization he was fighting a battle he most likely could not win.

If Annie and her grandmother hadn't come along when they did…he'd have surely died from Nalusa's snakebite.

"I've already caused you enough grief," he said gruffly. "Your grandmother may well die because of her effort to save me."

"I don't blame you anymore. For whatever reason, she made her own decision. Grandma Tia's always been that way." Annie gave a shaky laugh. "She's doing better, you know. She's awakened from the coma."

Relief lightened the pressure in his chest, where guilt and worry weighed like a boulder. Unfortunately, it was still heavy from other burdens. "Good to hear."

"Now, if you don't mind, could you give me some privacy to get dressed?"

The hurt in her eyes and the former frost in her voice had disappeared, but she was overly polite, distant. "Annie, I…" He stopped, unsure how to proceed. Wasn't this what he wanted? To put some emotional distance between them?

"I'll say it for you. The sex was mediocre and you aren't in love with me, so I shouldn't get any ideas that this is some kind of permanent relationship."

"What?" Shock and pain iced the blood in his veins. She was quite the actress if his lovemaking hadn't pleased her. Unfamiliar heat rose up the back of his neck. He'd been accused of being too fierce, too unfeeling and too bent on revenge, but he'd never had any complaints about his sexual prowess. "I could have sworn you were satisfied."

"I was, but you weren't. There, happy now?"

"Who said I wasn't?" Damn, she was confusing as hell.

Her eyes narrowed. "I thought that's what you were trying to tell me."

"Let's start over." Tombi folded his arms. "I only wanted to warn you that my number-one priority right now is defeating Nalusa. The situation is dangerous and headed for a breaking point."

"I already know this."

So far, so good. Annie seemed calm and accepting. If it had been Courtney sitting there in his bed…he'd be paying hell. She'd broken up with him because she wasn't first in his life. She resented the time he spent hunting during the full moon and the allegiance he had to his people.

"It doesn't bother you?"

"I worry about your safety."

"Which leads me to my next point. Nalusa and the shadows grow more powerful every day, and they have an inside track to our whereabouts and strategy, thanks to some informer. It could well be that the next full moon, Nalusa will go after me again. This time, I don't expect to live through it."

"Oh, Tombi." Annie dropped the sheet and climbed out of bed. Her body, only a shade lighter than his own, glowed in the pale dawn light. She approached him slowly and placed her hands on his shoulders. "Don't say that. Don't even think it. We'll find the betrayer. Together, we can work out a plan. And now that Grandma Tia is coming around, she'll help, too."

He wanted to believe Annie, but the years hadn't trained his mind to expect the best. "I wish I didn't have to involve you or your grandmother. But if there's any chance you could turn this war around in our favor, I need you."

"I'll help you."

Annie rested her head against his bare chest, and he stroked her hair, humbled at her willingness to stand with him and his people. "Thank you," he murmured in the comforting warmth of her scalp.

"I've never been needed before."

"Hard to believe." If he wasn't careful, he could grow to need her too much, could bask in her kindness and healing nature and let her brighten the dark, warring evenings.

She lifted her face. "It's true. I've always been the afterthought, never normal enough or smart enough to fit in with my own family, much less a boyfriend."

If he could, he'd erase every painful memory she suffered. Would kiss away every tear and chase away all her doubts and insecurities as mercilessly as he tracked down every wisp leading to Nalusa.

"Their loss," he ground out. Damn it to hell, if there was any way to keep from hurting her, he would.

Don't fall in love with me, Annie. He should tell her, warn her. But he couldn't bring himself to say the words. He bent down and kissed her full lips, hungry for her touch, her feel. As if last night hadn't been enough.

Tombi feared it would never be enough. There weren't enough days and nights in his lifetime for making love with Annie. He pressed his hands on the sides of her hips, marveling at her soft skin, at the way her body melded to his own, seeking oneness. He was selfishly taking all she had to offer. Eternal spirits help him, he couldn't caution Annie to guard her heart.

Because much to his chagrin, he needed the warning more than she did.

Chapter 12

The clear, pure melody of the flute danced in the breeze. As if a flock of birds warbled in the same octave, with high notes that trilled in a soaring ecstasy, tempered by a deeper undertone of mourning. And blended between was all manner of feeling: lyrical, haunting. Weeping whistles of warring hope and despair.

Tombi stopped playing, and the silence echoed in Annie's brain like a sudden death. "You're up early," he commented, his rigid back to her. His shirt was off, and the golden skin on his chest glistened with sweat. The red bandana on his forehead was wet.

It was one hell of a sexy sight.

Annie continued across the yard toward him, carefully maneuvering between workbenches and piles of wood and cabinet frames. The air smelled of cut pine.

She faced him, trying to evaluate his mood. Yesterday he'd been aloof, despite the previous night's closeness. He'd spent most of yesterday out speaking with other hunters and planning a meeting. All afternoon and into the evening, he'd worked his carpentry job, claiming to be behind schedule. But last night... She blushed, remembering their intense lovemaking. "Enjoying your break?" she asked.

"I was." He nodded at the pocketbook hanging from her shoulder. "You going to visit your grandmother again today?"

"Yes. Unless you're ready to give me another lesson."

He picked up a piece of lumber and placed it on the workbench. "Why don't you go ahead? The lessons can wait."

"Maybe for you," she answered sharply, frustrated with his aloofness during the day. He acted as if he wanted to shut her out of a large part of his life.

He raised a brow. "Problem?"

"Seems like you've been avoiding showing me how to control my hearing. We had a deal. Remember?"

He frowned. "Is that all that's wrong? I've been a little busy. Give me a break."

Annie tried another tactic. "I thought you said time was of the essence, that things were heading to a showdown between you and Nalusa."

"I have no way of knowing for sure, but that's my gut feeling."

"And you said you needed my help. So why aren't you putting me to work for you? I feel like you're shutting me out." Except when he wanted her body.

"All I need is for you to come with us during the next hunt to let us know when you hear something that we can't. Especially if Bo tries to communicate again."

"There must be something we can do between now and the full moon."

A knowing smile broke through Tombi's inscrutably calm face, and his pupils darkened. "I can think of a few things," he said with that deep gruffness she remembered from last night's bedtime talk.

"Well, there's always *that*." She cleared her throat. "My grandma's expecting me to eat breakfast with her at the hospital. Want to come with me?"

He picked up a saw and shook his head. "Not now. I have a couple client appointments today. Tell her I'll drop by again this evening."

"Suit yourself." Annie headed to her car, conscious of him watching her. She turned her face slightly to the side. Sure enough, he stood, saw in hand, staring at her ass. Her own lips upturned in a knowing smile as she climbed into her vehicle. She had the power to break through his remote facade whenever she wished.

Was it wrong to hunger for more? There must be something she could do to gain his respect, to make him see she could be a stronger ally. Some way to defeat Nalusa. As long as Nalusa lived and controlled the wisps and the birds of the night, Tombi wasn't free to live a normal life. His need for revenge consumed him.

"Be careful," Tombi called out.

Annie started the car and headed for the county road, her mind filled with possibilities. For starters, she could return to the cottage and study the grimoires she'd culled from Grandma Tia's collection. Maybe there was something there. She glanced at the dashboard clock. She had time for a little reading before visiting her grandma. Annie gunned the motor and arrived at the cottage quickly, filled with optimism. Must be some reason Grandma Tia communicated about the grimoires while she was in the coma, even if she didn't now remember why or how she'd done so.

Inside, she lit candles and settled at the kitchen table. She pulled the top one off the stack and opened it. Metallic ink shimmered on the pages with its flecks of crimson, forest green and ocean blue. The crinkling as she turned the page seemed an unnaturally loud rustle, as if a pile of dead leaves were stirred by a stiff breeze.

A sudden scent enveloped her awareness. An earthy, bitter greens top note sweetened with rich, dark undertones. Annie inhaled and analyzed the enticing mixture—it contained licorice, vanilla and myrrh. She'd noticed it before around the cottage, often when Grandma Tia performed a ritual calling on the guidance of an ancestor.

"Who are you?" she whispered, her skin tingling. The scent grew stronger, as if a spirit drew closer. Annie waited, hardly daring to breathe, but no other sign was offered. "Thank you for coming," she said, louder, more confident this time. She'd asked for help, and it looked as if she was getting it.

She ran her fingers down the cracked spine of the old grimoire. This book was the one. It whispered promises and answers. The strong premonition settled in her gut while her heart raced.

Primitive music sounded—so faint she wasn't sure she heard it at first. Annie strained and deciphered the vibration of a drum that provided a base to a flute. The music was subtly different from what Tombi played—there were fewer notes, less range of pitch, less sophistication. But instead of deterring from the sound quality, it made it more unique and poignant.

The pages began turning without any assistance, like an invisible hand leafing through the tome. It was like the time when she was twelve and playing with her grandma's Ouija board without permission. An unseen force had moved the planchette across the alphabet, spelling a slightly sinister message. Even now, Annie preferred tarot cards and crystals to seek help from beyond.

This time felt different, not sinister at all. As if the unseen hand was pointing toward a solution. Besides, an ancestor was in the room with her, one that smelled of strong femininity grounded by the earth.

The rustling stopped. Reverently, Annie pulled the grimoire closer and started reading. Excitement charged her body like an electrical shock at the story of an old Choctaw tale involving Nalusa Falaya and how his spirit was bound in an ancient ritual performed by the strongest warriors in the tribe.

Why had Tombi never mentioned this ritual? Annie tapped an index finger against her lips and gazed out the kitchen window, deep in thought. Maybe he hadn't heard of it, or maybe he did know about it and didn't believe it would work. Worry wiggled into her consciousness. Or maybe he knew there was a ritual, and he hoped to enlist her cooperation to perform it with him. And if that was the case, perhaps he didn't mention it hoping that in time she would become so bound to him through their relationship, she wouldn't refuse the request when he made it.

Annie shook her head, refusing to let negativity cloud her brain with such questions. If Tombi was trying to control her through a relationship, he'd be telling her he loved her and promising her the moon instead of keeping his distance.

She continued reading. In order for the containing ritual to work, the tribe leader needed to summon Nalusa with their sacred flute, crafted with the spirits' help. It was ancient, originally created at the time of Nalusa's first rise to power.

Chills tingled up and down Annie's spine. It all came together. Bo's words to find the music contained in the wind. The image of a flute Grandma Tia communicated from her bedside at the hospital.

Find that flute, and they would have the key to defeat Nalusa and his shadow creatures.

Kee-eeeee-ar. A hoarse screeching erupted as a large, rust-colored bird flew close against the windowpane and then jettisoned away in a flurry of beating wings. *Kee-eeeee-ar.*

Beating wings. Just like in her dreams. Annie jumped up and ran to the front door and down the porch steps, but the bird flew into the woods and disappeared. Some animal spirit guide; it did nothing but startle her. A small glint of dusty red and a shiver of movement by the kitchen window caught her eye. She walked across the grass and picked up a feather lying on the sill, fancying it still felt warm to the touch.

A memento from her bird, her guide. She held it in her hands, awed at the physical evidence left behind. Maybe it was like a courtship—every day it would draw closer and reveal more of its nature. Was there some way to thank it for appearing?

She scurried inside and returned with several pieces of bread. She crumbled them in her hands and cast them on the yard. "A little something for you," she called out toward the woods. She liked to think the bird was out there, watching—watching and protecting her from the birds of the night and snakes that crept nearby unawares, coiled to strike with deadly venom.

Annie spun in a dizzy circle of happiness, her heart lightened with optimism and hope. Even if Tombi was consumed with revenge and headed for a showdown with the bayou shadow world, she had not only an ancestor spirit guide, but also an animal guide helping her seek a way to defeat the evil. First, she would conquer evil and prove her trust and worthiness, and then she'd make headway into Tombi's heart and future.

She might just discover a real love.

Over halfway to the hospital, it struck Annie that she hadn't even considered her own need to control her hearing. If she hadn't alrseady lost her heart to Tombi, she was damn close.

Annie burst through his door and found him in the kitchen. Her eyes glowed with excitement, and her aura burst with energy. "Let's go on a hunt tonight."

What the hell had gotten into her? She hated hunting, the stumbling around in the dark and the fear of encountering a snake. Not that Tombi could blame her; she'd witnessed the worst of the worst after Nalusa had almost killed him and her grandmother. He set his glass of tea on the counter. "What brought about this change of heart?"

"I may have found a way to defeat Nalusa." She lifted up an old, thick book with aged, yellow paper poking out of its sides, and rocked on her tiptoes, grinning as she awaited his reaction.

Yeah, right. She'd never heard of Nalusa until last week, and now she had a plan to defeat the king of the shadow world? After he and the other trained hunters had been trying for years with no success? He crossed his arms and leaned against the counter. This should be amusing.

"Aren't you dying to hear?"

"Shoot," he said, lips curving into an indulgent smile.

"It's true. Grandma Tia and my great-great-great-great-grandmother, Belle Hamilton, led me to a possible way."

"I think you added a couple of extra *greats* in there. It would make her close to a couple hundred years old."

Annie blinked. "I didn't say she was *alive*. Anyway, we need to find the ancient flute that your ancestors used to keep Nalusa's power contained."

"Ah, so you heard that old tale. Surprising, though—it's not a generally known story." He nodded at the book she clutched in front of her. "I guess the story's in there."

The sparkle in her chocolate eyes dwindled. "You already knew about it," she accused. "You might have mentioned it."

"What's to tell? I've never figured there was any truth to it."

"But...but why not? It's a recorded legend by the Choctaws."

"And so are stories of the *Kowi anuskasha*—knee-high fairy creatures said to roam the bayou and play tricks on humans. I don't believe in them, either."

"It's worth a try."

"Only one problem. There is no such flute. Or if there ever was one, it's long since vanished."

"There must be. I heard it playing."

His heartbeat pounded in his ears, like the roar of a million insects on a rain-dampened summer night. This couldn't be. "Say that again."

"I heard the flute. Remember the grimoire Grandma Tia told me to find when she was in the coma? Well, I started reading it when all of a sudden I smelled this distinctive scent that was familiar. I couldn't place it, but when I visited Tia at the hospital she said it was my great-great—"

"Great-great-grandmother," he cut in impatiently. "Tell me the part where you hear the flute."

She frowned but continued on. "Anyway, as I was reading about the legend, the notes of a Native American flute drifted up from the pages. It sounded more primitive than yours. I even know what it looks like." She tapped the aged book. "There's a drawing and a description in here."

Excitement buzzed along his spine. "Let me see."

Annie opened it to a page marked with a red thread and pointed. "Right there."

He carefully took the book, afraid the fragile tome would crumble at rough handling. Tombi scanned the elegant cursive handwriting with its unusual glimmering ink and the dried brown bits of old flowers stuffed in its pages. Halfway down the right page was a drawing of the flute. A design was burned into the cane wood, but a long turkey feather tied at the base obscured the carving.

"Do you have it here in your bookcase?" she asked breathlessly.

He frowned at the description—it could belong to almost any of the reed instruments he'd collected over the years. Of course, the feather would have rotted away by now or have been switched out over the years. Tombi made his way to the den and stood in front of his music collection. Each one had given him so much peace over the years, had inspired him to learn to play and even craft several of his own flutes.

"Did you find these yourself?" Annie asked by his side.

"No. Tallulah works at the local museum, and she alerts me whenever they host a fund-raising auction. That's how I got most of these artifacts, except for the odd pottery shard or arrowhead."

Four of the flutes were made of cane wood and about the length described in Annie's book. He picked them up and showed them to Annie. "Do you think it could be one of these?"

Annie closed her eyes and lifted cupped palms. "Hand me each of them, one at a time."

He did so, despising the flash of hope that flared in his gut. *It's going to be another dead end.* But his gut didn't listen to his mind, and it burned on with unrestrained optimism. He carefully placed one of the flutes in her palms. Annie slowly shook her head "no," a gesture she repeated until he placed the final one in her hands, his hope at last in tatters.

Seconds—or an eternity—passed. "No. This isn't it, either."

Told you so, his inner voice mocked. Tombi put the flutes back on the shelf. "Well, that was fun."

"Are you giving up that easily?"

"You got any other ideas?"

"For starters, we can go to the ancestral land where it says the artifact is stored, see if we can find it."

"It's been tried, not just by me, but also many other hunters over the years. Face it, the flute is long gone—if it ever existed. I think it's all bullshit."

"You're wrong. I know it. I wouldn't have been sent messages if it weren't real. The least we can do is search again. Maybe it's mysteriously turned up?"

Annie was so enthusiastic, so full of optimism. He'd been like that once, so many years ago he'd forgotten what it felt like. Life would crush her spirits eventually, too, but he wouldn't be the one to do it. "Okay. We'll go look. But I'm warning you that the chance of it turning up is extremely remote. But hunting together at night will be good practice for you."

"Part of my training for the next full moon's hunt?"

"Exactly. Plus, it's an opportunity for Bo to speak with you again."

She clasped her hands together. "He might know where the flute's hidden."

"We'll go. I hate to put you in danger, but I promise I won't leave your side."

"I believe you, especially if you keep your other promise to me."

He raised a brow. "Which one?"

"I want you to teach me to control my hearing. I know you're busy with your work, but surely you can spare an hour every day."

It was only fair. "Let's do it now."

Annie bestowed a dazzling smile. "You don't know how much this means to me."

"Again, don't think this will be easy or a guaranteed success," Tombi cautioned. "I've never tried to help anyone this way, so it's all an experiment."

"I have faith in you."

Unease twisted him inside. *Damn, please, let this work.* Couldn't something go right for once in his life? "Normally, I'd do energy work outside. I have a circle set up with conch shells in the backyard. But right now is too risky. Not when there's a betrayer in the group and not when Nalusa's power's grown so strong he's been active during daylight."

"Inside is better for me anyway," Annie said. "More sound insulation. All the birds and insects drive me nuts, not to mention the rustling leaves and the tide."

"You hear the ocean way out here?"

"Yes, but it's not too bad—it's like a background sound, a white noise that's with me even in dreams." She clapped her hands and glanced about the den. "We can set up a circle right here. You do that, and I'll run upstairs and bring down my altar materials."

"The witchy stuff isn't necessary," he objected.

"I'm so excited right now I can't even get mad at you for that stupid comment." She ran up the stairs, paused halfway and leaned over the railing. "Besides, what could it hurt?"

True. He would need all the help he could get. Tombi walked to the backyard, braving the wave of heat, and gathered the conch shells. Back inside, he pushed the furniture to the walls and formed a circle with the shells. At the center, he unrolled a woolen rug woven by one of his cousins years ago. Amid an indigo background, a large golden sun was woven in the middle. The edges of the rug featured a series of intertwined pyramids.

As he lit a sage smudge stick, Annie returned with an armful of candles and statues and arranged them within the circle. Tombi walked to all four corners of the room, calling on his ancestors for their assistance and driving away any negative energy. He was as ready as he'd ever be. He settled on the rug and watched Annie.

She silently prayed at the altar, kneeling, moving her lips. After finishing, she picked up a spray bottle and walked on the outside of the circle, spritzing. The sweet herbal scent of sage melded with a strong floral scent.

"What are you spraying?"

"It's called Florida Water, one of the oldest hoodoo concoctions. It has bergamot, lavender and clove. I also mixed in a few drops of orange, ginger and pine for extra spiritual power."

They sat across from each other on the floor, cross-legged, letting silence settle in the room. At least, for him, all was quiet. "Do you still hear my energy field sometimes?" he asked, curious.

"Not often. Mostly whenever you let your guard down. Like when you're asleep at night or…" She blushed. "When we make love."

Fascinating. "Do I always sound like the flute?"

"No. When we make love you sound like a drum vibrating with the rhythm of your heart."

He could feel it pulsing now, as it always did when he was close to Annie. The familiarity of having her at his cabin did nothing to dispel his body's immediate reaction to her nearness. If anything, the link between them grew every day.

"We haven't talked about it, but the day I was drugged by Nalusa, I heard you in my mind."

Her eyes widened. "You did?"

"You told me to hold on, that you were near and help was on the way."

"That's what I was thinking."

"There's an energetic bond between us. My parents

said they shared one, and Bo and Tallulah shared one. But it's a rare thing."

Annie interlaced her fingers with his own. "I'm honored." She leaned forward and rested her forehead against his.

He felt oddly vulnerable as he absorbed the tenderness through their contact. "That bond will probably grow much closer after this," he warned. "Do you still want to try?"

Annie pulled away and nodded solemnly. "Yes. I trust you completely."

"And I trust you." Somehow, some way, she'd infiltrated his mind and body and…heart. He cared way too much for Annie. Worry about her safety and concern for her future weighed him down, at a time when he should be totally focused on Nalusa.

Her eyes clouded with tears. "Thank you."

"And now we begin. First—"

"Oh, wait, I forgot something that might help us." Annie withdrew her hands from his and stood. "My great-great-great-great-grandmother wasn't my only supernatural visitation today."

He watched as she went to the sofa and rifled through her purse, at last producing a feather. "You were right—my spirit guide is a bird. He made contact with me and left this."

"Some bird." He laughed. "I thought for sure it would be along the lines of a robin or a starling." Something feminine and petite like Annie. But the cinnamon-red tail feather was one he instantly recognized. "This is from a red-tailed hawk. Your bird is a highly intelligent raptor known for its hunting skills and partnership with humans through falconry. An excellent animal guide that will offer you its protection."

"It's huge. A little intimidating even. But I'm sure we'll

become great friends. Maybe the feather can help us with the ritual."

"Absolutely." He laid it between them as she resumed sitting across from him.

"All hunters have the skills of night vision, extraordinary hearing, a keen sense of smell or an intuition when the shadows arrive. We can even discern the marks and signs of shadow creatures. And some of us are better at various skills more than others. My specialty is blocking."

"Blocking?"

"I can prevent certain sensations from entering or exiting my energy field. When hunting, it allows me to maintain intense focus while at the same time I can stop others from sensing me. To a degree, that is. It's not like I'm invisible. If a shadow draws close enough, they will hear, smell and see me. But I have a definite edge no one else has. It's why I've been an unofficial leader of the group."

"That's not the only reason," Annie objected. "You would be a leader no matter what. You're smart and courageous and fair. The other hunters recognize those traits in you."

She had too much faith in him. He should warn her off; there was a certain ruthlessness to him that grew sharper from every contact with Nalusa and the wisps. He hated to imagine how much that ruthless nature would have overcome him after Nalusa's bite if Annie and her grandmother hadn't been there. She was truly his savior, although she was too insecure to recognize it.

"At any rate, I'll try to show you how I block sound. I'm not sure you'll be able to do it. I don't know if this is something I inherited, but I do know that over time I've been able to perfect this ability, so maybe some of it is learnable."

"It will be, I can feel it."

A smell of fresh-cut grass quickly followed by a flower aroma wafted through the air. "What the hell is that?"

"Ms. Belle, the great-great-great-great one. She's lending her support and approval."

Would he ever get used to this hoodoo witchy business? Then again, she'd adapted quickly to his fight against the shadow world. If she could deal, he could do the same.

"It's like this. During a hunt, when I'm blocking noise, I visualize sound waves floating toward me in slow motion. At the instant I hear a note, I picture a golden shield of light covering my entire body. As the waves advance toward me, I filter each note through the shield so that the noise is muted. If the will-o'-the-wisps are trying to fill my mind with negative messages, I can entirely block their attempt."

"That's so cool," Annie whispered.

"Let's try something. Describe any sounds you hear now."

She closed her eyes. "I hear the electrical hum of the air conditioner and the refrigerator. Far away, I hear the tide and the screech of a few children playing tag. I hear the whirr of the ceiling fan above and a car passing by on County Road 143."

"Can you hear my energy field?"

She shook her head. "Not at all."

He took a deep breath. He was about to open himself to someone as deeply as he'd ever allowed. He dropped the normal protective barrier that was his walking-around daily existence. Let it all go in a swoosh that felt like a boulder rolling off his shoulders.

Annie gasped.

Had he released too much? Quickly, Tombi blocked the flow. "Are you okay?"

She inhaled deeply. "Yes."

"What did you hear?"

"It's hard to explain, but the music from your aura was rich and deep and melancholy. I heard the flute, drums, a chanting, a rush of flooding waters, a snake's hissing and rattling, and the music of the wisps, only it was distorted. Instead of alluring, it was frightening and demented."

Rushing waters. Always, his parents' death weighed on his heart and mind. "You nailed it." He shook off the sad memories. "Let's try something. I'm going to play a few musical notes on my cell phone, and you try to picture the sound waves and block them with a golden shield." Tombi withdrew his phone from the back pocket of his jeans. Ready to try?"

Annie nodded.

He hit Play.

Annie screwed up her face. A minute passed.

"Annie? Are you okay?"

She waved him off. "I'm concentrating."

"Sweet Home Alabama" rocked on. When it ended, Tombi shut off his phone.

"Any luck, Annie?"

She opened her eyes and grinned. "Yes! Dammit, it freaking worked. Only for a few seconds, but it worked!"

What a relief, it actually worked. "Good. With practice you can do it for longer periods of time. Don't do too much at first, or you'll get exhausted."

Tears rained down her cheeks. "I can't thank you enough."

"I can think of a few naughty ways you can express your gratitude," he said with a wink.

Annie smiled. "Okay. I'm ready when you are."

"Right here in the circle? Right now? Suits me fine."

Annie sat up, resting on her knees and placing her hand on his shoulders. "Making love to you feels natural and right, whether in a sacred circle or not." A grin swept her face as she tilted her neck upward. "If you're still around, my dear great Ms. Belle, I suggest you leave immediately."

Chapter 13

Tombi pulled Annie's body against him so that his face nestled in her cleavage. For such a petite woman, her breasts were full and luscious. He knew she wore no bra, had been eyeing the peak of her nipples beneath her cotton T-shirt ever since she'd come home from the hospital and changed clothes. He liked that, with him, she was comfortable enough to let loose. Hell, he'd love Annie to loosen up enough that she'd want to parade naked whenever they were alone.

He cupped his hands beneath her breasts and turned his face into one of the ample mounds, kissing her through the thin cotton, until the fabric was wet and rough in his mouth.

Annie groaned and squeezed him tighter, reaching down and pressing her hand against his manhood. It bulged and chafed against his jeans, straining for release. She obliged by unbuttoning his pants and unzipping the jeans. Reluctantly, he withdrew from sucking a nipple, stood and hastily stepped out of his pants. He bent his knees to sit back down, but Annie had other ideas.

Her mouth was on him, taking in every inch. Tombi placed his hands on her head and ran his fingers through her soft hair.

Sweet, sweet Annie. It felt so damn good. This was what he wanted. Needed. To experience her in every way. But if she didn't stop... Tombi tugged at her hair, and she withdrew.

"What's wrong?" she asked, her voice rough and deep with passion.

"Not a damn thing. It's just your turn." He nodded at her clothes. "Take them off," he demanded.

Annie gave a slow, seductive smile and stood, taking her sweet time as she lifted the shirt up over her breasts and then her head.

He could never get enough of this woman. Ever.

Even slower, Annie hooked her thumbs over her pink gym shorts, taking her lacy panties down with them. She stood before him naked. The sun streaming through the rear window cast beams on her slim figure, as if she were an angel sent from heaven.

Maybe she was.

Her hair cascaded around her shoulders and hips like a curtain. She was the epitome of everything feminine and mysterious. "You're so beautiful," he said, knowing the words were inadequate, but hoping she'd glean the strong emotion behind them.

A blush stained her cheeks, and he even found her sudden modesty touching. Soon, very soon, modesty would have no place in what they were about to do. Annie ducked her head, dark hair falling over olive skin.

Tombi took her hand and tugged. Gracefully, Annie sank beside him, fluid as water, and stretched her lithe body against the woven rug, covering the sun design at its center. She was a goddess. A witchy goddess, and he was completely under her spell. She affected him like no other woman he'd ever known.

He allowed some of his tight reserve to break free. He wanted to give, to share everything with Annie. With time and practice, he might be able to completely relax his tightly held energy field that separated him from others. One which he donned every morning like an armor.

Tombi parted her thighs and pressed his face into the folds of her hot core and tasted her soft essence. And now she was the one with her hands on his head, pressing him deeper and deeper. His tongue lavished her folds until she writhed against him.

"Now. I want you now," she complained. "Please."

He couldn't wait, either. Tombi lay beside her and lifted her hips so that she straddled him. He entered her, and they moved together in the ancient dance of humankind.

It was an electrical storm of passion, as need rumbled in his heart and manhood. His blood pounded faster, straining and crackling in the tempest that was Annie. Her high-pitched moans roared in his mind, but he held back his own release until her thighs and core convulsed, signaling her climax. He let go all restraint, exploding like thunder deep within Annie.

She sank her body on top of his, and he ran his fingers through her hair, utterly sated.

"Am I getting heavy?" She slipped off him and folded herself against his side.

"Not at all." He rested his hand on the slim curve of her hips and ran his fingers over the small of her back.

Annie yawned.

"Why don't you take a nap?" he suggested. "It's going to be a long night."

"Does that mean we're going to go look for the flute?" She propped up on her elbow, eyes aglow.

"It does."

"This will be fun. A treasure hunt."

Huh. When was the last time he'd had an *enjoyable* hunt? Never, actually. He vowed not to get his hopes up about finding the flute. He could just enjoy the night with Annie and help her practice blocking skills and the ability to maneuver in the darkness together.

Tombi gently kissed her cheek. "Sleep well. For tonight, we hunt."

Kee-eeeee-ar. Three seconds elapsed. *Kee-eeeee-ar.* Another three seconds of silence.

Her hawk followed them as they went deeper into the woods, and after the initial surprise, Annie found the bird's calls reassuring. He was guarding her, offering his protection. She took it as a good omen. A sign that something special would take place this evening.

Annie gripped Tombi's hand firmly, determined to match his long strides. The waning moon didn't provide much light. Not even will-o'-the-wisp smoke glowed in the forest, not that she could see much at any rate.

Tombi stopped abruptly, and she realized she was on the muddy bank where she'd first met him and where Bo had first appeared. So much had happened since then, it seemed like months ago instead of a mere week.

"This is where my ancestors once prayed and petitioned the great spirits. And it's where they imprisoned Nalusa."

"Do you know which tree to check for the flute?" she whispered close to his ear.

"There's only one that has a hollow in its center."

Annie kept walking beside him and almost ran into the towering oak a few feet in front of them.

"This is it." Tombi dropped her hand and peered into the opening.

Suspense shivered along her spine. "Well? Do you see anything?"

He straightened. "Nothing. It's empty."

Shock doused her faith. "But... I don't get it. We were led here." She forgot to whisper, so deep was her disappointment. "Are you sure there's nothing in there?" She peered down the tree hollow for herself but couldn't make out anything in the darkness.

"Positive."

Annie kicked the tree, angry tears of disappointment welling under her eyelids. She hadn't realized how much she'd depended on the legend being true. She'd wanted to be a help to Tombi, especially after all he was doing for her. Instead, she looked like a fool. An optimistic, mystical idiot chasing unicorns. "Damn it. Why'd they even bother making contact with me if it's all nothing but a myth?"

"Hey, it was worth exploring," he said gently, wrapping his arms around her waist. "I didn't expect anything tonight. No harm done."

"No harm?" She laughed bitterly against his chest. "Feels like our last chance was snatched away."

"We'll keep trying to contact Bo. If he can identify who's destroying us from the inside, we might be able to regroup. And it's still possible you might pick up a sign around one of the hunters during an unguarded moment."

"I'll do anything," she promised.

Tombi pulled away and regarded her sternly. "Nothing risky. There's still much you have to learn."

"Then teach me. Now."

He looked around the woods. "Not here. Let's head home."

Home. The sweet sound of the word rumbled inside her with longing. *Don't make too much of it.* Tombi hadn't said he loved her, and he clearly had no designs for long-range planning, other than to do his duty by his people.

If only they could have met under different circumstances. Well, she wasn't giving up yet. There must be something she could do, some way to help Tombi, other than being with him on a hunt in case she heard Bo or an approaching wisp before he heard it. She vowed to find a way. She'd come out alone and find Bo, ask him what had happened to the flute. She'd work spells to find the betrayer, ask her hawk to lead her to the flute, if there was one, and visit every single hunter on her own in the hopes of catching them off guard—especially Tallulah. And if Grandma Tia came home soon, she could be a powerful ally in sorting out this dilemma.

Black shadows lightened by degrees to silver and ash. Perhaps Tombi was right that, with practice, her night vision would acclimate, or at least not be so dismally poor. There was so little time left, and she needed to work every second to hone her own skills and prepare for the next shadow encounter.

His battle had become her battle, as well. They were a team. No matter what happened the next full moon, Annie knew she'd never leave the bayou, would never leave Tombi and this dangerous, mysterious, haunting bayou world.

It was in her blood. Her crazy, mixed Cajun/Native American/Caucasian blood that fit in nowhere but Bayou La Siryna. Crazy Annie could live here in this crazy swampland. And she wanted to share this life with Tombi.

She loved him.

And she'd take what time they had together, whatever Tombi was willing to share, whatever the number of weeks before the shadow world might smother the light and capture their souls. Annie gripped Tombi's hand as they walked in the dark woods, aware of his hot body, his energy expanding to include her in a protective shield.

Back at the cabin, Tombi lit the fire pit on the deck. "I'd

hoped not to frighten you too much, but if you're going to go in the woods at night, you need to know about all the night's creatures."

"You mean, there's more?" Annie shuddered, remembering Nalusa as a giant snake.

"You've seen the worst, but there are others besides Nalusa, the wisps and the birds of the night. If you hear a fox bark or an owl screech, others of their kind will bark and screech in reply. You already know that these animal sounds foretell bad news. But if an animal makes a noise and there's no like response, it means that the *shilombish* is imitating the animal to cause trouble and grief."

"The *shilombish*?" she asked.

"A restless spirit who roams the earth."

"What do they look like?"

"They have no shape or form, but are merely spirit. They can't hurt you. Their only power is to frighten and confuse people."

She shook her head, bewildered at the news that the dark force was even stronger than she first realized. "Why don't the wisps capture these spirits?"

"Because they are the outside shadows. The wisps can only capture the *shilup*, men's inside shadow, which is supposed to cross to the land of ghosts after death."

"So the spirit that helped me that night was a *shilup*."

"Right. You have nothing to fear from them. They long to leave the bayou as quickly as they can. And there are a few other supernatural beings who won't harm you, but it's best if you know of their existence."

Wow. Annie wondered if her grandma was aware of all this. If so, she'd never even hinted at it.

Tombi poked the fire with a stick, and an arc of sparks crackled. "There's Kashehotapalo, who's a combination of man and deer. Even though he's frightened hunters in the past, our people admire him for his speed and agility.

He's harmless unless you rouse his anger. In that case, he will find your enemy and warn them of your presence."

Such a creature was hard to visualize; it sounded so far-fetched. "Have you seen him?"

"I caught a glimpse of him once. Otherwise, I would never have believed he existed and put the legend down as a fairy tale."

"Like you do the fairies. Maybe you just haven't seen them yet. Are they said to be dangerous?"

"No. Their worst trick is to throw stones or rocks at people as a joke. Supposedly, they're only a couple of feet tall and dwell in the deepest recesses of the bayou."

"They don't sound so bad. Anything else?"

Tombi hesitated.

"Go on," she prodded. "Nothing could be stranger than the half-man, half-deer creature."

"Just in case you're ever roaming the woods and decide to take a dip in the waters to cool off, be sure not to swim anywhere there's a white patch, because that's where the *Okwa Naholo* live."

"Underwater creatures?"

"Yep. The translation is 'white people of the water' because they have light flesh like the skins of trout."

Annie tingled inside. "Mermaids?"

He gave a crooked smile. "Exactly. And if you invade their territory, they'll capture you and turn you into beings like themselves."

"Pretty cool, actually. Not getting captured—but the idea that mermaids exist. Most little girls dream of being one. I think they represent the epitome of feminine power and beauty."

Tombi shrugged. "It's another one of the tales I'm skeptical about." He leaned back in his chair. "Anything you believe I should know about hoodoo?"

"Not really. We try to bend the natural laws for healing and to bring us luck in love and money." She laughed self-consciously. "Not that my life is an example of either."

Tombi regarded her soberly. "Your luck could change."

Annie's heart hopscotched along her rib cage. Did that mean he loved her? Secretly, she believed her fortune *had* changed. Despite the setbacks, she knew what it was like to love a good man. A man worth fighting for. A man worth risking her heart, her pride, her life.

Pop. A large ember from the fire flamed and jumped in the air, breaking the moment.

"I still can't believe we didn't get the flute," Annie complained.

"More than likely, it never existed."

She couldn't believe it. There was some reason Ms. Belle and the hawk had arrived at the moment she read about the legend. Some reason that Tia had visualized the grimoire while in a coma.

"All that was in the book was that the flute helped contain Nalusa and where to find it. Is there more to the legend than what I read?"

"It's said our ancestors used it whenever Nalusa grew too strong and disrupted the balance of light and shadow. If that happened, the tribe would gather for a full-moon ritual and play the flute. Nalusa would be drawn to the music, but could only appear in his visible, half-human form and not sneak up on them like a snake."

Annie shuddered, wondering if that version of Nalusa was less scary than the snake. "What does he look like in this half-human form?"

"He's named after his half-human form. In Choctaw, Nalusa Falaya literally means a 'long black being.' It was said he resembled a man but had tiny eyes and long, pointed ears."

She couldn't picture it. "I'm thinking of snake eyes and donkey ears, and the two don't seem to go together."

"Is it any harder to imagine than the religious tradition of a pitchfork-carrying devil with a red body, hoofed feet and horns for ears?"

He had a point.

"But why would your ancestors want to draw Nalusa to them—no matter what shape-shifting form he chooses? Personally, I don't ever want to see him again."

"According to legend, while he's exposed in human form, he's vulnerable. The legend also says that only in this form can we force him back into his resting place and bind his power."

She remembered the tightness in her chest as they approached the tree, the lingering miasma of evil. Some of his malevolent energy had marked his former prison. "He was trapped inside the hollowed oak, right? I felt a heaviness there, the way misery feels when it crushes you inside."

"That's his mark. He feeds on human grief and misery. It's what makes you vulnerable to his will. It weakens your fight and warps your thinking."

"Like it has the betrayer in your group," she said softly. And who among his circle had suffered the most?

Tallulah.

She'd been grief-stricken over Bo's death. And the mourning had left her susceptible to Nalusa's voice whispering in her mind, murmuring dissent as poisonous as his venom injected in a blood vein. Couldn't Tombi see the obvious? But Annie kept her mouth shut. *Blood's thicker than water.* He'd known her a week; he'd known his twin since the womb.

Time to pay Tallulah a visit. Maybe invite her over for dinner and slip a little hoodoo concoction in her drink. Once her guard was down, Annie would listen in on her aura. Not something she was looking forward to. Annie imagined the noise from her damaged aura would be akin to nails scraping chalkboard—times a million. And how could she ever break the news to Tombi?

His mouth pressed into a grim line. "Whoever it turns out to be, I'll have no sympathy. A warrior's mind and body never breaks."

"Not everyone has your strength."

"I would expect any of the hunters to confide in me if they were in danger of succumbing to the shadows."

He was in for a huge disappointment. "Could be they are too ashamed. Or maybe the darkness in their minds crept up on them so gradually they didn't realize the danger until it was too late."

"He should know better."

Or *she* should know better. But Annie wasn't brave enough to speak the words aloud. Tombi had been angry before when she'd suggested Hanan—how much more upset would he be if she suggested his sister? His twin, no less.

"Enough talk of Nalusa," he cut in, his voice as rough as oak bark. "We've done all we can do for tonight. Tomorrow will be here soon enough with its worries and duties."

Annie reached out a hand and touched his knee. "And whatever comes, I'm here to help. Anything you need me to do."

His mouth twisted. "If there's any way possible, I'll shield you from seeing Nalusa again."

"Don't even think it. You need me with you, and you know it."

Tombi stood and stretched. "We won't speak of it anymore tonight." He took her hand and lifted Annie to her feet. "We've better things to do."

She couldn't agree with him more. Tombi might skirt expressing his feelings for her, but his body had a language all its own. And his body said he loved her, too, even if his lips never formed the words.

Chapter 14

The dark of the moon settled into the night, smothering the bayou like thick fog. Annie lit every candle she'd gathered from her grandma's cottage, until Tombi's cabin glowed as if a thousand stars were contained within its rough-hewn walls.

The past two weeks had been filled with training sessions as Tombi, true to his word, initiated her more deeply into blocking external stimuli as well as containing the amount of energy she released into the world.

Too bad she and her grandma didn't call on the questionable, seamier side of hoodoo, since amoral spirits were more accessible at the New Moon. She'd been so tempted last week during the dark-moon phase. She could use some extra supernatural help—if the old tales were true that she'd overheard in whispered conversations behind closed doors.

Don't go there, Grandma Tia had warned a hundred times, wagging a finger. *The ends never justify the means.*

You start dabbling in that mess, you might get sucked into their evil forever.

As a child, whenever Annie had heard those warnings, she'd pictured a giant hand rising up from the swamp and curling its fingers toward her, beckoning her to come and sink into the murky depths from which it supernaturally emerged. A quicksand of destruction for the unwary.

Frightened the hell out of her.

For the second time in her life, Annie considered the consequences of calling on a dark spirit. Only a few weeks earlier she'd also contemplated the same—desperate to stop the blaring music that assaulted her mind. But the childhood nightmare of the beckoning hand always stopped her from such invocations. Better a quick death from a venom-filled fang than the agony of a slow drown in the swamp.

Pick your own poison, Annie-Girl.

The choice was easy.

Annie frowned at the kitchen window. The gleaming black pane seemed like the core of a pupil in a giant eye that watched her and waited. If Tombi had bothered with curtains, she'd have drawn them over the window like an eyelid, sealing shut the outside world. She quit stirring the large iron pot and rubbed her forearms that prickled with unease.

"Something wrong?"

Annie spun around. "I didn't hear you come in."

His smile was quick and warmer than the heat emanating from the stove. "I'm known for sneaking up on wisps, but for *you* not to hear me is quite a feat."

"All your lessons are helping me block sound for longer periods of time."

"Good." He sidled up beside her at the counter and peeked in the oven. "Chicken's done. Another fifteen minutes on the huckleberry cake."

"Hominy's ready and water's boiling for the banaha."

"I'll take care of the bread," he said, giving his hands a quick wash at the sink, before mushing together the cooked field peas and cornmeal.

Annie watched his dark, muscled forearms as he shaped small rectangles from the mush and set them to the side on a dish. Quickly, she removed the roasted chicken from the oven and put the dirty mixing bowls in the dishwasher. "I can help with that," she said. "Let me finish the patties while you wrap them."

They fell into a companionable silence as Tombi enfolded the rectangles in dried corn husks and dropped them in boiling water. She'd been skeptical at first, but the traditional Choctaw bread, banaha, was surprisingly good. Tombi had explained that for centuries, hunters had eaten this bread for the sustained energy provided by the complete protein.

"We make a pretty good team," she remarked.

Tombi shot her a slow, sexy smile that made her insides flame. A smile that promised another night of passion and enchantment. Heat chased across her neck and cheeks.

"Still shy?"

Tombi playfully slapped her ass, and she laughed.

Annie had never been this happy—so long as it was just the two of them alone in the cabin. Each day, Tombi let go of his reserve a fraction and spoke to her of happier times before Nalusa had broken his confinement and began wreaking havoc. Each day she'd opened up more on her difficult relationship with her mother. And each night they made passionate love, interspersed with such moments of tenderness that Annie felt sure of his affection, even if he hadn't professed his love—yet.

But to Annie's frustration, she could never catch the sly Tallulah unawares. They were no closer to naming their betrayer. As usual, she pushed the reminder aside, determined to enjoy their shared meal. Every moment they spent together was precious. In her heart, she tried to impress every detail to memory, wanting to remember everything in case... No, it didn't help to dwell on the possibilities of everything that could go wrong at the next full moon.

They sat down to eat the mini feast. Tombi eagerly eyed the golden and purple huckleberry cake throughout dinner. Annie delighted in his pure enjoyment of her cooking whenever he spooned in mouthfuls of the baked berries crusted in a butter and flour pastry.

"How's your grandma doing at rehab today?" he asked.

Annie swallowed a spoonful of the hominy. She still preferred grits but accepted hominy as its grainier cousin. "Grandma's giving the physical therapists hell. Which means she's feeling a whole lot better. They told me she can come home in another two or three weeks."

"When I visited yesterday, she was barking orders at the staff, saying all she needed was to go home and pray at her altar and drink her special tea. The staff thinks she's a bit of a crackpot."

Annie laughed. "I can't see her staying more than another week there before the doctors gladly sign off on the release papers just to stop hearing her fuss."

"She can complain all she wants," Tombi said firmly. "I'll never forget that she saved my life. If there's a way to repay her for—"

A heavy thud bumped against the kitchen window where a ruddy-colored ball of fur rustled. *Ker-thump.* Annie dropped her spoon and watched as it whacked against the window again. A scraping of talons against glass made her entire body wince and curl in upon itself.

"What the hell?" Tombi pushed away his plate and jumped up. "Your hawk's here."

The raptor had drawn closer every day while she hunted

with Tombi and had appeared with increasing frequency in her dreams, but it hadn't been this close since it had made its first appearance at her grandma's cottage.

"What do you think it wants?"

"Only one way to know for sure." Tombi hurried to the den, grabbing his knapsack filled with rocks and slingshots.

"Don't you dare hurt him," she said, following close behind.

"Of course I won't. I'm bringing ammo in case he's alerting us to trouble outside."

Trouble. Her stomach roiled, but she needed to buck up and go out there with Tombi and face the hawk. *Her* hawk. Annie sighed as she quickly slid into her shoes by the front door. Why couldn't her animal guide have been something friendly and nonviolent like a cute little chipmunk?

Kee-eeeee-ar. The screech erupted the moment they opened the door. The hawk beat its wings and flew toward the woods, glancing back at them in a command to follow. *Kee-eeeee-ar.*

Tonight, its squawks were higher-pitched and the cries closer together. Annie didn't need Tombi to explain that this signaled distress. Something was wrong.

Everything raced—feet, heart, mind—as she sprinted through the field after Tombi. Had Nalusa struck again? Had the wisps killed and captured another's soul?

The world darkened a shade as they entered the woods. Annie tried to keep up with Tombi as he forged ahead, chasing the hawk's cries. The crunch of twigs and dried leaves underfoot was a symphony of disaster. Over the jarring sounds of brokenness, musical notes clamored for attention. Annie halted and put her hands on her knees, panting. "Stop!"

Tombi came to her at once. "Out of breath?"

"Do you hear music?" she asked, holding a finger to her lips.

He cocked his head for a moment. "I don't hear anything."

The notes tantalized her memory. They were familiar, haunting... Excitement inched up her spine. "It's the flute!"

Tombi's expression was blank.

"*The* flute," she explained eagerly. "The one I heard through the pages of the grimoire. The one of legend. My hawk's leading us to it."

"How can you know it's the same flute?"

"It has a more primitive sound, with a reedy kind of twang. I'd recognize it anywhere."

His face tightened. "Who would have it? And why would they summon Nalusa? This might be another trap."

Annie shook her head. "My hawk wouldn't draw us into danger. He's trying to help us."

"Maybe."

A whoosh of wings, then a cry, bleated above them.

"We should go." Annie tried for a smile of encouragement, even while the thought of Nalusa made her lungs freeze with fear.

Tombi remained rooted to the spot, frowning. "I hate exposing you to danger."

Every cell in her body screamed *run*, but Annie overrode the scared demand. "You need me. Besides, this could be your chance. Get the flute, and Nalusa is yours."

He squeezed his eyes shut and nodded. "I know. Stay close behind me and let's try to be a little quieter."

Annie lifted her neck and stared at the piercing eyes upon her. *Quiet*, she mouthed, placing an index finger on her pursed lips. She placed a hand on Tombi's shoulder. "If you're planning a sneak attack, I'll lead since I'm the one tracking the sounds."

Tombi's mouth twisted in a grimace, but he nodded his acceptance.

Hesitantly, Annie walked forward, pausing every few steps to listen to the faint music. Above and in front, her hawk flew low, giving her confidence that she was headed in the right direction. On she plowed, heart hammering in anticipation. Tombi didn't say it, but whoever was playing the flute must be the betrayer. Any of the other hunters who came in possession of it would have alerted the group immediately, and they would have rallied together to fight Nalusa and his shadow creatures.

And if the betrayer was playing it, why did he want to speak with Nalusa? It could only be to share more damning information on the tribe's secrets and plans.

The flute grew louder, and she recognized where they were—the ancient tribal ground said to house Nalusa. Slowly, stealthily, they made their way to a parting in the trees. A person sat on the felled oak, elbows lifted and crooked, a flute held to their lips. A long black braid fell down their back, which could have been any of the hunters.

Annie studied the figure. As the betrayer shifted their position on the log, the profile gave away the identity. *Damn. Why couldn't it have been anyone else?*

Tombi's swift inhalation from behind meant he recognized the betrayer at the same moment she did.

Tallulah.

Na haksichi. The rogue, the betrayer.

His very own twin, the only one of two people in the world who had heard their mother's heart beat from the womb. Pain flayed inside Tombi, a vivid crimson that burned and coated his retinas like an infrared filter, obscuring his normally keen vision.

He plunged through dense saw palmettos, uncaring of

the noise. Let Tallulah see him, let her view his full fury, let her know that he found her utterly despicable.

"*Aholabi!* Liar!" he shouted, brushing past Annie's outstretched hand.

His sister jumped up and swung to face him, freezing like a cornered deer ready to take flight.

"It was you all along." He lobbed his words like darts. "*Na haksichi.* Betrayer. Why?"

Her eyes narrowed, and she gripped the flute tightly in her fist, holding it out with a defiant lift of her chin. "You would never understand."

"Tell me." He stopped before her, hands fisted at his sides. If this were anyone but his sister, he'd pummel the truth out of the man.

"I did it for Bo." Her voice was like torn strips of paper shredded from her soul.

"Bo?" Dread was a boulder weighting his feet to the earth, anchoring an urge to walk away from Tallulah's confession. He'd lost his parents and discovered his sister was a traitor. Was it too much to ask that the memory of his best friend be preserved? "Bo has nothing to do with this," he ground out.

"He has everything to do with this." She nodded at the flute. "This can bring him back to me."

"Where the hell did you get a crazy idea like that? You've no idea what you've done."

Annie stepped between them and cast worried glances around the woods. "Aren't you worried Nalusa is here? Tallulah's been playing it for at least a few minutes."

"Let him come. If he's hiding behind a tree, it's because he's vulnerable." Tombi raised his voice. "Come out, you coward. I'll take you on right now."

Annie shook her head, eyes wide with fear. "Stop. This isn't the time or place. Remember the legend? Wait for the full moon. Wait for the other hunters to be with you."

Tallulah laughed. A mad, eerie laugh fit for an insane asylum. "That old legend? This flute has no power against Nalusa."

"Give it to me," Tombi said between clenched teeth.

Tallulah snatched the flute to her chest, like a child protecting a toy. "No. It's mine."

Not for long. Tombi stepped forward. Sister or not, he *would* get that flute. "I said, give it to me."

Annie's slight head shake drew his attention. What was she about?

She turned to Tallulah. "If you don't believe the flute has power, why do you want to keep it?"

Her voice was calm and soothing. A mother placating an unreasonable child. Tombi wanted to shake sense into his sister, but maybe Annie's approach was best.

"I didn't say it was powerless." Her eyes watered. "Although it's done nothing for me yet."

Annie stepped a little closer to Tallulah. "What do you expect it to do?"

Tallulah dropped her head. A wailing, ruined cry spewed from deep within her.

He couldn't help it, pity snuffed out the worst of his rage. Tombi had seen her like this only twice before, at their parents' funeral and at Bo's death side.

"It's supposed to…to…" She swallowed hard. "I thought that if I stole this from the museum and played it in the woods, Bo would find me."

She raised her head and gave Annie a hard look. "But he never came to me. Only to you. Why would he do that? I hate you!"

Annie winced and took a step backward.

"Stop it, Tallulah," he ordered. His sympathy dried up at her treatment of Annie. "I can't believe you let Nalusa's shadows warp your mind this way. You betrayed us all for nothing."

"I knew you'd turn on me. You've never loved anyone in your life. You're a heartless robot. All you care about is fighting."

Indignation left him speechless. Tallulah had betrayed them all, and *he* was the bad guy now?

"That's not true," Annie said quietly.

In his anger, he'd almost forgotten she was there.

Annie gazed at him with a soft radiance lit within her brown eyes, like candle glow in the night. It warmed him inside. "Your brother is capable of great love," she said, a soft smile trembling on her lips.

"What do you know?" His sister's voice cut like broken glass. "So what if Tombi sleeps with you? Nothing's more important to him than his battles with the shadow world. You're just a…a…diversion."

Tombi sucked in his breath at the stark cruelty of his twin. Annie didn't deserve her vindictiveness.

Tallulah faced him. "That's what Courtney, your last girlfriend, told me."

"Is that so? And what is Hanan to you if nothing but a diversion?"

Tallulah gasped.

"You don't think I know about your late-night visits in his tent? Don't give me this crap about how much you loved Bo."

"Please, don't, you two." Annie looked back and forth between them, distress lines marring her face. "You're family."

Tallulah sank to her knees, sobbing. This was the worst he'd ever seen her.

"If you knew what it was like to love—really love somebody—you'd understand. Hanan helps me forget when the pain and loneliness are too much to bear. I would trade my soul to speak with Bo one last time."

"That's exactly what you've done. Traded your soul.

But the worst part is that you placed us all in jeopardy by keeping the flute for yourself. Every day, Nalusa and the shadows grow, and yet you selfishly said nothing about the flute. How long have you had it?"

"A few weeks. It's worthless."

So quickly, he could do nothing but watch, Tallulah stood and flung the flute into the air with all her strength. The wooden reed twirled and spun in the treetops, blending into the brown-and-green canopy of oaks and pine.

And then it began its inevitable fall back to earth. The fragile, ancient instrument that was the only hope of containing Nalusa. His heart fell along with it. Surely it would crash and splinter on the ground upon impact.

Kee-eeeee-ar. The hawk swooped down and gathered the flute in his beak.

Relief washed over him in a wave—until the hawk ascended back to the treetops, taking the flute with him. *Damnation.* Tombi hastily pulled the knapsack from his shoulders and opened it, gathering his slingshot.

"What are you doing?" Annie asked in alarm.

"Getting the flute back."

He placed a rock in the sling and drew back the elastic band.

"No!" Annie launched herself at him.

Just as he released the band, she grabbed his arm and changed the trajectory of the rock. It harmlessly thudded against a tall pine, several feet from the perched hawk.

Its loud screech thwacked the air, and Tombi could have sworn it mocked him. He shook off Annie's arm to try again, but the hawk flapped its massive wings and flew off, taking Tombi's last hope with him.

"We're doomed," he said flatly.

"We always have been," Tallulah lashed out. "I don't care, either. Not if I can't be with Bo."

Annie hugged her chest, wide eyes on him. "I'm sorry.

I… I couldn't let you shoot the hawk. He's my animal guide."

"I only meant to have the stone be a near miss. Enough to scare him into dropping the flute." He wanted to reassure her, to lie and say everything would be okay. But the lie died on his lips. To have had a chance, to be so, so close, only to have it snatched away at the last second. It was all too much.

Tombi turned to his sister. "You have no idea what you've done," he said harshly. "Hunters have been injured and placed in jeopardy, all because of your treachery."

Her tears dried up. "I had nothing to do with that."

"Liar. I don't believe anything you say. I'll never trust you again."

His sister's lower lip trembled. "I'm telling you the truth. I would never help Nalusa in an ambush. I was going to give you the flute eventually. I just wanted to contact Bo first."

"Always thinking of yourself and what you want." Tombi pulled his knapsack back over his shoulders. "From now on, you'll have all the time in the world to be selfish. You are no longer one of us. Don't embarrass yourself and show up at the next hunt."

Her eyes widened. "You're banishing me?"

He hardened his heart. After all, the lives of others depended on them working together as a team. As such, absolute trust among them was needed. There was no room for someone like Tallulah. He turned his back on his sister.

"Wait!"

Her anguished cry squeezed his heart, but his feet never hesitated. She had left him no choice.

Two more steps and he halted. "Annie?" Why wasn't she by his side? He didn't turn around, not wanting to face Tallulah again.

A rustle of leaves and pine needles, and Annie stood before him.

"You were pretty harsh back there."

He stared at her incredulously. "I can't believe you—of all people—would care. Tallulah's given you nothing but grief."

"It doesn't matter. She's your sister, your twin. You can't disown her."

The anger and frustration erupted once more. "I can do what I damn well want. You don't know what you're talking about."

Annie stiffened. "Stop being an ass."

The insult cut to the bone. After two weeks of staying together at the cabin, he thought of them as one, united. But at the first opportunity, Annie took the side of a woman who had shown her nothing but scorn. A woman who had betrayed him and the other hunters in the worst possible way. Annie had gone too far. "Fine. Stay here and let Tallulah cry on your shoulder. She won't thank you for it."

"I will stay."

Her stubborn streak surprised him. "Look, don't let her fool you. She's put all of us in danger, you included."

"Can't you bend a little? Show forgiveness?"

"Not on this. She's destroyed my hope."

"Don't you mean I have?" Annie asked with a gentle stillness that ripped at his conscious. "It was my hawk that flew away with the flute. Do you blame me, as well?"

The word *no* wouldn't come. He stood mute, unable to say it. Unable to give Annie the reassurance she wanted. Logically, he couldn't blame her; she didn't control the hawk. But something in him had snapped, was beyond reason.

At the prolonged silence, Annie flinched as if he had struck her.

"I see," she drawled. "I feel sorry for you, Tombi. Hate and revenge have consumed your heart. Tallulah's right about that. There's no room in it for love."

"Wait." He placed his hand on her arm, dismayed at the tears swimming in her dark eyes. "She's wrong."

Annie waited.

"It's just—I can't make any promises. The situation is too bleak. It wouldn't be fair to either one of us."

"I'm not afraid to say how I feel. I love you, Tombi."

No. Not now. He couldn't think about it. To fall in love would weaken his focus. How could he organize and fight Nalusa while worrying over a loved one's safety? "Don't," he said harshly.

"Too late." She attempted a smile and a light tone, but the hurt in her brown eyes muddied the light that usually gleamed in them.

He was responsible for that.

"I'm—"

She shook her head. "Don't say you're sorry. If you don't feel it, you don't feel it. At least you didn't lie to me."

She walked back to Tallulah, and he trudged back to the cabin. Alone. The weight of his aloneness smothered his hope even more than the loss of the flute and the betrayal of his twin.

They were right. He'd lost his capacity to love. Tombi shivered in the muggy heat. Nalusa had as good as won the battle.

Chapter 15

"Why did you come back?" Tallulah frowned and narrowed her eyes. "Go on. I don't need you."

Tombi was right. There was no winning with his temperamental sister. Annie sighed. She longed to run after him. But she had her pride, and she wouldn't beg someone for their love. He either felt it or he didn't. She had deluded herself thinking Tombi felt something stronger between them. Oh, she was convenient, and he liked her well enough, but Crazy Annie had struck out once again.

Tallulah swiped a hand across her cheeks and sniffed.

Annie couldn't help but sympathize. She was close to tears herself. "Come to my grandmother's cottage with me, and I'll fix you something to eat and drink."

"I'm not hungry." Tallulah frowned again, but her eyes threatened to spill tears.

An unexpected smile broke across Annie's face.

"What's so funny?" Tallulah asked suspiciously.

"You. You're just like your brother. So prickly." And so proud. Too proud to admit they ever needed anybody.

"What do you see in him? That relationship will never go anywhere. You know that, right?"

Annie's smile wilted. "Bet no one ever accused you of being a Little Miss Sunshine. Ever."

Tallulah snorted.

"That's what I thought. Stay here and cry your eyes out, then. I'm leaving."

Annie started down the path in the opposite direction of Tombi. To hell with both of them and their damn arrogance. She had her own dignity, and her temper was at a breaking point. She marched on, seething at fate. Useless, but it kept her heart from breaking at Tombi's silence after she'd spilled her guts. And why had her own animal spirit even betrayed her trust? Maybe she was as deluded and deceived as Tallulah by placing her faith in the wrong place.

Annie stomped through the path, crushing pine needles and twigs beneath her feet. Sweat steamed on her sticky flesh as she pressed on in the gathering twilight. Damn mosquitoes would eat her up before she arrived home.

A stinging pain whiplashed across her jaw and neck. She'd carelessly run into a thick, jutting limb.

A snicker sounded from behind. Annie turned, surprised to find Tallulah a mere ten feet away. Annoyance prickled her burning welt. "Are you following me or heading in the same direction?"

Tallulah shrugged. "Guess I could use a bite to eat after all."

Annie's temper melted at the admission, but she hid her smile. "Suit yourself." On she went until she reached the clearing. No light shone in the cottage. It wasn't the same without Grandma Tia. She longed for the light and warmth of Tombi's cabin. Instead, she was stuck with the cold Tallulah and an empty house.

"Is that your place?" Tallulah asked, stepping to her side. "It's so tiny."

Yep. A real ray of sunshine that one was. Annie kept walking, Tallulah close by.

"What does your name mean in Choctaw?" she asked, more to keep her mind occupied from Tombi's rejection than a burning urge to know more about his twin.

"Leaping water. Why?"

Annie thought of bubbling brooks, gurgling streams and effervescent bubbles. Happy, excited sounds and movement. Tallulah's name fit her about as poorly as Tombi's representing a warm glowing sun.

"Just curious."

Tallulah shot her a suspicious look. "Are you named after someone? *Annie* is so common."

"Meaning that I'm also common? You really shouldn't insult someone about to feed you."

"Whatever."

Annie retrieved the spare key from beneath a flowerpot on the porch and unlocked the door.

Stale incense and dust tickled her nose as they entered.

"It smells funny in here," Tallulah complained.

"Yeah, well, no one's been here in a couple of weeks." Annie flipped on lights and turned up the AC. "Let's go in the kitchen."

She was conscious of Tallulah's damning assessment of the cottage. Her face puckered in disapproval as she pulled out a chair and sat at the kitchen table. "Guess all the candles and herbs are for y'all's witchy stuff."

Annie didn't bother replying but retrieved a couple of glasses from the cupboard and poured tap water into them. "Here." She plopped one in front of Tallulah. "You hungry?"

"I could use a bite if you're eating, too."

"Tombi and I already ate." She pictured the simple meal they'd shared. How contented she'd felt a mere two hours earlier. That would teach her to think life had turned around for the better. Annie opened the freezer. "I can offer you a fried chicken TV dinner or a pint of salted-caramel ice cream."

"Ice cream."

Figured. Annie had wanted that for herself. She handed her guest a spoon and the pint, thinking longingly of the huckleberry cake at Tombi's. Resolutely, she turned on the stove burner to heat the teapot. A good cup of rosemary and mint tea to refresh their spirits. Annie mixed together some herbs into a sachet as Tallulah ate.

"Hey, what are you doing there?" Tallulah asked around a mouthful of ice cream. "I want plain black tea without that herbal stuff. Or coffee."

Suspicious as her brother. "You'll drink what I'm fixing, and I need this concoction."

Tallulah sniffed, but when the cup was placed in front of her she sipped it experimentally. "It's actually pretty good," she admitted grudgingly.

"So, how did you come in possession of the flute?" Annie asked, sitting down and leaning back in her chair.

"Does it matter? Your stupid hawk flew off with it. Not my fault it's gone." She bent over her cup and gulped down more.

Apparently, nothing was ever Tallulah's fault. Annie held her tongue. Tombi had been so angry, he'd neglected to get the details. But she wanted some answers.

"It's important we figure out everything together so we can get the flute back and find out who's really the betrayer."

Tallulah's neck snapped up. "You don't think it's me?"

"No."

"Why not?"

"I think you were duped. You weren't out seeking Nalusa and trading information for your own benefit. I believe what you said, only wanting to conjure Bo."

Tallulah set her cup down. "You're right," she answered softly.

"Tell me who put you up to it."

"Nobody. One of the archaeology crews found that old flute on a dig, and they brought it to the Cultural Center to be archived. I always guessed that it held powerful magic. Then yesterday, when everyone went home after five, something came over me. I *had* to have that flute. I can't explain it."

Annie nodded. "Go on."

"That's it. I went out to the woods, and this crazy notion wouldn't get out of my brain that if I played it, Bo would magically appear."

"Nalusa must have planted that idea in your brain, then."

Tallulah's brow furrowed. "But the flute makes Nalusa weaker, forces him to appear as himself and not in snake form. Why would he want me to play it?"

"Because, even weakened, Nalusa could take you on, one-on-one, without interference from the other hunters. Then he'd grab the flute and take it back into his possession. Your tribe would lose its best chance to capture him at the next full moon."

Tallulah nodded slowly. "Makes sense. Wish my brother had reasoned everything in his mind before jumping to conclusions."

"He's too close to the situation to react logically. He'll come around." Tombi might forgive his sister for bad judgment, but the fact remained that he didn't love her. Nothing about their relationship would change for the better.

"Don't hold your breath," Tallulah mumbled.

Annie stiffened in the chair, back to pondering the mystery. "I'm disappointed that it wasn't another hunter who gave you the idea that you had the power to contact Bo. Because if it had been one of them, we'd know the real betrayer."

They sipped their tea in glum silence until Tallulah spoke again. "Not only did the flute fail me, but if anyone at the Center finds out it's missing, I can kiss my job goodbye."

Well, she *did* steal the flute from her employer, but Annie bit her lip. Who was she to judge? Nalusa's influence must be a powerful thing. And at least Tallulah was opening up to her a bit.

Tallulah regarded her thoughtfully. "Why won't Bo talk to me? We were in love. He never even met you."

"Don't take it personal. I hear things no one else can."

"Can you try to contact him again?" Tallulah grasped Annie's hand. "And take me with you. Please?"

That was exactly what she'd do. Initiate contact. Many nights she'd wanted to sneak away into the bayou and try to find Bo, but Tombi wouldn't hear of it. They had sought him together, but no luck. Secretly, Annie thought Bo wasn't able to risk talking to anyone but her.

"I'll try to reach Bo tonight, but alone. You can't come with me. It won't work with you around. You're a distraction to him."

Tallulah's eager expression fell to one of resigned misery. "Okay." She gulped. "Thank you for trying and... thanks for believing in me when my own brother didn't."

So the seemingly unbreakable warrior woman wasn't all badass. She had a heart that had been broken and bludgeoned. A feeling Annie knew all too well. "You're welcome," Annie said softly. She rose and gathered up the dirty cups and saucers.

Tallulah placed a hand on her arm. "Tombi is a fool if he doesn't love you."

He was a damn idiot.

Tombi stood on the porch and stared out at the night. Where was Annie? Was she okay? He pulled out the cell phone from his jeans pocket and then angrily stuffed it back in. There was no need to call. She'd told him she loved him, and he'd just stared at her and said nothing. He'd lost the right to know where she chose to spend her evenings.

The cabin was silent and empty without Annie. How quickly he'd grown accustomed to her presence.

A spherical beam of light turned from the main road onto the dirt road leading to his cabin. About time Hanan and Chulah showed up.

Tombi pushed off from the railing and paced the porch. Telling them the news wasn't going to be easy. They would be almost as torn about Tallulah as he was. Hanan especially. He didn't know how deep their feelings for each other went. Or, as Tallulah implied, if they were merely friends with benefits. Ugh. Not how he wanted to think of his sister.

The old Chevy truck doors squeaked as the hunters jumped out of Chulah's pickup. Hanan's silver sheriff's badge glinted like a miniature star. "What's up?" Hanan asked, direct as always. His eyes were as sharp and focused as the eagle he was named after. Once he swooped in on a problem, he never let go until he was satisfied every stone had been turned. It made him an excellent officer.

"We have a problem," Tombi answered.

Chulah bounded the porch steps, face crafty and searching. "Where's Tallulah? She should be here, too. We always meet together when there's trouble."

"Tallulah *is* the trouble."

Fear danced in Chulah's brown eyes. "Is she okay?"

Best to just spit it out. "Tallulah's our traitor."

"No way. She'd never do that," Chulah said, voice pitched low and fierce.

Hanan stuffed his hands into his uniform pockets and frowned. "Hard to believe. How can you be sure?"

"The ancient flute that we once searched for and couldn't find? Turns out, it's a real thing after all. Tallulah has it. I caught her playing it in the woods today."

Shock registered on his friends' faces.

"But that's great news," Chulah protested. "She found it for us, and now we can use it to capture Nalusa."

"You say you caught her," Hanan said slowly. "Did she admit to revealing our secrets to Nalusa?"

"Of course she didn't admit anything. But she's desperate. Somehow she got it in her head that the flute would help her contact Bo's spirit. Tallulah would stop at nothing to hear from Bo." A kind of madness must have eaten away at Tallulah's mind. Her grief over Bo went far deeper than Tombi had realized. And someone suffering such grief was a target for Nalusa and the shadows. It made a person easy prey to whisper false promises. A seduction to the mystery of the night.

Chulah's face crumbled, and he stumbled down the porch steps, no doubt needing distance until he regained his composure.

"Where's the flute now?"

As usual, Hanan cut to the heart of their situation. His friend hid his emotions well, buried them under logic and a determination to attack problems. Tombi didn't see the attraction between Hanan and Tallulah, but there was no accounting for sexual chemistry. Personally, he'd rather

Tallulah had chosen Chulah, an honorable man who'd quickly become his closest friend in the past few months. Hanan was honorable as well, but in a detached, intellectual manner.

Tombi sighed. "My sister threw it in the air, and a hawk flew off with it."

"You didn't have the opportunity to kill it?" Hanan asked.

"Annie stopped me. The hawk is her animal guide. Or so she believed."

Chulah jerked around. "Where's Annie now? I bet she's behind everything. Not your sister." He stomped onto the porch, warming to his theory. "That's it. She's been the one whispering in Tallulah's ear about the flute, knowing Tallulah's grief. And Annie knew Tallulah gets to examine artifacts as soon as the archaeologists bring them in from their digs. She's the real traitor."

Tombi winced. No. Not Annie. It couldn't possibly be Annie. The porch tilted beneath his feet, and a rushing whirled like a tornado in his mind. Chulah had a point. A damn good one. He couldn't be so duped...or could he? What if it were true? What if his sister were innocent?

Shame pounded through his veins. He'd brought Annie into their inner circle, had come to completely trust her and taught her all he knew. Worse, he'd accused his own sister of being the traitor.

So which was it: Annie or Tallulah? Lover or sister?

Both choices were unimaginable.

"Let's not jump the gun," Tombi said.

Chulah gritted his teeth. "Oh, but you were quick to accuse your own sister."

True. Tombi didn't defend himself. He needed proof. "Have you found out anything yet from the computer records?" he asked Hanan.

"Not yet. Pisa says the tech expert he trusts to be discreet in reviewing the phone records is still on vacation for a few days."

"Isn't there anyone else that can look at them to see who sent the text messages?"

"No one we trust. Besides, if the person was smart, they'd use a throwaway cell phone that's untraceable."

Tombi slammed a fist into the railing. "I suppose you're right about that." How was he going to figure this out before it was too late?

"Isn't there anything you can do?" Chulah asked Hanan.

"Nothing. We could interrogate Annie and Tallulah, of course. But Pisa can't do it in his official position as a sheriff's deputy."

"I'll talk to Tallulah," Chulah volunteered.

Some interrogation that would be. In Chulah's eyes, Tallulah was an innocent.

"Might be best if I did it," Hanan said calmly.

Tombi studied his friend. Just what kind of relationship did he have with Tallulah? You would think that the news the woman you're sleeping with was a possible betrayer and could have killed you by sending information to the enemy would illicit a strong reaction. Yet nothing fazed Hanan, not even this.

Chulah, on the other hand, was distraught. Not for the first time, Tombi wished his twin had chosen Chulah. The man cared for her and was loyal in his defense of her character.

"I'll talk to both of them," Tombi said.

Chulah shot him a hard look. "I don't see how you can be fair. Considering you've been sleeping with the enemy for the past two weeks."

Heat burned his skin. "Careful, Chulah. My relationship with Annie is none of your business."

"It *is* my business when she's blinded you to the truth and disrupted our circle. What's the matter with you? Our tribe comes before all else. Are you going to throw away your family and our bond and duty for…for…a piece of ass?"

Tombi stepped up to Chulah, got in his face. His fisted hands twisted by his sides. "Don't you ever call her that again."

Chulah glowered, and anger crackled between them.

"Stop it." Hanan pushed them apart with both arms. "We have to work together."

He was right. Damn it. Tombi stalked off, needing distance between him and his friends before he landed a punch or said something unforgivable.

Everything was falling apart. The beginning of the end unraveled before Tombi. Nalusa was winning the battle before it even started. For all he knew, Hanan or Chulah might be the real betrayer. Maybe Chulah was emotionally unstable and Hanan a little too cool and calculating. His inner circle had collapsed.

"Where are you going?" Chulah called.

"To find the truth."

"We'll go with you," Hanan offered. "No sense in you walking in the woods at night by yourself. We can drive to Tallulah's place in the truck."

Tombi faced them. "I need to do this alone. Don't follow me."

Hanan nodded, and Chulah frowned but made no move to join him.

Tombi turned away from the faces of his closest friends, from the light and comfort of the cabin he'd built with his own hands, and marched into the gloomy darkness of the swamp. His arms prickled with a chill that defied the Alabama heat. He plodded forward, his heart hardening to stone—so hard it could be ripped from his chest and used to sling at a will-o'-the-wisp.

The fall of footsteps sounded behind him, but Tombi

didn't bother turning. He recognized the vibration of the footsteps, as familiar to him as a voice.

"Here." Hanan thrust something large and heavy against his right shoulder. "Don't be stupid."

Tombi grabbed the leather straps of his knapsack that was loaded with rocks and other hunting supplies and armored himself. How many times had he entered the woods laden with pounds of stones on his back? Too many to count. And yet he and the other hunters barely made a dent in fighting Nalusa and the night's shadows.

He kept moving forward. It was all he could do. Just keep showing up in the face of the odds stacked against him and his people.

"I put your phone in there," Hanan said. "Call me if you need backup."

Tombi flipped an arm in the air, acknowledging that he heard. But this was something he needed to do on his own. No one else knew Annie or Tallulah as well as he. Surely, whichever of them was lying, he'd be able to extricate their deception.

He stepped onto the path and into the woods. Cicadas and frogs chirruped and harrumphed in a bayou symphony. Mosquitoes buzzed by his ears and nipped at the unprotected skin of his neck and forearms. He swatted at them absently, eager to question the two women at the heart of the treachery. He could believe Tallulah had succumbed to grief, thus allowing herself to be in a weakened, vulnerable state that Nalusa preyed upon.

But Annie?

Sweet, sweet Annie. Memories flashed in his mind— the soft curve of her naked hips, her eyes darkening with passion, her fingers tracing his lips and jaw. Her sunny smile as she learned to block sound for the first time, her sorrow at her grandma's ill health, the special tea she brewed when he was hurt, the sound of her voice in their kitchen as they cooked together in the evenings.

Their kitchen. He'd come to think of the cabin as their special place. A mysterious, sexy, caring, complicated woman who had become a part of his life. Yet, he had to question her. Had to be sure she hadn't deceived him right from the start.

Chapter 16

The candle flame danced a red-hot tango, dipping and swerving to its own unheard music, leaving in its wake a hissing and popping of spent passion. Miss Belle was in the house, tripping the light fantastic. Annie knew it before she smelled the licorice and myrrh scent. She placed the grimoire on the altar top, opening it to the middle. She untied the strings of her mojo bag and placed it on the exposed pages marked with handwritten magical root-working recipes.

"Bless these herbs and infuse them with holy power. May they draw Bo's spirit close to me and help him speak this evening."

The pressure of a warm hand patted her shoulder. *It is done.*

Weeks ago, a physical manifestation of a long-dead ancestor would have sent her screaming from the room, but now, Annie welcomed Miss Belle's reassuring contact.

Tonight, she would speak with Bo and get the name of

the betrayer. After that, it was a matter of convincing her animal spirit to return the ancient flute. Her hawk wouldn't desert her and betray her trust. He just wouldn't.

A sharp rapping blasted the cottage's quiet. Annie glanced at the clock in the den: eleven thirty. Tallulah had cried herself to sleep in Tia Henrietta's bedroom over an hour ago. The muffled sobs from her grandma's room wouldn't have been audible to anyone but Annie. She and Tallulah might never become the best of friends, but Annie recognized there was some good in Tallulah. She was capable of great love.

Too bad her twin wasn't.

It had to be Tombi making that racket. Knocking in an arrogant, haughty way with no regard for the people inside. What did he care if she was asleep? He'd decided to talk at last, and that was all that mattered to him.

Annie worked up a righteous indignation. Better that than be a whining, pining fool who'd laid bare her soul. She jerked open the door. "What do you want?"

Tombi glowered, face set in harsh, grim lines. His brown eyes appeared hard as blackened, burned coal. What the hell was *he* mad about? He hadn't had his love thrown back in his face. She was the injured party here.

"We need to talk."

"Well, I don't want—"

He pushed past her and strode into the middle of the den, filling the feminine vibe of the cottage with a bit of the dangerous night that cloaked his aura. He smelled like smoldering wood chips and damp peat and moss and cypress. Intoxicating but dangerous.

Annie didn't budge from the doorway. "Say what you want and then leave. I was getting ready to go to bed."

A flicker of something—passion?—chased across his face, and Annie winced at her choice of words. *Bed* conjured up images of snuggling in Tombi's arms, of his skin golden in the moonlight, naked and smooth beneath her touch. Tangled bedsheets and groans and whispers and... Annie bit the inside of her mouth to stop the memories. "Why are you here?" she asked, knowing the hoarseness of her voice tipped him off to the passionate direction her mind had leaped to.

"Annie." He came to her and ran a calloused hand over her face, brushing back a curly lock of hair. "You're as much a mystery to me as the night we met," he whispered.

"There's nothing mysterious about me," she denied. "You know me better than anyone. I shared everything with you."

"Everything?"

"There are no secrets between us."

Tombi abruptly dropped his hand to his side. "I want to believe that."

"Why shouldn't you?" Annie countered. "I've been open. I've held nothing back." She swallowed painfully. She'd been too open, too trusting with her heart. And Tombi had crushed it.

He hardened his face and crossed his hands. "Tell me the truth. Are you in league with Nalusa? Does he have some kind of hold over you? Because if he does, I can help you break free."

"What?" Annie rubbed her temple, confused at the questions. "Why are you asking me that?"

"Because I believe the betrayer is you or Tallulah."

"Oh, yeah? On what evidence, you...you jackass?"

He ignored the gibe. "Ever since we met, the shadows have grown more powerful, Nalusa has infiltrated our ranks, and the inner circle has crumbled. No one trusts anyone else."

A cold fury tingled along Annie's spine. "I'm not in league with anybody. And neither is your sister."

"I want to believe you."

The anguish in his eyes softened her temper. "I understand that you have to suspect the worst of most people. But I thought we had something special."

He drew her to him, resting his chin on the top of her head. "We do."

The warm, husky voice made her tingle inside, and her thighs tightened. This part, the physical attraction, was so easy between them. If only everything else could be.

"Come back to the cabin with me," he urged, pressing his need against her core.

Annie's breath caught. She wanted to so much. To bury her heartache and disappointment in his kisses, to feel him inside her, pulsing, their bodies electric with desire. It took all her strength to step out of the warmth and safety of his arms.

"No."

"Why not? It's so damn good between us, Annie."

"In bed. But I want more than that. If you can't love me, I at least want your trust. One hundred percent."

"I'm working on it. Isn't that good enough for now?"

No. She'd tried to make Evan love and respect her, but it only ended with her doing all the giving. She wanted Tombi, but only if he could love her as she was. Nothing less would do.

"Don't hurt me any more than you already have. The longer we're together, the more I need to know you love and trust me. I'm done with one-sided relationships."

He gave a reluctant nod. "Best we end it now. There's nothing more I can teach you about blocking sound anyway." He started to the door and then stopped. "You'll let me know if your hawk brings you the flute, won't you? The full moon is in two weeks. We'll need it."

"I'll do my best to get it back," she promised. "I'll still help you any way I can. That hasn't changed."

He opened the door and stared into the night. "Will you be safe?"

"I managed twenty-seven years without your protection," Annie pointed out. "And at least for tonight, Tallulah's staying over."

"If you need me, call me."

Annie followed Tombi and shut the door behind him. She leaned her back against it and closed her eyes. It would be so easy to stop him, to go back to his cabin and enjoy his lovemaking. No, she'd done the right thing. Too much had been either said or left unsaid between them.

The rattle of his truck engine faded.

He was gone.

Annie took a shuddering breath. If Tombi knew what she'd planned for the evening, he would have never left. Quickly, before she lost courage, Annie went to the altar and picked up the mojo bag she'd infused with power. She tied it to a belt loop on her jeans and blew out the candle. On the way out, she grabbed a flashlight from the bookshelf near the entryway.

The black night was sticky with humid moisture as she gently shut the door, not wanting to wake her guest. But if Tallulah hadn't awoken when Tombi came over, she wasn't going to get up now.

Good. Best to proceed on this task on her own. Bo had never come to her while she and Tombi sought him together. She suspected his strength to communicate while trapped in a wisp was a difficult feat, easier attempted when he only had to concentrate on one human gifted to hear his voice.

With each step to the woods, Annie relaxed her mind and opened her hearing. The buzz of mosquitoes and the guttural music of bullfrogs were an instant, familiar backdrop. Amazing how the weeks training with Tombi had allowed her to adjust her supernatural hearing at will.

The elliptical beam of the flashlight guided her steps. Between its light and her night walk training with Tombi, her steps were quick, and the dark didn't impede her as much as before.

The smell and taste of salt tickled her nose and the back of her throat. Strange how often taste was enhanced by a stronger sense of smell. She didn't just absorb scent through her olfactory glands without it also arousing her taste buds.

Darkness descended further as she entered the woods. Annie stopped and leaned against the rough bark of a pine tree, switching off the flashlight. How far would she have to go in? She fingered the smooth flannel of her mojo bag.

The slightest snap of a twig and her breath seized. Was she being followed? She hardly dared breathe, straining to see or hear anything else in the silence of the swamp. Must have been a porcupine or squirrel. She shook off the fear and inhaled deeply.

"I'm here, Bo. Come to me," she whispered.

A faint blue-green light skittered from afar.

"Closer, Bo. It's okay, I'm alone."

The orb streaked through the forest, leaving a comet tail of sparkles that illuminated the twisting tree branches above and tangled vines and saw palmettos beneath. It stopped and hovered several feet away, its inner heart pulsing, breathing color.

It worked. She gripped the mojo bag, crushing the herbs and releasing more of the scent, bolstering her confidence. The glowing light twisted its shape, the upper half bending and pointing westward. Figured he would want to go back to the Choctaw sacred grounds where they'd first met.

"I'll follow you."

The wisp's glow made the flashlight unnecessary. A blue-and-green haze coated the air, painting teal brushstrokes everywhere. It felt like entering a strange, beautiful fairyland. She trudged along until the path grew less firm beneath her feet and became sludgy, the salt smell grew more pungent and her mouth puckered, briny as a pickle.

The light stood still.

"You came back," Bo said, his voice faint but clear. He sounded weaker than their previous encounter.

"Yes. Tombi wants to free you. But first we need—"

"Such a good friend," Bo said mournfully. "And Tallulah, my love, is nearby. She's followed you."

Aha. So that was what she'd heard earlier. "I thought I heard something. She's desperate to talk with you."

"No. It would only make her healing that much harder. I'm dead to her forever, and she must move on with her life."

"I'll give her your message. Knowing you care might help." Annie hesitated to bring up the purpose of her visit, but she sensed their time together was brief. "Please, can you tell me the name of the person who's been telling Nalusa the hunter's plans and secrets? If we don't find him soon, Tombi fears that they have no chance of winning. That, with the next full moon, Nalusa and his shadows will make a bold move to eliminate all of them."

"Tombi's right. *Na haksichi* is—"

"Bo!" Tallulah burst through from the path, long black hair streaming behind her, silver-streaked with moonlight. Her eyes were wild with a combination of grief and hope. "Is it really you?" She cast wild eyes on Annie. "What is he saying?"

The teal heart flame within the smoky wisp heated to an incandescent red that roared and cackled like an erupting forest fire. Annie took a step back from the wall of heat that singed her clothes and hair.

Tallulah dropped to her knees and held her hands out, imploring. "Take me with you, Bo. I only want to be with you."

Annie's own heart broke at seeing the proud woman so humbled and vulnerable. The woman warrior's loss was so intense, and seeing Bo trapped as a spirit had to be devastating.

"No!" Bo's voice rang out so loud it vibrated the earth beneath Annie's feet.

"It *is* you," Tallulah whispered in awe. "Even I heard you just now."

Annie knelt in front of Tallulah. "I need to talk to Bo. We have to find out the name of the betrayer."

"He approaches now," Bo warned. "Run!"

Annie scrambled to her feet and looked behind her. But this time she could make out nothing in the darkness. Except a stealthy footfall advancing toward them, one she had heard before. It teased the back of her brain like a spider crawling up her arm. "We have to go," she said, tugging at Tallulah's arm.

Tallulah didn't spare Annie a glance. She was transfixed by the fire that was once her lover, had eyes only for the conflagration burning at the wisp's center.

"C'mon," she urged, pulling harder.

The vibrations underfoot grew stronger, faster, more sure. *Na haksichi*, the traitor, was near. Annie dropped Tallulah's arm and stood, slowly turning around, dread prickling her spine.

Hanan's eagle eyes pierced the night, the topaz glints in his pupils like ground star chips.

"You," she breathed out, past the lump of fear in her throat. "You are the one."

His smile emphasized the sharp beak of his nose, and his white teeth were prominent as a chomping wolf's. "Just as you suspected at the start."

"Tombi had so much faith in you."

"Tombi." He spit out the name in apparent distaste. "He's leading us down a path of sure destruction. We are outnumbered. He should have compromised with Nalusa long ago."

"What kind of bargain have you struck with the devil?"

"One that allows me to live."

"And to hell with your friends? Your family? What kind of life is that?"

The wisp moved between her and Hanan.

"Be gone," Hanan commanded. His voice screeched like the talons of an eagle scraping glass. "You have no power here, Bohpoli. I killed you."

Tallulah shrieked, her banshee wail echoing through the swamp. She rose to her feet and stumbled past Annie. "You killed my Bo? Why?"

"Because he caught me with Nalusa. And because he was the most skillful hunter, the best shot."

Tallulah leaped at Hanan, screaming and clawing. He shoved her, and she tumbled several feet away.

"Stupid woman," he hissed. "You're weak. So weak you were in my bed only weeks after Bo's death."

The fire orb popped and hissed.

Hanan cast it a sharp glance. "By Nalusa's power, I command you to be gone, wisp."

The elongated smoky form of the wisp expanded, grew more dense and gray, smothering the light of Bo's trapped spirit. It skittered away in a heartbeat.

"Don't leave me behind," Tallulah wailed after the fleeing wisp.

Hanan said, face scrunched in contempt, "Shut up."

Annie stepped between them. "Why are you doing this?"

"The reign of Nalusa and the shadows is imminent. Might as well join them and share in the power. Tombi is an obstinate, stupid fool."

Anger burned in her gut. "He's not. He's a decent, honorable man."

"Who will die a horrible death." Hanan advanced slowly and deliberately.

"And so will you. Nalusa has no use for you. He'll kill you when this is over."

"I've worked out my deal. I'll be a rich man. All I have to do is provide him the flute." Hanan swooped upon her, grabbing her arm and clutching her, digging into her flesh, past muscle and to the bone.

Annie clenched her teeth, not wanting to give Hanan the satisfaction of hearing the whimper clawing at her throat.

Hanan's breath was hot on her face, and the topaz glints glittered like the eyes of a wild predator. "Call your hawk. I want that flute. Now."

So he knew. He probably knew everything, had hung back in the shadows and watched and waited for this opportunity.

"No," she ground out.

"Yes."

He shook her until her head bobbed like flotsam on the wave of a storm. "Do it," he growled.

"Or what?"

"Or you die. Tonight."

"You can't kill me. Without me, my hawk will never return the flute."

"Listen to me, witch. Call the hawk now, or you'll deal with Nalusa."

"And you won't get your reward," she shot back.

Hanan abruptly let go of her arm. "I don't have Nalusa's power, but I can give you a taste of what you can expect if I don't get your cooperation."

The screeching of a flock of owls and eagles erupted between her ears, a squall of birds of prey caught in a storm wind. Annie clamped her hands over her ears and bent at the waist, staggering backward. The sound stopped abruptly.

"It can get so much worse," Hanan warned.

Tallulah roused herself and came to Annie's side. "Leave her alone."

"That's rich," he sneered. "Only a couple of days ago, you hated Annie, said she was a witch who couldn't be trusted. You're a fickle lover and friend, Tallulah."

Fury wiped out the grief still evidenced by the tears on her cheeks. "And you're a bastard," she spat.

Hanan shrugged. "You're no longer important." He turned his eagle eyes on Annie. "Back to business."

Tallulah wedged between them, her back to Hanan, and raised her arms as if to hold him back. "Run, Annie! Go, get Tombi."

How she wanted to. Every cell in her body screamed *flee*. But she couldn't leave Tallulah alone with the enemy. Still…they would both be better off if one of them escaped and got help.

"You go," Annie urged.

Hanan laughed. "Run home, little girl. By the time you get your big, bad brother it will be too late."

Tallulah raised her eyebrows at Annie in a silent question.

Annie nodded.

Tallulah sprang from them and disappeared into the night.

A sardonic smile perched the corners of Hanan's thin lips. "Like I said. Fickle."

Her palms and underarms itched with sweat. What would he do now? "Even if I wanted to help you, I can't," she said calmly, hoping to reach some rational part of his mind not contaminated by Nalusa. "I've never tried to command my animal spirit. I don't know if I can."

"For your sake, this better work," he said quietly.

The kind of quiet that meant business.

The kind of quiet that was the whisper of the wind before the swooshing gale.

Infinitely more menacing than the noisy whirlwind he'd stirred moments before in her brain.

Some good her special petition and mojo bag had been. Annie's lips numbed with dread. She was alone and powerless in the midst of the most forsaken swampland on earth, alone with a heartless hunter who'd turn his own mother over to the devil if it meant gaining power.

"You left her alone out there in the woods?" Tombi slammed his fist on the counter and glared at his twin.

"I'm more help to her as a messenger than if I had stayed behind." Tallulah raised her chin. "Hanan would have taken us both hostage, and you would never have known until it was too late."

Hanan. Someone he'd known since childhood. Tombi remembered playing baseball with Hanan, their initiation into the hunter's world on their nineteenth birthdays. The friend who'd attended his parents' funeral, and the one who had helped him cut wood and hewn logs for the cabin he'd built.

His sister pulled out her phone. "I'm calling Chulah and the others. They can meet us here in fifteen minutes. Together, we might have a chance."

"You stay behind. I'm leaving now." Tombi rushed to get his knapsack and slung it over his shoulders. He had to get to Annie. Visions of Hanan torturing her clawed at his guts. He should never have left her earlier. Tallulah had been no protection.

"Don't be stupid. What difference can fifteen minutes make?"

"Every second I'm apart from her is agony," he answered shortly.

Tombi rushed to the den and grabbed his keys from

the fireplace mantel. If he drove his truck through the field to where the path started at the edge of the woods, it would save a couple minutes. More important, he wouldn't waste energy. He'd need every last ounce of strength to save Annie.

"Give me the keys," Tallulah snapped. "I'll drive you to the path and come back. You don't need to drive in your condition."

"Then move it." Tombi flew down the porch stairs and climbed into the truck.

Tallulah acted just as quickly, revving the engine and then slamming her foot on the accelerator. Headlights framed a square, narrow tableau of shadows and masses of swarming mosquitoes. The old truck bounced up and down on the uneven, rough soil, enough to make his teeth chatter.

And still it wasn't fast enough. "Hurry," he urged.

"I'm going as fast as I can. When I left they were on the edge of the salt marsh, near where Bo's body was found. You remember the spot?"

As if he could ever forget. "Yes. Anything else I should know?"

"No. Only…" She hesitated.

"What?" he asked brusquely. Could this situation get any worse?

"I have to give your lady credit—she insisted I leave. She stood her ground with Hanan. Never would have believed that tiny slip of a girl had it in her when we first met."

"She's not a girl, she's a woman." How many times had he said that same thing? Appearances were deceiving. Annie had depth and talent and compassion…and didn't even realize her own worth.

"And you love her," his sister stated matter-of-factly.

Love? Tombi scowled. Now wasn't the time nor the

place for thoughts of love. He gripped the door handle, ready to pounce as soon as the truck slowed.

Tallulah raised a brow. "It's okay to be in love. It doesn't make you weaker."

"So you say," he grumbled. The truck came to a shuddering halt at the path, and he prepared to leap.

His twin laid a hand on his shoulder. "And she loves you, too. I can tell."

He didn't want Annie's love. She'd be better off without him and his problems. Especially now that she'd learned to control her sense of hearing. There was nothing more he could offer Annie. Tombi shrugged off her hand. "Bring everyone as soon as you can."

He leaped out of the truck and hit the ground on a panicked run. *Must save Annie. Must save Annie.* The refrain echoed with every footfall, forming a rhythm of urgency. Heart and breath raced in despairing accompaniment.

Tombi wanted to kill Hanan. The rat bastard. After everything they had been through together. If the traitor harmed Annie, he'd pay with his life.

Chapter 17

Annie's arms, shoulders, back and legs dug into rough pine bark. Rope burned into her wrists like a bracelet of thorns. The more she struggled, the more it tightened, as if the cords were the sinew of a boa constrictor squeezing opportunistically with its victim's exhale. So this must have been what it felt like hundreds of years ago for women accused as witches and bound to a stake.

Hanan walked around the tree, inspecting his handiwork with the precision of a mechanical engineer. "That should hold you."

Annie bit her lip, struggling to hide her fear. Worse than the physical pain was the terror from being at Hanan's mercy. She was totally vulnerable, and he could do anything with her that he wanted. For as long as he wanted.

Had Tallulah gotten to Tombi yet? Her sense of time was as warped as an antique mirror. Every second dripped like a dollop of molasses. Tallulah could have been gone twenty minutes or twenty seconds for all she knew.

Defend yourself. Miss Belle's scent of myrrh and licorice teased the back of her throat. *I'm not alone.* She grabbed on to the belief as if it were a lifeline at sea.

What would Tia Henrietta do if she were in this position? Annie took a deep breathe. First, her grandma would admonish her to calm her mind, to find that quiet place deep inside that was still and peaceful and ever-present, an inner lagoon of peace and tranquility. There, she would find guidance—or the endurance to weather this ordeal. As long as her hawk possessed the flute, Hanan and Nalusa needed her alive.

He stood before her and crossed his arms. "Call your hawk."

She wouldn't outright defy him. Not tied to a tree. "I'll try." Annie closed her eyes and moved her lips in a flow of mumbo-jumbo words. It helped not to look at his eagle eyes dissecting her every move, watching for the slightest misstep. On and on she continued the charade, knowing each moment that passed brought Tombi closer.

Hanan interrupted her almost hypnotic reverie. "How long is this going to take?"

"I have no idea. This is new to me."

A sudden pressure pinched her chin, and Annie's eyes snapped open. Hanan's face was so close to her own that his hot breath fanned across her eyelids. His fingers dug into her flesh. Slowly, he increased the pressure until she feared he would break her jawbone. Tears stung her eyes, and a low whimper escaped her mouth.

"We don't have all night, witch."

"I'm… I'm doing my best." Her words were distorted from his grip on her chin.

"Try harder. I'll give you another minute. If it hasn't appeared, you'll force me to use other means to persuade you." He ran a hand down her breasts and painfully squeezed a nipple.

Bastard.

Annie clamped her teeth together to keep from crying out. Hanan would like that. She guessed he was the kind of man who would find rough sex a turn-on. What had Tallulah seen in him?

He took a step back and lifted his head, searching the night sky. She couldn't keep putting him off with the fake incantation. Perhaps the wisest course was to try to summon the hawk after all. Just because it came didn't mean it would bring the flute.

Come to me. If you are my animal spirit, meant to guide me, I need your help. Fly toward me. I ask this by the power of all the saints and by all that is sacred in our bond.

From a great distance, the swoosh from a spread of wings brushed against the synapsis of fear pounding inside her body. The hawk had heard her petition and would soon be here. The beating of its feather upon liftoff fluttered in her chest, and she sagged against the tree in relief. "My hawk's on the way," she whispered.

"Excellent." Hanan unloaded the leather backpack from his shoulders and withdrew a rounded stone.

Annie's breath caught. "What are you doing?" But she knew. She tugged against the ropes binding her wrist and ankles but only succeeded in further abrading the raw skin. Liquid trickled down her fingers. That blood would soon be a mosquito magnet.

"And now we wait," he said coolly.

"Please, can't you loosen these ropes a little bit? I'm bleeding."

"As soon as I have the flute, you'll be free."

Liar. She'd be trapped forever in a will-o'-the-wisp. Just like Bo. With the flute, Nalusa would defeat the remaining hunters, and there would be no one left to free trapped souls. And what would happen to Tombi?

Be careful, Annie urged the hawk. *Hanan is armed and means to kill you.*

Ca-ca-caw came a faint screech. The hawk understood her silent petition! There was still a chance to escape this disaster.

"What are you smiling about?" Hanan growled, his attention back on her. He stared up and down her body, slowly and deliberately.

She hadn't realized she was smiling. The blood drained from her face at this new menace.

Hanan abruptly grabbed her hair on both sides of her face and thrust his body against hers so hard she could feel his need pressed against her core. "You planning something, witch?" he growled into her right ear.

"N-no."

As suddenly as he'd been upon her, Hanan withdrew, and she gulped in fresh air.

"What the hell? Something's burning me." He slapped at the front of his jeans, and his brows knit as he studied her. Rough hands reached for her again, yanking and ripping the mojo bag from her belt loop. Smoke drifted through the cloth, and he threw it on the ground, shaking his fingers from the hot contact.

Annie smiled. This time a deliberate curling of the lips, a taunting. Hanan wasn't invulnerable against her hoodoo powers. He might hurt her, but she wasn't entirely defenseless.

"We'll have our fun later," he promised.

A flurry of feathers and wings beating in the wind sounded from above, so loud even Hanan heard it.

Thank the spirits.

Her relief was short-lived. Hanan gripped a rock, and his thin lips set into a predatory line.

"Look out!" she screamed.

Hanan rounded on her so swiftly she didn't see the blow

coming. Pain slashed her left cheek and cut her bottom lip—white heat pulsed and burned. A metallic taste tinged her mouth. Annie braced herself for more of the same, but Hanan's attention was directed upward.

The casual violence of the assault churned her stomach. This man would have no mercy in reaching his goal for more power and money. It was as if his soul had already blackened to match the pitch of the night.

A flick of the wrist, and his round stone was propelled upward. It pinged against a tree branch and fell harmlessly back down to earth. Hanan loaded his slingshot and attacked again.

Ca-caw. The hawk drew near enough she could make out the reddish-brown feathers spread in flight from one tree top to another. *Be careful*, she warned silently. *He's trying to kill you.* But her animal guide could probably see the enemy from afar better than she could only a few feet away.

Or so she hoped.

Another stone missile rustled through leaves and again fell harmlessly down.

"Damn it," Hanan muttered, loading another stone in the sling. The weapon whizzed in the night.

A sickening thud of rock hitting bird flesh rent the thick, humid air. *Ca-ca, ca-caw.* Its cry high-pitched and tattered. Wings fluttered and the sound of dead weight descending.

No! Not her hawk.

"Bingo." Hanan smirked, his voice pregnant with satisfaction.

Damn him. If she could escape her bindings, she'd make him pay for this.

A brown clump of feathers and claws appeared a few feet above Hanan's head, a motionless heap of dead weight.

"What the—" Hanan began.

The clump of bird stretched, wings spread open, feet and talons extended.

It lived.

Hanan flung his slingshot to the ground, one leg moved forward, set to run.

Her hawk swiped the man's forehead, ripping flesh. Hanan screamed and batted uselessly at his attacker. The hawk clung mercilessly to the top of Hanan's scalp, even as Hanan ran.

She was alone. Annie sagged with relief, muscles grateful for the reprieve. If only she could untie the bindings at her wrists. Her hawk would take care of Hanan, and Tombi should be along shortly. At least she was safe. Unless… Annie cast a nervous glance at the nearby underbrush. Unless Nalusa saw her predicament and decided to pay a visit.

She shivered in the sweltering darkness.

Tombi stilled at the unexpected scream. Could it be Annie? He pushed away the paralyzing terror and ran toward the sound. If it was her, at least she was alive.

For the moment.

He cut through to rough, less-traveled shortcuts on the main path. Limbs smacked his torso and scratched his face, but nothing mattered if it shaved microseconds in getting to Annie.

He'd never leave her alone again. Not for a second. Not for a chance to reclaim all the trapped souls in Bayou La Siryna. Not even for a chance to kill Nalusa. Tombi ran on, not bothering to consider the ramifications of his thoughts.

Still no sight of anything but the familiar, accursed swamp. "Annie?" he called. "Where are you?"

"Here!"

Relief jellied his knees for two seconds. The cry was weak but near. He pushed on with even greater determi-

nation. The path widened, and he rushed into the Choctaw sacred land by the marsh.

And found the most unholy sight—Annie tied to a tree,
blood oozing down her bottom lip, the left side of her face
discolored and bearing a hand imprint. Her eyes were wild
and frightened.

"Be careful," she warned. "Hanan might be back any
moment."

Tombi wished he'd show his traitor face. "Let him." He
walked to her and reached out to touch her swollen cheek.
"How bad did he hurt you?" Despite his intention to be
gentle, his voice was rough, and he choked down bile.
Hanan dared do this? He would pay with his life.

"I'll be okay," Annie whispered. "Untie me and let's
get out of here."

Tombi rounded the tree, and anger gushed like a geyser
at the sight of the blood-soaked rope. Grabbing the knife
from his backpack, he made quick work of cutting the
ropes binding her wrists and ankles. "Don't try to walk
just yet," he cautioned, returning to face her.

"We have to hurry." She took a step forward, and her
body collapsed.

Tombi caught her and lifted her slight frame in his
arms. "I'll carry you. It's going to take a few minutes for
the blood to recirculate in your feet."

She nodded, and he hurried down the path, holding
her in his arms. "You're a dead man, Hanan Sheffield,"
he yelled, itching for a confrontation. But first, he had to
get Annie to safety.

"He tried to kill my hawk."

Tears ran down her cheeks, salty as the bayou breeze.
He stopped abruptly and kissed her tenderly on the forehead. "Everything's going to be okay now," he promised.

She smiled in spite of the swollen, disfigured lips. "I
know. You're here. I knew you'd come for me."

Her trust humbled him. And to think he once suspected her as the *Na haksichi*. She deserved a man so much better than he. But he would never let another man touch her. Not now. Not ever.

"Always," he said, voice near breaking. He frowned. This wouldn't do at all. The battle was near, he knew the enemy, and it was a time for courage, not weakness.

"I love you, Tombi. Take me home."

"I can't leave you alone at your grandmother's cottage," he apologized, deliberately ignoring her declaration of love. "Come back to my cabin, where you'll be safe."

"Your cabin is my home," she said softly.

Her words felled him, touched the cold, dark spot deep within his heart. Resolutely, he resumed walking, intent on getting her to the safety of his cabin. Tallulah could protect her while he sought Hanan.

She laid her swollen cheek against his chest. Her absolute trust, after all he'd put her through, was his undoing. He might keep silent with Annie's declarations, but he could no longer deny the truth to himself.

He loved her. Loved her passionately, loved her tenderly, loved her with mind and body and soul.

Forever.

Violet-and-coral streaks radiated from the east, although the risen sun was merely a promise of the golden glory to come.

Annie snuggled in Tombi's arms, inhaled his unique scent. "Aren't you tired of carrying me? I can walk this last little bit."

"You aren't heavy." Vertical lines marred the bridge of his nose. "How are you feeling? You look like hell."

"Gee, thanks." She tried to smile, but her swollen bottom lip pulled and cracked at the motion. "Oomph," she mumbled.

Tombi's frown deepened. "Soon as we get home, I'll put some ice on it to stop the swelling."

"Perfect." They entered the clearing, and light glowed from the cabin. Tallulah and Chulah stood on the porch, watching them approach.

"Let me down," she insisted, wiggling out of his arms. She and Tallulah may have drawn a truce, but Annie didn't want to risk again being viewed as weak, as someone who needed her brother's attention and distracted him from his duties.

Her feet made contact with the earth, and her knees buckled. Some of the numbness had left and in its wake left sharp nerves flagellating in protest at bearing weight. Damn. She was about to fall and humiliate herself. Tombi slipped an arm around her waist, and she gratefully sagged against the support he offered. She might look a bloody mess, but at least she stood on her own two feet. Sort of.

Tallulah shoved off from the porch steps and approached, Chulah close behind. "You look like shit," she proclaimed.

Tombi stiffened. "Tallulah, what did I tell you—"

"I'm fine," Annie said hurriedly. "A hot bath and a good night's sleep is all I need."

Tallulah stepped to her side and wrapped her arm around Annie as well, lending her support. "Any of your special witch's herbs you want me to brew?"

Her words were brusque but not unkind. A cup of chamomile tea would be just the thing. "Sure. I'll go in the kitchen with you and show you how."

"Not necessary," Tombi said. "I've watched you make it, and I know where everything's at."

They slowly made their way to the porch, and Chulah stepped in front of them to hold the front door open. He regarded her with—could it really be?—concern in his warm brown eyes. "I'm glad you're okay."

"Seriously?" Annie clamped a hand over her mouth as if to call back the word, wincing at the contact with her tender lips. "Thanks," she mumbled, feeling foolish. Of course he and the others were glad she'd survived; they needed her to get the flute.

She hobbled to the kitchen table and sank into a chair, bones heavy and eyelids even heavier. One cup of tea and then it was bath and bedtime. She closed her eyes and sank her head in her hands, feeling the smooth oak of the table. Cabinet doors and low murmurs, the clanking of a teapot, the running of water—cozy sounds that invited slumber and a cocoon of safety.

Warmth pressed into the middle of her back.

"What—" She sprang up, dizzy and confused. The kitchen was packed with men. The hunters had come together, and they each stared unwaveringly at her.

Tombi set a mug of tea in front of her. "Drink this."

The heat singed the raw flesh on her lips, but she drank and cradled the warm cup in her hands as if it were a magical elixir. She took dainty sips, conscious of everyone watching.

It was evidently too much to ask that she be allowed some peace and rest. They were set on hunting Hanan, and they would want to know everything that had taken place earlier. Tombi kept his hand possessively on her shoulder. For all she knew, some in the group still suspected she was the traitor. That would be much easier for them to accept—a witch infiltrates the group, charms their leader and casts blame on one of their closest friends. So much more acceptable than the truth, that the evil sprang from one of their own.

"What do you want to know?" she asked wearily, setting down the empty cup.

Chulah spoke for the group. "Tombi and Tallulah have

filled us in on what happened. The only question remaining is—can you summon your hawk to bring us the flute?"

"I can try. I was able to contact him earlier. I don't see why I couldn't do it now, too."

"Not right now." Tombi's grip on her shoulder tightened. "She's been through enough. We'll summon the hawk tomorrow and hold our ritual next week when the full moon rises. Our best chance to defeat Nalusa once and for all is to have that flute and use it at the right time. Together."

"At least agree to let us track Hanan tonight," Chulah argued. "He's injured, and the odds of all of us against him are in our favor. We'll find him and keep him under lock and key until this is over."

Tombi's heartbeat grew stronger, faster, an angry tempo exploding sound waves.

"Go with them," Annie said, looking up at his tight, set face. He wanted to be with his friends, wanted to help capture the traitor. "I'll be fine."

"I've left you alone before, and it never turns out well. I'm staying."

Astonishment washed over Annie. He chose her instead of his men, instead of his duty. "You are? Really?"

"Of course."

Tallulah jumped up from the table. "Good choice, brother. I'll make sure that bastard pays for what he's done."

She plucked a feather from her braid and held it out to Annie. "You showed great courage tonight. You insisted I run to get help, and you faced *Na haksichi* alone. And you had enough presence of mind to summon your animal guide and escape."

Annie accepted the feather and nodded, too overcome with surprise and gratitude to speak. Tallulah nodded and marched out. One by one, each of the hunters stopped before Annie and gave her a feather, until the wooden tabletop was hidden beneath a pile of feathers in every dark earth and rainbow shade. When the last one had exited, she let the tears fall. This was the closest she'd ever come to feeling like part of a family. She hadn't even known how much she'd craved this until the sense of belonging and acceptance built to a crescendo of emotion.

"Be right back." Tombi withdrew and walked his guests to the door.

Annie dropped her head on the table, and feathers tickled her nose and cheeks. She heard a chorus of birds, each feather a note in a melody, as lovely as any she had ever heard. Sweet notes of love and home and family.

And she lost it. Totally lost all self-composure. She'd survived the ordeal with Hanan, but the acts of kindness were her undoing. If only Grandma Tia were here to see it, all would be perfect.

Strong arms enfolded her, encouraging her to stand.

"This has all been too much for you. Let's get you cleaned up and into bed."

She struggled to her feet, quelling the sniffling. Tombi smiled tenderly. He gently removed a blue feather stuck to her cheek with salty tear paste.

"Our tradition is to wear the feathers in our hair and not on our face."

"I thought y'all should start something new."

Annie shuffled to the back bedroom, leaning heavily on Tombi's arm. The sight of the familiar four-poster bed with wool patterned blankets folded at the ends and the handmade, sturdy furniture felt like an oasis in a storm.

"It feels like I've been away for weeks," she said with a sigh.

"It does. I've missed you."

The admission glowed her heart and numbed the pain in her wrists and ankles and face. It wasn't *I love you*, but she'd take it. In a heartbeat. Annie put her arms around his neck and kissed him enthusiastically.

"Ouch," she gasped as her cut bottom lip protested the deep kiss.

"Passion can wait." Tombi quickly guided her to the bathroom. "I've already drawn the water for you."

The scent of chamomile and sweet orange emanated from the Jacuzzi tub. "You even added my favorite essential oils," she marveled.

Tombi flashed a rare grin. "I pay attention," he boasted. "Now take off your clothes."

Annie mock saluted. "Yes, sir." She slipped out of the dirty, sweaty T-shirt and jeans, bra and panties. Hanan had touched her through these clothes. The whole lot should be burned. If she ever wore them again, she'd remember him.

Quickly she slipped into the warm, scented bath, ready to wash away the unsettling memory of Hanan's promise of more to come later. Impulsively, Annie dunked her whole body, face included, and let the water completely submerge her—a self-baptismal ritual to symbolically wash away all thoughts of *Na haksichi*. The raw skin on her wrists and ankles stung like a bitch, but they needed cleaning to prevent infection.

Tombi's face was above her own, its harsh, dear form and features rippled and blurred through the transparent liquid wall between them. His frown meant he was concerned. Annie immediately sat up, pushing through the water. She clasped her wet hands on his forearms and tugged. "Join me."

Tombi peeled off his shirt, and Annie smiled at his haste. No way was passion waiting until the morning. The sound and sight of him unbuckling his belt and unzipping his jeans wiped the smile from her face. This was what she needed. Him.

His erection popped loose from his briefs, and she swallowed hard. She squirted some body wash in her right palm, and when he sank into the tub opposite her, she massaged the wash onto his broad chest. White scars crisscrossed his golden flesh, and she lightly ran her fingers over them. "How did you get these?"

"Ishkitini. Horned owls known as shadow birds. They will sometimes attack if we slip past the wisps and get too close to Nalusa."

She shuddered to think of Tombi being sliced by the birds of prey. And she pictured her hawk carving Hanan's forehead and attaching his long talons into Hanan's scalp. "My hawk attacked Hanan today. Do you think my spirit guide might have once been on the dark side?"

"No. Once you've crossed, you can never go back. Any being, human or animal, is forever tainted." Tombi grasped her shoulders with his calloused hands and lowered his head to her level. "Now that we're alone, tell me…what did Hanan do? The swelling on your face and lips is proof he struck you at least once." He reached in the soapy water and raised her right hand. "And he cruelly bound you too tight. That was overkill."

"He only struck me once. Let's leave it at that."

Tombi placed his palm over her left breast. "You are bruised here, as well."

Annie hung her head. "Please. I don't want to talk about it."

He tried to gently lift her chin, but Annie jerked her head to the side.

"It will do you good to open up. We only have to talk about it this once, if you'd like." He paused a heartbeat. "Did he force himself on you?"

She shook her head, still refusing to meet his direct gaze. "It didn't get that far."

Tombi remained silent, and she rushed to fill the void.

"Once I was tied to the tree, he kissed me and...and then shoved himself against me and...pinched my breasts."

"You must have been so scared." Tombi wrapped her in his arms. "I'll never let him hurt you again," he said with fierce tenderness.

"I know," she said, her voice muffled against his chest. "Just hold me a minute, okay?"

"Always."

The steady drum of his heartbeat vibrated in every cell of her body, pulsing a message of love. He might not realize it, but he did love her. She knew it as certain as she knew she was the granddaughter of the most revered hoodoo practitioner in Alabama.

She soaked in every sensation, Tombi's heartbeat, the warm water a liquid caress against her bare skin, the sweet scent he'd so thoughtfully provided. Annie used her newly found abilities to block out the rest of the world—the distant noise of cars, the humming of electrical appliances, the birds beginning to awaken and stir, welcoming in the morning. By focusing on the here and now, the intimacy was more profound.

For the first time, she was thankful for her special gift of hearing. This moment obliterated the childhood pain of being an outcast. She'd been born and fashioned for this man, just as he had been destined for her.

He had to feel it, too. The stubborn man. Even if this were their last night together, her heart and soul had irrevocably linked to his.

"Annie, are you ready for bed?"

She opened her eyes and blinked. "Huh? Did I fall asleep?"

"Just for a moment. Let me wash your hair and then tuck you into bed."

She didn't feel like bothering, but it seemed to please him to take care of her. "If you want."

He climbed out of the tub and pulled the plug, turned on the faucet. "Stick your head under."

A splat of shampoo landed on the top of her scalp and expert fingers massaged it in, kneading her temples and working back down to the tight muscles at the base of her neck. Heaven. And to think she had wanted to pass this up. Tombi could wash her hair all day if he pleased. Satisfied, he rinsed away the suds and then wrapped her head in a warm towel.

"That was amazing," she said with a tired smile. "Thank you."

His face darkened. "It's the least I can do after failing to protect you."

He helped her out of the tub and rubbed a thick towel over her body to dry her off, taking care to avoid the abraded skin.

"Don't do that to yourself. Guilt is a terrible thing. It can destroy your spirit."

"Easy for you to say," Tombi grunted. "You're an angel."

Annie laughed until she caught his eye. He wasn't smiling; he'd meant it. She flushed, thinking of all the times she'd been angry with her grandma for not instantly curing her of her hearing gift. "Not true. I can be quite selfish. You're the one who's always sacrificed everything for your family and friends."

Tombi ruffled through a vanity drawer and produced a white tube. "Antibiotic cream," he explained.

"That's not necessary—"

"Lie on the bed, and let me dress your wounds."

He was in full master-doctor mode, so she followed him to the bedroom and obediently lay down. Tombi sat beside her, squirted a dollop on his fingers and, with incredible gentleness, took one wrist and applied the cream.

It still hurt like hell. Annie pursed her lips, determined not to make a sound. No reason to make him feel guiltier than he did. With gentle precision, Tombi applied the cream to all the raw flesh.

"Anything else I can do for you?"

She flashed a wicked grin. "Really? Do you need to ask? You're beside me in bed—naked. I can think of some naughty things you can do for me."

Tombi's eyes darkened, and he slowly leaned over and kissed along the side of her neck. She turned her head slightly, allowing him access to the sweet spot. He kissed the nape of her neck that always sent bursts of pleasure along her spine.

Right there. His warm breath tingled her nerve endings, just like he knew she liked it. Annie moaned.

Tombi pulled away. "Am I hurting you?"

"Quite the opposite," she assured.

He lowered his head and kissed the hollow of her throat. The man knew her weaknesses, had explored every inch of her body with intensity and curiosity. And she'd enjoyed every second of it, as much as she had loved learning every contour of his muscled frame, where scars crisscrossed his chest and shoulders, his long fingers and toes, his smooth flesh and solid jaw and cheekbones. Every detail thrilled her, made him more desirable each time they made love.

She pressed her hips against his erection, and his breath grew stuttered and harsh. She took delight in knowing she pleased him as much as he pleased her. It was as if there was no space between their bodies, no barrier between their souls, as they explored one another.

Tombi placed his mouth over one of her nipples, his tongue lathing the sensitive bud. His hand felt her core, and he inserted a finger. Annie bucked against it, her muscles contracting. The roaring in her head was like that of an incoming train—a powerful force bearing down and that couldn't be stopped.

She fondled his erection, and Tombi groaned. He entered her, and she squeezed her thighs and core, desperate for release from the building crescendo.

It came, crashing like the Gulf tide at high waters. He plunged in and out, advancing and retreating, dominating and surrendering, until together they climaxed. She held on to his muscled back, an anchor in the passionate maelstrom. Her breath gradually slowed down, and her heart returned to a normal rate.

Tombi rolled beside her, a soft music of flute and drumming played like a lullaby. She was so tired...slumber beckoned. Before she surrendered to it, an unexpected quiet filled her mind and body.

A perfect silence blanketed her world for the first time—blissful, peaceful silence. And all because of Tombi. Annie sighed and snuggled under the crook of his arm, knowing she was safe and loved—even if he didn't know his own heart yet.

Chapter 18

Tonight was The Night. Two weeks had passed since Hanan had tied her to the tree, and her wounds had scabbed over.

Morning rose with twin orbs gracing the sky—the bright sun to the east and the pale slip of the full moon visible and awaiting its hour to usurp the heavens.

Annie had glanced fretfully at the moon for hours, knowing that with each minute that passed, she was either a step closer to a future with Tombi or a step closer to losing him forever. Various hunters had come and gone throughout the day, conferring with Tombi on tonight's battle strategy.

Annie shyly moved among them, her hair adorned with two skinny plaits at the front, the hunters' gifted feathers braided in the strands. She gleaned from snatched conversations that in the prebattle ritual, she was to summon her hawk for the heirloom flute to defeat Nalusa.

Talk about pressure. If only Grandma Tia were here, but she'd be in rehab a few more days.

She fully understood what Tombi had dealt with for years; the weight of responsibility pressed down, smothering her lungs until her breath grew shallow and her stomach leaden. What if the hawk had been injured or killed? The hunters had found no trace of Hanan, no clue as to who had been the victor in that skirmish.

The murmur of voices grew louder in the cabin's den as the whisper of twilight approached. A furtive glance behind, and Annie snuck out the back door, certain no one saw her. The heat had cooled from near one hundred degrees to the low nineties. Tolerable. Nothing like the cool night air of the North Georgia Mountains, but she'd been a summer visitor to the bayou ever since she was a baby and had acclimated to the heat and humidity, as much as humanly possible.

Not to say she enjoyed it. Annie grabbed the front of her T-shirt and fanned the cotton cloth back and forth in a futile effort to dry the perspiration gathered in her cleavage. Quickly, she scurried down the back porch steps, eager to reach the patch of trees that would shelter her from human eyes. There she could beckon her hawk without the prying…

"Where do you think you're going?"

Caught again. Annie's shoulders sagged, and her head lowered. Slowly, she turned around to face Tombi. "Just getting a little air," she called nonchalantly over her shoulder.

"Nice try."

Annie sighed and faced him. "I thought you were absorbed in business."

"I'm never so busy that I don't notice where you are."

"So I see."

"Why do you keep sneaking off? You're welcome to join us. I just didn't think you'd be interested."

Might as well tell him the truth. Annie kicked the toe of her sneakers in the red clay dirt. "We've tried every day to summon my hawk together, and it hasn't worked. Let me try to do it alone without everyone watching. It might work this way." She sighed heavily. "I feel like such a failure when my summons don't work."

"No one will consider it a failure if the hawk doesn't ever show. You can't control an animal guide. He'll show or not, depending on its own will. We all know that." Tombi walked to her and held out his hand. "Come back inside where it's safe. I don't want the distraction of worrying about *you* on top of everything else."

Annie folded her arms under her chest. "Y'all don't stand much of a chance without the flute. Everything depends on my hawk. And me."

Tombi dropped his outreached hand. "This wasn't your battle to start with."

"Well, it is now."

"No. It's too dangerous." He ran a hand through his long hair. "I won't lie. That flute could be crucial, but not at the risk of putting you in more danger."

"I'm already in danger," she pointed out. "I overheard you telling the others that I'll be included in the ritual dance and that we'll try to contact the hawk as a group. But I need to do this on my own."

"No. We do it before the battle, and then you'll stay here in the cabin with one of my hunters on guard."

Anger scraped the back of her throat. "And when were you going to tell me this? Right before the ceremony? It's already dark, almost time for the gathering."

"The less time for you to argue," he said with a rueful grin. "C'mon. Remember how much you hate snakes?"

She glared at his pitiful attempt at humor. "I'm going with you tonight."

"No."

"Yes."

"No."

"You can't stop me. I'm going to contact my hawk now, and I'll be with you and the others this evening." Annie spun away.

She made it all of three steps before Tombi caught up to her and placed a heavy hand on her shoulder. "How about a compromise?" he suggested.

She raised an eyebrow.

"I come with you now and stay by your side while you connect with your hawk. In turn, you'll agree to stay at the cabin this evening."

One step at a time. Get the flute and then renegotiate. "Okay. But stay at least a few feet away from me when I petition my guide. He'll be more likely to show up."

Annie had no idea if that were true, but Tombi's proximity made it impossible to concentrate on anything but the music of his heart.

He nodded and dipped forward in a mock bow. "I'm following you. Lead on."

Annie smiled to herself. Victory was won a battle at a time. She strolled to the path to the woods, Tombi close on her heels.

The temperature mercifully dipped several degrees under the canopy of trees. Annie located a fallen log and sat on the makeshift bench. Tombi backed off a few feet and stood, watching.

"Don't stare. You're making me nervous," Annie complained.

Tombi gave a long-suffering sigh. "I'll be over here." He gestured at a tree a few feet behind him. "No farther."

"Fine."

Annie deliberately turned her back on Tombi and drew three deep, calming breaths. She let down the shields Tombi had taught her to erect and fully opened her senses. Wind whistled in the treetops, twigs crunched with the scurrying of small animals, the swell of an ocean wave breaking from far, far away, the hum of insects, Tombi's heartbeat. Annie drew the cinnamon stick sprinkled with frankincense essential oil from her mojo bag and inhaled. She held it between her palms as she pressed them together into the prayer position.

"I beseech thee, hawk," she whispered. "Your will is your own, your heart wild and free to roam the bayou. But if possible, I need your help. By the power of the universe that created you to fly and me to walk on land, I ask that you appear."

She paused and cocked her head to the side, straining to hear its presence above. A cold chill chased down her spine. What if Hanan had managed to free himself of the hawk's talons and kill it?

No. Surely she would have heard or felt some sign of such a catastrophe. Annie tried again.

"Please, help. We need that flute. Just this one favor is all I ask. With the flute we can stop Nalusa and contain the birds of the night—*ishkitini*—that prey upon you, as well In the name of all the holy saints, please, come. Amen."

She kept her eyes pressed shut, hardly daring to breathe Every second that ticked increased her agitation, and her fingers stroked the soft feathers braided in her hair. Annie crumpled the cinnamon stick in her hand and held it to her nose. The sweet spice odor calmed her mind, allowing her to focus. She pictured her hawk, flying high above the oaks and pines, wings spread majestically, eyes sharp and probing, searching below. Seeking, seeking. In its left talon, its gnarly claws clutched the thin reed—the flute that held their hope and safety. Salvation. How very frag ile and small it appeared in the sky. So much rested on such a fragile instrument.

Have faith.

Grandma Tia's voice commanded—pristine and visceral—cutting through the static of the cacophony and doubt swirling through her mind.

That's all ya got to do, child. Faith moves the mountains and makes all things possible. Yer stronger than ya know. Make me proud.

If only her grandma were sitting beside her, holding her hand. She could do it then.

But Grandma Tia was miles away. This was something she had to do alone. Something sacred and holy between her and the hawk.

"I'm waiting," she whispered. "For as long as it takes, I'll wait for you."

The beating of wings roared above, loud as a hovering helicopter. Annie looked up. Her hawk screeched and flew close, so close its rapid heartbeat fluttered in her ears, and she heard the wind rustle its feathers. The flute was clamped in its hooked beak.

Annie tentatively held out a trembling hand. The hawk was upon her; she smelled the dusty scent of its skin beneath the feathers, felt its hot breath on her face. She wanted to run, wanted to tell it to give the flute to Tombi, but to do so would betray its trust, would repudiate the their bond.

She sank her heels into the red clay, determined to stay rooted.

The hollowed tube thudded onto her opened palm, and she curled her fingers on the warmed wood...

And nearly dropped it when the hawk took flight, disappearing in a loud roar, as suddenly as it had first appeared. Annie clutched the flute to her chest, watching in humbled awe as the hawk became a speck of brown in the darkened sky and then became one with the shadows. Would she ever see him again?

"Thank you," she whispered.

Tombi stepped in front of her, waiting for her to gather her emotions. "Your hawk came through. I'll be damned."

"No. You'll be saved."

He laid his dark hands over her own. The flute pulsed like a living creature. Joyful notes teased her mind; the Choctaw artifact knew it had come home once again.

"This belongs to you," she said, placing the flute between his fingers.

Tombi lowered his head and rested his forehead on hers. The moment was as sacred and precious as a wedding kiss, a vow of love, the promise of a future. All the things that could now be theirs.

He pulled away. "It's time. Thanks to you, we have a chance."

"More than a chance. You can't lose now."

"We won't." He squared his shoulders and took her hand. "Wait until the others see this. Tonight's ritual will be one of celebration."

Sparks of fire crackled and swirled upward, whipped by the Gulf breeze. The scent of burning oak, salty air and purifying sage signaled the welcoming of the full moon, sights and sounds he'd experienced since he was a young boy. The murmurs of his people were solemn and hushed, even more so than usual. Not finding Hanan had been a blow to their confidence.

Tombi came to an abrupt halt. "Wait."

Annie skidded to a stop beside him. "What's wrong?"

"Nothing. Thanks to you." Tombi pressed the flute into her hands. "You should be the one to carry this in."

She shook her head and tried to hand it back. "I don't care—"

"No argument." He took long strides away from her, emerging from the wooded path and into the field, Annie trailing behind.

The murmur of voices halted as they all stared at their approach. Annie hung back, and Tombi motioned her forward.

"We've got great news," he declared.

Tallulah broke from the group. "Did you find Hanan?" she asked, peering behind his shoulders.

"Even better news." He turned to Annie. "Show them."

Hesitantly, she raised the flute.

"The ancient instrument that will help us defeat Nalusa has been returned to us."

Tallulah was the first in line to celebrate. She eyed it critically and then faced Annie. Her throat worked. "Thank you," she said gruffly. She threw her arms around Annie and hugged her.

Tombi grinned at the round *oh* of astonishment on Annie's face.

"—knew she could do it."

"—never doubted her—"

"Tonight we win—"

"—Hanan is dead meat."

One by one, every hunter shook Annie's hand. Pride swelled Tombi's heart at her humble acceptance of their tributes. She'd won them over, had become one of them.

And had won his heart, as well. If they defeated Nalusa this evening... No. Tombi gritted his teeth. Tonight was all about the battle. Nalusa and his shadows would pay for the deaths of his parents, for Tallulah's suffering, for the suffering he'd caused everyone in the bayou. He would *not* be distracted from his destiny and duty.

Mela, the drummer, began beating the hand drum. Its rhythm was a call for celebration. Chulah and Pisa took Annie by either hand and led her to the fire. Tombi gathered with the others, and they encircled the bonfire piled with dried sage. The drumming stopped. Through the smoke and heat waves, he saw that all eyes were on him, awaiting the signal to begin. He raised his right arm, and the drumming began, slow and measured. Each put their right hand on the back of the hunter in front of them and stepped forward on their left foot, then slowly dragged their right foot beside the other and stomped.

The tempo increased, then slowed back down to its original pace, his signal to begin the antiphonal chorus. Tombi released two war cries and sang an old, old song calling upon the sun for power. After every stanza, the hunters repeated the verse until the song had been sung three times through.

He looked back at Annie and winked. She had a look of dazed excitement. This full-moon ritual was undoubtedly more colorful and exciting than the paper-burning ritual she and her grandmother shared.

"Enough," he said. "Let's save our energy for capturing Nalusa."

A large cheer erupted.

"You each know your assignments. Release as many wisps' souls as possible, and then at the first note of the flute, we attack."

Chulah raised a fist. "Tonight it ends!"

Tombi waited until the resulting cheering died down. "We have every reason to be confident, but don't take anything for granted. Even in a weakened condition, Nalusa is powerful and cunning," he cautioned. "Plus, Hanan may still be out there. So be on the lookout."

He stared each hunter in the face, and they nodded grimly. Childhood faces of friends he'd played stickball with, had wrestled with, gone to school with since kindergarten. "Courage and luck be with you, my friends."

In groups of twos and threes they disappeared into the

darkness of the woods, until it was just Annie and him standing by the dwindling fire. Silently, she handed him the flute, and he carefully placed it in his backpack.

"I'll put out the fire, and then I want you to stay inside the cabin until I return. Don't open the door for anyone."

Annie lifted her chin. "I'm going with you."

Why was he not surprised? "No. You've done more than enough." He dragged over a bucket of sand by one of the tents and threw it on the fire.

Annie grabbed another one, her small body bent over double from lifting the fifty pounds. "I want to be with you."

"You would be a distraction," he argued, relieving her of the bucket and tossing it on the dying embers.

Which was partly true, but the thought of Nalusa sinking his fangs into Annie would destroy his soul like a battalion of shadows couldn't. If she didn't want to save herself, at least she'd listen to reason about hindering his safety.

She opened her mouth, as if to offer more objections, but he kissed her—hard and swift. If all else failed, he had to know that Annie lived on, that his life had been worth something, that he had helped her control her gift.

Annie loved him, but he'd held a bit of himself back, and she knew it. If he died, he wanted her to move on and find someone who could give her all of himself. Someone who could put her happiness first.

Tombi told her none of this.

He ended the kiss. The longer he waited, the more difficult the parting.

"Go inside," he said gruffly.

She shook her head.

"Please."

Annie bit her lip. "Maybe I could help if you take me with you."

"No. I would be looking out for you and not focusing on anything else."

"If you're sure—"

"Very. Go." He stepped back and crossed his arms. "I'll watch until you get inside."

With a sigh, she nodded and walked slowly back to the cabin.

Her silhouette appeared in the den window, and she pressed her face against the glass.

He longed to go to her, to the warmth and light of the cabin. But his duty was clear, and he would not stray. Tombi turned away and headed into the inky blackness of the bayou swamp.

Annie restlessly paced the cabin; burning some energy moderately helped manage the terror. She'd done everything she could do, lit incense, prayed at her makeshift altar and called Grandma Tia and asked her to do the same. She stared out the window, willing Tombi to materialize from out of the darkness, to walk across the field and back into her arms. Alive and safe and victorious.

Nothing but night's black veil. She drew the curtain and started to turn when a speck of light appeared in her peripheral vision. Annie stared again into the night.

A blue-green orb skittered to within a few feet of the window. Its shaped wavered and flickered like a candle in the wind; the green color pulsed rapidly within its core.

High-pitched wailing assaulted her ears. She recognized that voice.

Bo.

Tombi was in danger. Annie flew to the door and ran down the porch stairs. "What's happened?"

"You must come. Quick. Bring your herbs."

"Is it Tombi?" she asked, already rushing back up to the door.

"No." She could have sworn she heard sobbing. "It's Tallulah. Hurry."

Relief washed over her, followed by a tinge of guilt. She didn't want anybody hurt or killed. Annie grabbed her pocketbook and went to her altar, stuffing in everything available: candles, herbs, essential oils, Florida water, tea.

Back out the door she followed the flickering, agitated wisp that held Bo's soul. Even without the light, she could locate Bo from the grief-stricken melody that flowed out of him like a mighty river. On and on she stumbled through the swamp until a stitch cramped her side, and each breath felt like inhaling flames of fire.

Annie stopped and leaned against an oak, trying to catch her breath.

"Almost there," Bo urged.

Reluctantly, she straightened and pressed on.

Another few feet and Annie heard a low moan of pain.

"Here. Help her!" The wisp pulsed in and out with agitation above a cypress, and then its light faded away. Underneath, Tallulah cowered, hands clutching her temples.

She rushed over and dropped to her knees. "Tallulah, it's me, Annie. What happened to you?"

Eyes fogged with pain looked up at her in confusion. "Wh-what are you doing here? Dangerous. I sense a wisp is nearby."

"We're safe for the moment. Where are you hurt?" Annie pushed Tallulah's hair from her face, searching for blood or a wound.

Tallulah placed a hand on the back of her skull. "Here."

Annie felt the baseball-sized knot. "How did this happen?"

"Felled by my own weapon," she said bitterly. "I shot a wisp, and one of the *ishkitini* grabbed my stone and threw it back at me." She whimpered as Annie probed the damage. "Strange. That's never happened before." She stopped and drew a shaky breath. "Wasn't…expecting it."

"Nalusa and his shadows grow stronger," Bo said.

Tallulah stilled. "Did you hear something? Or did this blow to the head make me crazy?"

Annie scrambled in her bag and pulled out a bottle of water. She added a tincture of willow bark. "This might help the pain," she said gently.

Tallulah lifted the bottle to her lips and drank greedily.

"Is she going to be okay?" Bo asked anxiously.

"I hear something again." Tallulah straightened. "I swear it sounded like… Bo? Are you out there? Can you hear me?"

The wisp glowed and flickered before them.

"Tallulah. My love."

Wonder clouded Tallulah's eyes. "Bo! I can hear you." Tears ran down her face. "I've missed you so much. Come back to me."

"If only I could."

Bo's voice was filled with such sadness, Annie felt her own eyes fill with tears. She couldn't imagine how awful it would be if something were to happen to her love.

"But it's time to let go of the past," Bo said. "For better or worse, the battle ends tonight. Before it starts, I need you to do one thing for me."

"Whatever you want," Tallulah promised at once.

"Release me. There's nothing more I can do to help."

"But…if I release your spirit, I'll never be near you again."

"I'll still be with you. I'll be there when the birds sing at morning's awakening, when the wind lifts the hair from the back of your neck during the noonday heat, and when the stars glow in the heavens at night, I'll be watching over you."

Tallulah wept, and Annie cried, too, for the gentle man

who had been Tombi's best friend and who had been taken so young and had been so in love.

"And I'll look for you and remember you. Always." Tallulah dried her eyes and struggled to her feet, a rock in her hands.

Annie turned her back. The moment was too intimate and personal to witness.

A whoosh of sound and the air shimmered with a splintering of light, until one lone glow remained. It hovered a few seconds and then sped up into the heavens.

It was done.

"I thought he'd never leave."

Tallulah spun around, but Annie absorbed the shock in the pit of her stomach. She turned slowly, as if her body was weighted by cement blocks. As if some small part of her mind had known this was inevitable.

Hanan, sporting a grotesque, bloodied scar across his forehead, gripped a leather belt in front of him, snapping it open and shut, the sound a riptide in Annie's ears as she imagined the strap cutting into her flesh.

"Run, Annie," Tallulah demanded.

"No." Annie stepped close to Hanan. She had her hawk and her hoodoo, while Tallulah was only armed with a bag of rocks.

Hanan roughly pulled her tight against his body and jerked her so she faced forward; the bite of the belt choked into her neck until she could barely breathe. "Leave or I'll kill her now," he warned.

"You son of a bitch," Tallulah snarled. "I can't believe I ever—"

"Screwed me?" Hanan asked, amusement lacing his words. "You quite enjoyed it. Over and over again. Remember?"

An *ishkitini* screeched nearby. Annie lifted a hand and signaled for Tallulah to go. Pain erupted as Hanan twisted her neck, so fiercely Annie heard sinew and tendon pop from deep within. She whimpered.

"Stay and watch your friend suffer," he spat. "The *ishkitini* will do much worse to you."

Tallulah scowled at Hanan and turned to Annie. "I'll get help," she vowed.

Annie stared at the promise in Tallulah's eyes until the acorn-brown pupils disappeared and blurred into the stygian darkness.

The night was alive with the drone of stinging insects, the thrashing of tree limbs, a rumble of distant ocean waves and the rasping breath of her captor hot in her ears. Through the symphony of terror, she heard her own heart thump as violently as a trapped rabbit's quivering.

She'd never felt so utterly alone.

Chapter 19

The eerie shrieks of the *ishkitini* prickled the flesh on Tombi's forearms, yet he continued on, ever deeper into the woods, until the air became dense with a suffocating miasma, which meant wisps were nearby.

Lots of them.

Above the treetops, flocks of *ishkitini* shadowed the full moon. Will-o'-the-wisps, *Hashok Okwa Hui'ga*, lit the ground in a ghostly festival of lights, outnumbering his hunters by a large margin.

An overwhelming despair threatened to slow his steps, but Tombi pushed on, heading for the sacred land of his ancestors. Nalusa knew he was in a compromised position and had gathered all his forces to even the fight.

He pictured Annie, remembered his sister and friends who were circling around the edge of the wisps, coming together to encircle Nalusa and his shadow beings. He threw back his shoulders and fingered the backpack straps holding the flute. He took comfort in possessing the ultimate weapon and that Annie was safe in his cabin.

Another fifty feet to go until reaching the sacred land border. The wisps sensed the danger; they darted across the swamp erratically, moaning with the souls of the trapped spirits. The squall of misery that combated the *ishkitini* screeching. Tombi drew a deep breath and focused on the human footsteps advancing along with him. All was according to plan.

He plunged forward until he was a good ten feet inside his ancestral land. It was time. Attack the wisps now, and free as many spirits as possible before playing the flute and confronting Nalusa. If he did it too early, the shadow king would cower behind his following. And Tombi wanted the chance to wrestle him, one on one. Tombi cawed, mimicking a crow.

And ran. All of the tribe rushed inward, compressing the circle's circumference. They threw rocks, careful not to throw strong enough to hit one another. A few wisps escaped, light blinking upward, the inner hearts glowing and pulsing. If they defeated Nalusa, they would do a cleanup operation later to find and free the remaining trapped souls. But if Nalusa won, the poor souls would be trapped forever, roaming the swamps with the parasitic wisps controlling their movements. Tombi doubted any of them had Bo's incredible will and strength to briefly take control of the wisps and communicate with the outside world.

Puffs of smoke erupted from the glowing wisp hearts— like a million sparklers waving in the sea breeze. The sparkles burned out, and the souls coalesced into pure white light that spiraled upward. If Annie were here, she could detect a symphony. At least, that was how Tombi imagined it would be—utter joy at the sudden freedom.

The screeching above intensified. A great horned owl

flew directly at him, eyes aglow with murderous intent. There was no time to grab another stone and fend him off. Tombi clutched the dagger in his left hand, his own eyes focused on the owl's breast, its most vulnerable place, housing its beating heart.

The owl would scratch first, before his knife could strike, and it would be a vicious slice into flesh, or worse, it could rip out his eyes. A quick glance around, and he saw the *ishkitini* bearing down on them all. Damn birds. To be defeated by these winged creatures would be humiliating.

A burst of light appeared between him and the owl. Tombi blinked and threw his right hand over his eyes to protect himself from the blinding conflagration.

It was a trapped spirit who, instead of flying up and away, had remained.

A loud screech of pain rent the night air. A smell of burned feathers and singed animal flesh clogged his nose and throat. Tombi crouched low and removed his arm from his eyes. The *ishkitini* lay before him—dead.

The lone light rocketed up and away, chasing its freedom with the others released. All around him, his tribe took aim and fired at the advancing *ishkitini*. Nearly a third of them were taken down, and the rest turned tail.

Tombi smiled in grim satisfaction. The tribe moved closer until they formed a tight circle. A few of the men were bleeding, but all looked well. Yet...

"Where's Tallulah?" he asked, fear thickening his tongue.

Chulah stepped forward, his face haggard. "No one's seen her in over an hour."

"Go find her," he ordered.

His friend nodded and left the circle, eager to ease his mind. *She's okay. She can defend herself.* Tombi respected her defense abilities and sharp mind. He couldn't worry about his twin until Nalusa was defeated.

They would never have a better time than this moment. Two of the hunters quickly gathered twigs and started a bonfire in the center of the circle. Each of them threw bundles of sage on the flames, the pungent scent that helped counter evil and allow the holy to enter.

Tombi dug the flute out of his backpack and blew on it, beginning an ancient song of victory. The notes drifted, pure and compelling, filling him with purpose and resolve.

A rustle shook the underbrush a few yards away, and the grinding metal whir began, drowning out the flute music. Tombi stopped playing. A whiff of decay permeated the land. Tombi's heart tripped, and all his senses heightened. His friends turned and stared, and they waited as one for Nalusa to appear.

Dark shadows melded into the form of a tall, thin man who stepped into their vision. He had small pointed ears and red, glowing eyes that sought Tombi.

"So you've got the flute," Nalusa said in a voice that rumbled like thunder. "But you are still no match for me."

"We'll see about that. Seems all your help has disappeared." Tombi lifted his hand, ready to signal for his friends to begin the attack.

"That doesn't mean I am without power. I have something you want. Something you consider precious."

Tombi hesitated, arm held midair. His heart skittered up to his throat. Nalusa had his sister. What else could it be? Unless…

Another rustle from behind a clump of cypress trees, and more dark shadows emerged. Two of them. A blond male and a slight woman with a familiar shock of brown hair curling down to her hips.

"Annie!" Tombi's hand dropped to his side, and a numbed shock bolted through his body like a current. His fingers loosened, and the flute began to slip. He fisted both hands, and the cane reed almost snapped in two pieces while he willed his mind to catch up to his racing heart. *Not Annie. Not Annie. Please, not Annie.*

Nalusa's deep-throated laugh jangled through the bayou. "Ready to make a deal? The flute for your girl-friend."

"Don't do it, Tombi!" Annie pleaded. "This is your chance."

Hanan jerked the leather strap, and Annie's knees crumpled, face contorted in agony.

No. What mattered most was no longer revenge. It was love. He would fight Nalusa not just for his sister's ruined life or the tribe that was his family now. Not for his dead friend and not for the greater good of humanity, but he would fight to save Annie. He'd do whatever necessary to keep her safe.

She was his world.

"How about this," Tombi said, slipping the backpack off his shoulders and letting it drop to the ground. "Have Hanan release Annie, and we battle for the flute. Just you and I."

Nalusa ran a hand over his long, pointed face, ears twitching and teeny eyes surveying Tombi.

"I'm a mere human," Tombi goaded. "This shouldn't be hard for you."

"You are more than a puny mortal." A fine drizzle of spit foamed at the corners of his thin lips. He pointed a finger at Hanan. "Release the girl."

Hanan scowled but took a step backward.

Damn traitor. If he defeated Nalusa tonight, he'd show no mercy dealing with Hanan later. Annie took great gulps of air, and Tombi winced at her suffering.

He stepped toward Nalusa, fists raised, and they commenced circling one another—watchful, with deadly intent, gauging their first moves. By the bonfire's light, Tombi saw that Nalusa's face was largely featureless, with only a shadowy patch of skin where a nose and cheekbones should appear. His flesh was black, but patterned copper designs shimmered on his skin in the firelight, making him appear half human, half snake. Even though the eyes were human-shaped, the red embers of his pupils burned with the misery of a thousand souls.

Tombi stared harder. Did he see human faces contorting in misery within those red eyes? He took a deep breath. *Focus. I can't let him invade my mind, or I've lost before the fight has begun.*

Nalusa struck first, swinging a right hook, aimed at Tombi's face.

Tombi ducked at the last possible second and put out a foot to trip Nalusa. The soul-eater danced away and regained his balance.

"Not bad," he muttered. "You've been training for this fight for years, haven't you?"

Tombi didn't respond, waiting for Nalusa to show a moment's loss of concentration before he tried to volley a series of punches.

Melancholy roiled over him in waves. A bitter miasma invaded his lungs, his heart. Fighting seemed…too hopeless, too futile. Who was he to think he could battle the Shadow King? He stiffened his spine and shook off the dreary thoughts.

Go for the neck. According to ancient lore, if Nalusa had a weakness, it was this one part of his anatomy.

Nalusa lunged, swinging wildly with his right fist. Tombi pushed at the advancing arm, spinning and hammering Nalusa in the back of the neck with his right elbow. Numbness shot through his right arm. A stinger injury. The Shadow King's neck muscles were as heavy as cement, muscular and flexible beneath a wall of sinewy muscle.

So much for ancient legend.

Nalusa staggered, but at once regained his balance and threw a few fake jabs, obviously trying to find a weakness in Tombi's defense. Tombi stayed alert. He wanted to shake the numbed right arm and get the blood flowing, but to do so would clue in Nalusa on his injury. He couldn't let that happen.

Time for a little testing of his own. He threw a fake punch but overcommitted, leaving the one side of his body open and vulnerable. Pain exploded in his right hip, and he was thrown to the ground from a vicious kick. Didn't take Nalusa but a nanosecond to react to an opportunity. Tombi rolled a couple of yards and leaped back to his feet, body semi-crouched and fists up in the defensive position.

That had been close, a near thing. It was believed that if Nalusa grabbed a man, there was no escape. His strength was equal to a thirty-foot boa that could constrict and crush muscle and bone.

Nalusa advanced and delivered a barrage of left and right punches. Tombi's quick reflexes deflected each one, but the assault still weakened his strength. His hip ached, and his right arm still tingled. No doubt his enemy realized this and was toying with him like a broken-winged bird being bitch-slapped by a hungry cat.

At last, Nalusa seemed to grow impatient. He scowled and drew his arm back and then forward, ready to deliver a killing blow.

Tombi turned to the side at the last possible second, which left his opponent startled and off balance.

There would never be a better chance.

He gathered all his strength and power and kicked Nalusa in the head, knocking him to the ground.

Nalusa stood and slowly smiled. "No one has ever lasted more than a minute fighting me. Finally, I have a worthy opponent."

Despair again threatened to engulf Tombi's mind. He'd

delivered his best move, a kick that would have killed any man. Yet, his enemy shook it off. Nothing had worked. Not the sacred relics in his medicine bag, not Annie's charms and not his years of training for this fight.

Annie's scream ripped the air. Ripped his heart.

Tombi spun around, ready to rush to her defense. A giant hand clamped on his left shoulder bore down, guiding him to face forward again.

Scalding pain ripped the front of his chest, and the scent of blood assaulted his nose. His blood. Dazed, he glanced down and saw shredded flesh. How had this happened?

Nalusa laughed and licked a bloody finger that sported long, razor fingernails as lethal as the *ishkitini*'s talons. "Mmm…delicious."

Chills prickled his arms and chased down his spine. He'd been warned that Nalusa's saliva was poisonous, no matter what form he appeared in. Now that venom was invading his bloodstream, would spread to every inch of his body. He had to stop this. Had to get to Annie. In desperation, he opened the medicine bag belted at his waist and removed a blessed bottle of tannic acid mixed with spring water from their sacred land.

He poured it over his lacerated chest, praying for the best.

The pain stopped immediately. Tombi tossed the empty bottle aside. "Fight's not over yet."

Nalusa's eyes flashed, the banked fires of his pupils flamed. Enraged, he swooped down and grabbed a large branch and charged.

The loss of blood had left him dizzy, but Tombi clamped his jaw shut and stiffened his shoulders. If he failed tonight, he'd have to trust that his friends would carry on the fight against evil. That Annie would go on to live a long and happy life. That his death held some meaning and purpose.

* * *

Shrill screams echoed in Annie's brain like the death throes of a wild cat in a canyon. Only the raw burning at the back of her throat clued her in that it was her own voice.

Blood. So much blood. It seeped and oozed from Tombi's chest in crimson ribbons. She'd tried to scream a warning, but all she'd done was make it worse for Tombi.

"It's almost over now, bitch."

A thousand needles of fire prickled the back of her scalp as Hanan jerked her to her feet.

"And we can continue where I left off last time." His arm went around her stomach, and Hanan shoved her against his hard body. "But this time, it's going to hurt so bad," he whispered in her ear. "You are going to pay for what that hawk did to me. It will be long and painful, and when I'm through with your body, I'll kill you."

"You're crazy."

Hanan took one of her arms and pinned it behind her back. "Shut up and enjoy the show. Tombi was a fool not to join Nalusa. He's paying for it now."

Annie's gaze swept the ring of warriors and their grim, set faces. Couldn't they see Tombi needed help? Damn their pride and honor. *I have to do something.*

Annie closed her eyes and took long, shuddering breaths, willing the noise and the smells and Hanan's painful grasp to fade. She pictured herself falling down a long, dark tunnel, falling, falling...to a safe, quiet space where none could intrude. *Help me, Grandma Tia. I beseech the saints and all that is holy and good, be with me. Help me escape Hanan and help Tombi. Don't allow evil to soil this sacred land and destroy the one I love. I ask for a sign.*

A strong cadence, a marching music, lifted her out of the tunnel, speeding Annie back to present reality. Tallulah was near.

A thud, like the sound of a cracked egg, vibrated along her spine. Hanan's arm dropped, and he fell backward.

Annie whirled around and instinctively cowered.

Tallulah shoved Hanan's back with her foot, and he rolled lifelessly beneath her. "Good riddance," she muttered.

"Forget him. Tombi needs our help." Annie tugged at Tallulah's shirt, desperate to save Tombi.

Tallulah shook her head. "No. I was behind the trees and heard the deal. Nalusa and Tombi, one on one. We wait."

"To hell with that." Annie turned, but Tallulah grabbed her arm and held her.

"No. My brother must win it on his own merit. You can't dishonor him and our people."

Annie's eyes sought Tombi's, looked for some reassurance that he could win.

Tombi staggered like a drunken sailor; blood ran in rivulets down his chest. It didn't look as if he could win anything in his condition.

Annie sank to her knees and prayed. *One more request. By the power of all the elements and roots and all the magic of the bayou and the saints...protect my love. Shield his mind and body with a golden aura that Nalusa cannot penetrate.*

She hardly dared open her eyes, afraid of what she might find. If Tombi died...the sun would set on her happiness. Once, her only wish was silence, but Tombi had helped her achieve so much more, had opened her eyes to love and possibility and what it meant to live a life of courage and honor.

Be brave now. Be there for him if the end is truly near. Annie took a deep breath, preparing for the worst, and opened her eyes.

Light as vivid as marigolds surrounded Tombi's body.

Her spell had worked like nothing she'd ever before even thought to attempt. Awe and hope flushed out the pit of dread she'd fallen into.

Nalusa snarled and bared his teeth; the grinding noise of metal whirred from within his thin body, sounding like the wailing of thousands of souls trapped in hell. His eyes flashed, red and crackling like fire.

Music as pure as harps and flutes played a symphony from Tombi's golden aura.

Nalusa thrust his right hand at Tombi, attempting to cut into his flesh once more. The long, gnarly fingers extended and sizzled upon contact with the light. Nalusa screamed and jerked his hand to his chest, as if he'd been burned.

Tombi's brows knit, and he turned, seeking understanding. Annie scrambled to her feet, and he gazed directly at her and nodded. *Thank you*, he mouthed.

Before she could respond, Tombi whirled back around to face Nalusa and charged, throwing his weight onto Nalusa. They fell to the ground, Tombi on top. His hands encircled Nalusa's neck, and his thumbs bore down into the soul-eater's windpipe.

She couldn't watch. Annie looked down at the ground. The metal grinding noise slowed, decreased in volume. And stopped.

Was he dead?

From behind, Tallulah cheered, and the other hunters joined in. Tallulah put a hand on her shoulder and gave a little shove. "You can open your eyes now. It's over. Did you have something to do with that light?"

Annie opened her eyes. Nalusa had been reduced in size until his height only reached Tombi's hips. A thick cord was knotted around his neck, and Tombi, whose aura had dimmed until all that remained was the suggestion of a yellow haze, held the end of the rope.

"I... I thought Nalusa was dead. What's happening?"

"You can't kill Nalusa Falaya. Not completely. All you can do is contain his power." Tallulah pumped a fist in the air. "And we've done it!"

Tombi held up a hand and silenced the cheers. A hush settled over the bayou, as profound as the windless calm before a hurricane. Tombi jerked on the rope and led Nalusa forward; the hunters fell in behind the two.

"C'mon," Tallulah urged.

Mystified, Annie tagged along.

Tombi broke out in song. His rich, deep baritone formed Choctaw words she couldn't understand. He'd sing a chorus or two, and then the hunters would repeat the same lyric back, like a church reading.

All singing stopped abruptly as Tombi approached a gigantic oak that looked as eternal as the land itself. The circumference of the tree must have been at least six feet, and its trunk and branches seemed to extend forever to the sky.

"Please, let me go," Nalusa whined like a toddler. "I promise to be good. Really. I won't cause any more trouble." His voice was high-pitched and scratchy.

Tombi shook his head. "You cannot be trusted. Time to return to your home." He picked up Nalusa and stuffed him into the large hollowed-out hole in the tree.

Nalusa screamed and kicked, but he was no match for Tombi. He disappeared into the hole with a long wail that lingered and echoed through the bayou.

A single coral ray from the rising sun cracked open the sky, and birds began chirping.

Real birds, normal birds. Not the piercing shrieks of the *ishkitini*. Their voices were like a blessing and benediction, nature's omen of the triumph of good over evil. A great weariness settled in Annie's bones as the pump of adrenaline crashed, recognizing Tombi was out of danger and her work was done.

Tombi retrieved the ancient flute from his jeans pocket

and blew on it three times—short, staccato bursts. He raised both arms, lifting the flute skyward. "Let peace return to Bayou La Siryna. May Nalusa Falaya and his power over the shadow beings be forever constrained to this ancient tree until the end of time. May our ancestors look upon us now with favor, and may the sun's warming shine bless our work here today. We ask in the name of all that is holy and right and just."

"Ikahli. Amen," Tallulah muttered at Annie's side.

Tombi lowered his arms and placed the flute inside the hollowed oak and turned to them. "It's over," he said simply. "Finally. Thank you, my friends." He nodded at his sister. "I see we are all one again." A shadow crossed his face. "Except for Bo."

Tallulah spoke up. "Bo's spirit was released tonight. He's at peace." Her voice broke slightly at the end, and Chulah made his way to her, encircling her waist with an arm.

Annie smiled at his act of caring. Surely one day Tallulah would recognize he loved her, and she could move on from her grief.

"But there is still one thing left to do," Tombi declared.

The hunters looked at one another quizzically.

Tombi marched to where Annie stood and took her hands in hers. "I owe you my life. *We* owe you our lives. Without you, this wouldn't have been possible. At last, I can tell you what is in my heart."

He dropped to one knee, and Annie gasped.

"I love you, Annie Matthews. Will you marry me?"

Chapter 20

"The Blood Moon of October is a-comin' tonight. Yer life will never be the same," Tia Henrietta announced, sprinkling herbs and roots into a mojo bag. Despite the dour words, a broad smile chased away the deep hollows in her face. "Bet you won't be burnin' no slips of paper at midnight, prayin' for the Good Lord to remove yer hearin' gift."

"I have everything I want." Annie patted her grandma's hand, still frail from her recent ordeal, but once again adorned with rings in an explosion of crystal colors. "It's good to have you home again. You concentrate on getting your strength back."

Tia sniffed. "I'm fine now I'm back home. And I intend to be around a long, long time."

"Your heart—"

"Is fine," Tia interrupted. A flush darkened her cheeks, and she dropped her gaze to the mojo bag. "Never nuthin' wrong with it in the first place."

"Wh-what are you saying?" Annie stammered.

"Now, don't you be givin' me that look. I had to get you down here and to visit longer than a few weeks. A little fib never hurt nobody."

"Little fib?" Her spine stiffened, and she took a step back. "How could you lie to me like that? I was worried sick about you."

Tia Henrietta grabbed Annie's hand. "Don't get yer dander up. I had a vision you were needed in Bayou La Siryna and that you would learn to appreciate yer special gift." Tia's lips trembled. "Yer all I have in the world."

Annie softened at the admission. It wasn't easy for her grandma to swallow her pride. And until a few weeks ago, Grandma Tia was all she truly had in the world, as well. How could she be angry when this morning she was right where she was meant to be, surrounded by love? She bent down and kissed the top of Tia's head. "I'm glad you're all right. But no more secrets between us. Okay?"

"Deal." Tia resumed her work, and the ethereal scent of crushed rose petals filled the den. "I intend to be around to see my great-grandchildren one day."

Annie rolled her eyes. "We're not in any hurry for that. I'm going to the kitchen to see if Tallulah needs any help."

Cozy kitchen smells replaced the herbal scents from the den. She watched Tallulah transfer hoecakes from an iron skillet to a plate on the counter, and marched over.

"Mmm." Annie spread butter on a cake and bit in. Creamy sweetness melded with the crispy fried corn bread in an explosion of awesomeness.

Tallulah shot her a sideways glance, a smile tugging her lips. "Heard y'all wouldn't be doing one of your witchy ceremonies tonight at the full moon. Good thing my brother will be keeping you busy until dawn."

Warmth flooded Annie's cheeks, and she almost choked

on a bit of hoecake. Hastily, she poured a glass of sweet tea and took a long swallow.

A sharp ping bounced against the front door.

Annie grinned. "Is that—"

"It is."

Annie put down her glass and turned toward the front door.

"Not so fast." Tallulah tugged at her sleeve. "Our custom is to make the groom wait. He can't think you're too eager."

Annie groaned. "Really? Or is this some sibling thing where you take any opportunity to tease and torment each other?"

"He's too arrogant for his own good," she said, laughing. "I try to take him down a notch when the opportunity arises."

A barrage of thuds assaulted the door.

"What's all that racket?" Tia called from the den.

"Don't worry, I've got it," Annie said, rushing to the front porch. She jerked open the door and blinked. Tombi stood on the steps—tall and dark and long black hair glistening in the sun. In honor of the occasion, he wore a colorfully beaded leather vest and had two narrow braids by the sides of his face with crow and eagle feathers woven in the plaits.

Every time she saw him, her heart rang to know that this magnificent man was hers. Crazy Annie had struck gold.

"About time," he muttered.

Tallulah smiled as she walked up. "Impatient, Tombi?"

"Very," he answered shortly.

The heat from his eyes warmed Annie to the core. He longed to make love again as much as she did, to spend the night together and wake up in the same bed come morning. Ever since Grandma Tia had returned from the hospital three weeks ago, she'd insisted her granddaughter return to the cottage. Arguing about her old-fashioned notions of living together before marriage had been fruitless.

Annie gave him a quick hug. "It won't be long now," she whispered in his ear. He squeezed her in a bear hug, and she laughed and pushed at his chest.

He stepped back with obvious reluctance. "You look beautiful," he said gruffly.

She ran a hand down the front of the vanilla, lacy dress that flowed down to her ankles. Grandma Tia had sewn it with much love and skill. Annie had woven fresh flowers into the bodice and made a matching floral garland for her hair. Like Tombi, she'd also braided two thin strips by her face and threaded in a few of the feathers Tombi's hunters had given her after her ordeal with Hanan.

"Thank you," she said shyly. She bent and picked up one of the smooth, tumbled pebbles Tombi had thrown at the door. "So this is the heralded messenger of love?"

He grinned and gave a mock bow. "A token of my affection."

"You accept it, and there's no going back," Tallulah warned with a snicker.

"I'll keep it forever." Annie stared straight at Tombi as she spoke. Their ancient custom for a man to make an overture to a woman by tossing a pebble her way filled Annie with whimsical delight. She'd honor this stone as much as she did her engagement ring.

Grandma Tia's voice rang out from the den. "That you, Tombi? Come in," she ordered.

Tallulah took off her apron. "I'm going to gather with the rest of the guests outside." She stood on her tiptoes and brushed Tombi's cheek with a swift kiss. "You've got a good woman there," she whispered, before slipping out the door.

Annie took his strong hand in her own, and they entered the den.

"For you," Tombi said, holding out a beaded leather pouch to Tia. "It's filled with natural cures and relics and blessed by our medicine man. He claims it will help strengthen your weak heart."

Annie suppressed a snort. Barely.

Grandma Tia gave her a sharp stare before nodding to Tombi. "Thank you. Please, sit down."

They sat together on the edge of the sofa, across from Tia.

"I have something for you, as well." Tia placed a small red felt mojo bag in his hands.

Tombi held it to his nose and sniffed. "What's in here?"

"Juniper berries, for passion and stamina. You know, in the bedroom."

"Grandma!" Annie blushed, mortified. As if Tombi needed that. He'd kill her if he had any more passion and stamina.

Tombi winked at her.

But, oh, what a glorious way to die.

"I take it this means we have your blessing," he said drily. "Thank you for the gift. I'll be sure to put it to good use."

"You have something for me, too?" Annie asked, trying to turn the conversation.

Tia produced a pink mojo bag tied with lavender ribbon and bulging with her grandma's garden goodies. "I fed this here gris-gris with a bit o' everything while I anointed it with my special marriage oil and recited verses from Song of Solomon. There's catnip to captivate, red clover flowers fer a prosperous marriage, lavender fer romance and harmony, rose petals fer luck, and some juniper berries fer your passion to match Tombi's."

"Sounds like you covered all the bases." Annie suppressed a smile. "Including having the ceremony during the full-moon phase."

"Ain't no use takin' chances." She fixed Tombi with a stern look of warning. "You best take good care of my Annie-girl."

"Yes, ma'am." He reached for Tia, his strong fingers closing over her frail hand. "I promise."

She grinned. "Well, don't tell me. Tell it to the preacher." Tia waved a hand. "Shoo."

Tombi rose and squeezed Annie's shoulder. "I'll be outside waiting for you."

It wouldn't be long now. Annie stood and nervously adjusted the garland in her hair. At the door, Tombi paused and gave her another slow, sexy wink that made her knees turn to jelly.

"Go on now," Tia chuckled.

The front door clicked shut, and Annie paced the pine floorboards. Tia stood watch at the window.

"It's time," Grandma shouted. "Go!"

Annie took a deep breath.

"I'll be joining the rest of the folks out there." She kissed Annie's forehead. "Yer Tombi's a good man. Now git going."

No more waiting. No more lonely nights. No more unlovable Crazy Annie. Excitement bubbled inside. She couldn't wait another moment.

Annie burst out the front door and into the warm sunlight. They were all there. Off to one side of the field stood Tallulah, Miss Verbena, dozens of Grandma Tia's friends and customers, Chulah and all of the former shadow hunters.

And Tombi. Looking as handsome and sexy as she'd ever seen him. Chulah stood at his side, holding his arms. Tallulah broke from the pack and waved her arms at Annie. "Run!"

She bounded down the porch steps and hit the ground running, conscious of all eyes upon her. No simple wedding march would do for this occasion. She bunched a fistful of the ankle-length dress and ran through the field, feet pounding red clay. No high heels, but the dainty white sandals were an impediment nonetheless. Her heart pumped stronger, truer, in a joyful celebration of love and life. Halfway across the field, she spared a glance over her shoulder.

Unleashed from his friends, Tombi began his chase. Long, loping strides that could easily outpace her. That wouldn't do at all. Annie kicked off the sandals and pumped her legs faster. According to their custom, if he captured her too quickly, it meant either her love was weak or she was uneager to mate.

Neither was true.

Her lungs filled to bursting, and her labored breath echoed in her ears, loud as an oncoming freight train. Had she run far enough and hard enough? Annie eased up slightly at the slight hitch in her right side.

For the first time in her life, she wasn't really running away *from* anything but *to* something. For every step alone in the field, Tombi would match it and then, at last, overtake her. That was, if he truly loved her and wanted to claim her forever.

Only ten feet away, a line of ripened blackberry vines edged the woods where the fattened deer grazed within. The Choctaw called this the Hunter's Moon season, a time of celebrating the harvest and taking stock of provisions for the coming winter. An auspicious time for a wedding. From far away, friends and family shouted their encouragement for Tombi to hurry and claim his bride.

So why hadn't he swept her up yet? He should have caught her by now. If he loved her and wanted her forever, then why—

The soles of her feet vibrated with the pounding of his footsteps from behind. A great whoosh of air, and Annie was upended, caught up in strong arms that braced her securely under her back and legs. She shrieked and wrapped her arms around his neck.

Tombi's normally somber face was transformed by a triumphant smile. "I've got you now," he said, and the low baritone of his voice strummed against her chest, thrilling her with its promise of complete possession.

"Only because I let you catch me." Best not to let him get too smug. Annie traced his lips with her fingers, marveling at the depth of their love.

"Kiss her!" Chulah shouted.

Amid the whistles and catcalls, Tombi pressed his mouth against hers. A passionate kiss with the promise of more to come. Annie opened her mouth, welcoming him in, deeper.

The harsh sound of beating wings penetrated her haze of passion. Dread tightened her lungs. Had the *ishkitini* returned? She broke away from Tombi and gasped at the sight of a large brown bird swooping down, pale eyes piercing her soul.

Her hawk.

"Thank you," she whispered, weak with profound relief at the recognition. Without her spirit animal, this day wouldn't have been possible. "Thanks for everything."

The hawk slowed, flew closer. Close enough that Annie was able to reach out a hand and brush it against the reddish-brown feathers of his breast. The hawk's heart pulsed beneath her fingers, fast, proud, strong.

And then it was gone. Left in an explosion of movement as abruptly as it had first appeared.

"I was afraid the birds of the night were back," Annie admitted. Tears blurred the edges of the tree limbs and turning leaves as she raised her head, searching for her animal spirit. "I wonder if I'll ever see my hawk again."

"The *ishkitini* can never harm us again. Nalusa's no longer a threat," Tombi assured her.

"And what about my hawk?"

"An animal spirit is yours for life." He planted a tender kiss on her forehead. "Just as I am yours for life."

He carried her in his arms the few remaining yards left to cross in the open field. More good-natured cheering erupted from the gathered witnesses, and Annie laid her head against his broad chest, perfectly at peace.

They reached the forest, a place none of them had reason to fear anymore. Tombi slowly set her back on her feet, and her body brushed the strong, hard length of him. Desire coursed through Annie, pooling at her core. Forever wasn't long enough to love this man and be loved by him.

He took her hand and raised their joined arms. According to custom, this signaled to everyone that they would complete the journey of life equally yoked as husband and wife.

Together.

* * * * *

THE WORLD IS BETTER
WITH
Romance

Harlequin has everything from contemporary, passionate and heartwarming to suspenseful and inspirational stories.

Whatever your mood, we have a romance just for you!

Connect with us to find your next great read, special offers and more.

f /HarlequinBooks

🐦 @HarlequinBooks

www.HarlequinBlog.com

www.Harlequin.com/Newsletters

HARLEQUIN®

A Romance FOR EVERY MOOD™

www.Harlequin.com

SERIESHALOAD2015

Turn your love of reading into rewards you'll love with

Harlequin My Rewards

**Join for FREE today at
www.HarlequinMyRewards.com**

Earn **FREE BOOKS** of your choice.

Experience **EXCLUSIVE OFFERS** and contests.

Enjoy **BOOK RECOMMENDATIONS**
selected just for you.

PLUS! Sign up now
and get **500** points
right away!

Earn
FREE
REWARDS
Join
Today!
HarlequinMyRewards.com

MYR16

JUST CAN'T GET ENOUGH?

Join our social communities
and talk to us online.

You will have access to the latest
news on upcoming titles and special
promotions, but most importantly,
you can talk to other fans about your
favorite Harlequin reads.

Harlequin.com/Community

Facebook.com/HarlequinBooks

Twitter.com/HarlequinBooks

Pinterest.com/HarlequinBooks

HSOCIAL

Love the Harlequin book you just read?

Your opinion matters.

Review this book on your favorite book site, review site, blog or your own social media properties and share your opinion with other readers!

Be sure to connect with us at:
Harlequin.com/Newsletters
Facebook.com/HarlequinBooks
Twitter.com/HarlequinBooks

HREVIEW